Tell Me I'm Dreamin'

EBONI SNOE

AVON BOOKS NEW YORK

This is a work of fiction. Names, characters, places, and incidents either are the product of the author's imagination or are used fictitiously. Any resemblance to actual events, locales, organizations, or persons, living or dead, is entirely coincidental and beyond the intent of either the author or the publisher.

AVON BOOKS, INC.
1350 Avenue of the Americas
New York, New York 10019

Copyright © 1998 by Eboni Snoe
Published by arrangement with the author
Visit our website at **http://www.AvonBooks.com**
Library of Congress Catalog Card Number: 97-94767
ISBN: 0-380-79562-0

First Avon Books Printing: June 1998

AVON TRADEMARK REG. U.S. PAT. OFF. AND IN OTHER COUNTRIES, MARCA REGISTRADA, HECHO EN U.S.A.

Printed in the U.S.A.

WCD 10 9 8 7 6 5 4 3 2 1

This novel is dedicated to pioneer publisher Leticia Peoples, who had a desire and saw a need for novels like this . . . and filled it.

Tell Me I'm Dreamin'

Prologue

Eros, a Caribbean island
1971

 "Ulysses." The name crackled from her mouth. Layla's eyes emitted shock and concern in a way only a mother's eyes can. "What happened to you?"

He clamped his seven-year-old mouth together in stubborn determination, making the thick line of blood running down from his nose tumble over his sealed lips. The drops spread like dark ink on his shirt. Aghast, Layla disappeared from the foyer and returned with a damp linen cloth. She dabbed gently at his nose while maneuvering his face so she could get a better look at his rapidly swelling eye. "My little one, who did this?" She trembled, switching from heavily accented English to her native Egyptian tongue. Ulysses removed his face from her hand and looked down at the floor.

"You must tell me, Ulysses," she insisted softly. "What happened?"

He tried to maintain his cover of stubborn strength, but when his dark, misty eyes locked with hers a tear escaped over the rim. "They called me

1

bad names because of you. Because you look so different from their mothers. Your skin is darker and they say you sound different.'' He wiped away a matching tear with the back of his hand. ''They said you shouldn't be living at Sovereign, that you should be working here and living in the settlement along with the other Africans because you're not high white or even Bajan. They say, because of you, I'm a mutt. A worthless dog.''

''So you fought for me?'' Layla asked, trying to hide the quiver in her voice.

Ulysses nodded. ''And I did fine in the beginning, but Michael and Dominique are older than I am, and bigger.''

''Thank you,'' she kissed him tenderly on the cheek, ''for protecting my honor. It was brave of you. But I don't want you to ever do it again,'' Layla told him in measured tones.

Ulysses looked away.

''You must promise me, Ulysses, if the odds are not even, you will not do it again.''

The slight concession on Layla's behalf was rewarded by a hesitant nod.

''Good. Now there is something I want you to always remember.'' She took his small, mahogany hands in hers. ''Your father and I have much more in common than people realize. Although his immediate ancestors are British, generations before that your father's ancestors were adventurers. They traveled and married in Greece, Portugal, all over the world long before they settled here in the Caribbean. Because of his rich ancestry, his love of knowledge, and his appreciation for different cultures we named you Ulysses, a Greek name. Your father believes the best scholars base much of their knowledge on Greek and Egyptian understandings. He sees important links between my people and the Greeks; even our gods and goddesses are similar in many ways. Your father gave you a name from a culture he loves and whose blood flows in his veins. One that is built on the same foundation as mine, a foundation of legendary proportion.'' Ulysses' dark eyes widened as he listened. ''This foundation was the original home of the cliff dwellers. It was a continent called Lemuria. So our ancestral taproot, your father's and mine, is the same no matter what they may believe. And you,'' she touched his cheek, ''are special to all of us.''

Layla kneeled down and hugged Ulysses, holding him close until she forced herself to let him go. ''Now,'' she looked into his eyes, ''go to the kitchen and get one of the fresh codfish balls Catherine just fried. Then find your Aunt Helen. She missed you while you were at school today.'' She rose. ''I must go out for a little while.''

Layla headed down the path from the estate, Sovereign, images of her child's battered face haunting her. The further she advanced, the faster she went. Finally, she kicked off the shoes that she hated to wear, leaving them carelessly in the dirt as her bare feet reintroduced themselves to the earth. Layla recognized the names of the boys Ulysses had mentioned, and she knew where they lived. She was determined to tell their mothers what they had done. She could not let it go unpunished.

Out of breath, and with sweat trickling down her face from her short, coarse hair, she arrived at the small house. Impatient to have the issue resolved, Layla knocked, but did not wait for an answer as she opened the door. The room smelled of rum and was hazy with smoke. She stared into the faces of three men playing cards. Layla had not expected to find the men at home this time of day. Normally, they were at work on the neighboring estate, Sharpe Hall. Two of them were the boys' fathers.

She watched as three pairs of surprised eyes turned in her direction, exhibiting a growing curiosity. Layla could tell the men had been drinking heavily and felt a spark of fear. But she took control of the emotion, transmuting it into assertiveness. "I need to talk to two of you about something that happened between our children today."

The men simply stared.

Disconcerted by their lack of response, Layla rushed head on, describing what had taken place between Ulysses and their sons. In the end, despite their aloofness, she sought what she hoped would be common ground between them. "And I believed if I told you this, as adults, you would not go along with this kind of fighting." She waited for some kind of answer as one man slowly put out his cigarette and another turned up his glass, tapping it on the bottom with his fingers. After an incubating silence the first man spoke.

"What kind of woman are you, coming down here confronting us men?" White smoke flowed from his nose and mouth as he spoke. Then the bottom portion of his face began to quiver. "But I don't need to ask that. You're Peter Deane's black Egyptian whore, who he calls his wife. You think you are something because you live better than most of us here on Eros. It's a crime that white men work harder for the little money we earn than you, a black Egyptian, child of slaves."

The words dashed over Layla like ice-cold water, and she realized she had lived within the protective confines of Sovereign too long, had forgotten the prejudices that some of the islanders harbored. At first his words made her angry, and her eyes narrowed as she prepared to give him a verbal lashing. But the expressions she saw on the men's faces changed her mind. Layla realized she was in the worst kind of danger.

She turned to rush out of the door, but a hard body slammed into her, stealing her breath away. She recovered in seconds, turning into an animated ball of panic as she was lifted up by a strong pair of arms. A dirty kerchief quickly silenced her screams and she fought with everything she had as two of the men took her outside behind the house. The other man followed.

They were cruel beyond what she thought was humanly possible. They had their way with her, they beat her unnecessarily, and when they were done the men laughed as they dumped Layla on the lonely path that led back to Sovereign.

Her candle of life was almost out when her husband, Peter, found her. His distraught cry seemed to fill the forest around her as well as every cell within her body. Layla would have cried out against what he was preparing to do if she had possessed the strength, for she understood how deeply he loved her, that during their nine years of marriage his love had grown with each passing day, just as hers had. He loved her more than anything or anyone else in this world. But when she saw him raise the knife above his chest, all she could think of was What about our son, what about Ulysses? But Layla was unable to speak and her thoughts went unnoticed. She died when Peter's body slumped over hers, the knife deep in his chest.

At the brink of dusk the child, Ulysses, found his parents. He stood in hardened silence a few feet away from their bodies until his Aunt Helen caught up with him. When she saw the gruesome scene she screamed until her sun-browned skin turned white. She attempted to embrace and protect Ulysses' rigid body from the horrifying sight, but he would not allow it. He struggled against her as if a demon had possessed him, then snatched himself away and ran into the forest.

Chapter 1

25 years later . . .

Nadine Clayton tried to imagine how long the dusty artifacts had lain on the shelves untouched by human hands. Perhaps it had been as long as she had been untouched by a man. A total of twenty-six years. The number of years she had been in this world. Distracted by that haunting fact, she stared off blindly.

She knew plenty of sisters back home who had screwed their brains out, gotten married, had babies, and divorced by the time they were twenty-six. No one had asked Nadine to marry him, not that the thought of being a divorced mother was that appealing. Maybe she should have done like some of the others, slipped around, or made herself desirable enough, open enough despite her Pentecostal upbringing, where some brother may have tried to get with her. At least she would have gotten the basics about sex out of the way, and wouldn't feel like she had some big V tattooed on her chest. Frustrated, Nadine looked down with regret.

She forced her thoughts back inside the cluttered room and took on a protective attitude. I'm not even going there today; I will not down myself like that today. Why, it would be like blasphemy to do it here of all places, here on the island of Eros.

Boy, she was a long way from Ashland, Mississippi. She tried to think of how long she had dreamed of traveling outside of the United States. Nadine had probably wanted to travel from the very beginning of her love affair with literature and art, which felt like forever. Then the unbelievable happened, she was assigned to a consulting project. She had been given a choice of two locations, Athens, Greece, or a small island near Barbados that had become known for its literary and artistic treasures. For Nadine the choice was simple. It had to be the Caribbean. A place that held her ancestral roots. A place she had heard strange, intriguing tales about. A place she felt drawn to. So the job was sheer luck, or safer yet—Nadine looked at the cross that hung around her neck—a bountiful blessing from God.

She continued to gaze at the delicate cross. Grandma Rose had polished the necklace to perfection the day before Nadine left. It was her grandmother who had told her the stories about the Caribbean, and she knew, to Grandma Rose, the cross symbolized protection, something her grandmother believed a woman traveling alone would need. Yet Grandma Rose also believed that as long as Nadine kept the Lord in her life she would be safe and she would never be lonely.

Grandma's words were good words, the kind of thinking that had guided her safely through the years. But it was not Grandma's words that had kept her living in a glass house. It was Nadine's zeal for the Apostolic faith. She had adhered to it like there was no tomorrow. Now she was beginning to fear her inflexible views had kept her from living the life of a full-blooded woman. Ring or no ring around her third finger.

A shiny, black object amongst a slew of books drew Nadine's attention as she looked around the room. She walked over to it and picked up an onyx slab, but she was shocked when the table and the books upon it began to rattle. The entire room shook uncontrollably. Terrified, Nadine threw up her arms to protect herself from falling objects and clods of dirt. Even so, she found the law of gravity was against her, and she fell back against a trembling bookshelf, clutching the black stone to her chest. Several smaller pieces cluttered with clay tumbled from another table and shattered on the floor as the room continued to shake violently.

Terror mounted inside Nadine. She was forced to slide down with her back pressed against the case until she made contact with the dirt floor. Afterwards she was grateful for the sense of security the floor provided as her mind struggled to make sense of what was occurring. The turmoil ceased in a matter of moments, but still she found herself afraid to move, afraid the awful quaking would begin again during the unnatural silence that replaced the deep-throated grumblings of the earth.

Badly shaken, Nadine clambered to her feet, softening the iron grip with which she'd held the slab. A dull pain throbbed in the center of her chest where she'd clutched it so tightly against her body. She could feel her heart pounding as she took concentrated breaths to slow her breathing down to its normal pace. Nadine couldn't remember ever being so frightened, and all her senses remained on alert, anticipating a moment when the quaking might start again.

The silence was shattered by a panic-stricken voice shouting an alarm outside. Soon it was joined by several others. In her haste, Nadine crushed a tiny bowl as she rushed outside. She nearly collided with an elderly man running and pulling a child along. They were not the only ones running toward the center of the small marketplace that edged the island wharf. Dozens of people were running and screaming. The mass hysteria was frightening, but even so, Nadine felt compelled to follow the crowd. High, white-capped waves crashed against the shore. The waves were continuing proof that the earth had shown her displeasure.

It was her first day on Eros, a small Caribbean island near the more popular Barbados. She knew nothing about the people who inhabited the island, and only a little about the Caribbean culture in general. Her knowledge was limited to what she had managed to read in a couple of library books prior to her arrival. Because of her quick research Nadine knew that volcanic eruptions triggered by earthquakes were not an unfamiliar occurrence in the islands.

Nadine's adrenaline continued pumping. The rush itself was frightening. Through the years she had trained herself to remain outwardly calm, no matter what the circumstances. Her calm demeanor shielded her from the prying eyes of the world, and was a thin but adequate veneer to hide her insecurities. But this was different. She was a stranger here, and the strong tremors of the earth made her realize how far away from home she actually was. It was emotionally unraveling.

Nadine's steps quickly turned into a sprint as she rounded the corner of the tiny library/museum. Several yards ahead she could see a group of islanders pointing at a large statue in the middle of the antiquated business district. One elderly woman, wearing a scarf that nearly covered her eyes, wailed with fear, then covered her mouth with her hand as she stared in front of her. Nadine gently moved her aside as she approached the object through the gathering crowd. She had seen the British influence on Eros through the buildings and the language, but now a massive Greek statue rose before her. She read the inscription beneath it.

DIONYSUS, GOD OF FERTILITY AND WINE,
MAY HE FOREVER HOLD AND PROTECT
THE ISLAND OF EROS IN THE PALM OF HIS HAND
AS HE DOES THE BELOVED GOD, EROS.

Nadine placed her forearm over her brow, shading her eyes from the setting sun as she looked up, studying the immense bronze god. As frightened as she was, she couldn't help but marvel at the workmanship and artistic talent the vast object embodied.

Her gaze trailed upward over grapes and vines, sandaled feet, and strong muscular legs. A type of loincloth encased Dionysus' hips, topped by what Nadine knew to be a fawn-skin shirt. Dionysus held a drinking cup in his left hand, and his right arm was raised straight over his head. It ended in a flexed wrist that was cracked, yielding a sporadic stream of white dusty powder trickling from the wound. The immense wrist curved into a large, cupped palm with the tiny god, Eros, lying inside.

Another gasp rose from the growing crowd.
"What's wrong?" Nadine heard herself ask just as
another tremor struck the island. The small statuette
of Eros tumbled to the ground, shattering before
the horrified crowd.

Blind panic took over as the islanders ran toward
several twisted paths leading up a steep hill. Automatically, Nadine looked for someone she recognized. But of course there was no one. So she
ran behind the crowd, her mind a total blank. Her
survival instinct forced her legs toward the hill,
compelling her to follow the people who knew the
island. It said the islanders would know a safe place
to go.

Nadine struggled to keep up with the sure-footed
group. But even though she wore flats, the slick
bottoms of the department-store shoes were not
made to travel so quickly over a rocky area. Almost
falling when her foot struck a jagged rock, Nadine
caught her balance and realized she was still holding the black slab in her hand. Her first instinct was
to throw it to the side of the path, but a little voice
inside stopped her. She studied the slab for just a
second. It was a work of uncompromising beauty.

Carved on top of it was a sublime unicorn wearing a decorative medallion about her neck, and a
small crown upon her head. The lines were feminine and sleek, and Nadine could not bring herself
to discard it.

She unzipped her fanny pack, threw out a notebook pad, some pencils, and a package of Kleenex,
then placed the slab inside. It had taken no more
than seconds to complete her task, but when Nadine looked at the islanders in the distance, it might
as well have taken half an hour. Determined to

catch up, she began to run as dusk embraced Eros.

Darkness was fast approaching when she reached a hairpin turn in the path and another tremor rocked the island. Crashing and splintering sounds erupted all around, and Nadine covered her ears against the assault. Sheer instinct forced her to her knees, eyes squeezed shut. There she remained, praying, until the awful noises ceased.

When Nadine found the courage to open her eyes she remained in her protective huddle, and it was more than fortunate that she did. Mere feet in front of her a shower of stones and rocks rained down from the hilltop, completely blocking the foot-trodden path. Stunned, she surveyed the natural barrier. She began to tremble, realizing how grave the situation might have been. Tears stung her eyes. The path was impassable.

Nadine clutched her cross in a clammy hand. "My God, what should I do?" she cried out to the ghostly silent island, and forced herself to remain calm, knowing she teetered on the brink of hysteria. Should I chance venturing off into the woods to bypass the stones, not knowing what kind of damage has occurred inside the forest or still might occur? She stared at the ancient trees beside the path.

Nadine thought all of nature appeared to be against her as dusk turned to night. "Damn!" A rare cussword spewed from her mouth. "I should have stayed my black butt back in the States," she whined, looking at the darkening sky. Nadine tried to calm herself and think of what to do next. Then she had it. The only thing she could do was go back the way she came. She had seen a small cave as she climbed. Yes! She would go back to the cave.

Forcing herself to stand, Nadine cautiously felt
her way back down the footpath. Sheer determination kept her going. One thing at a time, she
reassured herself. I'll figure out what to do once I
reach the cave. She kept her left hand against the
warm and sometimes sharp rock that bordered the
path. But as the sky turned to a midnight blue it
seemed she would never reach the opening, and she
began to doubt if it ever existed.

Suddenly, her fingers wavered in midair. Relief
flooded inside her. But she hesitated as she turned
toward the dark cavern. What if some wild animal
sought shelter there like herself? When she stepped
into the pitch-black interior her nose crinkled at the
damp, musty smell, and her hands went to the
fanny pack to search for a book of matches. Once
she found it, she hastily extracted it from the pack,
but in her nervous state the matches slipped out of
her hands.

"Oh, no!" she gasped, falling to the floor of the
cave. She began to feel in the dark with uncertain,
anxious hands.

The hiss of sulfur striking a matchbook cover
stunned her. Suddenly, the cave came alive with a
dull light.

"I presume this is what you are looking for." A
vaguely accented voice slid into the darkness.

Nadine's head jerked upward with alarm. She
could see a pronounced circle of yellow light surrounding the face that appeared above her. The
match was only inches away.

Midnight, intense eyes peered down at her, further shadowed by a curly wedge of ultra-dark hair.
Nadine made a gagging sound at the sight of him,
the man was so near. Near enough to reach out and

touch her. There was something sinister about the image, but before she could focus on his features the match went out, and they were plunged into total darkness again.

"Lord," she gasped. "What are you doing in here? You nearly scared me to death," she said as she jumped up.

"The answer is rather obvious, don't you think?" the low voice replied.

Nadine stood in the dark only inches away from the stranger, and she became aware of his interesting but pleasant male scent. To say she was unnerved would be inadequate. The silence that filled the space between them was so unbearable, it was asphyxiating. "How long have you been in here?" Nadine spoke just to hear her own voice.

"Not long."

"Well . . ." her discomfort was increasing, "how long do you think we'll have to stay?" She waited for his answer, which came after a long pause.

"Not much longer. The timing of the earth's tremors are as rhythmic as a heartbeat here on Eros. Once they start, the spaces of time between them can be measured. If the earth is silent a short while longer, there will be no more tremors tonight."

Who in the heck was this character? He spoke with a distinct, unusual accent. His strangeness frightened her, but Nadine knew not to show that. Instead she asked, "How can you be so sure? Earthquakes are so unpredictable; without equipment even a seismologist would not be able to determine exactly when another tremor is going to occur."

His response was a low grunt. Once again silence followed as they waited. For Nadine it was like torture, and she was about to speak again when the stranger abruptly announced his departure.

"Good-bye," the voice said, and she heard the faint movement of clothing. "Now the earth is content and will remain so until the next time."

Almost like an apparition, the shadow of a man appeared in the mouth of the cave, his form etched against the pale moonlight. Panicked at the thought of being left alone, Nadine blurted, "You can't leave me here like this! I don't even live on Eros. I was over here today doing some preliminary work. I don't have any place to—"

"The truth is, your problems are not mine," was his indifferent, abrupt reply. "You can follow me if you wish, but that's up to you." No sooner than the words were spoken, he stepped out on the path and into the woods.

Nadine hesitated only a moment before she bounded after the mysterious figure. She was nobody's fool. She wanted to holler out and call him everything but a child of God, but she didn't. She followed him.

The quarter moon did not provide much light, but the white shirt the stranger wore helped to keep him within view. The trek through the ancient trees would have been perilous by day, but at night it was nearly impossible. She was frustrated within minutes because her nylon-like top seemed to get snagged on every other branch, and although she wore her hair close to her head, the ball in the back was still a magnet for low-hanging tree branches.

The stranger's actions backed up his words as he moved swiftly ahead. It was evident he was not concerned about her welfare, and if Nadine hadn't clearly heard his reluctant invitation she might have assumed he was trying to lose her.

Suddenly, a ripping sound erupted as Nadine leaped over a large, decaying branch. She stopped, knowing the pants she had bought especially for this trip had torn. "Is there anything else that can happen?" she moaned and tried to continue, but one pants leg had gotten caught on a protruding stump of the dead plant. "Wait!" she yelled as she bent over to free the material, ripping the seat of her pants even further. Her request was met by dead silence, and her heart jolted when she could no longer hear the stranger crashing through the woods ahead. The sound of man had totally been replaced by the night sounds of nature.

Alarmed, Nadine rushed forward, only to emerge on a well-formed dirt road. She desperately looked in both directions, her head swiveling back and forth. She knew luck was with her when she caught a glimpse of the stranger's white sleeve reflected by the pale moonlight. Mentally and physically drained, Nadine pushed herself to follow the fleeting sign as the stranger rounded a bend. Even though she was terribly frightened, and should have felt thankful for any assistance the man offered, she could not help but feel anger welling up against him. But Nadine continued to follow him, wondering if he had been sent from heaven or hell.

Chapter 2

The house was so much a part of the forest it would have been invisible if it were not for a light billowing out of a tunnel-shaped entranceway. Nadine entered it with caution. She stopped near the wavering flame of a wall-mounted candle beside the door. For a moment she allowed herself the luxury of marveling at the flat shell shape of the base filled to the brim with wax. Reality would not allow her to dally for long, and Nadine was forced to confront the full impact of her predicament. She was deep within the island facing the unknown. "This is ridiculous," she said, staring at the large wooden door. "He tells me I can follow him, then he leaves me, and now I'm forced to figure out how to get into the place." Frustrated, Nadine looked down at the limestone floor. "I bet he doesn't even live here." She could feel beads of perspiration forming above her lip as she contemplated what to do. Alright, just be calm, she told herself. Whoever comes to the door, you'll just have to tell the truth about how you got here. What can they do to you, anyway? She raised her hand and knocked before her mind conjured up answers she was afraid to acknowledge.

It took several efforts, each one more nerve-racking than the last before a strained female voice called, "Who's there?"

"Uh, excuse me," Nadine stammered, not knowing where to begin, "I know this is going to sound a little strange, but I was invited—"

"I cannot understand you," the woman replied, cracking open the thick oak door just enough to create an opening that resembled a straw filled with light.

"I'm sorry." Nadine spoke inside the cranny. "This is rather difficult to explain. My name is Nadine Clayton. I'm an American. I am here with the World Treasures Institute to do some preliminary work."

"Yes?" The crack widened until Nadine could see a middle-aged woman in a colorful dress wearing a wrap on her head. The woman looked at her with a skeptical curiosity, then with an increasing look of astonishment.

"A man led me here after the earthquake, but he was going so fast I couldn't keep up. I'm embarrassed to say I don't know his name," Nadine continued, feeling a need to get it all in. "I hope you can understand how frightened I was under the circumstances, and how following him here seemed to be the wisest thing to do at the time." She trailed off under the woman's steady stare, before starting up again. "If you'll just allow me to use your telephone so I can call my boss, Dr. Steward, I promise I won't inconvenience you any further."

"Please, forgive my rudeness," the woman seemed to acquire a sudden burst of energy, "and by all means, come in," she offered, opening the door for Nadine to step inside. "Madame Deane will never forgive me if I turn you away.''

Nadine didn't know why, but she felt the woman's words held an underlying meaning. But she had enough on her mind, and she gratefully obeyed the woman's request, brushing her feelings aside, attributing them to a bad case of nerves and stress.

No sooner had she stepped into the foyer than she was overtaken by the sensation of being surrounded by hundreds of white doves in flight. Seconds passed, and soon she realized the key to the illusion was a simple candelabra. It offered up countless reflections of a statue of doves flying in V formation in tiled mirrors that decorated the foyer from ceiling to floor.

"This is amazing," Nadine exclaimed, unable to resist taking a closer look at the marble statue. "For a moment I thought I was surrounded by flying birds."

"It is wonderful, isn't it?" the woman replied as she watched her. "I have worked here for many years, and I still find myself giving in to the beauty of the place. Master and Madame Deane would have had it no other way."

"They must be very special people to have such an artistic eye."

"Yes, the entire family has been that way for as long as I can remember. Amongst the islanders they are known as 'the Protectors of Eros' Treasures.' Each generation has done its share of contributing to their large collection. I guess that's why Madame Deane is taking it so hard now," the woman added almost to herself.

Nadine felt uncomfortable with the woman's frankness, but she was grateful that she had let her in. "I really do appreciate your allowing me to use your telephone. I was beginning to feel a little nervous, everything was happening so fast," Nadine said gratefully.

"Telephone, miss? But no one has a telephone here on Eros. Messages are either hand-delivered or mailed. The nearest phone is on Barbados."

"But I asked you if I could use your telephone when I was standing outside," Nadine replied, confused.

"Once again I'm sorry, miss. Seeing you surprised me. I guess I wasn't really listening to what you were saying."

"Well, I don't know what to do at this point, if there's no phone. I guess I'll just have to—"

"You'll just have to come with me," the anxious housekeeper cut her off. "Like I said, Madame Deane will never forgive me if I don't tell her you are here."

"That is very kind of you. I suppose you don't get very many . . . stray visitors here."

"That's true, and surely not one like you," the woman added with a hint of excitement in her voice. "By the way, my name is Catherine. And your name once again?"

"Nadine. Nadine Clayton."

"So Miss Clayton, if you'll just follow me, I'll let Madame Deane know you are here." Acting as if the matter were settled, Catherine proceeded out into a courtyard.

Nadine followed her into the enclosed area with bronze lamps lining the walls. Only a few of them were lit, but they provided a soft light throughout. Her shoes clicked as she crossed the well-polished terra-cotta floor, and Nadine found herself almost

walking on her toes in an effort to preserve the
peaceful feel and sound of the place. Groups of
chairs accompanied by stools and tables were
placed decoratively about, but it was the extraordinary well that caught Nadine's eye. The outer
walls had been sculpted, and despite the poor lighting Nadine could see it was painted in vivid colors,
enhancing the sculptures. The smell of tropical
plants was strong, and a melody strung together by
a guitar and flutes created an exotic musical backdrop.

A little light-headed, Nadine placed her open
palm above her breasts. She closed her eyes for just
a second, and blew out audibly through her mouth.
The sound of her own breath startled her. Embarrassed, she looked up to see if Catherine had overheard her case of the nerves, but to her relief the
woman had not. She was reaching for the handle
of another door, seemingly oblivious to Nadine's
unrest.

Catherine ushered her into an artfully decorated
room. "Please feel free to make yourself comfortable," she told her before she left her alone.

Nadine realized this room was the source of the
music she had heard out in the courtyard. It was
coming from a turntable mounted in an antique
cherry-wood cabinet. She knew a lot about antiques
because she had grown up in a house that was quite
full of them. Grandma Rose had a strong fondness
for antique furniture. Through the years she had
accumulated a wide array of chests of drawers, tables, desks, beds, and sideboards. Everyone in Ashland knew how Auntie Rose, as she was known by
most, loved old things. So as elderly family members passed away, if the residents of Ashland had

a barn or shed cleaning, Grandma Rose was always notified just in case she wanted some of the furniture that wasn't worth anything to anyone anymore. Not once did Grandma Rose come home empty-handed from these ventures. She always managed to find something of value in what others considered worthless. Maybe that's where Nadine had acquired her love for old, beautiful things.

A reminiscent smile surfaced as she traced the floral pattern carved along the edge of the well-preserved cabinet with her finger. Grandma Rose's eye for things that were worthless to most of the people in Ashland, Mississippi, ended up being a main source of funding for Nadine's college education. Time and time again Nadine watched her strip the furniture and restore it almost to its original beauty, telling her all the while how the dents and marks gave the piece character like moles and wrinkles did for a human face.

People began to travel from Tennessee and Arkansas to bid on Grandma Rose's antiques, and it didn't take her long to realize how "these well-to-do folks," as she called them, valued the furniture. From that point on, the majority of her time was spent gathering pieces from all over Russell County and restoring them.

Nadine recalled how Grandma Rose always paid the owner "a little something" so that her conscience wouldn't bother her so bad when she made what she termed "a killin' " off of each piece.

A female voice interrupted her thoughts. "I am Madame Deane. I must tell you, most people are more enamored with my collection of Waterford crystal than that old cabinet."

Remembering the split in her pants, Nadine

whirled around to face her hostess. "The cherry-
wood cabinet reminds me of the house that I grew
up . . . in."

Nadine hoped the shock she felt did not show on
her face. Because of the strong, self-assured tone
of the woman's voice, she had expected to see a
well-manicured elderly woman with every hair in
place, and a posture that signaled her feelings of
inherent superiority. Instead she found before her
one of the strangest white women she had ever
seen. She was a slip of a female, with her hair
elaborately arranged like the Athenian women of
ancient Greece. A headband of artificial olive
leaves had slipped precariously low on her brow,
allowing a white bang and frayed side tendrils to
protrude underneath. The band continued, wrapping itself around a large braided ball that sat at
the nape of her neck. It was like looking at a comical character from the past.

Nadine couldn't help but stare. Brooches held
two dress-length pieces of rectangular material together at her shoulders, while a cord belt encircled
her small body, creating soft folds of material
above and below it. Her large, dark eyes twinkled
in a well-worn face that showed not even a hint of
disillusionment over being confined to a wheelchair.

Nadine could tell she was not the only one making a full appraisal as the woman's eyes narrowed
in speculation, then slowly opened wide with a
dawning recognition. In an elegant manner she
placed frail fingers over pleated lips, and an unnatural gleam filled her eyes as she said to Nadine,
her head nodding with each word, "So you finally
decided to come."

Chapter 3

Nadine made a half turn and looked behind her, although she thought she and Madame Deane were alone in the room. Reassured that they were alone and thinking, What in the heck have I gotten myself into now? she squeezed her hands together, faced her strange hostess, and searched her mind for the right words to say to this crazy white woman.

"I must say this is a first. I had to come all the way to Eros for somebody to tell me I remind them of someone they know," she quipped, then turned serious as she tried to cut a path to any sanity Madame Deane might have. "I'm sorry to inconvenience you like this," Nadine continued, "but there was a bit of miscommunication between your housekeeper, Catherine, and me. I thought you had a telephone here on the premises. I wanted to call my boss and tell him what had happened and that I was here." She felt a sudden need to tell her story again. "You see, everything was happening so fast. I was led here by—I'm sorry, I haven't even introduced myself. My name is—"

"I know who you are, Lenora. I knew you would come. *She* told me about it," her thin mouth set in

25

a grim line, "and I in turn told Catherine. But of course Catherine did not believe me. The cliff dwellers also knew you would come, but it's been a long time since we've visited their side of the island. The accident has caused all sorts of problems," she explained.

"Wait a minute, Madame Deane." Nadine showed the woman her palms to ward off any further misunderstandings. "I'm Nadine Clayton. I live in the United States. I'm working on an international project that will—"

"There is no need to be shy, Lenora," the eccentric woman broke into Nadine's explanation. "I know why you are here. The time has almost come. Catherine," she called, raising her voice slightly.

Seconds later a composed Catherine walked into the room, and Nadine surmised she had to be listening around the corner to appear so quickly.

"Prepare the third bedchamber for Lenora, and see to it that she has everything she needs for her stay here, would you?"

"Yes, of course, madame."

"Now," Madame Deane paused, inhaling deeply, "all of this excitement has begun to tire me out. So you two go away now and leave me alone."

Nadine watched as Madame Deane tried, unsuccessfully, to push a low-hanging artificial olive leaf away from her eye.

"I've got so much to think about now that Lenora has come." She began to wheel herself toward a wall of books as she waved them away with a flip of her hand.

Nadine looked from Madame Deane to Catherine who was following her mistress' requests. She beckoned for Nadine to do the same. For the second time that day she found herself following someone with a total sense of helplessness. As the two women crossed the threshold, Madame Deane called out another instruction to Catherine. "When you are finished with Lenora, come back. I should be ready to retire." Her high-pitched voice trailed off behind them.

Without a word Catherine proceeded down the wide hallway, passing distinctive three-legged tables topped with black- or red-figure vases. At any other time the decor would have caused quite a stir for Nadine, but not now. She was trying to determine if both Madame Deane and Catherine were mentally unstable. Maybe she had a few screws missing as well for going along with them!

Lord, Nadine thought, how the folks in Ashland would have a field day with a story like this if they ever got wind of it. It would probably be talked about for generations. How that strange grandchild of Auntie Rose claimed she was mistaken for someone who lived on a Caribbean island. They probably would recount how as a child she had a habit of stretching the truth a bit, and now as an adult her ability in that area had definitely increased. Lucky for her, she was out of the country and there was no chance of them ever finding out.

Upon entering the room where Nadine would sleep, Catherine produced a box of matches from the folds of her dress and lit a lamp near the door. She released a heavy sigh, and began to talk in hushed tones.

"You have to understand Madame Deane, Miss Nadine. Her world is made up of the past and the present. For her, in some ways, they are one. But don't you think for a moment that she is not aware of what is going on around her. She is. Sometimes she just interprets it a little differently than other people. To tell you the truth, through the years I've come to enjoy it," Catherine confided as she turned back the bed. "It brings the mystery and the power of the past into a somewhat uneventful present. And I knew she would react the way she did when she saw you." She waved her index finger. "I believe it did me, as well as Madame Deane, some good to see that old spark return to her eyes. It used to burn all the time before her accident. But you need not worry about any of that." Catherine tugged at her head wrap. "Just get a good night's sleep, and you will be able to go on your way tomorrow. I'll get Clarence, he's the handyman around here, to take you," she remarked as she fluffed the pillows. "I believe it was Clarence who told you to follow him here. His ways take a little getting used to, but he's really not so bad." She put her hands on her boxy hips. "Would you care for anything to eat?"

Nadine watched the Bajan woman puttering around as if she were her maid and it hit her again, how far away she was from Mississippi. "I really hate to put you through any more trouble than I already have, but I *am* hungry," Nadine confessed. "I had a half of a sandwich for lunch, and that seems like eons ago."

"Is that all you had during the midday meal?" Catherine leaned back. "Here, lunch is our main meal of the day. Don't worry." She waved her hand. "I will bring you some codfish balls and cakes that were left over from supper today."

Nadine had no idea what codfish balls were, but

it didn't matter. She was hungry enough to eat anything. "Alright," she replied.

"Good. But first you might want to clean up a bit," Catherine said, removing a couple of leaves from Nadine's hair. "I'll be back with some towels, and something for you to sleep in. The bathroom is down the hall between this bedroom and Master Ulysses' bedchamber. He went to Barbados about three days ago and is not expected back until tomorrow," she said before shutting the door behind her.

Glancing about the room, Nadine could see that it was tastefully decorated with an antique dressing table and bed. She walked over to the mirror that rose above the dressing table and was stunned by her appearance. She looked like she had been through a major ordeal. There was a strained look on her face and large pieces of leaves and twigs were sticking out of her hair. Nadine began to remove the debris and decided this had been the most harrowing day of her life. She comforted herself by thinking it was all coming to an end, and somehow, tomorrow, she would contact Dr. Steward to put her life in order again.

Her hands felt heavy as she removed the flexible ponytail holder from her thick, light-auburn hair. Once freed, it reached just below her shoulders. Nadine looked at it. Gloria, her dearest friend, had always encouraged her to wear her hair down. She said that Nadine's hair was one of her best assets, but Nadine had never worn it that way. She had felt it would call too much attention to herself, which would be a vain thing to do, and of course, in the Lord's eyes vanity was a sin.

With her thoughts far away Nadine unconsciously arranged her hair attractively around her face, but when she realized what she had done she stopped abruptly, and smoothed it back with her hands.

"It needs washing, that's all," she said to the strange surroundings.

She steered her thoughts to the moment at hand, and how ill-prepared she was to spend the night away from her hotel room. She had very little with her in the fanny pack. Nadine unzipped the small bag, thinking of the toiletries she did not have, and was surprised to see the onyx slab. It had been forgotten in the midst of everything else that had taken place.

She attempted to take it out, but the task was difficult; the stone was stuck inside the pack with her large-tooth comb. When she was able to remove it a conversation surfaced in her mind. She had overheard her boss and a colleague discussing a collection known as the Gaia Series, a set of stone carvings that some believed were tied to a legend on Eros. Either way, for their artistic value or for their mysterious origins, they felt the set was very important. Nadine thought they said one of the pieces was an onyx unicorn. For a moment she considered the probability that the unicorn carved on the slab was the one they referred to, but she quickly discredited the thought. It would be highly unlikely that she had discovered one of the rare pieces during her first day on Eros. She placed the onyx slab in the lower drawer of the dressing table.

Nadine looked at the remaining items in the pack, her comb, her glasses, and a small care case for her contact lenses. She had bought the lenses the day before she left Memphis, but did not put them in her eyes until she arrived at the airport. It was her way of lessening her chances of running into someone she knew. Nadine wanted to anonymously get accustomed to living without the thick-lensed glasses she had worn her entire life. On a deeper level, she had decided the contact lenses and the trip to the Caribbean were the first steps toward a new approach to her life. Although the notion was quite scary, she was determined to be a changed woman when she set foot in the United States again. A woman who was open to new, stimulating situations. A woman who was not afraid to live and to love.

Of its own volition Nadine's brow lifted. Yes, she was open to new experiences on Eros and Barbados, but not the unexpected situations she had thus far encountered. Here it was her first day: there had been an earthquake, she had nearly been killed by a rock avalanche, and now, at this very moment, she was staying in the bowels of this island at the home of some strange white folks, led here by a mysterious man, while the owner of the place, eccentric to say the least, thought she was someone called Lenora.

But even today's events hardly dimmed the sparkle of Nadine's delight over being in the islands. Her love for her work was unshakable. She was here to do the work she had aspired to: historical research. The Caribbean was a land she had always dreamed of visiting and this house and its occupants surpassed even her wildest imaginings. Nadine believed the Deane family had lived on Eros for many generations. Perhaps before she left tomorrow she could talk to Catherine, or even Madame Deane, although she was a little unbalanced.

Yet Catherine had said she was well aware of the past and the present.

Nadine heard a warning tap before Catherine opened the bedroom door. The housekeeper brought in the towels and clothing she had promised.

"The food will be here by the time you return from your bath. The bathing area is behind the first door you come to, where the two hallways connect. I lit all of the lamps before I went to get the towels, so you shouldn't have any problem finding your way."

"Thanks," Nadine replied.

"I've already run your bathwater. I suggest you hurry before it gets cold. If you leave your clothes here while you're bathing, I can repair your pants and have them washed and ready for you sometime in the morning."

"Wow. Such service," Nadine exclaimed as she continued to be surprised. "Thank you. I really appreciate it."

Catherine nodded then disappeared into the corridor.

Nadine removed her pants and top, and donned the homespun linen robe which had been provided for her. It felt soft and pleasant against her skin. Catherine had also given her rawhide thongs for her feet.

Finding the bathing room was easy. Carefully, Nadine opened the door which had carved dolphins on the surface. She kept thinking about everything that had happened to her within the last few hours. It was almost unbelievable, and the research possibilities were beyond belief. Nadine let out a shriek. The cause for her scare was her own reflection in an oval mirror.

"Oh, God," she gasped, laughing to herself and shaking her head. "I can't stand it. I am nothing but a ball of nerves," she explained to her image with exaggerated movements. "Now what would the ever-prepared Gloria advise?" Nadine leaned closer to her image in the mirror before she began to mimic her friend. "Just chill, girlfriend," she said, then laughed nervously.

Gloria. The only real friend she ever had. Nadine wrapped both arms around the towels and held them close to her chest, placing her chin on top of them. I wonder what she is up to, she thought. I am sure she is the life of the party, picnic, community meeting, or wherever she may be, and out-dressing everyone at each event. But of course if things did get just the slightest bit dull, Nadine could see Gloria "throwing a little party," and inviting everybody who was anybody in Atlanta's black community. Nadine smiled at the familiar images.

They had been such opposites at Spelman College. Gloria was the socialite originally from Atlanta, and she was the shy introvert from a small country town. All of the young women who felt self-confident and good about themselves loved to be seen with Gloria Turner; it enhanced their clout and their image on campus. But Gloria was no snob. She was as adaptive as a chameleon and could get down with the best of them. Yes, Gloria knew what was happenin' and she knew how to call upon her cultured side, whatever best served her purpose.

Nadine knew, in the beginning, Gloria had felt

sorry for her. Most coeds thought she was a Holy
Roller with country-bumpkin ways. Could be kind
of cute, the guys would say, but you had to look
hard to see it. As they put it, it was all going to
waste underneath long dresses and skirts, and wide
tops. The word was: she just didn't know what to
do with what she had.

But fate had thrown Nadine and Gloria together
in several classes. With time, and despite their differences, they discovered they genuinely liked one
another. Eventually, Gloria took Nadine under her
wing and taught her all sorts of female things that
Grandma Rose had felt she did not need to know.
Makeup. The colors that best suited her, and the
kinds of clothes that complemented her curvy
frame. She also picked up some tidbits about socializing on the way. But Nadine had never found
any real use for her friend's lessons. So, she stored
them away in her mind, as she stored away the
beautiful lingerie she felt compelled to buy. Finding comfort in the knowledge that they were there,
but never daring to wear them.

The last time Nadine had seen Gloria was at their
college graduation, three years ago. They promised
to always write or call, and for a while they did.
Meanwhile Nadine furthered her education at the
Brooks Art Institute in Memphis while teaching
part-time in an optional school for exceptional students. Whenever she saw a very smartly dressed
woman with class to match, she thought of her
friend, and even though she admired such things,
she felt they had no place in her life.

Gloria's letters were the highlight of those years.
Filled with events and people that Nadine could
only dream about, written from cities and countries

she had only read or heard of. The last letter she received said Gloria was embarking on a trip to India, and she'd be hearing from her soon. But soon ended up being a year, and it was only a couple of months ago that she received a short note, nothing like the letters of old.

Nadine walked over to one of the long counters lining the walls of the room, put down the towels, removed her contact lenses, and placed them in the case. She noticed shampoo and body oils were neatly placed on one side of the marble slate, while bottles of varying scents huddled together in the center. Another huge mirror in a sculpted, painted frame hung above it, while stools crowned with ample cushions were spaced out below.

Nadine's attention was drawn to a spacious opening that led further into the interior of the unusually shaped bathroom. It grew darker as she progressed. Catherine had said she had lit all the lamps, so Nadine assumed one of the lamps had gone out on its own. She hurried out to get the matches Catherine had provided. Upon her return, she stepped inside the dark area. The wall felt finely textured as she rubbed her hand along the surface, feeling for the candle-like lamp that she assumed would be there.

"Ah, here it is," she announced, striking the match and placing the flame against the used wick. Amazingly, an impressive sculpture of Poseidon sprang into view between clouds of steam. The massive object dominated the huge room with his furling beard and poised three-pronged spear. His scaly tail divided a mammoth sunken tub. Nadine could hardly believe her eyes. Had she lived a thousand years, never in her wildest dreams could she have imagined such a sight inside someone's home, let alone their bath!

The flame from the lamp created many foreboding shadows, and the sea god's icy stare did not help matters much as Nadine looked warily at the imposing, powerful figure.

"My, aren't we fancy." She spoke aloud, finding comfort in her own voice. "Well, I tell ya. I've never undressed in front of a man before," she professed teasingly. "So if you'll just close those big eyes of yours, I'd be awfully obliged." She mimicked the Southern belles she'd heard so much about as a child.

Nadine began to untie the belt around her waist. Just as she had almost completed her task, she heard a husky, masculine voice coming from Poseidon's direction.

"I would love to see what is underneath that robe, but I do not know if you are ready to show it."

Chapter 4

Nadine stared with disbelief at the magnificent statue.

"I can tell from the conversation you have been having with yourself," the silky voice continued, "you probably believe this statue is the one who is talking. I hate to disappoint you and tell you it is not so." There was ill-concealed mirth beneath the words.

Instinctively, Nadine grabbed the folds of the partially open robe around her. She stood there at a loss for words. The sound of parting water followed as Nadine watched a faint figure emerge from behind the sea god's tail. His movements were inappropriately calm, considering the circumstances. Slowly, the shadowy figure took on a more distinct shape as he progressed toward the front of the marble structure.

Loose, glistening, dark curls, heavy with water, clung to a well-formed head that topped a broad chest, matted with curly hair. His movements revealed an animal-like grace, and Nadine had the distinct feeling he could be as virile as any. There was quite a bit of space between them and the lamplight was hampered by the ever-rising steam, preventing her from discerning his facial features.

Then it hit her, just as the mysterious stranger spoke again, if it were not for the dense vapors about his lower frame, she would be staring at a stark-naked man.

"Even though *I* have undressed in front of a woman before," he announced, tauntingly, "unless you want to see something you obviously have not seen in living color, I suggest you close your eyes or do whatever makes you feel most comfortable." He continued to advance.

Nadine snatched around like the devil himself had commanded her, facing the lamp she had just lit. She was totally speechless as she listened to the splatter of his wet, bare feet crossing the room in her direction. He stopped not far behind her, and bent over to pick up a towel that was almost beneath her feet. Nadine glanced down and saw his hand retrieve the bundled object. She thought she could feel the heat from his nude body he stood so close.

"Do you always follow directions so well?" he asked, his voice indicating he was enjoying her discomfort.

"Only when I'm in the room with a naked man I've never met before!" was her exasperated reply.

"But that is not true," he continued in his mild accent. "We met earlier today in the cave. Or have you forgotten? By the way, you can turn around now."

Nadine looked, cautiously, to the side. She could see him folding the towel in around his waist. Feeling more secure now that the stranger was at least half-dressed, and incensed over the fact that he had not announced his presence earlier, she turned to confront him. "Is this the way you usually act, inviting strangers to your employer's home, then leaving them in the process?" She glared, flustered by the situation. "You probably didn't tell me you were in here because you don't have any business here in the first place."

But even under the extraordinary circumstances, when Nadine finally stopped talking and looked into his eyes a kind of sinking feeling began in the pit of her stomach. Unspoken chemistry bolted between them and she was stunned by the foreign sensation. Despite her sincere anger Nadine could feel herself being drawn into the inky depths of his eyes. She felt light-headed, and for a moment she feared she might faint.

Ulysses looked down into the captivating expressions crossing the woman's face. He guessed she was in her early to mid-twenties, and he realized that rarely, if ever, had he seen such a strange mix of emotions. Fear, anger, anxiousness along with hopeful anticipation. He could smell a fading scent of floral perfume about her, and the single candle flame provided an enticing backdrop for hair and skin whose tones were so much alike, it gave her a surreal appearance. Hazel eyes hauntingly searched his and her petite but bountiful bottom lip became slack, as tiny audible breaths passed from her. Ulysses felt he had no choice but to comply with the woman's silent bidding.

Nadine had no idea what was happening to her, but she could not withdraw from the magnetic hold he seemed to have. Their gazes remained locked as his dark head descended slowly. At first she thought she was imagining it; the gamut of emotions she had experienced that day were so far from normal, perhaps she was taking leave of her senses. But when his soft but firm lips touched hers, the sensations that began to smolder within Nadine were real. Like dry tinder that had been waiting to be ignited, her entire being began to respond to his kiss. The feel of his lips was devastating. Just the slightest touch made her knees feel weak and she longed for more. But somewhere in the back of her mind reality muscled its way forward, and when Nadine was fully cognizant of the inappropriateness of her actions, she yanked her head back.

"Just what are you doing?" she exclaimed, totally surprised by him, but even more surprised at herself.

"I never pass up invitations like the one you just gave me," he countered, his voice husky, seductive.

"I don't know what you're talking about." She was completely shaken by what had just transpired.

"Well, you are in deep trouble if you do not." A knowledgeable gleam entered his eye.

Flustered, Nadine shifted her approach. "You're the one who will be in deep trouble if you don't tell me what you're doing here. I'm going to have to report this to Catherine or even Madame Deane."

"Is that right?" His dark gaze raked over her insultingly. "I do not feel I owe any kind of explanation to a woman who talks to herself, *and* to statues. But if you must know, my name is Ulysses Deane, and I do have business, as you put it, here. I own Sovereign."

Embarrassed, Nadine watched Ulysses' back after he passed by her. Quickly, her discomfort and surprise turned into anger. "I don't care if you do own the place. You are one rude, presumptuous man!'' she blurted as the door closed behind him.

The gall of this guy, Nadine thought as she stood staring at the door, her latest encounter with Ulysses Deane flitting through her mind. Needless to say by now she was in no mood for a long leisurely bath. Mr. Deane had spoiled all that. Instead she marched over to the bathroom door and locked it from the inside, then turned and flattened her back against it as she thought he might return. Yet deep inside Nadine knew barring him from the room could not rid her of the feelings he had created inside of her.

She closed her eyes to better feel the warmth that was still there. The sensation called up disdain in one part of her, while another longed to embrace it, explore it. The kiss was so new and deliciously frightening; it seeped into and caressed the most private parts of her. She felt embarrassed again, and automatically, her hand covered her mouth. How could she dote on these ungodly feelings created by a man who was a complete stranger? He was so different from the men she usually found attractive. They were all very dark-skinned with hair that was close-cut and neat. Ulysses Deane did not fit either one of those molds. His looks reflected his heritage. He was a foreigner, not a brother, and Nadine's old friend, guilt, prodded her again, but this time it was for being attracted to a man outside of her race.

Nervous and ill at ease, Nadine decided that tonight, a quick washup would do just as well as a bath. She ran the water and started the task, her ears keen to every sound around her. Her senses ready. But for what?

She held the soft towel up to her face, burying

her features in it, then patted her flawless skin dry. Nadine chastised herself for the direction of her thoughts, but it was like scolding a child for desiring sweets. The feel of Ulysses' bare body so close to hers as he gazed knowingly into her eyes kept surfacing. It was as if he sensed beneath her affront some deeper feelings. Then he had kissed her. She had been kissed before, but never like that, and never by such an attractive man who, but for a square of terry cloth, was naked.

Although Nadine's eyes had been riveted upward, focusing on Ulysses' face, she had been very much aware of his muscular arms and chest, and the thick hair on the latter which was almost level with her face. Nadine shut her eyes, tight, for she dared not think what lay beneath that cloth, but the images continued to come. She could see him as he walked away, how his torso tapered into a thin waist and slender hips, his towel pressed against firm buttocks with muscles that tightened and released as he moved.

Looking at Ulysses Deane sparked the ache that occurred whenever Nadine had the unsettling dreams. A teasing warmth deep inside bubbled up, eventually becoming a threat if it was not released. A couple of years ago she had written and told Gloria about the dreams. There was no one else she felt close enough to, to reveal such personal things about herself. Gloria had written back making light of her dilemma. "Girlfriend," she had penned, "nature is letting you know you weren't born to be nobody's nun. You better take care of that," and she went on to describe ways that Nadine could do just that. It made her feel flushed even now just to think of some of them.

Nadine recently had begun to look outside of the more restrictive religious practices that she had embraced. Although her high moral standards had cost her more than one budding relationship, Nadine was determined she would not become intimately involved until she was ready. At twenty-six she was feeling more than prepared.

Her mood changed when she searched her reflection above the silver-embossed basin. Her hair was a voluminous brown cloud surrounding her face, sprinkled with remnants from the forest. There was a sparkle in her eye and a wildness about her that was unfamiliar but invigorating. She claimed the free being that she saw in the glass as part of her new identity, and Nadine submerged her hair under the running tap water. It was a kind of baptism and acceptance of that budding part of her.

As Nadine dried her hair then managed to gather it together, braiding it into a single French braid from the crown down the back of her head, there was a sense of anticipation, an impending awakening. Her eyes were extremely bright when she looked in the mirror for the last time, and she hurried into the hallway, attempting to discredit the feeling as she returned to her room. Tomorrow she would be leaving this place and the strange people within it. Nothing would make her happier. She looked up apprehensively in the direction of her maker.

After eating the codfish balls Catherine had left, Nadine climbed into bed and placed another towel on the pillow. As she closed her eyes she prayed that denying her true feelings would not also be a part of her new identity.

Chapter 5

"Catherine, you cannot let Lenora sleep too late this morning. We have all kinds of things to discuss. I know the poor woman must get antsy whenever she thinks about her fateful meeting with the cliff dwellers." Madame Deane clicked her tongue several times for emphasis.

Clarence's dark eyebrows rose as Madame Deane made the assertions, but he continued to tend the pink and white orchids growing in a large flower box. Madame Deane rolled her wheelchair behind Catherine, who was bringing in the morning meal.

"I like having breakfast on the lanai," Madame Deane commented as they entered the screened-in room. "I enjoy the fresh morning air."

"It is good for you, madame," Catherine replied. "It helps put color back into those papery cheeks of yours." She looked back at her mistress and displayed surprise at how much Madame Deane looked like her old self this morning as she rattled on about the new houseguest.

"Do you think Lenora's awake, Catherine?"

"Now Madame Deane, the young lady calls herself Nadine. She does not know anything about this Lenora story you keep talking about.''

"I know. I know," she shook her white head agitatedly, "but that does not make any difference because I tell you she is the one spoken of in the Legend of Lenora. Don't you think it is rather strange the way she turned up here last night?'' Madame Deane continued before Catherine had a chance to answer. ''And you cannot tell me she does not resemble the Lenora I have been telling you about. She has the same strange features. Her hair, skin, and eyes are virtually the same color, almost blending one into the other. You must admit that is very unique.''

Catherine did not answer. She simply looked up at the screen above.

Madame Deane placed her finger on the tip of her nose. "Did you do what I told you to do, Catherine? About the dress, I mean?''

Nodding, Catherine answered, "Yes, madame, I did.''

"Good. Because you see I've got it all right here," a charged-up Madame Deane announced, patting a small roll of animal skin. ''Well, a part of it. The last page is missing, but most of the story is here. Right here," she said emphatically. ''I've just got to remember where I hid that page. I was trying to hide it from everyone else and I hid it from myself. Even if I do find it *she* wants me to keep it a secret until the proper time.''

Catherine looked at the dirty piece of animal skin and sighed. Madame Deane was always claiming to have found some special treasure, but the objects were treasures to her because of how she perceived the world. "Madame, I do not like you exciting yourself like this,'' Catherine warned. "Miss Nadine has plans to leave today, and I do not think she is going to take too kindly to our replacing her clothes with that getup you provided.''

"Getup? What do you mean, getup? Why, it is a woman's duty to weave her own cloth right here in her home. I do it every day, Catherine. Do not try to confuse me.''

"Yes, madame,'' Catherine replied as she rolled her eyes. How very well aware she was of the madame's weaving. Each time she saw her begin a new color pattern it became increasingly more difficult to find a store-bought or hand-woven one to replace the bungled mess.

"And what is this about Lenora wanting to leave?'' Two whisper-thin white brows knitted together in consternation.

"I do not think anyone is going anywhere,'' Clarence announced, "at least not for a while. All the main paths and roads are blocked. I talked to one of the servants over at Sharpe Hall. He told me some of their workers are still stuck down by the lower wharf.''

"Well, they are better off down there than they are with those two-faced Sharpes,'' Madame Deane spat out disapprovingly. "They have too many servants anyway.''

"Did I hear my name mentioned?'' A rather short man with brown hair approached the screened door. The black collar of his shirt overlapped a bright-red vest, giving his ruddy skin an even redder tone.

"Yes, you did. And if you ask me—''

"Good morning, Master Sharpe.'' Catherine cut Madame Deane off before she could do any more damage. "Madame Deane was just saying how hard it is to get good help these days. With your having such a large estate and all, it would be easier if you had a competent overseer to head up the workers in your sugarcane fields."

"You could not be more right, Catherine, and it is because of that very thing that I am visiting Sovereign today. I must say, it makes me feel good to know my neighbors are concerned about my welfare."

Madame Deane eyed the young man suspiciously, then slid the animal skin between the folds of her dress as she gave a sarcastic "Humph," which Catherine attempted to cover up by clearing her throat.

"Would you care for breakfast, Master Sharpe?"

Madame Deane looked at Catherine as if she had sided with the enemy. Then she leaned over and placed a protective arm about her portion of fresh fruit, cheese, bread, and honey, making her feelings about sharing obvious.

Rodney Sharpe put forth his most engaging smile, ignoring his cantankerous neighbor. "Thank you, Catherine, I would love a cup of coffee. By the way is Ulysses back?"

"No, he is not," Madame Deane responded in a refined, mature voice. "We are expecting my nephew back tomorrow."

Her tone was completely different from moments before, and Rodney looked at her as if he expected to see someone else. And in a way she was. Madame Deane's posture now appeared regal, and the wild look in her eyes had been replaced by an almost genteel glow. Rodney sat down in the chair across the table from her. He appeared unnerved by the change, as if he were more comfortable with her initial persona.

"I am truly beginning to miss him." She looked up from her plate wistfully, her back arrow-straight in her wheelchair, her frail chin holding an aristocratic tilt. "And now that all the roads are blocked, there is no telling when he will return."

"Well," came a deep voice from the doorway, "you can stop worrying, Aunt Helen. The most beautiful woman on Eros should never worry." The words reflected Ulysses' admiration for his only aunt. "And with the way you look this morning, even Cleopatra of Egypt would be envious of you."

"Ulysses! You are back!" Madame Deane's frail shoulders seemed to straighten as he bent and kissed her withered cheek. Her eyes twinkled as she followed his movements, watching him fold his six-feet-two frame into the chair beside hers. He was taller than his father had been, taller than most of the people on Eros, but height wasn't the only thing that made Ulysses Deane unique.

His bountiful black curls brushed his neck in a virile, disorderly fashion. One curl managed to escape and hang provocatively low on his forehead. Madame Deane recalled when he was a child how she would twirl it on her index finger, tweaking it repeatedly to watch it spring back and forth. She had always loved his curly hair. Her lips turned up in an attractive smile as she thought of how Ulysses blamed her for training the stray curl whenever it materialized at inopportune times.

Helen Deane continued to look at her nephew. His eyebrows were uncharacteristically arched as if

drawn with a fine hand. The word "uncharacter-
istic" came to mind because there was nothing
about his character that was not explosive, even
unruly. He was his own man, and all of his life he
had paid the price for it.

It was hard for her to see her heritage, the British
heritage, in Ulysses' face with his strong nose,
mouth, and jaw. But his mother's heritage, Egypt,
was quite obvious in his skin color and his hair,
setting him apart from the group at the table. His
hair texture was curlier and coarser than her own,
and to her, his complexion was a most interesting
hue, for his skin was decisively darker, a deep car-
amel. Because of Ulysses' coloring, his perfect
teeth shone brightly as he surrendered an uncom-
mon, but nevertheless melting smile in his aunt's
direction.

Ulysses had always been fond of his aunt. When
Helen Deane was completely present, like this
morning, it reminded him of the times before her
accident. Her Greek dress and the artificial band of
olive leaves were the only obvious signs of her eccentricity.

"Catherine, bring Ulysses his favorite, coconut
water and conkies," Madame Deane called. "And
check on our guest as well, would you please."

"Of course," Catherine replied and went back
inside the house.

Catherine opened the door to Nadine's bedroom
and peered inside to see if Nadine still slept. She
saw the bed was empty and made up, and she announced herself in a proper manner.

"Miss Nadine, it is Catherine. May I come in?"

"Of course, Catherine. How are you this morning?" she inquired from her seat on a divan.

Nadine had been awake for a while, but without her clothes she was confined to her room. In their place were two pieces of finely crinkled linen draped across the end of the sofa.

"I am fine, thank you," Catherine replied. "Madame Deane sent me to check on you. I told her you would be disappointed not seeing your clothes this morning, but she insisted that I leave the pieces of cloth so you could wear a chiton today. I tried to explain to her about your plans to leave Sovereign, but she would not hear it. Now Clarence says the earthquake made all the major paths and roads on the island impassable. So it appears you are stuck here with us, at least for a day or so."

"Impassable." Nadine repeated the word as if she did not understand, so caught up was she in the inevitability of seeing Ulysses Deane again. Yet she made sure her response to Catherine did not convey her thoughts. "What in the world am I going to do? I need to let my boss, Dr. Steward, know where I am. He's got to be worried about me, and each day I remain here I am getting further behind in my assigned work."

"There is nothing you can do about that at the moment," Catherine stated flatly then added, "Come down and join everyone for breakfast. Master Ulysses has returned. He and Rodney Sharpe are with Madame Deane on the porch."

Nadine rubbed her fingers across her forehead the way she always did when something was on her mind. "I believe I met Mr. Deane last night. As a matter of fact he was the one who led me here."

"Is that right?" Catherine replied, mildly amused. "Ulysses is Ulysses, the handsome devil.

If I had not seen him grow up and go through some things no child or adult should experience, I don't think I would ever understand him. I tell you this family has had its share of problems.''

"I'd say he is quite an enigma, and he likes the dark too.'' Nadine's last words trailed off as she thought of her second meeting with Ulysses.

"Pardon me?'' Catherine looked at Nadine, confused.

"Never mind,'' she replied quickly, then changed the subject. "Catherine, I can't possibly go down there wearing this piece of material. They'll think I'm crazy,'' she proclaimed, while admitting to herself that Ulysses probably already did after hearing her talk to herself and to the statue in the bath.

"I can understand how you feel, Miss Nadine, but I do not want to upset Madame Deane. You see, it's not really her fault that she has such an obsession with Greece. If you are to blame anyone, you can blame her brother, Master Peter. He wanted to claim all of his ancestors, he used to say, and he swore way before the British Deanes settled in this part of the world they were adventurers and pirates whose blood was a mixture of Greek and Portuguese. When the Deanes came here back in the late sixteen hundreds, they brought plenty of proof of that heritage with them in the books and art they owned. It was the Deanes who gave that statue of Dionysus to the island of Eros.'' She nodded her head proudly before taking on a somber look. "So Greece holds a certain fascination for Madame Deane that she inherited for good or bad from her brother. And with the accident and all . . .'' She looked down at the floor before look-

ing up again. "When I left her a few moments ago
she was the perfect lady of the house. If I told her
you refused to wear it, I just know it would bring
out her . . . other side." She looked away momentarily. "Besides, with my help, you would look
wonderful in it."

Nadine did not like the thought of meeting Ulysses again wearing an ancient Greek dress. She
would feel awkward enough if dressed in her best
suit, pumps, and a single strand of pearls. But a
Grecian costume! She looked at the housekeeper
who was waiting for an answer. Still, Nadine
thought, she had to consider, it was because of Madame Deane's hospitality that she had a place to
stay after the earthquake. Nadine was reluctant to
admit Ulysses Deane had a part in it as well.

"The longer we take, the more agitated Madame
Deane will become," Catherine added. "Soon we
will hear her wheelchair roll up to your door and
believe me, you will not like what you see if she
is upset. It is not a pretty sight," she concluded,
pleading her mistress' case.

Nadine hesitated only a moment longer. "Okay.
Fine. I'll wear it. But you're going to help me."

"But of course I will," Catherine replied, removing the soft pieces of material from the divan.

Nadine watched as she held them up lengthwise,
then folded them over about a quarter of their width
and placed one of the pieces in front of her, the
other at her back. "Now, hold the material right
here," she instructed, bunching the cloth together
above Nadine's slender shoulders.

Absorbed in what Catherine was doing, she
obeyed. The housekeeper went to the dresser and
took two brooches out of an intricately woven con-

tainer. Afterwards she used the trinkets to fasten the cloth together on top of Nadine's shoulders. Nadine was amazed at how quickly the dress was completed with no sewing or cutting, as well as how it fell in graceful folds about her upper body, creating a sleeveless look. As a finishing touch Catherine placed a piece of decorative cord to serve as a belt. She fluffed and bloused the garment above the belt, and below it, creating large ripples that continued down to the floor.

Once Catherine's handiwork was completed, Nadine turned to look at herself in the full-length mirror. She simply stared, barely recognizing herself. The only physical reminders of the woman she knew were the dark spots that remained beside her nose from wearing eyeglasses, and her round butt that was a Clayton trademark.

"My, my, my. You are a picture," Catherine crooned, standing behind her. "That shade of green brings out the color of your eyes, and with your hair pulled back like that, it gives them an exotic look." She tilted her head to the side. "And if you don't mind me saying so, I do not think I have ever seen anyone whose skin was such a color. Your hair almost matches it to a tee," Catherine proclaimed. "It reminds me of one of my spices. Cinnamon, that is what. It reminds me of cinnamon. But I have to tell you it's those unusual-colored eyes that are your best feature. They are nothing less than captivating."

Nadine could feel herself blushing under such unadulterated praise, but she had to admit she was pleased by what she saw in the mirror. Somehow the chiton had transformed her from the lackluster woman who grew up in a small Mississippi town into an almost ethereal being. It was a new beginning and Nadine knew that Gloria would be impressed.

"I can't believe it," she heard herself say softly. "I look like something out of a book." She studied her own image. "As a child I loved reading stories about faraway places, and I would have dreams of being there. Many of the dreams took place on islands like this one. I would go there as a stranger, but I would always be very well received, as if I was coming back home. I would be given gifts of jewelry, clothing. Once I was even given a story that had been written about me. It became my childhood secret, believing in and vowing to find that written story."

Nadine's awe over seeing her gossamer image in the glass had goaded her into professing some of her most private thoughts. Aware of what she had revealed, Nadine looked into Catherine's wary features. "Don't you tell anybody I said that, Catherine," she threatened. "As my grandma used to say, sometimes I get beside myself."

"No, you are right, Miss Nadine," Catherine replied, her eyes becoming cow-like. "It is amazing how well the style and color suits you. Almost like you had worn clothes like this before." Her words were breathy. She avoided Nadine's eyes as Nadine sought hers in the mirror.

"You're thinking about Madame Deane, aren't you?"

Catherine nodded.

"Lenora." Nadine sampled the name out loud. "That's the name she called me, isn't it?"

"Yes, it is."

"It's such a beautiful name. Did she really exist?"

"I really cannot say, Miss Nadine. I only know the bits and pieces Madame Deane has told me and they were a ball of confusion," Catherine rushed on. "We would need all the time in the world to make sense of it. Sometimes in her world a plain rock is a precious gem and an old animal skin is an ancient manuscript. So I can assure you we don't have time to make sense of the things Madame Deane talks about, not if we want to get down to breakfast before madame comes looking for us."

Nadine could tell Catherine did not want to discuss the matter. If the housekeeper believed that the story surrounding this woman, Lenora, was just the mental meanderings of an eccentric old woman, why would she avoid discussing it? "I guess you're right. All I need to do is slip on these sandals." She placed her feet into the leather shoes. "There. A perfect fit."

Feeling the spirit of the costume overtake her, Nadine held the material up daintily above her ankles. "After you, Catherine."

The housekeeper beamed a generous smile. "Madame will be pleased when she sets eyes on you."

Chapter 6

Nadine stood motionless in the doorway, watching the three people at the breakfast table. Catherine had led her to the lanai, but had continued down the hallway to get more food for the morning meal. Nadine thought the scene was a unique blend of old and new. The furnishings, the landscape, and Madame Deane's clothing appeared to be from another time, while the two men were of the present. Nadine found herself focusing on Ulysses. She could feel her confidence, bolstered by the pleasure in her appearance, slipping away when Madame Deane spotted her. Immediately, the woman's eyes took on an unnatural glow, reminding Nadine of how bizarre the occupants of Sovereign really were. She wondered what was going on in Madame Deane's mind as her gaze darted from her to Ulysses.

"Well, our guest is here, Ulysses." Madame Deane motioned for Nadine to come closer as Ulysses turned his eyes toward her. Rodney also watched her advance.

As she approached them, Nadine was grateful for the feel of soft material flowing about her. She felt elegant, and judging from the expressions on everyone's faces, she looked it as well.

Nadine then decided to take advantage of the situation life had offered. No one knew her here, or had ever heard of Nadine Clayton of Ashland, Mississippi. Here, she could be the woman she had secretly yearned to be. A woman with worldly experience, cultured, knowledgeable. There would be no one here to say she was putting on airs. Here, Gloria's lessons would be of good use.

Nadine knew she would need all the self-confidence she could muster as Ulysses watched her advance. His penetrating gaze seemed to take in everything. When she reached the table both of the men stood. Ulysses towered considerably above his breakfast companion.

"Ulysses, Rodney, this is Le—excuse me, Nadine. Your last name escapes me, dear." An almost imperceptible nervous twitch tugged at Madame Deane's wrinkled lips.

"Clayton. Nadine Clayton," she replied in her most impeccable style.

With one well-formed eyebrow slightly raised, Ulysses studied the young woman who sat across the table from him now. This poised creature was nothing like the woman he had observed talking to herself the night before, nor the near-hysterical female he had met in the cave. She had been unpretentious, almost transparent. He could never see this woman displaying the raw expressions that crossed her face the night before.

"Miss Clayton and I had the . . . pleasure of meeting yesterday," Ulysses announced.

Nadine glanced down for only a moment. Ulysses' pause behind the word "pleasure" went unnoticed by Madame Deane and Rodney, but his meaning was not lost to her. Controlling the heat that was rising to her face, she pursued his line of conversation.

"Yes, we did. It was Mr. Deane who invited me here in the first place. I am thankful to the two of you for your hospitality," she added graciously, displaying her most accommodating smile.

"Well, I for one am glad that he did," Rodney interjected with an appreciative boyish grin. "It is rare that we have outsiders travel so far inland. And I must say I cannot remember ever seeing one so lovely."

Nadine flashed a sincere smile. "Why, thank you. But I have to admit the earthquake forced me to take refuge here. My visit with Madame Deane and Mr. Deane was not planned. And I hope to be able to return to my work as soon as possible."

"What kind of work is that?" Madame Deane queried as her fingers busied themselves with her olive-branch headband.

Nadine noticed a slight change in the pitch of her hostess' voice. Her shoulders had begun to slump forward in her chair, and the nervous quiver about her mouth was more apparent than before.

"I work with the World Treasures Institute gathering information for a centralized computer located in Paris. This particular system is similar to a giant library where you will be able to find out about literary and art treasures from all over the globe. I . . . lead a project which is responsible for historical research of the people, literature, and artifacts native to this area." Nadine's brownish-jade eyes opened wider as she heard the little white lie come out of her mouth.

Now why did I have to say that? It wouldn't

make any difference to them if I were an art consultant or a historian, she thought. Actually, I am a little of both, though on this project, I am the lowest person on the totem pole. Still, I must admit, "historian" sounds so much more elite.

"I am sure you will find we are quite an interesting people," Ulysses remarked with veiled eyes.

"And fate could not have placed you in a better spot than this, Miss Clayton. The Sovereign estate is known as 'the Protector of Eros' Treasures.' There's no other place richer in the history of Eros than right here," Rodney added. "And I see you are most definitely dressed for the part. I do not believe even Ulysses would have artifacts to top that."

A bizarre giggle surfaced from the end of the table. "That shows how much you know, Sharpe," Madame Deane replied with a hawkish glare. "But you don't need to know any more than you do," she goaded him. "Now that Lenora's come back, all the evil that has been going on around here is going to stop."

Nadine felt unnerved by the tiny woman's outburst, while Ulysses and Rodney passed perturbed understanding looks between them, though the latter was obviously embarrassed by the vehemence of Madame Deane's verbal assault.

"I believe it is time for your morning medication, Aunt Helen," Ulysses declared in a comforting but firm voice.

Like a dog caught stealing scraps from the dinner table, Madame Deane nodded her head sulkily, lowering it even further than Nadine thought physically possible.

Rodney took advantage of the moment and announced his departure. "I must be going now. It was nice to meet you, Miss Clayton." He extended his hand to Nadine. "And Ulysses, Basil says he has some important business to discuss with you if you can find time today. He is too busy to come to Sovereign. So drop by when you get a chance."

Nadine could see the muscle in Ulysses' jaw contract and expand.

"That is, if you have the time, Ulysses," Rodney added sheepishly.

"I will see," was Ulysses' only reply.

Rodney left as Catherine entered with a steaming pan of hot conkies and a pitcher of cold coconut water. The spicy smell of pumpkin, sweet potato, raisins, and coconut floated beneath Nadine's nose, making her stomach reply quietly to the aroma.

"Like Master Ulysses said, it is time for your medication, madame," Catherine stated as she placed the food on the table.

At first Madame Deane snatched away from the housekeeper, and pushed her lower lip out like a pouting child. Then her tiny head turned in Ulysses' direction, and she looked up at him with cowering eyes. He gazed back with a compassionate but firm look. She sat back in her wheelchair, and with a resigned sigh allowed Catherine to roll her away.

Nadine had no idea what to say, so to busy herself, and appease her hunger, she placed fresh slices of mango and tangerine on her plate along with a cup of yogurt. Ulysses preferred the conkies and coconut water that had been provided especially for him, and for a few moments they prepared their plates in silence.

Now that they were alone Nadine's confidence

in her charade began to ebb. Feeling nervous, she tried to give the impression of finding the slices of fruit and the yogurt more interesting to look at than the man that sat before her. Ulysses on the other hand seemed content to sit back, relaxed, with an open banana leaf in hand, never once removing his eyes from Nadine's face.

"I have never met an African-American historian from the United States before," Ulysses stated as he continued to watch her.

"Oh, well. Here I am in living color." Nadine let go a nervous laugh. "Some of my ancestors were from Africa and even this part of the world," she lamely explained.

"I see." He placed more food in his mouth. "It is different for me. My mother was African. She was an Egyptian. So my blood is half-African and half-British. I believe I know which one runs the hottest inside me." He stared into her eyes. "I claim both of them. But I was born of my mother's body, and therefore I hold my Egyptian heritage close to my heart."

"I can understand that," Nadine replied, somehow relieved. It made her feel Ulysses Deane was not as taboo as she first thought.

"So, Miss Clayton, does your research into our history include interviewing the people of Eros?"

She released a breath she did not realize she was holding. Nadine felt safe with the subject at hand. "Why, yes, it does, Mr. Deane. Along with reading your literature and uncovering your legends, if any. Could you tell me where to begin?"

Ulysses' dark eyes narrowed before he answered, "Yes, I could. With me."

Nadine let go a laugh that sounded to her ears

similar to Woody Woodpecker's. "I believe you
may be right. What did Mr. Sharpe call your estate,
'the Protector of Eros' Treasures'?"

"That is correct. And I must add we have treasures of all kinds. Tangible and intangible," Ulysses added in a husky voice.

"Well . . . I'm . . . sure you do," Nadine replied,
almost choking on a piece of mango at his innuendo. "Your house is a virtual museum from the
little I've seen of it. It must have been in your
family for a long time."

"According to our family records, some, if they
are authentic, and we have no cause to believe
other than that, date back hundreds of years. Sovereign has been in existence since the early seventeen hundreds. Many of our books and art date
back even further than that."

Nadine was fascinated to discover she was actually staying in a place that was rich in island history. Her facade forgotten, spellbound hazel eyes
soaked up the source of information. "You've got
to be kidding."

"No, I am not. If you do not believe me, you
can always ask the statue of Poseidon to verify his
origins."

At first Nadine was taken in by Ulysses' serious
tone. His quip had gone right past her. His eyes
were the only thing that reflected his jest. They
sparkled mischievously.

"Why, Mr. Deane," Nadine put on her best im-
itation of a mother chastising a naughty child,
while at the same time trying to recover her composure, "we all have our fantasies. Mine just happen to be rooted in an overly active imagination."

"Is the fantasy undressing before a merman or just undressing before a man?"

"Believe me, Mr. Deane—"

"I believe as of last night we are well enough acquainted for you to call me Ulysses."

"Uh . . . Ulysses," Nadine uncomfortably complied. "My fantasies are no different from any other woman my age."

"Is that so?" His voice was low, his eyes piercing. "I intend to make it my business to find out."

Nadine felt a twinge of fear and excitement from Ulysses' mild but definite threat. With an all too flowery wave of her hand, she patted the French braid at the back of her head. Now what would Gloria say to that?

"I wouldn't be too hasty if I were you. You may take on more than you can handle." She forced herself to look directly into his eyes, but underneath the table a nervous hand clenched and unclenched the silky chiton. Nadine pushed away from the table and rose to her feet, attempting a graceful getaway. "If it's alright with you, perhaps later on today I could see some of the books and artifacts you have here at Sovereign."

Ulysses' ebony eyes watched her with mild amusement. "You have my permission to do so. As a matter of fact, I will show you around myself."

"I'm sure with your having been away for a few days you're far too busy for that. So I'll just—"

"I think I would be the best judge of how busy I am, Nadine." His silky voice caressed her name. "I shall see you at two this afternoon if that is convenient." It was more of a statement than a question.

"That sounds fine." Nadine managed a brittle smile before turning away. *Now how are you going to handle this?* She entered the hallway. *My goodness, I wonder if all the men from this part of the world are so direct.* Once Nadine was alone she fanned herself with an open palm. *But I can't blame it all on him,* she chastised herself. *If I wanted to throw out sexual innuendoes I should have done it with someone a little more in my league.* She could feel her stomach fluttering from the undercurrent of their conversation. *Alright. Alright. Just get a hold of yourself. Nothing has happened yet, and nothing will, if you don't want it to.*

Nadine stared blankly at the painting of a Caribbean sunset in the dim hall, her mind racing. *What you are thinking about is simply sinful. Sinful I tell you. You had never laid eyes on that man before yesterday and you are thinking about allowing him to be your first. What would people say?* Nadine stuck out her chin stubbornly as her inner battle raged on.

For twenty-six years you have waited chastely, and where has it gotten you? Nowhere. People have poked fun at you, and had another reason to add to their list for calling you strange. And it's not like you still believe in saving yourself for your husband. The way your life has been going you will be as old as Methuselah before a potential husband is anywhere near the picture. Anyway, you know plenty of women who didn't wait, and they are living healthy, happy lives. Married or not. So what if you do allow something to happen between you and Ulysses? This way you can get the preliminaries out of the way, and gain some experience to boot. And when you are back in the States no one will be the wiser.

Nadine smiled to herself. *You never know. Gloria might be right. Maybe I have been like a bud whose blossoming is well overdue. After my rendezvous here, I can return to the States a full-fledged rose. Who knows? It's possible, if I don't seize some opportunity real soon, the bud may just wither and fall off the bush.* She giggled to herself, but underneath it all Nadine knew she had a real fear of growing old and never tasting the virtues of physical love.

With that Band-Aid of self-advice, Nadine decided she would let things flow naturally with Ulysses Deane. She turned away from the painting feeling more at ease, and headed back toward her bedroom.

"Did you enjoy your breakfast, Miss Clayton?"

"I sure did," Nadine answered, eyes sparkling with harnessed anticipation. "But I wish you'd call me Nadine."

"Nadine it is then." Catherine's wise eyes noticed the glow on Nadine's face. She threw a glance in the direction of the house where Ulysses remained. "If you do not have anything else planned, would you care to join me in my walk to the sugarcane fields? There is a small festival today at our rum still, and I usually bring some fresh molasses back to the house." Catherine placed folded knuckles on her boxy hips. "Sovereign produces enough rum for most of the folks here on Eros. From what I understand we have the only still in these parts outside of the West India Rum Refinery near Bridgetown on Barbados." Catherine lifted her chin a bit. "But their rum isn't nearly as good as what we make here."

"I bet it isn't." Nadine smiled with understanding, picturing the homemade wine that Grandma Rose sometimes kept in the back of the kitchen cabinet. "I do have something planned a little later on today, but I'd love to see a real rum still." She looked down at the green material that lay against her body. "But I'm sure this isn't what I need to be wearing."

"Do not worry about that. Your clothes are waiting for you in your room, along with a couple of blouses and skirts I was able to dig up."

"You're a blessing, Catherine," Nadine stated appreciatively. "I'll go change and meet you on the lanai, say in about fifteen minutes?"

"Yes. Good. That will give me enough time to finish up a few chores."

Nadine felt more alive than she had felt since she was a child. She walked through the house, staring. On an American scale, this would have been considered a very large house with extraordinarily spacious rooms. Unlike the majority of the structures in the States, the rooms were very rarely placed directly off hallways. You simply stepped out of one room into another.

Nadine felt a heightened sense of anticipation as she closed the bedroom door. Removing the cord belt and taking off the chiton was simple. The pieces of material fell soundlessly to the floor when she unfastened the two brooches upon her shoulders. She turned the jewelry over in her hand for a closer look and was amazed at the weight and intricacy of the ornaments.

A satyr holding a wineskin in his hands was

carved upon one of the pins. The other displayed an olive-wreathed nude male riding a panther. Both appeared to be made out of solid gold. Carefully, Nadine placed them back in their original container, conscious of their apparent value, and the trust placed in her by allowing her to wear them.

She felt almost buoyant as she dressed. What Nadine had experienced so far and what she hoped to experience was intoxicating. The island of Eros was proving to be more of a treasure than she ever imagined. Why, here, at Sovereign alone, was Ulysses, a rich historical, literary source, and a possible source for more intimate things.

With her thoughts in overdrive Nadine looked in the mirror. Her regular clothes were anticlimactic. The oversized top, like the majority of her wardrobe, had been bought to conceal her figure. Looking at it now, Nadine knew that it more than accomplished its purpose. A purpose contrary to her current plans. If she was going to play up Ulysses' interest in her as a woman, these clothes wouldn't do at all.

With a lifetime of being inconspicuous to encourage her, Nadine sorted through the small pile of clothes Catherine had provided. She chose a white linen blouse with long sleeves and large, lazy ruffles trimming a V-shaped neckline, knowing it was just what she needed. Nadine held it up in front of her. It was soft and utterly feminine. Quickly, she put it on, tucking the tail into her navy-blue pants. Looking in the mirror again, she noticed a little cleavage at the bottom of the V, and decided she had been progressive enough for one day. She arranged the bountiful ruffles to conceal it, her upbringing still influencing her.

With practiced fingers she unraveled her hair and found it was still a little damp from the night before. Through habit she began to comb it all to the back, placing it in its customary ball. Nadine stopped, then turned her face from side to side, examining it in the mirror. On impulse she let go of the auburn fibers, and shook her head vigorously. Using brisk movements she combed it out with her fingers. Nadine was pleased with the end result, and her eyes shone with more than the physical effort.

When she arrived Catherine was not waiting for her in the designated area. Nonplussed, Nadine assumed she was still completing her chores and she went to look for her in the kitchen. As she entered the room she could hear muffled snapping noises coming from the direction of a screened door. Through it, she could see Catherine shaking out a square linen tablecloth in the midst of a flurry of white flakes. The delicate hand-woven diamond designs that edged the fabric seemed to blend with the floating chips, creating an illusion of snow. Catherine's nose and mouth were covered with a red kerchief, protecting them from the flying material.

Nadine watched the housekeeper take another tablecloth, identical to the first, and cover it with a bucket of white wood ash that she removed from a large beehive-shaped oven. After treating the material with the ashes and removing them with several hardy shakes, the linen was the purest of whites. Nadine stepped aside as Catherine brought the neatly folded squares into the kitchen and placed them in a convenient linen closet. She dusted off her hands.

''Do you need to tell Madame Deane that we are leaving?''

''No, she iş fine. I mentioned the festival to her before she took her medication. I'm pretty sure she is sleeping by now. It will be a while before she wakes up again. Usually, she reads after her morning nap. She should be content until we get back,'' Catherine assured her.

Chapter 7

The two women set off together down a well-trodden path lined with evergreen trees. The inspiring smell of pine helped to heighten Nadine's sense of adventure. The scent reminded her of the woods that bordered Grandma Rose's house, where she had embarked on countless flights of fancy as a child. She had always dreamed of traveling to far-off places. Books had been the medium that transported her there, and she loved the pictures and paintings of ancient cultures the most. In the Mississippi woods she had created her own imaginary world, using nature as her inspiration.

Nadine felt content. She followed the path that opened onto a grass-tufted hill sprinkled with rocks and pebbles. In the distance she could see various shades of green.

Seeing Nadine's delighted expression, Catherine felt compelled to praise her homeland. ''Those are the sugarcane fields. Barbados is known all over the world for its rum and its sugar. The ones you are looking at belong to the Sharpes. They own the largest sugarcane fields on Eros. Some of their fields are hundreds of years old. But it has not been all good for them, the Sharpes I mean.'' She pulled her head wrap further down upon her forehead until it nearly covered her eyebrows. "Through the years they have been accused of stealing land from innocent people. Madame Deane says their entire northwest field used to belong to Sovereign." She whispered conspiratorially, as if she could be overheard. "There have been similar stories passed between the workers from other estates as well."

"Do you believe it?" Nadine inquired, concerned.

"It does not matter what I believe. People like me have no power here. I only feel sympathy for madame. Her word along with the word of a few field hands or house servants carries no weight."

"What does Ulysses think?" Nadine asked with contrived nonchalance.

"Ulysses believes in evidence. He says there is no proof to back up the stories, but if he had proof there would be hell to pay." Catherine raised her head haughtily. "But as it is they remain just that, stories." Reaching the top of the knoll she pointed at the view below. "Ah. There are some of the workers headed for the still."

Several donkey carts filled with sugarcane were methodically making their way toward a large building. Bunches of men, women, and children followed on foot, some carrying bundles and baskets, others musical instruments. Unlike the carts filled with sugarcane, the workers and several other carts continued toward a clearing where a few islanders were busy near what Nadine assumed was the rum still. She took in the scene with appreciation.

A magnificent azure sky framed the backdrop of

countless blossoms of red, yellow, pink, and white. She could hear cheerful voices carried toward them on the wind. Nadine was bewildered by the apparent joy generated by the group. "Are they always so happy about going to work?"

"Bajan people are merry by nature. But our emotions can run high no matter what the direction. Yet I believe happy music and dancing are our first love. See there," Catherine pointed to a small group of men walking together, "some of them are carrying instruments. That is because we always look for a reason to have a festival. Running the still gives us a good reason."

Descending the hill, Nadine enjoyed the wind whipping through her hair. The weather was breathtaking, and she wondered how Catherine and some of the others kept their heads bundled up beneath the head wraps. But she did not ask.

Greetings passed back and forth between Catherine and several of the workers as they merged with the crowd. They cast curious looks in Nadine's direction, along with low welcomes. She met them all with an enthusiastic nod of her head and a smile. As they reached their destination the men and women began to split up. The women and children situated themselves near a group of trees growing close to the still. Nadine couldn't help but notice the group that had gathered were all white people with hair that varied from straight to semi-wavy. Somehow they did not reflect the ethnic blend she had expected.

The women went straight to work, transforming their bundles into blankets to sit on. Once done, they put out baskets and containers of food and drink, buffet-style. Several yards away pots over open fires were being tended.

"Miss Nadine, do you like the black pudding?" a smiling Catherine inquired. She was helping another woman tie what looked like sections of intestines on both ends with string, then suspending them over waiting kettles of boiling water.

Curious about the white cylinders that she recognized as stuffed pig intestines, Nadine felt squeamish when she realized the black in black pudding was blood. But she did not want to spoil Catherine's obvious pleasure. Nadine hunched her shoulders and smiled as she thought, Oh, God, don't tell me I'm going to end up eating cooked blood! Why couldn't they be fond of turnip greens or sweet potatoes?

"You will! We will boil it until it is cooked well. It is delicious with a glass of rum."

Nadine kept the smile in place as she walked toward the still. It fascinated her. She watched as several men with sleeves and trousers rolled high began to scrub their feet in a nearby stream. Others removed medium-sized barrels of molasses that hung along the sides of the carts, then carried the ponderous objects upon their heads while holding convenient handles. Soon a production line of sorts had formed. Some men, usually the older ones, removed the barrels while others transported the molasses. Still another set stood by to ensure the molasses tumbled directly into the openings of the still, and not on the ground. Large vats were placed at the end of tubular shoots, ready to catch the precious vapors that transformed into rum once the distilling process had begun.

Conversation was at a minimum during this

process. Nondescript grunts and sounds passed between the men, who knew the job as well as they
knew themselves. Only the men working near the
still talked and laughed as if pumping themselves
up for a football game. Nadine smiled when an
occasional lyric burst forth from an extremely motivated worker.

As the men traded jobs, keeping the molasses
supply high, the vapors filled the tubes, forcing
brown rum downward into the colorful vats. As
time passed Nadine wondered if more rum was
flowing from the still or was being consumed by
the men working there. The potent liquid flowed
all around. The women drank more modestly than
the men; the musicians imbibed the most.

Catherine had been right. Nadine found black
pudding delicious, and even the small glass of rum
she drank along with it was beginning to taste
pretty good.

"You know what? This is the second glass of
alcohol I have ever drank," Nadine confided to
Catherine. "The first time was about five years ago.
Afterwards, I was a total mess. Everything was
funny to me, and on top of that, I fell asleep while
the party was still going on."

"Sometimes it is good to be free of control, Miss
Nadine. Enjoy yourself, I will make sure no harm
comes to you here," Catherine encouraged, passing
her another piece of pudding.

Nadine took the pudding and Catherine at her
word, but she also determined to make the one
glass of rum last her until she returned to the house.

A stirring melody from a flat string instrument
rose above all the other sounds as the musicians'
festive mood heightened. The workers' movements

became dance-like. Amorous females even handed them an occasional blossom. The men laughed boisterously as they placed the flowers behind their ears with undaunted flair.

The musicians had set up their ensemble near the donkey carts. Not far away, three men stepped in unison from side to side, dipping, swaying, then leaping. Nadine snapped her fingers along with the dancers as their steps became faster and more elaborate.

Suddenly, the sounds of gaiety trickled into silence. One of the workers pointed in the direction of the hill. A small band of people approaching the still could be seen in the distance. All eyes fixed upon them. As they came closer, Nadine realized all of the men were wearing their kerchiefs like headbands, while the women wore no head wraps at all. Instead they too wore headbands made of tiny stone tablets strung together like beads. As a matter of fact, all of their jewelry was made from the same beautiful material, carved with intricate patterns. The strangers wore it on their ears and necks, wrists and ankles. The sunshine amplified the polished earthen colors which ranged from orange to a slate-gray.

The strangers were somewhat darker, more muscular, and shorter than the workers. Somehow Nadine knew they *were* different in more than looks. Their clothing reminded her of the traditional clothing worn by some Native Americans. They used the same linen material worn by the workers, but the strangers decorated the cloth with stones and patterns of woven reed. The men's tops were long, accompanied by calf-length trousers, whereas the women wore skirts fringed and decorated with a combination of frayed reeds and stones. Their waist-length tops were finished in the same manner.

Even Catherine, who had become quite animated under the influence of the rum, was observing them with a watchful eye.

"Who are they?" Nadine asked, curious about the effect the group was having on the workers.

"They are cliff dwellers. It is unusual to see them in such a large group. I have seen them often enough, but usually it is down at the wharf selling things like jewelry, baskets, or wild game. They do not usually associate with the other islanders." Catherine leaned closer to Nadine. "As long as I have lived on Eros the only cliff dweller I got to know personally was a woman name Kohela. She used to work for Madame Evelyn Sharpe when she was still alive. And I can tell you that did nothing but worsen the relationship between the islanders and the cliff dwellers."

They watched as one of the men who appeared to be the leader advanced, leaving the other cliff dwellers behind at a comfortable distance. The oldest male among the workers met him.

"That is Elmo. He is always in charge of the still at Sovereign," Catherine informed Nadine.

A quiet, short exchange ensued, then three of the male cliff dwellers were motioned forward. Elmo headed back to the still. His announcement to the group was brief. The only word Nadine recognized was Ulysses' name.

"He says Ulysses has given the cliff dwellers permission to help here at the still," Catherine explained. "I guess with the roads being blocked they can't get down to the main wharf to sell their goods. Ulysses has always had a good relationship with those people. It is probably because as a child he spent a lot of time playing with their little ones on their side of the island. Some of the islanders resent it when he gives them work. They say the cliff dwellers feel they are superior because they rarely speak to anyone outside of their group. If the stories that have been passed down are true, for years it was the other way around, and as a result of that the cliff dwellers kept to themselves because of how they were being mistreated.''

It took an additional wave from Elmo's hand for the musicians to start playing again. When they did the uneasy feelings amongst the workers slowly began to dissipate.

Nadine watched as the three cliff dwellers scrubbed down in the stream and joined the other workers in the still. The remaining cliff dwellers kept their distance.

Soon the workers were joined by another party of islanders who Catherine explained came from the Sharpe estate. "The lady in the bright embroidered dress is Melanie Sharpe. You met her brother this morning during breakfast."

Nadine noticed the petite woman's natural grace. Unlike the others, her head wrap was white, trimmed with the same flower motif on her dress. Her serene smile poured out to everyone. Still, there was an aloofness about her as she circulated among the workers.

Eventually, the music reached its previous heights and the dancers increased in number. Now there were men and women from both estates sliding, dipping, and swaying. One exceptionally sensuous female had removed her head wrap and was causing quite a stir. Her flashing ebony eyes teased the men as she shook her equally dark tresses. She called out to her girlfriend who danced on the opposite side of the circle. Intentionally, they exchanged provocative words, enticing the men even further.

A disapproving Catherine clicked her tongue. "Those two are always trouble if you ask me. Especially Cassandra. She always offers more than she intends to deliver. At least to the men in this group," she added meaningfully.

Nadine heard Catherine's innuendo, but by now her glass of rum was empty, and she was feeling its full effects. She had decided Catherine was nice enough, but she was also one of those people who always had to focus on the dark side of life. At the moment, Nadine felt she had absolutely no space for negativity. The world was hers to explore, freely. She had accomplished one of her lifelong dreams, to travel to the islands, and her journey as a woman of the world had begun. She wouldn't have it dampened by judgmental talk.

Standing to the side, Nadine followed the steps of the dancers with uncertain movements, snapping her fingers with the music. She never danced at home. It was forbidden. So it felt good when her high-pitched laughter mingled with the laughter of the others. Somehow, she managed to keep up with the vigorous performers.

She was enjoying herself immensely, but the sound of Ulysses' voice behind her brought a jolt of surprise. She did not see him join the group, and she wondered how long he had been there. Her first thought was to stop her solitary performance, but that would be too obvious. Nadine knew the way she was acting now did not gel with the demeanor of the woman she had pretended to be earlier that morning, but the effect of the rum was strong. It had roused the free spirit in her, and she liked it.

"My aunt is in need of your services, Catherine." His deep voice carried to her ears.

"Is she really? I guess I have been here longer than I intended. Miss Nadine seems to be enjoying herself so." She laid the burden of her indiscretion on Nadine's shoulders.

"Catherine, if she was not putting up such a fuss I would not bother to tell you. But she thinks she needs you back at the house. I will stay here with Nadine."

"I guess I better hurry." Catherine's tone was less than enthusiastic.

Ripples of excitement fluttered in Nadine's stomach as she listened to the exchange. Sheer reflex drew her hand to her abdomen to quiet the growing sensations. This is not going to work, she thought. The man has not said one word to you and you feel as if he is nibbling on your neck and speaking loving words in your ears. She smothered a rising giggle. Slow down, Nadine, she warned herself, the afternoon has just begun.

Nadine felt a touch on her elbow, and she turned to look up into Ulysses' probing gaze.

"Come. I have been watching you," he told her. "You were not too bad for a beginner. Now," he reached out his hand, "let us try it together." Ulysses nodded toward the circle of dancers.

Nadine didn't know if it was the rum, but without the slightest hesitation she allowed herself to be led forward. They entered the circle, met by surprised looks; Cassandra alone looked displeased.

Nadine was caught up in the magic of the moment. Hastily, the musicians brought the current number to an end.

" 'Come to My Web,' " one of them shouted as the others waved their instruments high in a salute to Ulysses.

He stretched out his arms to acknowledge the announcement that they were about to play his favorite. A rousing cheer rose up as the guitarist struck the first slow, sensuous chords of the melody. Awestruck, Nadine watched as Ulysses' body responded to each note.

His chest began to rise, very slowly, as his chin sloped down to meet it in the most sensuous display of male sexuality she had ever witnessed. At that moment Ulysses turned his magnetic gaze toward her. Pure, contained fire was in the depths of his eyes as he focused his power upon her, his firm lips forming the word "Now," commanding her to dance.

Every nerve in Nadine's body tingled as she watched him and tried to emulate his steps. First, his foot formed a slow, exacting circle on the ground, followed by a smooth, gliding move to his right. Nadine forced her eyes to remain upon his feet, but as the dance progressed it was not easy. Whenever she focused her attention on his polished, short black boots the movement of his hips and pelvis in fitted black pants was the first thing that met her. His hips rose and rotated outward as his feet made their moves, and Nadine's body responded as if it had been shocked by an electrical current. She felt a nearly overpowering need to have him hold her, and she nearly swayed with the weight of it.

She looked up at his face with smoldering hazel eyes, hoping he was not aware of what was happening to her. To Nadine's relief, they were met by a face wearing a mask of control. The only hint of what he felt was the fiery glow within his own dark, thickly fringed eyes.

Nadine could feel when Ulysses' unwavering gaze focused on her face, but she was afraid to return it, knowing her feelings would be transparent. Even the rum did not give her the gumption she needed. She knew returning his look would seal an intimate agreement between them. No words would be necessary, the sexual energy that flowed was so strong. Potent desire ripped through her, thwarting her ability to continue the act she had started that morning. Her sexuality broke loose after years of repression, and Nadine finally experienced how much a woman's nature it is to have a man.

The slow deliberate tempo of the song began to pick up speed like a train pulling off from a station. Through her peripheral vision she watched Ulysses' emotional response to the tune. It was as if the music had entered his soul, and he was consumed by the pulse of it. Nadine felt herself being swept away on a similar current of exhilaration.

Back and forth, around and around they pranced. Feeling an earth-shattering wave of need overtake her, Nadine turned her revealing gaze toward the man beside her. She felt no shame in what she knew was blatantly written in her eyes. Like the response of her body to the melody, what she yearned for was only natural. Seductively, her eyes locked with those of the dark, magnetic stranger;

the music helped to free her of any residual fears. She gave in to its attuning powers.

Nadine threw back her head and closed her eyes. Her body jerked rhythmically to the beat of the music, paying tribute to the vibrations. Ulysses watched the woman's transformation from a timid, unwilling creature to a vision of captivating beauty. The white ruffles about her neck fluttered back and forth, revealing a small, cinnamon cleavage. Her thick mane danced, bathing in the rays of the sun as she shook it in time with the beat. The American had taken to the dance as if she were born to it, and the elated expression on her exotic features showed the music had entered her heart. Ulysses could feel the power of her feminine nature, and he wondered why she struggled so hard to keep it confined.

"Ulysses," a persuasive voice called to him.

Cassandra sauntered into the center of the circle, her arms outstretched to the side. In high-stepping fashion she thrust her ample bosom forward. Her red painted lips opened temptingly, and her face mirrored the look of a woman in the throes of deep passion. Cassandra's hot sable eyes raced intimately over Ulysses' body as she danced for him. She was sure of herself and her body language was clear.

Ulysses said nothing. His expression remained unreadable as he watched her dance in front of him. Everyone stopped their dancing and watched, for Cassandra knew how to create a spectacle.

All of a sudden, like a hot-air balloon falling from the sky, Nadine's feeling of exhilaration plummeted as she recognized the exchange that was going on between Ulysses and the carnal female that paraded before him. There could be no doubt in her mind or anyone else's that they were much more than friends.

Nadine was grateful when the music finally stopped. She could not have stood it much longer. The shame of her abandonment washed over her, and before she could remove her arm that had been entwined with Ulysses' for the traditional dance, a coarse hand removed it for her. Nadine allowed it, even though a part of her wanted to lash out. But she had to consider maybe Ulysses was this woman's man.

Ulysses stood still as he watched Cassandra's blatant display of ownership, although the heat of their sexual escapades had begun to cool some time ago. It was evident she could not tolerate his showing interest in another woman. Ulysses allowed himself to be led away by a triumphant Cassandra. He would not disrespect her in front of her peers. But he intended to make sure she understood how he really felt, and that it was to never happen again.

Nadine could feel the workers' eyes on her as she left the circle. Her eyes burned with an immediate need to cry, but she would not dare let anyone know how deeply the incident had affected her, so she walked away with her head held high. Nadine no longer felt like joining the women she had befriended through Catherine, instead she stood a safe distance away from their furtive glances.

"If I had not seen you learn that dance, I would have sworn you had been doing it all of your life," a comforting voice called from behind her. "I am Melanie Sharpe." The woman came up and stood beside her. "You must be the young lady my brother, Rodney, came back to the house raving about.''

Relief flooded inside Nadine as she looked into the smiling face of the attractive woman. "Thanks. Once I got started it was easy. I didn't even have to think about the steps.'' She stretched out her hand in greeting. ''I'm Nadine Clayton. And yes, I did meet your brother this morning. He was quite flattering.''

''Rodney is the charmer of the family. Sometimes I am afraid he is too forward and is going to get himself in trouble again. Once his aggressive admiration for one of the islander's daughters rewarded him with a black eye.'' Melodic laughter accompanied the confession.

Nadine gladly took to the light mood with a modest smile. ''Looks like Rodney is not the only one who can be aggressive around here.'' She looked at the receding backs of Ulysses and Cassandra.

''Cassandra has always had an eye for Ulysses. Even when we were little children. At first he paid her little attention, but as the years went by and he began to change he started doing many things he had always promised himself he would never do.''

''You seem to know him very well.'' Nadine tried to keep the tremor out of her voice, but she knew it was still apparent.

''I guess you could say that. I've known Ulysses for practically my entire life. His aunt had a birthday party for him when he was nine. My brother Basil and I attended it. Basil was thirteen and I was seven. That was when our friendship began. That was twenty-three years ago.'' She looked at the rum still, then looked down. ''He has always been bursting with life. Half the young girls on the island were secretly in love with him. Including me.'' A forlorn look blanketed her poised features.

Nadine sensed a quiet uneasiness about Melanie Sharpe, but she was grateful Melanie had reached out to her at a moment when she needed it so badly. Yet despite her outward calm, Nadine could tell Melanie was haunted by her own ghosts. She decided to bring an end to the awkward moment. ''It's time for me to get back to the house.'' She glanced self-consciously over her shoulder. ''I think that should be pretty easy if I follow the path leading over that hill.''

''Yes, that is the best way. It will lead you straight to the entrance. I would walk with you if I had not already promised my brother Basil that I would stay with our workers until our vats were beneath the shoots.'' Melanie turned, pointing to some black and yellow containers that stood beside the wall. ''You see, we do not have a still. Sugar is our main business.''

''Oh, I see.'' Nadine nodded with interest. ''Look. I don't know how long I'm going to be here, it depends on how long it takes to get the roads cleared. But I hope we get to see each other again before I go,'' she said earnestly.

''So do I,'' Melanie replied.

The two women smiled at each other before going their separate ways. The conversation had given Nadine a chance to regain her composure before heading through the watchful gazes that were still upon her. She could see the cliff dwellers sitting in a group not far from the base of the hill. They had remained quiet and detached the entire afternoon. None of them had joined in the festivities, and they displayed no obvious signs of even hearing the music. Now, with concentrated curiosity, they watched Nadine's approach. Numerous pairs of sable eyes consumed her every move. As she walked along the outskirts of the cliff dwellers' cluster, Nadine saw the leader signal to one of the women in the rear. With the agility of an acrobat she rose to her feet, and crossed to stand directly in front of Nadine.

Even though her movements were not hostile, Nadine was completely caught off guard. She found herself staring directly into the face of the unusual female. The woman's demeanor was calm, but her eyes were filled with a curious excitement as she made an evaluation of Nadine's facial features. With a quiet look of approval, she bent her head and removed one of several necklaces from her own neck. Without a word she held the object suspended in the space between them.

Nadine's first instinct was to question the woman. Confusion mixed with a strange feeling of wonder as she studied the hands that held the article out to her. She could see a tattoo in the palm of the female's right hand. It appeared to be a double circle with an eight-sided star within it. Nadine took note of the ancient cross, and she wondered what significance the symbol held for the woman.

Without further thought a force from deep within compelled her to accept the necklace. The diminutive tablets felt cool to the touch as she took them from the cliff dweller's hands. It was only after she accepted the necklace that the woman looked into Nadine's face again, and waited for her to place the ornament about her neck.

The stones made a light clattering noise as she

worked her hair from between them, then straightened the necklace so it lay against her skin beneath the ruffles of her blouse. Once the woman saw her task was complete, she rejoined her group with the same swift but quiet movement. Nadine watched the cliff dwellers draw their gaze away from her and look, as if with the same mind, toward the still. The necklace was the only evidence that the uncanny incident had even occurred.

Chapter 8

 "You should have told me you were about to leave," Ulysses called to her as he emerged from the evergreen trees beside the path.

"Well, I didn't," Nadine countered without even turning to look at him. Her anger at his deserting her burned close to the surface.

"No, you did not." He looked down at her stern profile. "Are you ready to see some of the collection of works we spoke of earlier? Or is the poised Nadine too upset to think of business?"

She stopped, her flashing hazel eyes lashing into him. Now he was treading water where Nadine was extremely confident. "Look. I am a professional. I am on this island because of my work. So please, don't misjudge me. I'm ready any time you are."

"Maybe we will both need to remember the real reason why you're here."

"You don't have to worry, I won't forget it."

"It is a shame," his husky voice chided her. "You dance so well."

"It's all relative. Dancing is a part of the island culture. What better way for me to understand a people than to join in their traditional festivities,"

she replied with one generous, well-shaped eyebrow arched high.

A wry smile crossed Ulysses' lips as he allowed
Nadine to walk in front of him. The rapid sway of
her round, slim hips emphasized her no-nonsense
mood. He was not accustomed to being brushed
off, and initially he was amused. But that shortly
changed to aggravation as she walked further
ahead, ignoring him as they advanced up the road.
Among the islanders Ulysses was known for his
short patience, and that reputation doubled when it
came to women.

Under normal circumstances Nadine would have
been unnerved by Ulysses' presence behind her.
Watching her. She had never been comfortable under the watchful eye of men. But her outrage at his
leaving her for the wanton Cassandra was more
than her pride could take. Let him watch her. She
was glad he had plenty to watch. Her breath blew
out forcefully through her nostrils. Who did he
think she was? Somebody he could use as a toy?
She could feel the heat rising to her face as she
thought about the decision she had made earlier.
Let him be the first? Over my dead body!

Ulysses caught up with Nadine as they reached
the kitchen door. She stood and waited for him to
open it. Her eyes showed disdain and a challenge
before she looked down at the handle.

"Does business also include small courtesies
like opening the door?" Ulysses asked her calmly.

Nadine refused to answer the needling question.
Without a word she swiftly opened the door, almost
hitting Ulysses in the face. It took all her concentrated control not to smile at the irritated look she
had managed to put on his dark features. And to

think, she did not even conjure up Gloria for that. "Now where do we start?" she asked, feigning ignorance about what had just transpired.

This time it was Ulysses who took the lead. "Right this way, Miss Nadine."

She waited quietly while he lit a lamp beside the heavy oak door. His attitude toward her could be described as no less than icy when he was leading her up the stairs, uttering a mere "Up here" as he proceeded in front of her. He had searched through several keys before settling on the newest one in the bunch.

Nadine could not remember how many times as a teenager she had sat and watched the old movies where the trusting female was being led to a secret chamber by a not so trustworthy male. The thought amused her, but it also unnerved her, and she wondered if she had pushed the man in front of her too far. The little she knew of him would not be considered normal by a long shot. The odd meeting in the cave. His less than conventional actions in the bath, and the strange magnetism he developed as she watched him dance. Eros was a long way from Ashland, Mississippi, and Nadine decided to tone down the antagonistic approach she had taken only minutes before.

She entered the room behind Ulysses as a single lamp gave eerie life to the myriad of objects within. Statues and busts looked blindly about, carved in marble, bronze, and limestone. Detail and color grew in clarity as Ulysses somberly ignited a series of lamps revealing bookcases filled with books. His chilling silence added to the breathtaking aura of the place. Rodney had said Sovereign was considered "the Protector of Eros' Treasures," but Nadine had not been prepared for the abundance of treasures that were kept within the room.

Her lips parted in awe as she surveyed the treasures around her. The black velvet floor-length drapes that covered the walls and windows supplied an appropriate backdrop; like a velvet-lined jewelry box, they displayed the numerous works of art in the best possible manner. "It's overwhelming," she breathed, her eyes sparkling with the wonder of it.

Despite the frostiness that had encapsulated his feelings, Ulysses had no choice but to warm to Nadine's sincere appreciation of his beloved collection. "Right here in this room you will find the richest source of Eros' history. But this collection," he passed his hands across the leather bindings of several books before caressing a female statuette, "spans many centuries and tells much about people around the world, their lives, their dreams, and their beliefs."

Had the statue been a real woman, Nadine thought as she watched him, there would have been no doubt in her mind how much Ulysses loved and treasured her. As she gazed at the plethora of treasures Nadine discovered there was no need to ask Ulysses about the pieces that graced the second floor of his home. He began to talk about them out of a need born of pride and love, like a parent bursting to share the accomplishments of a cherished child. After a while, Nadine found herself joining in his recitations, citing periods and styles. Each one of them fed on the other's enthusiasm and true appreciation for the paragons that surrounded them.

Ulysses' vast knowledge of his people and their

artistic accomplishments enthralled Nadine, and he in turn had never had a more captivated audience. Any awareness of time dissolved, and the wall of mistrust crumbled between them.

"They look so real," Nadine said as she looked at the ivory statue of a man stabbing himself above the limp body of a woman. "Pain and agony are so clear in his eyes, whereas her eyes and body convey death compellingly."

"Yes, it is an old replica of the Dying Gaul." Ulysses' words were spoken in wistful tones. "It is a tangible example of pain and courage. It shows what a human being will do, knowing his enemy's capacity for cruelty."

The pang in Ulysses' voice as he spoke was unexpected. Nadine could tell from his posture, as he turned to look at the painting on the easel behind him, that it took extreme effort for him not to show his feelings, and yet she didn't know if it were hurt or anger that he was trying to subdue.

Nadine turned her attention to several marble statuettes displayed within a glass case behind lock and key. "These are lovely. They are most definitely Dionysian. There is such an erotic feel about all of them, and some of their hair is so close and tight to their heads, as if they were of African descent."

The first one was a nude Eros embracing and kissing a half-nude Psyche. The others featured men and women in several positions indulging in amorous pleasures.

"That is the one continuous theme that I have found throughout the artwork believed done here on the island, love and passion." Ulysses crossed the space between them. "It is said that long before the settlers arrived, the island of Eros was actually named by the goddess Aphrodite after her son. And with the name, she cast the spell that all whoever lived here, even for the shortest time, would eventually taste its sexual pleasures in some way or another.''

"Is there no other record connected with the name of the island?" Nadine asked, suddenly feeling giddy, the heady sensation brought on by Ulysses' tale and his close proximity.

"None that we know of." His voice plunged to a seductive purr as he came even closer. "There is no reason to be afraid of yourself, Nadine. I watched the change that came over you while you danced in the sugar fields. I know that your battle is not with me, but with what you Americans call your convictions. Here on Eros, the island of love, the only conviction is *not* to deny yourself pleasure. Take it if it is offered to you."

He raised his hand to caress her cheek, allowing the back of it to trail down the curve of her jaw, only to open his palm to softly stroke her slender throat as he looked searchingly into the hazel eyes that watched him.

Passion and panic rose simultaneously within her, and Nadine searched for something that would provide an escape from the rapid change in circumstances. Two gold busts of Egyptian origin caught her eye and she started toward them, then stopped abruptly. "My goodness. What is that?" she asked, pointing to an intricately carved bronze chest.

"This container houses my pride and joy." Ulysses allowed his attention to be diverted. "If you are good to me, one day I will show it to you."

Nadine felt a quiver run down her spine, a natural reaction to the seductive invitation lying beneath his ambiguous words. She began to babble. "It is most intriguing. I've heard so many stories about the islands from my grandmother that I've always dreamed of coming to a place like this. I wanted to find out if her stories were true. You know, launch my own private treasure hunt. It's why I love my work." She kept her eyes on the case covered with figures and symbols that somehow looked familiar, but she had no inkling why. Bending closer for a more detailed assessment, Nadine saw the symbol that was tattooed in the cliff dweller's hand. The ancient cross was carved on a thin bronze shield covering the lock.

"This has something to do with the cliff dwellers, doesn't it?" she asked, pleased with herself and wondering what could the container possibly hold that was more precious to Ulysses than anything else among the slew of priceless pieces. Nadine looked at him with expectation, but Ulysses' face had changed from soft and yielding to a distrusting mask.

"How do you know that?" The words were low, threatening.

Before Nadine could answer, Ulysses had grabbed her by her arm and was leading her toward the door as he badgered her. "That case is none of your concern, do you understand me? And if I find out you are here for reasons other than you have told us, you will regret it!"

He forced her out of the room, shutting the large door in her face. Shocked by his reaction, Nadine stood listening to Ulysses turning the key in the lock from the other side. She was shaken by his actions, and her arm actually ached where his hand had held it in a vice grip.

Her eyes burned with tears of confusion for the second time that day. Nadine took the stairway nearest to her to put as much distance as she could between herself and the irate man. Once she considered herself out of harm's way, Nadine loosened the button on her cuff to see what damage had been done to her arm.

What is wrong with him? One minute he is trying to get next to me, and the next he's acting like some fool off the street. I'm not going to be bothered with this kind of insanity, she fumed, her eyes still glistening with unshed tears. Nadine pushed up her sleeve, searching for evidence of the pain she was still feeling.

"There you are." Madame Deane's voice reached her through an open door. "Come here. Right now! I've been waiting for a moment alone with you."

Nadine wanted to disobey the shrill voice that called to her, but she thought better of it. Catherine had already warned her of madame's moods. She wished someone had warned her about Ulysses.

"Hurry up! Close and lock the door before somebody sees you," Madame Deane ordered in a conspiratorial tone. "She told me to tell you that you should be thanking us for keeping this safe until you returned. We have kept it hidden for years." A dangerous, somewhat demented gleam accompanied her irrational claim. "This story is one of the reasons I am in this wheelchair today." She looked up from the dirty object she held wrapped in her lap. "They thought they could get rid of me, but we were smarter than they were."

A perturbed look descended on madame's wrinkled features. "What is wrong with you *now,* Lenora?"

Nadine looked at the pitiful creature before her, and all of a sudden she felt very tired. "Madame Deane, I am not Lenora."

"Never mind all that. What is wrong with your arm?"

"You tell me. It's your nephew's fault," she spat out in exasperation. Then, looking into Madame Deane's glassy eyes: "Oh, what's the use!"

"Pay no attention to Ulysses. He has been moodier than ever since someone broke into the house and stole some of the collection. Before that he never locked the room. Now, you can't get Ulysses to part with that key ring of his. I think he sleeps with it." An irritating hissing sound passed between her clenched teeth.

"Madame Deane, are you in there?" Catherine called from outside the door. "You know I've warned you about locking these doors, especially so close to your medication time."

In an exaggerated whisper madame urged Nadine to come forward. "Here, hurry up and take this. And do not show it to anyone! No one, you hear!" Madame Deane seemed unusually strong as she shoved the animal skin into Nadine's hands, then changed her tone for Catherine's benefit. "I was just in here talking to Nadine. I guess she must have locked the door when she came in." The woman extended her neck outward, reminding Nadine of a vulture.

Nadine took the skin without protest, simply to get away. Then she unlocked the door. A perturbed Catherine stepped inside.

"Miss Nadine," Catherine's emphasis on the

word "miss" accentuated her discontent with Nadine's actions, "if you do not mind me saying so, I do not think it is a good idea for you to lock any of these doors unless it is your own. What would happen if Madame Deane had one of her spells? I could not get in to help you, and I assure you, you would not be able to control her," she warned with a final snub.

Frustrated, Nadine threw up her hands in surrender. "Yes, ma'am." She exited to Catherine's announcement of dinner in forty-five minutes, and the distasteful hissing of Madame Deane's snicker behind her.

Entering her own room, Nadine firmly closed the door and locked it. She thought of the things Catherine had told her about Madame Deane while she helped her dress earlier that morning. Nadine looked at the roll of matted skin and hair the eccentric woman had given her, and dropped the unsightly object onto a slat of wood behind the headboard of the bed.

Nadine felt she had taken more than she wanted to take from the occupants of Sovereign. After the events of the day she lumped the entire household into one category. Psychotic. In her opinion, the entire place was full of people with, to put it mildly, extreme personality disorders. She thought if all the islanders were like the people here at Sovereign it would be a very difficult place to live. Nadine placed her forehead in her hands. God, I don't know what to expect next.

"Miss Nadine?"

She exhaled long and hard at the sound of Catherine's voice breaking in on her mental tirade.

"Yes . . . ?"

Catherine paused, waiting for Nadine to open the door, but when she didn't she continued. "Just thought I'd let you know Clarence says the roads should be clear by tomorrow."

"Thank God."

"Pardon me?"

"Thank you, Catherine," she replied with as much patience as she could muster.

Nadine listened as the woman left muttering to herself, the word "rude" being more audible than the rest.

Ulysses stared long and hard at the two empty spaces inside the open case. It was like picking at a festering wound, and his mind raced as he tried to figure out why the carved slabs containing the manuscript had been taken.

The set had remained in the collection room for years until two weeks ago when the jade and onyx slabs were stolen. He guessed he was lucky the thieves had not taken the entire case. By sheer co-incidence the two stones had been left in the treasure room. The others had been taken to his room where he continued to tediously clean the intricate etchings that covered the bronze case. It was a process that had been going on ever since he found the case half buried in an abandoned cave on the south side of the Sovereign estate. During the cleaning process he had discovered two paper-thin pieces of bronze on the inside of the lid that slid in and out, masking two extremely shallow compartments.

But the secret compartments were not what occupied Ulysses' thoughts. Now, since the theft, only three stone carvings, three pages remained of the Five Pieces of Gaia. The carvings had been in his family's possession for many years, although it was just recently that Ulysses discovered the manuscript pages hidden inside the slabs.

A coin that Ulysses had been given when he was a child playing in the cliff dwellers' caves was the key, literally. He discovered this when he realized the cliff dwellers' symbol etched into the coin matched the size and shape of the medallions carved on the Five Pieces of Gaia. Ulysses placed the coin inside one of the medallions and it fit so perfectly it was hard to remove, so he turned it, and the slab slid apart, revealing the manuscript inside.

This time Ulysses used the coin with intent. Carefully, he opened the rose quartz slab and gazed at the papyrus filled with hieroglyphs. The airtight stone had preserved the paper and ink through time, and he wondered for the hundredth time what the writing meant. Ulysses also wondered if the thieves knew about the manuscript pages hidden inside the stones. He had never noticed the hairline fracture encircling the carvings. Ulysses believed one would almost have to know about the manuscript to find the pages inside the slabs.

He closed the stone and held the rose quartz in his hands. Ulysses traced the smooth pink carving of the Moon Goddess. Her slender outstretched arms held a small sphere high above her head. About her neck hung the one symbol that connected them all. The sign of the cliff dwellers. The ancient cross within an eight-sided star surrounded by a double circle.

As Ulysses traced the gentle lines of the figure, his mind visualized the narrow jaw and smooth skin of the woman, Nadine. Her skin had felt like satin, and he could see the longing mixed with fear in her eyes as he touched her. Eyes that were so full of fear they were almost as green as the jade slab.

His instincts told him Nadine was no more than she professed to be, although he admitted there were times when her actions were contradictory. But there was one message that was constant. Nadine Clayton was a woman whose passions ran deep. So deep that even she was afraid to explore them.

Ulysses' dark eyes stared at the Moon Goddess. But how did she know the Gaia Series was connected with the cliff dwellers when she claimed she had only been on Eros for one day? His brows knitted together. Unless Nadine Clayton was involved with the theft.

Ulysses could not, and would not allow himself to be blinded by the feelings she was able to invoke in him. She could very well be his enemy. A lovely, enticing enemy. The deadliest kind.

He rose, crossing over to the desk that held all of the notes on the family's private collection that his father and grandfather had written through the years. He took out a key and unlocked the drawer; a cracked leather ledger lay inside. He studied the yellow pages filled with a list and description of Sovereign's special treasures. Ulysses thumbed through the book until he came to the page entitled "The Five Pieces of Gaia." Beneath this his father had written:

Of all the collection, these five slabs house the greatest mystery and history of Eros, the cliff

dwellers, and the Deane family. They are my
favorites, and they hold a special meaning for
you, Ulysses, my son. One that I am on the
brink of truly understanding.

Ulysses stared at his father's incomplete message. Peter Deane had not known about the manuscript pages inside the slabs. If he had, Ulysses
would have known. But for some reason he still
felt the Five Pieces of Gaia were the most important pieces of their entire collection.

Ulysses read his father's words again. The passage created a void that reminded him of the painful loss he felt as a child growing up without his
parents.

Looking up, his gaze was drawn to a jade pa-
perweight on top of the desk. Ulysses recalled how
he had acquired it from a merchant selling articles
to tourists on Barbados, then his thoughts drifted
to Nadine again.

Yes, she was different. She was not the average
American who had traveled to a foreign country
taking in its sights and treasures with greedy apa-
thy. He knew the feelings that stirred within her
were real, but that didn't mean they were all good.

Ulysses ran a searching finger over the round
edges of the jade rose petals as he told himself he
could not afford to feel anything else for this
woman. He had learned the hard way. He knew
forming emotional attachments of any kind brought
nothing but pain and sadness. In the long run you
would try to protect those you love, like his mother
tried to protect him. But it would be to no avail
because you would still lose them, and as his father

had proven by his suicide, the pain of that loss was worse than death.

"I cannot allow myself to ever become involved in that way. Never!" His raspy voice rang out amongst the lifeless faces that watched him. Ulysses realized that his outburst before his deaf audience resembled that of the woman he had made up his mind to keep at arm's length, Nadine Clayton.

Chapter 9

Nadine recognized the distinct taste of fish and coconut as she bit into one of several codfish balls Catherine had placed before her. It was a taste she had not become accustomed to, and she would have done anything for some fried chicken and spaghetti. Her eyes kept straying to the empty place setting at the head of the table where Ulysses usually sat.

It was difficult for Nadine to accept that the poised creature, albeit still dressed in her usual chiton and olive headband, was the same person she had seen no more than an hour earlier.

"I must say I am thankful that my evening dose of medication does not put me to sleep like the earlier ration. It simply would not do for me to miss supper," Madame Deane commented, then glanced at Ulysses' vacant chair. "It is so unlike him to be absent from supper. This is the time when we usually go over household matters, and talk about other things that need to be taken care of. Catherine says he has locked himself upstairs inside the collection room again." Her dark eyes clouded over with concern.

Nadine studied her hostess, her hazel eyes suspicious, curious. It just did not make sense. None at all. There was no medicine in the world that could change a person like Madame Deane's medication changed her.

The older woman seemed oblivious to Nadine's silence. "Sometimes I wish there was a pill Ulysses could take to get rid of the anger and hurt I know he still harbors about his parents. They died so long ago. As a matter of fact, next weekend it will be twenty-five years that they've been gone. If that's not enough time for a person to purge themselves of such damaging feelings . . ." Her gaze sought Nadine's compliance. "I am not saying he should not miss them, but you would think a child of seven would have grown up and left a bit of the pain behind. But some of the islanders," she looked down, "well, they just would not let him forget. People can be so cruel, you know."

Nadine had wondered about Ulysses' parents. She was surprised to find out they had died when he was so young.

"I know just how cruel people can be," she admitted. "But it seems when things happen to you when you are a child," Nadine sought the right words, "so innocent and trusting, they stay with you somehow. Like an impression in wet clay, it hardens." She looked at Madame Deane who was listening intently, as if she were searching for an answer.

Nadine continued. "I only saw my mother a few times when I was growing up. There were pictures of her and my father that kept them alive for me. For a while I *chose* to believe they were dead." She looked directly at her hostess. "But then I accepted the truth, and the hurt was different, because

I realized they were alive but they didn't want me with them. They had *chosen* to leave me with Grandma Rose. My grandmother tried to make me feel better by saying they didn't have the means to provide for me. But from time to time the pictures of different cities would arrive. They were always accompanied by a short note, describing the places where they were working. My mother would be dressed in extravagant clothes, posing glamorously outside of places with names like Dixie's Dollhouse and Lacy's Girls.''

Nadine looked at Madame Deane, embarrassed over revealing so much about her past, but as with Ulysses the pain of her childhood was still real. She would not lie to protect her parents' dignity. They had not cared enough to protect hers.

''Did your parents ever come to visit you?'' Madame Deane asked.

''No. But after a while I grew accustomed to it,'' Nadine added quickly. ''And for a short period of time I felt rather special. I thought it was wonderful to have parents who were able to travel all around, and I would boast to my playmates about it,'' she continued, almost as if she were talking to herself. ''Then I began to hear the rumors. 'Nadine Clayton's mother and father actually have a working relationship. That's why she can't live with them. The things they are involved in aren't fit for a young girl to see, and that's why Auntie Rose had to keep her. With the way things are, there is no way to really tell if Slim is really the girl's father. After all, who else in the Clayton line has those strange hazel eyes,' they would say.'' Nadine became silent.

''You know,'' Madame Deane jumped in,

"Ulysses used to be teased all the time about his skin color and his curly hair. It used to make him furious," she told her. "And I know deep inside it hurt him more than anything else."

"Yes. It always hurts when people ridicule and degrade things you cannot change," Nadine confirmed. "I remember one conversation Grandma Rose and I had about my eyes. I was already having a hard enough time when the incident happened. Just about all the children would tease me." Her lips turned up into a smile, although it wasn't a real one. "They called me the praying mantis because I was long and thin, and the color of my hair nearly matched my skin. But it was my large, hazel eyes, and the long periods of time my grandmother and I spent at church that had really earned me that name. My other features were merely icing on the cake," Nadine continued.

"One particular day, several of the school bullies followed me without my knowing it. As usual, before going home from school, I went to my secret spot in the woods. It was springtime, and a couple of days before, I had managed to find a tree branch with butterfly cocoons attached to it." This time Nadine smiled for real. "How excited I was at the prospect of watching the ugly caterpillars inside their shells, eventually turn into beautiful butterflies. And then to watch them fly up into the sky. Free! Free to experience the world, no longer hampered by their ugliness. It was just what I wanted to do," she explained. "Well, I remember I didn't want to disturb the cocoons, so I lifted the branch oh so gently to have a closer look. Suddenly, a loud voice screamed, 'Hey! Look! The praying mantis is gonna eat those cocoons. Let's take them away from her!' And before I could stop them the three boys had snatched the branch out of my hand. Two of them held me, while the third took the cocoons off of the branch. I remember screaming, 'No! Please! They'll die!' and feeling as if my little heart was being crushed inside my chest.'' She sort of laughed. ''But one of the boys turned to me with this ugly look on his face, and said, 'What does it matter to you? You're just an ole stick! You don't have a mother or father. Those people that you talk about in those pictures don't even know you. Just look at yourself. Does either one of them have those bug-colored eyes?' ''

''No,'' exhaled Madame Deane, her olive-leaf headband dipping a little too low.

''Yes, he did,'' Nadine told her. ''And boy, when he said that, this surge of anger and hurt came up in me like a roaring fire. I pulled away from the two who held me and hurled myself onto the boy who had said it. I started beating him like he had stole something.''

Madame Deane covered her mouth with her hand, almost laughing behind it.

''I sure did,'' Nadine continued. ''I mean I scratched and kicked as if my life depended on it— that is, until his friends pulled me away. Then I heard Grandma Rose calling my name, and they heard it too.'' Her eyes got larger. ''They ran away, but not before they attempted to smash the cocoons. When my grandmother found me I was holding the branch. It only had one cocoon on it. Somehow it had been spared.'' Nadine paused. ''Of course, when I saw Grandma, a new crop of tears started to fall, and I told her what the boys had said. Grandma just shook her head, sat down beside me in the forest, and put her arm around me.

" 'Look, honey,' " she said. " 'Don't you worry about what people say. I love you, and in her way your mama does too. And as far as your eyes go, there have been stories passed down in our family that some folks say originated on an island called Barnado. It talked of a child who would be born with the proof of her ancestry in her eyes. She would be important to all humankind. Who knows,' Grandma Rose shrugged, 'perhaps that child is you.' She looked deep into my eyes, then she said, 'And you know what else?' I remember shaking my head. 'With us Black folks here in America and our history, it's hard to tell what color a baby is going to be, or what he or she might look like. You know, it's like throwing a couple of dice, all kinds of combinations are possible.' "

"I like that," Madame Deane exclaimed, a subtle gleam in her eyes. "And you know what? It is kind of interesting how you and my nephew are somewhat alike when it comes to dealing with prejudice, even from your own people." She straightened her headband. "It is a shame how we allow color, and different physical characteristics, to separate us." Madame Deane looked down at the entree Catherine was placing before her. "From the very beginning we knew it was going to be hard for Ulysses' parents, but what can you say when two people are in love." She raised her thin hands expressively. "Ulysses is definitely a combination of the two. He was named by my brother, and that's where he got all of his charm." She smiled reminiscently. "But he took his height and some of his color from Layla. She was an Egyptian. There are very few on the island, but there are several African families. Ashanti. Ibo. A lot of the slaves who ended up on Barbados were from those tribes. Most of them are spiritual, peaceful people.'' Madame Deane paused. ''Boy, was she fiery.'' She spoke with her fork and knife suspended in the air as she conjured up images from the past. ''I am talking about Layla. And she was beautiful too. Her skin was a shiny, dark brown. Her ancestors were among a group of Africans brought here from Barbados as slaves. That was hundreds of years ago.'' She placed a small amount of food in her mouth and chewed pensively. ''Slavery was ingrained in our culture. But by the time my grandfather took over Sovereign, slavery had been abolished. Still, on some of the estates you wouldn't have known it. And the folks here on Eros had been operating independent of the mainland for decades, so it was like a separate country. But my grandfather was determined to treat the African families that had been connected with Sovereign as fairly as he could. I'm not saying he didn't have his prejudices.'' Madame Deane waved her fork. ''Inevitably that meant my brother Peter and I grew up with a different mind-set about them than most of the islanders,'' Madame Deane continued to explain.

''My brother was always a true art lover, just like his son. Rare things of beauty always intrigued him.'' She patted her wrinkled lips with a napkin. ''One day he spotted Layla in some woods that edge our secluded beach. He said from the very first moment he saw her he knew she was the most beautiful woman he had ever seen. Her beauty captured him, but he said the way she was acting roused his curiosity. You see, Layla kept looking

over her shoulder as if she didn't want to be seen.
Peter said she appeared to be very scared, so he
hid himself and continued to watch her. Finally,
when she felt secure she was alone, Layla removed
two stones near the edge of the woods and began
to dig. In no time at all Peter said she unearthed
this magnificent bust. He said the sun reflected off
of it like gold as she held it in her hands.'' Madame
Deane gazed off as if she too were looking at the
scene. ''Peter said seeing her hold it with such reverence was a work of art within itself, and out of
pure excitement and overwhelming curiosity he
came out of his hiding place. From what he knew
about the African workers, he had expected her to
flee or cower with fright. But not Layla. Peter said
she pulled herself up to her fullest height and
looked him dead in the eye, claiming the piece as
her own. Her stance dared him to challenge her.''
Madame Deane's eyes sparkled with pride. ''He
said he could barely understand a word Layla was
saying she was so excited, but he said her gestures
were plain and clear. At that point Peter did his
best to reassure her that he had no intention of taking the bust from her, and he expressed his appreciation for its beauty. He said they stood there
staring at each other for a long time, and that Layla
would not leave until he left. After that, for several
days around the same time he revisited the spot
where he had seen her, but she never came. Then
finally Layla showed up again, and to his surprise
she told him she had secretly watched him each
time he visited the spot. It was only after the third
time he had come, and had not tried to dig up the
bust, did she feel she could trust him.

''Yes,'' Madame Deane's eyes clouded over

with sad acceptance, "from that point on their visits together became the highlight of their days.
Eventually people knew they had developed some
kind of relationship, but none of the islanders expected Peter would ever marry Layla. But being the
kind of man my brother was, he did. For a while
they were really happy. I hate to say it," she looked
down at the food that was getting cold, "but they
were happier after Father died. He really did not
approve of the marriage. He knew the problems
they would encounter. Then Ulysses was born, and
their lives seemed so fulfilled, for a while." Madame Deane paused as the ghostly images took
over.

"He was seven years old when it happened.
Ulysses had been beaten pretty badly by some older
boys on the island, and Layla decided to take the
matter up with their parents. Unlucky for her, two
of the fathers were drinking together at the first
home where she stopped. Instead of listening to
what she had to say, they turned it into an opportunity to take advantage of her. From what I heard
they did all sorts of horrible things. Then they
brought her battered body and left it on one of the
paths that led to Sovereign. My brother found her,
and in his grief he stabbed himself in the heart. Sad
to say Ulysses was the one who found the two of
them. The crime went unpunished because we were
never able to prove who did it."

"How awful!" Nadine's heart went out to Ulysses, and she looked up at the ceiling, picturing him
locked inside his room.

"Here on Eros we have such a blend of the awful and the sublime, the old and the new. And it is
only because of the recent tourist trade that things

have changed as much as they have. It is a place
rich in myths born out of ancient cultures.''

"Yes, the cliff dwellers appear to be living proof
of that.'' Nadine studied Madame Deane's expression as she mentioned the name that had sent Ulysses into an unexplained rage. But madame showed
no feelings at all as she took the conversational
tidbit offered by her dinner guest.

"They are definitely an interesting people.
Theirs is the oldest culture on the island. Their settlement sits among the cliffs on the far east side.
Can you believe they actually live beneath cliff
overhangs and in shallow caves?'' She leaned forward. ''Personally, I've never seen their houses.
But of course the entire island knows about them,
and Ulysses has visited them many times.'' She
pushed the cold pastry and sea eggs around on her
plate. ''It was not always the way it is now. I heard
in the beginning their ancestors came here from a
sunken continent that was located in the western
part of the world. It was called Lemuria. They
chose to make their homes among the caves and
cliffs, and later, when outsiders inhabited the island, they tried to become more a part of the island
community. At first they were well accepted. It is
said they were a very demonstrative and expressive
people, and because of this, they brought harmony
and rhythm to the island of Eros. The outsiders
began to enjoy their lives in ways they never had
before, and before anyone realized it, the cliff
dwellers were looked up to as leaders.

"Soon the islanders found out that they were
very different from the cliff dwellers. Not just in
looks and the sort of things that are obvious. But
something,'' Madame Deane looked up in the air,

"something less tangible. You see, the cliff dwellers believe in following what they call their inner voices. They call this voice the Will. Also they believe their bodies hold a sort of awareness, maybe consciousness would be a better word. It is not just flesh and blood." She examined her own hands as she explained.

"To the islanders the cliff dwellers appeared to be so much more attuned to their emotions than they were, and for hundreds of years the outsiders' gods and goddesses were the only deities they believed in and worshipped. Therefore the outsiders' nature was much more cautious, mainly because they did not want to offend the gods. In contrast, the cliff dwellers tended to heed their own callings from within. Eventually the two found it very hard to get along. The islanders began to fear the gods and goddesses would find the cliff dwellers offensive, and thereby bring death and destruction to the island. It took many generations, but eventually the cliff dwellers were ostracized and driven back to the caves. Then, for reasons unknown, the outsiders disappeared from Eros."

Nadine thought about the things Madame Deane had told her, and she realized how different she was from the people of Eros with their mystical tales.

Madame Deane had barely touched her food, she had talked so much during the meal. Nevertheless when Catherine came to remove Nadine's empty plate, madame insisted she take hers as well.

"Well, young lady. I have some reading I would like to do before I retire for the night. I really regret that Ulysses did not show up this evening. He knows the book sale is scheduled for the end of the month, and we really need to get started organizing it. There is so much that needs to be done.'' She maneuvered her wheelchair away from the table. ''Poor thing, I know he has feelings against it.''

Shocked, Nadine asked, ''You mean you plan to sell the books in the collection upstairs?''

''My word, child, no,'' Madame Deane replied. ''We have an entire slew of books and other things in an antechamber below the house. We will be selling them. We have a real need for money right now.'' She looked discreetly at Nadine, and began to almost whisper. ''Not that we're broke or anything like that. Ulysses just hates it when I talk about financial situations with what he calls outsiders. He says he doesn't want me to worry about money.'' She gave a long deep sigh. ''I just wish I could be of more help to him.'' A thin hand absentmindedly fiddled with her headband. ''I wish that you were staying longer, Nadine. You did say your business involves literature and art, didn't you?''

''Yes, I did.'' Nadine was pleased with this opportunity to tell the truth.

''Well, that is a shame. We could really use your help around here. At least until after the sale.'' Madame Deane removed her napkin from her lap, and began to propel herself toward one of the doors. ''I shall see you tomorrow before you leave. I'm sure you are planning to do so tomorrow. I mean, with the roads clear and all?''

''Yes, ma'am, I do.''

''What a shame,'' Madame Deane remarked as she disappeared into the next room.

Chapter 10

 Nadine wrapped the robe snugly around her before she entered the expansive hallway. This time her bath had been uneventful, if not solemn. Her clash with Ulysses and hearing the horrible events surrounding his childhood had left her feeling numb. It made her realize no matter where she traveled, prejudice and the negative side of human nature would always be a reality. She guessed it was one of man's frailties.

Nadine moved along the lamp-lit corridor deep in thought. As she advanced, a light-headedness overcame her. She stopped to brace herself against the wall to rid herself of the sensation. When Nadine opened her eyes to the hallway ahead, an uncanny metamorphosis had occurred. The walls were now covered with ancient drawings accompanied by strange hieroglyphics, and three people had appeared in the midst of them. Two men were seated at a table made from the same kind of stone as the cliff dwellers' jewelry. It was oddly shaped as if it had been sliced from a larger article similar in form. There was a third person, a woman, standing with her back to the men. Nadine could tell from her stance and the droop of her shoulders, she was feeling heavily burdened. One of the men rose from the table and went to put his hands on the woman's shoulders. He turned her to face the largest drawing on one of the walls, and Nadine's heart began to beat uncontrollably as she looked upon the mirror image of herself being led closer to the etchings. The man was gentle but firm. He pointed out the different images to the woman, underlining the hieroglyphics. Suddenly, all three of the people looked up as a gong sounded in the distance. Almost simultaneously a man's form appeared in a doorway. Nadine could not see him clearly—his face remained hidden in the shadows. As he moved forward two other forms seemed to materialize behind him. Just as their bodies took on definitive shapes, flames ignited in the doorway, engulfing them. Nadine's mirror image screamed and fainted. All of the images faded as Nadine's own scream erupted with no sound, she was so frightened.

Nadine stood rooted to the spot as the hallway dissolved into its natural form. She tried to rationalize what she had just seen. Automatically, she searched for physical evidence to prove that what she had seen had actually occurred. There was none.

"I don't believe this. Oh, God! I must be losing my mind!"

A muffled thud sounded to the left of her, coming from behind a door. Consumed by panic and fear Nadine pushed it open, expecting to see a scene similar to the one she had witnessed only moments before. Instead her astonished brownish-jade gaze landed on a half-dressed Ulysses. He was sitting on his bed with a cumbersome record book at his feet and a startled look on his face. Pages were hanging out of the book, and several were scattered on the floor.

"Did you hear that?" The question was more of a demand as Nadine urged Ulysses to substantiate what she had just experienced.

"Did I hear what?" His voice was skeptical.

"Look, don't mess with me." She pointed with impatience. "Did you hear the people who were out here in this hallway?" Her voice rose with frustration as she took in his disheveled hair, and noticed the almost-drained glass of rum near his bed.

Ulysses narrowed his eyes as he studied her. He could tell from the look on her face and how large her eyes were she was physically shaken. "No. I did not hear anything."

"But you had to." Nadine's chest began to rise and fall visibly beneath the robe. "They were standing near your door. If you didn't hear them talking you had to hear the woman scream before she fainted," she insisted.

"I tell you I heard nothing." His tone was aggravatingly calm.

"Look here. I don't know what sort of games you people are playing around here." She took a step back. "There must have been something in my food," she said with an air of discovery. She squinted suspiciously before threatening, "Don't make me show you how crazy *I* can act. I can act a fool like you've never seen before if you push me far enough." She could feel her fingernails pressing into her palms as she clenched her hands into fists.

In silence, Ulysses approached a decanter that sat on top of a large wooden chest. He poured an ample amount of rum into a crystal glass, and offered the drink to Nadine.

She started to refuse it, but her immediate need for calm changed her mind. She belted down the beverage in several quick swallows. Afterwards she thought, This is horrible, and she wondered if grain alcohol or Mad Dog 20/20 could have tasted worse as the liquid burned her throat.

Ulysses waited for the brown liquid to cause the inevitable rush. As he expected, seconds later she began to teeter on her feet, reaching out to take hold of anything that would steady her. Ulysses made his arm available, and led her to a divan placed against the bedroom wall. He watched perspiration break out on her forehead while she attempted to cool down by using her palm as a fan.

"Whoa! That's some strong stuff."

"Yes, it is. And it is even stronger when you drink the entire glass within a moment's time," Ulysses admonished her.

"If you had seen and heard what I just did, you'd do the same thing."

"Maybe," was his only response, giving no indication if he believed her bizarre story or not.

"You said you didn't hear anything, but I tell you I did. Not only did I hear them, I saw two men," she paused before she continued, "and a woman who looked just like me. But she was dressed differently and speaking a language I couldn't begin to understand. Don't you think that's more than a little strange?"

"Under regular circumstances I would say yes. But maybe not for a woman who I know talks to herself, and to objects that cannot talk back."

Nadine's anger and frustration increased. Ulysses was not taking anything she said seriously. "So are you suggesting that I made all of this up?"

Ulysses shrugged his broad shoulders.

"And tell me, puh-lease, why would I do that?"

"In order to have an excuse to come into my bedroom without an invitation," was his quick reply.

His dark gaze trailed down Nadine's robe that had loosened with her not-so-ladylike plop onto the cushioned divan. Ulysses' eyes rested at the top of her smooth, bare thigh where the garment had naturally parted.

Nadine flipped the trailing part of her robe up from the floor and covered her exposed limb.

"Now tell me the truth," his voice turned threatening, "why did you come in here?"

"I just told you. I heard and saw some really bizarre things a moment—"

"Do you expect me to believe that?" His eyes narrowed. "You should not. I think you had another reason for coming into my room. Did you think you would find out more about the little bronze case if you came in here half-dressed?"

She opened her mouth to protest, but he grabbed her face in his hand, applying pressure to her jaws. "Thinking maybe I would get so excited you could get me to tell you whatever you wanted to know. Is that it?" He tilted her oval face upward, forcing her hazel eyes to look into his. "Or is it just that you could not resist my masculine charms any longer, and you decided to sample them since this is your last night at Sovereign?"

Nadine's face filled with anger. "I have heard it all," she spat out between clenched teeth. "You must really think a hell of a lot of yourself, and your . . . collection, don't you? Well, I'm sorry to have to be the one to burst your little egotistical bubble, but I want you to know I don't have to use my body to get what I want in life." She forced his hand down from her face. "And on top of that, I've come across men much more desirable than you, Mr. Deane," she lied, "and managed to keep myself intact. So believe me when I tell you, I didn't need to make up a ridiculous story to burst into your bedroom to get information from you, or to give up my virginity to a man I don't even like."

A spark of surprise appeared on his face, then slowly his gaze began to smolder as he raked her up and down insultingly. "You may not like me, Nadine. But I know when a woman wants me. Even if you are too inexperienced to know when you really want a man." He stood closer to the divan, a harsh chuckle surfacing from within him. "I should have known your display of being a worldly woman was a farce. Here I was thinking the desire I saw in your eyes burned so brightly because you were such a well-experienced woman. But now, I really understand." He paused to give his words the full effect. "The light was simply the suppressed fires of a reluctant virgin."

Ulysses' brash statement cut to the core. Her virginity was a touchy subject that she discussed with no one besides Gloria. Had he said those same words a year ago her reaction would not have been the same. She would have been proud of her virginal status. Only recently had she begun to regret it. Her thoughts seem to focus more and more on how difficult it was to find a good man to love her, and even more difficult a good husband.

"Re-reluctant," she stammered, embarrassed. "I

am not reluctant. At least I wouldn't be with the right man.''

"And so you are telling me you have never come across a man who wanted to make love to you? Or one that you wanted to make love to?''

"I didn't say that.'' She looked away from his dark, piercing eyes.

"Well, if that is not true, why have you not tasted the pleasures of love? I can see you are well beyond the age of consent.'' He knelt intimidatingly close, his face only inches away. There was a fresh scent of rum on his breath; his eyes were slightly red from the liquor.

"First of all, twenty-six is not well past the age of . . . anything. And I wish you would show me the international law book that says a woman must make love by a certain age. A man and a woman should join together when they really love one another, not just to fulfill some passing desire.''

"But my sweet Nadine, life is far too complicated for that to be the reality. It may be the ideal. But believe me, most idealists end up having their dreams shattered. My parents were idealists. In the end it brought them nothing but pain and sadness. I believe we should all live for the moment.'' His thickly lashed gaze bore down on her. "You never know what fate has in store for you.'' A brown finger began to trace the neckline of Nadine's terrycloth robe, stopping at the bottom to rest between her softly bronzed breasts.

"Ulysses . . . look—''

"No. You look.'' His voice turned into a silky purr. "Look at how the slightest touch of my hand makes you quiver with anticipation.''

Nadine was praying he would not see the small

tremors she was experiencing, but no sooner had
he said those words, an even stronger one coursed
through her, visible to them both.

"Well, you would be trembling too if you had
seen what I just saw," she countered, trying to
keep the breathless tone out of her voice.

"That was over ten minutes ago, and your
breasts are rising and falling faster now than they
have since you first entered my room. You do want
me, Nadine, just as much as I want you. It is just
that I am not afraid to face my desire, and to
quench it."

"See? That is the whole problem in a nutshell."
She pressed her back further into the divan, putting
as much space between them as she could. "I don't
want to be another woman that you add to your list
of females who have quenched your desire. If I
wanted to be on that kind of list I could have offered myself to any number of brothers on the
street back in the United States." She paused.
"Yes, I must admit at first I had decided to let go,
and let things just happen naturally. But then I really saw what you were like at the rum still, and
heard how the majority of the women were enamored of you, including Melanie. Also there were
subtle hints from Catherine and your aunt," she
continued to explain. "Now on top of all that, you
kneel here and tell me because of some quirk of
fate that refuses to allow life to be a bed of roses
for all of us, that I, Nadine Clayton, should take
whatever I can get and be happy with it?" Searching hazel eyes looked deeply into the eyes that
peered into hers. "I just don't buy that."

"That is simply the way I see life." Ulysses'
eyelids formed a cynical hood. "I am what I am,

Nadine. A product of my experiences, and the world around me. I take what pleasure and momentary happiness that is offered to me, and I expect little else. Are you so much the wiser to look for rainbows and happy endings in a world blanketed with misery and sorrow? I do not think so.''

Nadine could feel the buried hurt and disappointment beneath Ulysses' fatalistic words. She knew all too well how easy it could be to give in to hopelessness and accept whatever life decided to throw your way. She used to see that kind of surrender every day on the faces of the men habitually standing on the corners in the small town that edged Ashland, and in some of the eyes of the inner-city children she taught. Eyes that she felt were too young to have experienced such pain-filled realities.

But Nadine knew there was something different about Ulysses. There was no pain or hurt visible in the black depths that she gazed into now, only acceptance, and a hardness that was the support beam for his strange personality. It made Nadine wish that she could be the one to open the way for hope and love in his life.

At that moment Nadine guessed Grandma Rose was right when she called her a rescuer. Grandma always said she had the fortitude and the foolhardiness to look for sunshine even in the darkest hour. Nadine knew for her there could be no other way. She believed the immobility of hopelessness was worse than dying.

Nadine's small, but steady hand reached up to touch the profusion of midnight curls crowning Ulysses' head. She watched as he closed his eyes and turned his face toward her palm, nuzzling it as the young calves on her farm used to do. But the sensations that flooded within her now, as his arms encircled her and he lay his head upon her breasts, were far removed from those childhood experiences.

Nadine's body tensed beneath Ulysses' embrace, and she tried to reason through the pros and cons of the situation. Instantly her mind began to conjure up all of her old fears and judgments, even though her hand, as of its own volition, continued to stroke the thick, coarse locks beneath it. A warm tingly sensation began to mount inside Nadine, the result of Ulysses' closeness and his large hands sensuously kneading her flesh. Over and over her breath was forced audibly from her body as he squeezed gently, easing away her reservations with each stroke. "I don't expect rainbows from you, Ulysses, but I expect you to give me all that you can of yourself as I would want to give you all of me." The hushed words came from a place and a need deep within.

"The way you say it makes it sound so simple." He looked up at her open, sincere features. "And I believe for you it would be. But there is one thing that I have always been, no matter what my other faults may be, and that is honest. The truth is, Nadine, I am not good at giving of myself. Especially not in the way your words imply. I have had no need to be. Physically? Yes. That is my forte. So let us look at this straight on. You and I are here tonight, and the opportunity is ripe for many things; after tomorrow, we may not see each other again. That is the reality."

Nadine turned her head to avoid his eyes as she felt the sting of tears resulting from the truth he had spoken. Regardless of what she had told herself earlier that morning, Nadine knew she was not the kind of woman who could love, especially for the first time, and not expect some semblance of love in return. For her, sex could not be an act without love. They were inseparable.

Nadine's hands pressed down on his shoulders as she attempted to extract herself from his embrace. "Ulysses, I'm no different from you when it comes to changing the way I am, and I can't allow myself to do this. I've waited all these years, and I guess I can wait a while longer." Her hazel eyes narrowed as she spoke. "I'll admit I want you, but I know I deserve more than a man who has consciously decided he does not want to give or receive love."

She struggled to rise from the divan, but Ulysses' arms remained like steel bands around her, yet the fear and anger that gripped her heart were just as strong. She had to get away from this man whose heart had been voluntarily hardened against the most tender of emotions. "I may be inexperienced, Ulysses, but I'm no fool. I believe that love is the strongest and most powerful emotion that we as humans have to offer. Without it we are nothing. If you are afraid to open up to the possibility of feeling love for another person, I feel sorry for you." She spoke the words as she shook her head.

Ulysses looked at her as if he was seeing her for the first time. Then his hands dropped and rested outside of Nadine's thighs as he pressed his face closer to hers, his eyes lighting up with a searing intensity. "A few moments ago you said all you wanted was what I was able to give, and that is what you will get, Nadine Clayton. It is too late to change your mind now.''

Roughly, his lips descended on hers, forcing her head against the wall behind it. Ulysses was no longer able to stand their lush closeness without partaking of them. Looking into her frightened eyes, he lessened the pressure and spoke with his mouth still pressed against hers. ''It is not that I do not want to give or receive love, Nadine.'' His tortured stare held hers captive. ''I need help,'' he huskily pleaded as he nibbled at her full bottom lip, ''your help.''

Ulysses began to press his hard frame against hers, and Nadine could feel the rigidness of his desire as he blazed kisses down her face, her throat, and onto the soft flesh that swelled, forming her breasts. ''Say you will help me find the love I need so badly.''

His intensity alarmed Nadine, and she grabbed for any straws of rationality she could to dissuade him. ''Stop, Ulysses. No, I can't do this. I won't! I've waited so long to find someone worthy of sharing my love,'' the words tumbled out, ''I simply can't waste myself or my love on this situation . . . on you.''

She watched as pure pain flashed in his eyes then disappeared beneath an emotionless blanket. Regret filled her seconds later as Ulysses sat back stiffly, then rose to his feet, never removing his eyes from her face. For seconds on end he stared at her, an ugly cynicism marring his handsome features.

''So you think that your love would be wasted, do you? Well, do not flatter yourself, Miss Clayton. You are not the first person to feel I'm not good enough for them, and you won't be the last.'' He looked at her with distaste. "I will leave the job of making you into a woman up to some cold, pompous little fool that can promise you everything you want, including himself. And he will be able to deliver it too." A guttural laugh made mockery of her. "But believe me, he will not deliver anything the way I can." He paused, his stare intensifying. "But you need not concern yourself with that, because we will never see each other again." Ulysses took one step back, giving Nadine just enough room to leave.

The look of disdain on his dark features made her feel all the more self-conscious as she gathered the robe about her body. She felt her self-confidence ebbing away under his scathing gaze. Yet something inside Nadine would not allow her to accept all of the burden of this dark stranger's emotional ghosts. She reminded herself, I am not the root of his problems, and I am worthy of some man's love, even if it is not yours, Ulysses Deane.

As she stood, Nadine returned Ulysses' stare with a confident look of her own, and with her head held high, she made no hasty retreat as he watched her close the door.

Chapter 11

Silent laughter erupted from the people inside the minibuses as they waited for the streetlight to change, while others moved back and forth on the sidewalks with shopping bags and bundles under their arms. Inside a building across the street Nadine idly gazed at the scene through a window. The only sounds she could hear were street noises: horns blowing, the purr of motors, and the sound of calypso music. Everything on Barbados felt as different as night and day when compared to Eros. The narrow lanes of traffic bustled with activity from tourists and locals, making her short stay on the nearby island seem even more surrealistic.

With each passing day Nadine questioned herself about the things that had happened there. Today was no different from the rest. Time only made her feel more uncertain about what her heart and mind told her had been reality.

Nadine's slender fingers involuntarily touched the cool stones lying against her skin. It was as if her body wanted to remind her of the only tangible thing she possessed that made her stay on Eros more than a fantasy—the necklace the cliff dwell-

ers had given her. She had left behind the animal
skin Madame Deane forced upon her. It did not
belong to her. It belonged to Sovereign and Eros.

When Nadine returned to her room from breakfast that last morning to retrieve her fanny pack and
the onyx carving, she discovered it was gone. She
searched the drawer thoroughly but the slab was
not there. Clarence was waiting outside with the
donkey cart, ready to take her to the wharf, so she
decided there simply was not enough time to do
anything about it. Yet Nadine knew if she were
more truthful with herself, there was nothing she
wanted to do about the carving being missing. She
had never mentioned the stone to anyone at Sovereign, and she thought it would be rather strange,
almost ungrateful, to accuse someone in the household of taking it when there were so many priceless
possessions on the estate.

Throughout that last morning at Sovereign Nadine had felt very tired; she had barely slept the
night before. The two emotional days she had spent
on Eros could be seen in her pinched features. So
when the opportunity came for her to leave she was
glad to go. Nadine had said her good-byes to Catherine and Madame Deane after the morning meal.
She never saw Ulysses.

That had been over three weeks ago. The work
on Barbados had kept her busy, even though Dr.
Steward, her boss, had gone to Paris and had remained there for the last two weeks. His calls came
frequently, leaving brief instructions, promising a
quick return that never happened.

She had to admit she thoroughly enjoyed cataloging the literature and art that had not been cat-
egorized by the institute. The work was tedious but

interesting, and the personal satisfaction was high. It felt good to be a part of an international team, one whose goal was to create a centralized computer database of the world's treasures. There were only three members of the team working in the islands, including Dr. Steward, but it was wonderful knowing there were many others like her working in offices around the globe. Their tasks were the same, finding and cataloging the world's treasures, and entering their existence into computer terminals whose messaging systems linked them all to a host computer in Paris, near the Louvre.

"If you're not going to use the terminal, I've got something I'd like to enter, if you don't mind." Claudia's clipped tones broke into Nadine's retrospection.

Nadine looked up into her coworker's judgmental features. She and Claudia had not hit it off well from the beginning, if they had hit it off at all. Claudia seemed to think that Nadine had only been accepted on the project because of a racial quota. So it peeved Nadine no end to be caught daydreaming at the window. As rare of an occurrence as it was, she did not want to give Claudia anything to feed her preconceived notions.

"Sure," Nadine responded, "you may use it. I guess I have been dominating the station. Look how many entries I have made compared to yours," she quipped, smiling with a doe-like innocence, then keyed out of her program. That should shut her up for a while, she thought. I am not in the mood to deal with her narrow-minded views today.

Nadine rose from the only comfortable chair in the room, allowing Claudia to take her place. She reflected on how, in the beginning, she believed they could be friends. But Nadine learned Claudia did not share her belief.

At first Nadine had made excuses for Claudia. Claudia told her she had grown up in a small isolated town in Oklahoma, and had not had much contact with African-Americans. But after several weeks of working with Claudia and getting to know her, Nadine discovered she was satisfied with her tainted views, and had no intention of trying to open her mind to the reality of good and bad in all people.

Once during a particularly belittling conversation, Nadine had fought back with comments about Claudia's close, personal connection with Dr. Steward. Claudia had turned as red as a beet, making the black roots of her blonde hair even more pronounced.

Nadine looked at the casual slacks and sweater Claudia was wearing today, and she knew she had not been far from the mark. When Dr. Steward was around the only thing Claudia ever wore were form-fitted sweaters and tight skirts that inched up whenever she sat down.

"By the way," Claudia called, aggression in her tone, "Dr. Steward will be back tomorrow. So if I were you I'd make sure I had all my ducks in a row *before* he arrives."

Nadine didn't bother to respond as she walked out of the office door.

"We have had this conversation over and over again, Melanie. I do not have any intentions of joining Sovereign's sugarcane fields with Sharpe Hall," Ulysses told her.

"I am only thinking of you, Ulysses," said Melanie softly, obviously hurt by his curt remark. "And you must admit this conversation is quite different from the others."

"Do not think about me, Melanie. I can take care of myself, and Sovereign."

"Why won't you let me help you?" She touched his arm.

"You call asking me to marry you helping me? Marriage should be much more than that. You deserve much more than that."

"It could be." A seductive tone entered Melanie's voice. "You know that." She let her hand slide down to Ulysses' hand, then slowly moved his hand upward until she placed it on her small, firm breast. "We would be good together, Ulysses. I have always loved you. It has just taken me all this time to tell you. Maybe I was waiting for you to come to me. But you never did. You went everywhere else, Ulysses. But you never came to me." Her words revealed her injured pride.

"Melanie, we have been friends for so long. Do not do this," Ulysses urged, surprised by her forward actions. He had always known her to be extremely proper. She never revealed any indication of a strong sexuality. Somewhere inside, her sudden change unnerved him.

Too many things had happened over the last few weeks. Things he could not ignore. Finding the onyx slab in Nadine's room with her belongings had only been the beginning.

Ulysses could not force himself to say good-bye to Nadine the morning she left Sovereign, not after what happened between them the night before. So he settled for visiting her room while she had breakfast on the lanai.

His previous night had been restless. His mind was filled with thoughts of Nadine, who lay only a few yards away in the bedroom down the hall. Her unguarded sincerity haunted him as much as his need to physically have her. The urge to possess her had been strong, but her words of rejection had been even more powerful, delivering a blow to a very vulnerable place.

As a child, the feeling of rejection had been overwhelming. Ulysses had come to believe his parents had left him because of his unworthiness. Especially his father, who had chosen death over a life with a weak son. As an adult the sharp edge on the pain had worn a little. Now it only surfaced as a dull throb when he felt his inadequacies or was reminded of them.

As Ulysses looked around Nadine's room, her only visible possession was a comb lying on top of the dressing table. He sat on the bed, bewildered. He was not able to say good-bye, but he was reluctant to let her go. In deep thought, he began to systematically open each drawer of the dressing table. The first two were empty, but in the third drawer, he saw Nadine's fanny pack stuffed inside. Compelled by a desire to know the truth about her he took hold of the bag, but found it was snared upon an even heavier object. A mixture of shock, disappointment, and distrust erupted within him as he removed the onyx slab.

For a while Ulysses stared at the smooth, black object as it lay inside the drawer, his feelings volleying between anger and betrayal.

The manuscript pages had been stolen over two

months ago. Why would Nadine still have this one in her possession if she was the original thief? She would have had plenty of time to sell it, if that had been her objective. And why would she return with the object to Sovereign, the place from which it had been stolen? Did she intend to secretly return it? Why? And why hadn't she carried out her task if that had been her goal? Did Nadine know about the manuscript hidden within the carved stone?

Ulysses' first instinct was to confront her, but something else persuaded him to wait. Maybe she had come upon it by accident. If she were innocent, when she found out it was missing she would simply report it to Catherine or his aunt. So Ulysses decided to give Nadine that chance. For whatever reason, he needed to prove to himself she was innocent. But she never reported it. That morning Nadine left without saying a single word.

"Do you find me so undesirable that you would not marry me, even if it meant saving Sovereign?" Melanie pushed her point further, a harshness descending upon her usually serene features.

Stern, dark eyes regarded her. "Sovereign is my affair, Melanie. And it's not such a desperate situation that it needs saving, at least not yet. Or do you know more about the group of workers who have refused to harvest my sugarcane than you are letting on?" Ulysses looked at her suspiciously. "Thank God the cliff dwellers haven't gone into seclusion for the spiritual ceremony they hold every year around this time." He ran an exasperated hand through the tangle of black curls on his head. "I am fortunate that most of the sugarcane crop was cut and sent to the mill before this rebellion got started. Things were bad enough, and now

all this. What do you know about this, Melanie?''
He watched for a change in her expression. ''Is
your brother Basil behind it? He has always dis-
liked me and would not hesitate to pull something
that would put all the sugarcane fields of Eros under his control.''

''I do not know what to say.'' Melanie looked
down. ''I never thought the day would come when
you would not trust me.'' Two injured obsidian
eyes accused him. ''I am the one who has always
defended you, Ulysses. In the village, and even
against my own brother. But ever since your aunt's
accident you have changed . . . toward my family
. . . and me. I knew you never looked at me the way
I wanted. The way a woman who wants a man she
loves to look at her.'' Melanie let go an ironic
laugh. ''You treated me like your sister. The way
Rodney treats me. I hated that, but after Madame
Deane was injured you even took that away.''

''What did you expect?'' Ulysses looked at Melanie, needing her to understand. ''There were so
many questions left unanswered, and the accident
did happen on your estate. If Clarence hadn't been
trying to see that cook of yours, Aunt Helen would
have died at the bottom of your well. To this day,
Melanie, my aunt swears she received a letter from
Sharpe Hall with your family seal on it, telling her
if she met with the sender secretly, they could piece
together all the things that had been kept secret
about our family's histories.''

''And you believe her?'' Melanie asked deri-
sively. ''One minute that woman is hissing like a
serpent and the next she's as calm and composed
as a dove,'' she retorted. Ulysses' countenance
hardened against Melanie's harsh words. She ac-

knowledged it and softened her approach. "All I am saying is, there are obvious reasons why you should not believe some of the far-fetched things your aunt says."

Ulysses began to walk away in offended silence.

"Let us just forget about it," Melanie offered, trying to make amends.

"You know that is not possible," Ulysses declared, turning abruptly. "After all these years the stories still have not died down about your father, Henry, and Aunt Helen. How he wooed her, although he was still married to your mother. Wooed her when she was at her weakest. When she was grieving over the death of my father, her only brother." Ulysses stopped himself before he said what he really felt. That Henry Sharpe had been like a spider devouring an immobilized prey, taking total advantage of his aunt's distressful condition after his parents died.

"I remember how he called on her at least twice a day," he continued. "She was so relieved there was someone to help her through the difficult time. Aunt Helen totally relied on him, and your father began to direct the workers and keep up the paperwork at Sovereign. She was grateful for his presence and his companionship." Cynicism rose in his eyes. "Eventually, he took over running Sovereign's affairs, and he ran them for seven years until he died. After that Clarence took charge of the workers and Aunt Helen looked after the records." Ulysses paused. "Until this day she has never admitted they were having an affair, but after he died she never married, or pursued any other relationships," he stated pointedly.

"It was not until I was eighteen and was truly

master of Sovereign that we discovered the discrepancies over the borders between Sovereign's sugarcane fields and Sharpe Hall's. I went straight to Basil and we had words over the matter. I told him it was mighty strange that the oldest of the documents clearly stated that the northwest fields between our properties belonged to Sovereign, and the ones your father had handled said they belonged to Sharpe Hall. He would not even listen." Ulysses' dark eyes burned passionately. "You see, there were three sets of records. Two at Sovereign, and one at Sharpe Hall. The one that stated the sugarcane fields belonged to Sovereign had been hidden in my father's personal belongings for years. The other document had been filed away with Sovereign's records by your father. Needless to say, the latter agreed with the papers at Sharpe Hall." Ulysses began to look out over the fields of Sharpe Hall. "Well, I wasn't about to give up, so I took the matter to the authorities on Barbados. They looked at the documents and decided the situation was a common one. They said that discrepancies were often found between old records; therefore they declared the two sets which agreed on the property lines had the most weight."

"None of that is my fault, Ulysses," Melanie insisted. "And I would think if you accepted my marriage proposal it would make up for all of that."

Ulysses looked back at the picture Melanie made, standing between the columns supporting the porch of her home. Her eyes were soft and compelling, but there was something else there he could not quite describe.

"No, it is not your fault. But it is something you

alone could never make up for, Melanie. And you know with Basil being the oldest boy of the family, Sharpe Hall is his to do with as he pleases. Your marrying me would not change that.'' He turned, making his way down the spacious stairway.

''Ulysses.''

He stopped and turned toward her.

''Please think about what I've said.''

Ulysses simply looked down at the stairs.

Melanie made one last attempt to solicit an acknowledgment. ''If you need any help getting ready for the book sale, don't hesitate to ask me. It is two weeks away, is it not?''

Ulysses nodded his compliance, waved, and began to walk away. He took in the lay of his land as he traversed back to Sovereign. As he approached the hilltop he could see his home nestled between a forest of evergreens.

The exterior of the structure was deceiving. It did not reflect the riches that abided inside. Unlike Sharpe Hall, with its imposing columns and archways insinuating even more marvelous things to come, it was Sovereign which housed the treasures of Eros, and Ulysses intended to keep it that way.

He watched as a donkey cart driven by Clarence advanced steadily up one of the island paths. Upon reaching the house the elderly man got down and hobbled into the side entrance. Clarence, like Catherine, had been with his family for years. Never a man much for words, but a good man. Ulysses' handsome features contorted with anger as he thought of Clarence being assaulted during the last break-in at Sovereign.

The intruder had waited to do his dirty work until the one night Ulysses was out of town. He had come across an unsuspecting Clarence when making his escape. The criminal struck him down, then kicked him repeatedly to ensure he would not get up and follow. It made Ulysses apprehensive about his next visit to Barbados, but he simply had no choice, he would have to go again for his business.

He remembered arriving back from his trip and finding that the lock on the collection room bore marks of an attempted forced entry. His own room had been searched thoroughly, and so had the library. What puzzled him was that some of the valuables that could have been taken remained intact. Catherine and Aunt Helen had slept on the main floor and heard nothing.

Ulysses was sure the would-be thief was looking for the Five Pieces of Gaia, but he did not understand why. There were many objects strewn idly about within Sovereign that were much more valuable. But for him and his family, the collection was priceless for sentimental reasons. Could someone else have similar reasons for wanting to possess them? Would the inscription on the bronze lid, if it could be deciphered, answer all of these questions? Against his will, Ulysses wondered if Nadine could have been an accomplice in the latest attempt. It happened one week to the day after her departure.

Chapter 12

The old guard looked at her suspiciously as she advanced up the side stairwell. It was 10:30 P.M., and she knew he wondered why a young woman would choose to return to work in a small, cramped room filled with old papers and artifacts.

Nadine was asking herself the same question, although in the back of her mind she knew why. She was having problems sleeping ever since her return from Eros. Her nights had been an accumulation of snatches of sleep, mixed with strange dreams that left her uneasy. But when she tried to remember them, she could not. That was bad enough. But the thoughts of Ulysses that kept her awake for long, endless hours deep into the night were the worst.

She would find her nipples tightening, and a demanding yearning building inside her abdomen as she lay alone in her twin-size bed. The sensations were always the same, varying in intensity, as her mind replayed the last meeting she had with him. The feel of his arms about her as he pressed his body against hers. His kiss was urgent, hungry. It was as if she had been seared, branded by the passion that poured from him that night. Nadine knew she had done the right thing by not giving herself to this man who remained a puzzling stranger. She believed his ability to be cruel was just as potent as his ability to make love. Lovemaking of a kind he promised she would never receive from any other man. Just as she was accepting the pain of knowing she would never experience Ulysses' lovemaking, the guilt would set in. Guilt from wanting him. Over her body's reaction to just the thought of his touch. She would feel the weight of the years of her Pentecostal upbringing, which taught her she had no right as a single female to any of the things she was feeling or thinking. All her life she had tried so hard to be the epitome of righteousness, combating the endless rumors about her parents.

Listlessly, Nadine unlocked the office door and turned on the wall switch. She found the quiet of the musty room comforting, and its clutter reminded her of Grandma Rose.

Nadine walked over to one of several bookshelves. Many of the books were studies of ancient art, and writings compiled by various scholars over vast periods of time. She found reading the yellowing, torn pages relaxing.

During the past two weeks she routinely returned to the office during the late-night hours to read. If it wasn't for the unbendable rule, "None of the books or paperwork are to be removed under any circumstances," she would have saved herself the trip by taking a few of them back to her room. But it really wasn't so bad. Dr. Steward had found them housing in a building a couple of blocks down from the library. Of course, for many of the locals and tourists, 10:30 P.M. was the time to be out and about in St. Phillip, the largest parish on Barbados.

With the desk light on, Nadine settled down with a book in the secretarial chair. An open window let in a tiny breeze, but soon beads of perspiration formed on Nadine's face. She realized how warm the office had become. Nadine fumbled with the knot of the scarf she had tied around her neck after buying it earlier at a boutique at Sam Lord's Castle. Moments later the knot was undone, but the scarf had become entangled with the cliff dwellers' necklace beneath it. Nadine put the book down, and removed both the scarf and the necklace. The objects slid apart as she placed them on the desk.

The light from the desk lamp beamed on the diminutive tablets, playing up the craftsmanship of the distinctly carved figures on each stone. Nadine studied the characters, noting the repetition of some. Others were unique, and like many times before, she wondered what meaning they held.

A short gust of wind rushed through the window, causing several papers to take flight and the pages of her book to flutter in its path. Nadine held down the ones that she could as she waited for the strong breeze to subside. As she picked the papers up from the floor, Nadine noticed a thin collection of onionskin writings floating down from the highest point of the wooden shelves. She waited for it to complete its descent, fearing the pages might crumble if she attempted to grasp them too quickly. The paperwork opened like a fan as it made contact with the tiled floor, revealing the symbol of the cliff dwellers on the bottom of one of the pages.

A chilling apprehension overcame her as her hazel eyes traveled from the papers to the necklace spread out on the desk. She stared at the window through which only a slight breeze drifted.

Ever since Nadine experienced the vision in Sovereign's hallway, she had tried to ignore an ever-present feeling. The feeling was linked to the dreams she could not remember and information about Eros and the cliff dwellers that would surface without provocation. They were inner murmurings that told her she had mystical links to the island and its people. Nadine did not want to accept these feelings. They scared her. Nothing had frightened her so much since she was a little girl, and actually, what she experienced then had not frightened her, Grandma Rose's reaction had.

Nadine was seven and had been ill when the woman appeared in her bedroom as she lay in her bed. She was beautiful, with dark-brown skin and tranquil eyes; her hair was swept back from her angular face. She had worn a nondescript robe, tawny in color.

Nadine's fever had broken, and Grandma Rose had gone to get a cool glass of water because her throat and mouth felt dry. The woman entered her room through the door, and at first Nadine thought it was Grandma Rose.

"You forgot my water, Grandma," she had barely whispered.

The woman moved closer, and Nadine could see she was smiling as she shook her head from side to side in a silent no. She stopped beside the bed near Nadine's feet, and raised her right arm out in front of her. Dangling from her fingertips was a tiny scale. It hung still and unbalanced, though Nadine saw nothing in the small cups.

The woman's soft eyes seemed to beckon to her. She wanted Nadine to place her hand upon her own. Nadine knew this even though there were no words that passed her lips. She remembered sitting up with effort and stretching out her arm, then placing her hand upon the stranger's ghostly hand. With Nadine's slightest touch, the silver scale balanced, the woman smiled, and disappeared into thin air. Grandma Rose entered the room directly after that.

"Honey, what are you doing?" She walked over to Nadine, feeling her head, concern in her eyes.

"The lady wanted me to touch her hand and help balance the little scale she was holding."

"What?" Grandma Rose looked around the room apprehensively. "Nay-Nay, what are you talking about?"

"There was a woman here. She was very nice. And she was pretty too. She just wanted my help."

Grandma Rose slowly looked around the room again. "Now child, I know you've been sick, but you can't go around saying things like this. Folks down here don't take too kindly to it. They'll have you in the crazy house before you know it. You hear me? Let this stay between you and Grandma Rose, okay?"

Nadine remembered nodding numbly.

Grandma Rose started to leave the room but she turned around again. "Nay-Nay."

"Yes, ma'am."

"You know Grandma Rose believes in God and I hope that you do too."

"I do, Grandma," she had replied.

"Well, there's one thing you got to remember. Everything comes from God, even the things that might scare you." She pulled her bottom lip between her forefinger and her thumb. "Even Satan was made by God. Why?'' She looked Nadine directly in the eyes. ''Because there's nothing like a good bout with Satan that will make a man turn to God faster than anything else.'' She nodded authoritatively. ''So you just remember that, you hear?''

''Yes, ma'am.'' Nadine laid back down on the plump feather pillow as Grandma Rose left the room. But she remembered for the rest of that night, whenever Grandma Rose checked on her, she seemed nervous and ill at ease. Out of all the things that happened during her childhood, Nadine realized that was the only time she had truly seen Grandma Rose afraid.

Nadine's shaking fingers lifted the document and made room for it upon the desk. She realized some of it was missing. There was no cover page. It had probably gotten lost along with several other beginning passages. The work commenced bluntly, describing several ancient sacred symbols, amongst them the symbol of the cliff dwellers, which it called the ''Royal Escutcheon of Mu.'' Mu, better known to some as Lemuria.

''That's the place Madame Deane had spoken of,'' Nadine exclaimed, amazed. She skimmed the small group of pages for a direct reference to the cliff dwellers. There was none. But she did find a chart showing the symbol, and explaining how it had been deciphered and then translated. The chart displayed the same characters that were carved upon her necklace. It called them the hieratic characters of Mu.

It was 12:45 A.M. when Nadine laid down her ink pen, and read her rough translation of the tiny stone message. Her heart seemed to pound in her ears, reflecting the fear and turmoil growing inside her. She read the startling message out loud. Nadine knew, as she read the prophetic words, the message was intended for her. It read "Lenora, the Bringer of Light."

Chapter 13

 "Did it occur to you to ask about the stone after you realized it was missing?" Dr. Steward quizzed her, trying to remain calm.

"Yes, it did. But under the circumstances I thought it would be best to leave things as they were," Nadine replied.

The seemingly endless interrogation over her leaving what Dr. Steward thought might be one of the Five Pieces of Gaia at Sovereign had been going on for the last five minutes. Nadine believed the conversation would have been easier to handle if Dr. Steward showed the anger that lurked behind his questions. She could tell from his heightened color he wanted to raise his voice, but that would have been beneath his cultured, intellectual upbringing. Nadine thought if Dr. Steward would only admit that he was upset, it would have had a calming effect, but that was not going to happen. She saw his jaw quiver with restrained anger.

"Ms. Clayton, you have not been brought all the way down here to make decisions that work against the goals of the World Treasures Institute."

"Maybe the slab had no significance at all for

our purposes. I kept it just because of a hunch. It wasn't among the articles that were designated for me to catalog,'' she added lamely in her own defense, wishing she had never mentioned it.

There were so many things on her mind when she arrived in the office early that morning; the deciphering of the necklace the night before, and its significance, had been foremost in her thoughts. She was glad when Dr. Steward arrived shortly afterwards, and inquired about her stay on Eros. She needed to talk to someone about her experiences there. But the conversation had not progressed any further than her discovery of the carved onyx slab.

''It was a hunch, an intuitive feeling, that motivated some of our greatest minds to create their most sublime works. Hunches should not be taken lightly when it comes to the arts,'' Dr. Steward preached, his well-manicured hand rubbing the thin spot on the crown of his shiny head.

''I agree with that,'' a robust accented voice echoed from the hall.

A gentleman much taller than Dr. Steward's five feet six inches rounded the door. Claudia entered behind him moments later.

''Why, Mr. Richarde.'' Dr. Steward seemed surprised. He glanced surreptitiously about, as if he wished he had had an opportunity to prepare for the stranger's arrival. ''I did not expect you to come to the office so early this morning.'' He put on his best smile. ''I thought you would prefer to sleep in after your late arrival last night, and then perhaps do some touring of the island today before we dine this evening.''

The neatly dressed visitor smiled tolerantly as he addressed Dr. Steward, while his eyes remained on

Nadine. "I assure you, Dr. Steward, I have no desire to *tour* Barbados. I've been here many times before. There may be several places that I'd like to visit in order to check on some longtime acquaintances, but touring is hardly ever on my agenda."

Dr. Steward's cheeks turned a slight pink as he stuttered his understanding. "Of course, of course." He changed the subject. "Well, I guess you've had the pleasure of meeting Ms. Claudia Edmunds?" Dr. Steward motioned toward the young woman as she maneuvered herself into the stranger's line of view. A pink sweater and beige skirt clung to her voluptuous figure, playing up her naturally pretty face.

"Not officially." He took the hand she offered. "*Enchantez, mademoiselle.* I am Etien Richarde." Then, turning to Nadine, he offered her his hand. "*Et vous?*"

"I'm Nadine Clayton," she responded, aware of the enamored sparkle in his eye.

"Both of these ladies are working with the project," Dr. Steward chimed in, and then as to let Nadine and Claudia know the importance of their visitor he announced, "Mr. Richarde is one of the World Treasures Institute's greatest benefactors. We are very grateful for the support he has shown us through the years." An indulging smile crossed his thin lips.

"I am sure you are," Mr. Richarde commented without a smile. "I thought I'd come by this morning and pick up that paperwork we talked about last night. I want to get this business out of the way so my day can be free for other things, if you don't mind."

"Why, certainly. I have it tucked away right

here.'' Dr. Steward scurried over to an antique dresser-turned-desk, and retrieved a manila envelope from one of the drawers. He handed it to Mr. Richarde.

''*Merci beaucoup*. And now I will leave you to your work.'' He turned toward the doorway, hesitated, and looked back over his shoulder. ''By the way, I am sure you have also invited Mademoiselle Clayton and Mademoiselle Edmunds to dine with us tonight, *de vrai?*''

A startled Dr. Steward gave the only answer he could. ''Why, of course.''

Mr. Richarde gave Nadine a clandestine wink before responding, ''*Bon*. I am off then. *Au revoir*.''

It was difficult for Dr. Steward to keep his spectacled eyes from straying to the low neckline of Claudia's cream-colored dress. Nadine found it was almost comical how the thick lenses of his glasses magnified their every move, making it impossible for him to sneak the furtive glances without being discovered.

As the tallest of the group, Claudia stood out obtrusively. But her height was not the only projecting part of her. Her breasts strained against the knitted material, just below Dr. Steward's natural plane of view, causing small beads of sweat to appear around his receding hairline. Nadine felt the urge to laugh and could have enjoyed Dr. Steward's restrained response to nature if Mr. Richarde wasn't standing so close beside her. Now she was glad she had broken down before leaving the States and bought the chic burgundy dress she was wearing. The scalloped neckline revealed just enough of her slender shoulders, giving way to a simple cut that ended with tiny pleats two inches above her knees. There was no way for Mr. Richarde to get a direct look at anything besides her legs, but from the look in his eyes his imagination made up for what he could not see.

Nadine looked around the crowded restaurant while they waited for the maitre d' to come back and seat them. Mr. Richarde had spoken very highly of this particular establishment during their short trip in the taxi. He said the owner grew his own vegetables, and if they enjoyed beef, guinea corn, and green peas, they would have to try the jug-jug served here. It was the specialty.

Nadine thought the cave-like interior of the restaurant was very different from the lights and ambience of the other parts of the resort. The pottery and woven baskets reminded her that she was on a Caribbean island.

The maitre d' efficiently escorted them to one of the better-lit tables. Nadine was thankful that all of the tables that provided privacy had been taken. She hoped the light would help curb Mr. Richarde's amorous attention.

Once the menus were placed before them, Mr. Richarde took the liberty of ordering a bottle of what he called the most unique rum of all. It was obvious as he threw out bits of wisdom concerning Bajan cooking and customs that he was quite knowledgeable. Nadine might have even found him to be a little attractive had he not been so aware of his own attributes. A well-cared-for hand constantly rubbed and patted his perfectly shaped mustache and goatee after smoothing the edges of a precisely tapered haircut.

"Mademoiselle, nothing but the best for you tonight," he said, his smile gleaming as he placed a soft palm on top of Nadine's hand.

A small, courteous smile crossed her lips, acknowledging Mr. Richarde's generosity, but Nadine opted not to meet the eyes that sought hers, and she used a contrived cough as an excuse to extract her hand from the bejeweled one that held it.

Dr. Steward's two frail eyebrows fused together at his displeasure toward Nadine's tactful rejection of one of the institute's chief benefactors. "Mr. Richarde, I want you to know how grateful we are for your invitation this evening, and that the institute will pick up the tab for your meal."

"*Excusez moi.*" An annoyed Mr. Richarde sized Dr. Steward up with one look. "The institute will pick up the tab for Nadine and Ms. Edmunds as well. Of course, you will be responsible for your own."

A stunned Dr. Steward lowered his head and nodded his agreement.

Nadine knew that her boss wanted her to be more "friendly" toward Mr. Richarde. He had made his feelings known earlier by pressing a pointed elbow in her side when she declined to sit up front between Mr. Richarde and the taxi driver. She did not like his actions one bit, but Mr. Richarde's constant belittling of Dr. Steward was uncalled for, making her feelings even less favorable toward him.

After they placed their orders, the meal proceeded quietly. The group sampled a variety of conkies as appetizers. By the time the entrees were placed upon the table, Mr. Richarde was ordering the second flask of rum, having drunk most of the first. Nadine and Claudia's initial glasses were more than half full, and Dr. Steward had just finished his first. As the waiter hurried away to grant Mr. Richarde's request, the smell of flying fish and prawns garnished with peppers and other spices demanded their attention. The dishes were accompanied by the jug-jug. Wary, Nadine tasted the food on her plate. It was different, but to her surprise it was good as well.

While they ate Nadine noticed that some couples were dancing. Like shadows they emerged from the hidden tables around them, finding refuge in movement to soft, rhythmic music. There was a variety of sounds ranging from tuk band to reggae. It was an interesting combination, an appropriate background for the unique meal. Everyone but Claudia had traditional sweets, coconut sugar cakes and tamarind balls.

"I don't know if I'll ever get accustomed to the foods here. They are so unlike the dishes we cook back home." Claudia's expression reflected her discomfort. Nervously she glanced back and forth between the two men seated beside her. "But I guess it just goes to show how different people can be," she added, trying not to fuel the tension that already existed at the table. For the first time Nadine found herself in the peculiar position of agreeing with Claudia.

Donning his most dashing smile, Mr. Richarde downed his fourth glass of rum and agreed, "*C'est vrai.* How boring life would be without variety." He cast a meaningful look in Nadine's direction. "Mademoiselle, would you care to dance?"

The slow, rhythmic island tune made her hesitate. It was smooth, alright, and music as smooth as that would give the most well-intentioned male ideas. But Nadine saw a look of utter apprehension surfacing on Dr. Steward's features, so she complied with her escort's wishes.

Despite all the space on the almost vacant dance floor, Mr. Richarde chose to lead Nadine to a secluded spot that received little light from the tables behind it or the pendulum-shaped lamp that hung above the circular area. Immediately, he enfolded her within both his arms, and put pressure on her lower back, attempting to make her body flush with his.

"Mr. Richarde, I don't mean any harm, but I'm not comfortable like this," Nadine protested, trying not to turn it into an ugly situation.

"*Ma chérie*, it is because you are being difficult. It would not be so bad if you would simply amuse me a bit. I am not a hard man to please. You know as well as I do that money, power, and sex make the world go round. I happen to have plenty of money. I wield a little power in my circle. And as far as sex goes," he brought his rum-laced breath closer to her ear, "it is one of those things that one must constantly do to obtain excellence. That's what makes it all the more exciting."

Nadine pressed her palms against Mr. Richarde's chest. She decided to be more forceful in her reproach. "Sorry to tell you this, but I didn't take this job to find *this* kind of excitement."

"But that's what I mean, mademoiselle. You took this job because of the money, and let's not forget the power or prestige it gives you amongst your colleagues. It just so happens sex is the one thing that can keep you in the treasured position you find yourself in now.''

Nadine's eyes flashed angrily as she looked into the pale-blue ones eyeing her like a cat with a mouse in an easy-to-capture situation. ''Are you telling me my position on this project would be threatened if I didn't take you up on your . . . offer?'' Her voice rose with astonishment as she freed herself from his clasp.

''*Mais non.*'' An icy chill coated the patronizing words. ''I am only advising you of how precarious of a predicament a woman like you could find herself in so far away from home.''

''And you, Mr. Richarde, what brings you to this side of the island?'' a low, male voice inquired. ''Far from your loving wife, Jean, and two wonderful girls, Lisa and Elise?''

Stunned, Nadine and Mr. Richarde both turned to see the interloper. Mr. Richarde was too jolted to reply, and Nadine was having the strangest feeling of déjà vu. The voice was all too familiar and reason fought with what her feelings told her was true. The battle did not last for long as Ulysses stepped out of the shadows.

Chapter 14

Nadine and Mr. Richarde said Ulysses' name in unison, then looked at each other.

He bowed his dark head slightly in greeting. "Nadine. Etien."

Quickly, Mr. Richarde regained his composure and extended his hand to Ulysses. "*Mon Dieu.* Imagine meeting you here. It has been over a year, hasn't it, since I've seen you? Have you seen Pamela lately?"

"As a matter of fact she is here with me this evening," Ulysses replied. "She stepped out to the ladies' room."

Mr. Richarde had to work to keep his composure. Removing a handkerchief from his dinner jacket pocket, he dabbed at what Nadine assumed to be perspiration on his forehead. "I saw John Castle earlier today at his office. You see, I've got several business deals working on Barbados and John's legal advice is indispensable." Mr. Richarde took a deep, cleansing breath. "What brings you to Barbados?"

"Business . . . with John." Ulysses replied to Mr. Richarde's question but his attention had become focused on Nadine's lowered head.

"So, I see." Mr. Richarde rubbed his hands together nervously. "Well, obviously, there is no need for me to introduce you to Ms. Clayton." Mr. Richarde looked from one of them to the other. "Small world, isn't it?"

"Yes. Small world." Ulysses' voice was nearly a whisper.

"May I be so bold as to ask how you two met?"

Nadine's full lips rounded to form the word "We" but was cut off by Ulysses' quick reply of "Business." Then he turned the spotlight once again in Mr. Richarde's direction, pushing his marital status to the forefront. "So how is Madame Richarde?"

"She's fine. So are my girls. They were here vacationing about two months ago. They stayed with Chloe and John."

"It's remarkable how much Pamela resembles her Aunt Jean," Ulysses commented as the young woman approached.

"Uncle Etien! How delightful to see you." Pamela kissed him on both cheeks. "Goodness, this has been a day for reunions. On our way over Ulysses and I bumped into Mr. Tim Johnson, the tutor who taught him and the Sharpes. Mr. Johnson and my dad attended Georgetown University together. You wouldn't happen to know him, would you?"

"No, I can't say I do," Mr. Richarde said with contrived gaiety.

"Oh, please excuse me for being so rude. I'm Pamela Williams," the winsome young woman addressed Nadine.

"Nadine Clayton," Nadine replied, her smile genuine despite the circumstances. Pamela radiated a sincere air of friendliness.

"What brings my favorite uncle to the Sly Mongoose tonight?" Pamela asked.

"You know how Jean and I are always supporting charities and the arts." Mr. Richarde straightened his tie with a nervous jerk. "Tonight I'm dining with one of the directors of the World Treasures Institute and two of the consultants assigned to the Caribbean islands. Ms. Clayton is one of them."

"Isn't he wonderful? He's always been so freehearted." Pamela beamed a trusting smile in her uncle's direction.

Placing a light kiss on Pamela's cheek, Mr. Richarde attempted to bring an end to their little chat. "Well, we don't want to take up any more of your time. I'd invite you to join us, but I'm sure you're enjoying your evening alone."

"On the contrary," Ulysses protested, "Pamela and I were thinking about leaving. We'd be glad to join you for a few minutes and hear more about the institute."

Nadine's eyes widened as she looked at Ulysses and then Pamela, whose flawless features displayed a small trace of disappointment.

"That's right. If my memory serves me correctly, Ulysses, you are quite a lover of the arts," a thwarted Mr. Richarde replied. "Well, right this way. I'll introduce everyone."

The introductions were made while the waiter provided two additional chairs. Dr. Steward was pleased to find out that Ulysses had expressed an interest in the institute.

"This is such a wonderful bonus for the evening." His eyes began to shine. "Perhaps, before the evening is over, you may consider becoming a benefactor for the institute as well, just like Mr. Richarde.'' He nodded appreciatively. ''If I may say so, it is a wonderful organization, and I'm sure with your being an art lover you can truly understand the importance of our work.'' Dr. Steward leaned forward dramatically. ''We want to ensure that years from now the majority of the world's treasures can be located with little effort. It is our goal to make the treasures of the world available to everyone.''

During the entire exchange Nadine remained very still and quiet, never once looking at Ulysses, who sat to the right of her.

''Nadine,'' her first name seemed to hang in the air like a specter, ''so this is the institute that you were working for when you stayed at Sovereign?'' Dark, fringed eyes pinned her to her seat.

Before Nadine could respond Dr. Steward threw two more questions in her direction. ''You two know each other? And it was his estate that you stayed on while you were on Eros?''

''The answer to all three questions is yes,'' Nadine replied, the picture of composure.

The entire table waited for a more elaborate response, but she was determined not to give one. Her mind and feelings were still reeling from the fact that Ulysses Deane had once again entered her life, but she wasn't *even* about to show it.

''It is quite amazing that we would bump into you like this tonight. Isn't it, Ulysses?'' Pamela leaned forward to rally her companion's support. ''Tell them about the book sale that you plan to hold at Sovereign next week.'' She turned her attention to Dr. Steward who was seated beside her. ''It is going to be one of the most extravagant and memorable evenings of this region. Ulysses' family has quite a reputation when it comes to literature born here in the islands and abroad. Sovereign is known as 'the Protector of Eros' Treasures,' and even though I am sure he will not be parting with any of his favorite works, their collection is so large no one will be the wiser.''

''My goodness, I am definitely impressed.'' Dr. Steward's small eyes twinkled behind his tortoise-rimmed glasses. ''This would be a prime opportunity for the institute to catalog the rare and valuable works on your estate, and to record the new owners once they purchase them, of course. That is, if you don't mind?''

''You have my permission to catalog any of the works that are presented at the sale, but my own private collection is just that, private,'' Ulysses stated flatly.

''Sounds fine to me,'' Dr. Steward added, satisfied. ''Nadine, since you and Mr. Deane are already acquainted, I will send you over to Eros the day before the sale to record everything. Then you can return to the island the following evening for the sale itself.''

''I have a better idea, Dr. Steward.'' Ulysses drew the man's excited gaze in his direction. ''I have just begun organizing the items to be sold during the event, and it would be to your and my advantage if Miss Clayton would be allowed to come to Sovereign several days before the event is held. Her knowledge of literature and art would be quite beneficial, and with her help, it will ensure that all of the pieces that can be cataloged and made available for the sale will be displayed.''

''We-ell, I don't know. I truly appreciate the

hospitality that you showed Ms. Clayton while she was stranded on Eros, but we have so much work to do here.'' Dr. Steward chewed pensively on his bottom lip.

Nadine gave her support to her boss' misgivings. ''That's true, Dr. Steward. I am quite busy. I have several stacks of entries that I plan to finish by the end of the week.'' Her leg shook uncontrollably beneath the table, the thought of spending several days working alongside Ulysses nearly unbearable.

''Dr. Steward, I would not think of using one of your workers without compensating the institute,'' Ulysses pressed his point. ''A sizable donation would be made to your organization from the proceeds generated by the book sale.''

''I say.'' Dr. Steward squirmed in his chair with the mention of money. ''How could I possibly turn down such a generous offer? It is settled then. Claudia will take up the slack where you leave off, Nadine.'' Then he turned his most appeasing smile in Ulysses' direction. ''When would you like for Ms. Clayton to begin her work at Sovereign?''

Nadine watched as the tension seemed to leave Ulysses' body, and he settled back in his chair. ''As soon as possible. And don't worry about Miss Clayton's sleeping arrangements. Sovereign is well equipped to accommodate her.''

Chapter 15

Nadine held her suitcase close to her side as she shuffled down the exit ramp between an excited tourist couple and an islander carrying a crate full of oranges. She noticed a variety of festivities taking place on the colorful shore as she looked for Clarence among the busy crowd.

She had arrived in the office early that morning, bringing the suitcase with her. There were a few things she wanted to finish up before going to Eros, and she would not have time to go back to her room before the ferry embarked. Nadine was glad Claudia had some errands to run before coming to work that morning, and she knew Dr. Steward rarely showed his face before ten. That suited Nadine just fine. She did not want to answer any more of their prying questions about Ulysses and Sovereign.

But luck was not with her entirely. She bumped into Dr. Steward as she was leaving the building. He took the opportunity to remind her of how important her work was, and to keep her eyes open, especially for the carved onyx slab.

Getting down to the wharf in a timely fashion proved to be more difficult than Nadine had expected. Several of the streets had been blocked off, and groups of people had begun to camp out along the curbs. It was not until she overheard a conversation between several tourists that she realized today was the beginning of the Crop Over Festival. The residents and tourists were out in full force to celebrate.

Long before the ferry pulled up to Eros' shore, bright bunches of red, yellow, blue, and pink could be seen in the distance. As the gap shortened they took shape as parade floats. The parade was over, but the proud owners had parked their magnificent displays of intense work and patience along the wharf. They would be one of the first things visitors would see when they arrived on the island.

The constant activity jostled Nadine back into reality. She had passed the last forty-eight hours operating on automatic, spending longer hours at work, not taking lunch, and doing what needed to be done at the office to keep herself occupied. Dinner the last two evenings had been food from a street vendor not far from the library. It was convenient as she continued to work late into the night.

Instinctively, Nadine's fingers touched the small tablets that hung about her throat. She had not worn the cliff dwellers' necklace since the night she discovered the meaning of the petroglyphs. She had been afraid. But after her chance encounter with Ulysses, and Nadine now doubted whether she should call it that, she no longer felt that fear. Instead there was a feeling of resolution. Only so many things could be summed up as chance, coincidence. Nadine decided her return to Eros had to be some kind of fate.

As she focused on the island and not on her

thoughts, she noticed three cliff dwellers who had stopped selling their wares to look at her. Once she acknowledged their presence they were content, and went back to their work.

Convinced more than ever that she was destined to come back to Eros, Nadine walked further into the business district. She sat on a large boulder near the front of the makeshift library/museum. From her vantage point she could see the majority of the little lanes that served as streets. They all converged at the huge statue of Dionysus. White-washed buildings sparkled in the sun as visitors and islanders alike went in and out of the shops where jewelry, pottery, and colorful cottons were sold. Behind her, several sailboats with their sails wrapped around their masts rested at the dock, which was outlined by the Atlantic Ocean in all its splendor. The water was the bluest of blues and as smooth as a sapphire.

A band near the statue of Dionysus played vibrantly for an attentive audience who snacked on travelers, syrup-covered snowballs, lead pipes, glass cakes, and peanut brittle. Nadine did not mind that Clarence was not there to pick her up as soon as the ferry arrived. It gave her an opportunity to take in the flavor of Eros during a holiday. The sights and sounds helped to lighten the feeling of foreboding she carried within her.

As she waited, Nadine decided to take a closer look at the festivities. She reintroduced herself to the proprietor of the library/museum, and asked if she could leave her suitcase there for a while. He obliged her happily, waving merrily as she departed.

Music could be heard everywhere, from makeshift family bands to the more professional groups. Further down the shore a beach tavern was packed with patrons. They ranged from little children to elderly couples. Huge spits sizzled not far from the water, the smell of roasting pork foretelling great meals to come.

Nadine stopped in one of the taverns to admire a group of people dancing to constantly changing tempos. Bunches of men and women alike pranced and shook to the invigorating sounds. One young man became the center of attention as he began several chains of leaps, squats, and spins, then stretched out inviting arms to a delighted pregnant woman with ignited coal-black eyes.

Nadine found the smiles and laughter to be contagious and shouted "Goat heaven" in unison with the gleeful, grateful crowd. Shouting the words felt strange, but it allowed her to release some of the tension that had built up around her return to Eros and Sovereign. Afterwards the people in the tavern threw money to the band. She guessed it was compensation for the good job they had done.

"You too have become a victim of the music," a deep voice announced beside her.

"A victim?" Nadine acknowledged the pleasant stranger who spoke English.

"Good feelings that the music brings," he returned with a wide smile.

Nadine met the man's offer of friendship with a smile of her own.

"Are you a tourist?" he asked.

"No, not really. Are you?" Bright hazel eyes reciprocated the question.

"No, I live here on Eros. Basil Sharpe," he extended his hand in introduction, "is the name."

"Oh, Mr. Sharpe. I've already had the pleasure of meeting your brother, Rodney, and your sister, Melanie."

Thick eyebrows framed Basil Sharpe's curious eyes as he made a closer appraisal of the young woman beside him. "Is that right?"

"It sure is. About three weeks ago I was a guest at the Sovereign estate. I met your brother during breakfast one morning, and later on that same day I met Melanie at the rum still."

Basil Sharpe continued to smile down into the animated features in front of him, but an almost imperceptible jerk started about his curved lips. "Eros is quite an intimate island; I am disappointed that I am the last of the Sharpes to meet you. Are you a friend of Ulysses and Madame Deane, Miss . . . uh?"

"Clayton, Nadine Clayton," she complied. "No, actually I'm here to do some work for them, in conjunction with a project that I've been assigned to through the World Treasures Institute."

"Oh, I see," he said.

Nadine stepped back just in time to avoid a collision with a swirling couple whooshing by. The reaction caused her to step on Basil's foot that was planted firmly behind her own. "I am so sorry." The sincere apology poured out as she quickly removed her sneaker-clad foot.

"I do not know that sorry will be enough." He feigned extreme pain. "I will accept no less than dinner at Sharpe Hall, so our family can officially welcome you to Eros," Basil insisted. "At your convenience, of course."

Nadine's look of concern turned to relief as she

regarded his teasing features. "I think that can be arranged," she acquiesced.

Basil Sharpe raised both arms above his head. Snapping his fingers in unison, he shouted, "Goat heaven!" as the band struck up another vibrant tune.

Catherine gave Nadine a warm welcome as she apologized for Ulysses' and Madame Deane's absence. "Sorry neither of them are here, Miss Nadine. Madame is napping after her noon medication and Ulysses is out on the grounds."

"It's okay, Catherine. I'm here to work just like you, so no grand reception was required," Nadine replied.

Actually, she felt relieved when she heard Ulysses was not inside the house. It would give her an opportunity to pass a few moments with Catherine, who did not hesitate in updating her on news.

"Other than that, things are about the same around here," Catherine informed her. "A few things have gone awry, but Master Ulysses has it under control now." She gave Nadine a white envelope. "It is from Master Ulysses," Catherine said. "He told me to give it to you once you arrived. Just between you and me, that handsome devil has been nothing but one headache after another lately. Now that you are back, maybe things will get better."

Surprised to hear her say such a thing, Nadine looked up from the envelope to Catherine's face.

"You know what I mean. To help with the book sale and all." Catherine's eyes darted to the left as she tried to cover up her all-too-meaningful words. "He says you can get started in the antechamber whenever you like,'' she stated after walking Nadine to her room, then continued on her way.

Nadine was given the same room she had occupied during her initial visit to Sovereign. Everything was the same, including the animal skin she had hidden behind the bed. She looked at the dresser, and couldn't help but think of the onyx unicorn that had been taken.

She stopped and stared at her reflection in the mirror. Slender fingers touched high cheekbones as she leaned closer to the glass for a more intense inspection. There was something decidedly different about her. But as she examined her image she didn't quite know what it was. Before coming to the islands she could say she had admirers, if you could call them that. Men, although Nadine could count the number on one hand, who had told her they found her to be attractive in her own way. But never had she received the kind of attention she was getting here.

Once again thoughts of Mr. Richarde, Basil Sharpe, and Ulysses passed through her mind as her slim eyebrows knitted together. Why does it seem like men are finding me so much more attractive here? She had heard stories that foreigners were attracted to African-Americans. The French were known for embracing and exalting African-American artists from singers to clothes designers, and the Swedes, she had heard, found African-Americans to be very attractive. But most of the stories she had heard about the islands involved the women being attracted to African-American men, not the reverse.

Nadine tilted her oval-shaped face to the side. She had to admit, since Ulysses Deane appeared in her life, she viewed herself differently. She felt more alluring, more feminine, and there were physical changes as well. Gone was the wrapped-around ponytail at the nape of her neck that she always wore. Gone were the days when she would wear only loose-fitted tops and blouses outside her long skirts and pants. Gone was the timid woman unsure of her own capability to love and desire. Now Nadine knew far too well what kind of searing fire desire could be. Especially when the object of those feelings had expressed that he no longer wanted to have anything to do with her.

She continued to stare at her reflection in the glass. Hope entered her eyes as she remembered Ulysses' conversation with Dr. Steward. He had persisted with the conversation until Dr. Steward agreed that she would be returning to Sovereign. Maybe there was still a chance. Nadine covered her mouth with a tense fist. But a chance for what?

She had let her hair dry naturally that morning, creating soft, but tight, amber twists which sat out from her face. Nadine's eyes enlarged as she thought, Maybe the things the town gossips used to say about a woman named Miss Lisa were true. Miss Lisa always had some eager male after her. "It's nature taking its course," they would say. "The male animal always knows when the female's in heat. Be he two-legged or four." She could feel the blood rising to her face. She was definitely in heat for Ulysses.

Nadine pushed away from the antique dressing table and completed her unpacking. Only then was she prepared to look inside the white envelope Catherine had given her. She turned the sealed package over in her hands; something slid to the

corner. Nadine took a deep breath and opened it.
She removed a single page of stationery with gold
stalks of sugarcane embossed at the top corners. A
metal key remained inside.

Nadine—

*This is the key to the antechamber. You will
find all the supplies you need down there.
Matches for the wall lamps can be found in
the kitchen.*

U. D.

That was all. Nadine had no idea what she had
expected to read but this plain and simple message
was definitely not it. She stared at the clean, crisp
handwriting that flowed on the linen paper.

What did I expect, she asked herself. A profes-
sion of love? Or maybe I thought he would pour
out his heart and tell me how much he missed me,
that he was glad I had returned. Nadine gave a half
laugh as she shook her head. Love did not bring
me back to Sovereign, work did. That is what I
need to accept, she thought, although she could feel
the disappointment. Nadine took the key from the
envelope, flipped it into the air, and caught it with
a snap. Seconds later she placed it in the pocket of
her jeans and headed for the antechamber.

Chapter 16

Nadine stopped by the kitchen and picked up a book of matches from a utility shelf.

Afterwards she moved into the room Catherine called the hall. It was an extremely large room, sparsely decorated with stools, chairs, divans, and tables.

Six large bronze statues of gods and goddesses contrasted deliciously with the painted terra-cotta floor, resulting in a feeling of majesty. Nadine's mind conjured up pictures of boldly dressed male and female dancers, rhythmically moving their bodies and arms to the music of wind instruments and drums, honoring one or more of the deities looking on.

She traced her foot against the colorful patterns on the floor before crossing to the antechamber door. When she reached the bottom of the stairs Nadine illuminated her work area.

It was fairly large and filled with boxes of books and art. Despite the quantity, Nadine could see books were stored in an orderly fashion. The statues and paintings were separated from the vases and smaller objects, and the boxes of books were marked according to the country of their origin.

There was very little, if any, dust or dirt to contend with, and a table had been set up with pads and pencils, as well as tags and labels. The tools for her work looked out of place in the antechamber. Their newness conflicted with the antiquities around them.

Nadine had not expected to be responsible for deciding the prices for the sale. Even with her brief visual assessment of the collection, she knew some of the books and objects would be considered priceless. Why would Ulysses give such a responsibility to a total stranger?

Her gaze rested on an especially delicate object. She picked it up, placing the carved ivory lyre with bronze-cast tips in the palm of her hand. She thought of the last confrontation she and Ulysses had the night before she left. He had told her in so many words he did not trust her. Ulysses questioned her reason for bursting into his room, even for being at Sovereign, although he was the one who had invited her. How could he be so sure she would not tuck the beautiful object away in her belongings and carry it back to Barbados? Had his feelings toward her changed? Something must have happened to change his mind, for him to allow her in the antechamber alone, without supervision. Maybe he had checked on the World Treasures Institute and found it *was* a prestigious organization that would only hire the best. Whatever the reason for Ulysses' change in attitude, his obvious trust made Nadine want to prove she was worthy of it.

Then a bothersome possibility entered her mind. Or could this be a setup? Nadine thought of the missing onyx slab. She did not want to think that Catherine or Clarence could have been responsible for taking it. But who else would have without saying something? For sure Ulysses would have no reason to steal an object like a thief in his own home and then say nothing, and it was highly improbable that Madame Deane was responsible. She pondered the issue even further, her thoughts becoming darker. Perhaps Ulysses was involved, without Madame Deane's knowledge, in some black market dealings, and she, Nadine, had unwittingly become a convenient pawn. Madame Deane had admitted they needed money, badly, and Ulysses hated to talk about it with outsiders. Could it be possible that he had found a way for the institute to help legitimize his transactions? This time she looked at the collection that surrounded her with apprehension.

I have got to stop this, Nadine admonished herself. I have not been on Eros but half a day, and already I am off on a tangent. There is something about this place that tends to do me that way, she thought. There will be plenty of time to rationalize the things that had occurred during my first stay at Sovereign. But now it is time to get started on the work at hand, and no matter what the circumstances are, I am determined to do an impeccable job.

She walked over to inspect an old set of leather-bound books entitled *The Caribbean: Eden Found*. Nadine could tell from the look and age of the novels that they were priceless literature. This is what I am going to do, she decided. The objects that I can suggest a price for I will, and those whose value that I think are beyond my ethical capacity to determine, I will say just that.

Nadine decided to start with a box filled with an

assortment of books. She pulled up a chair, and shortly thereafter time and space were forgotten. The work became a labor of love as she wrote down each title, then recorded it in two places. One record would go to Ulysses and the other to the institute.

Nadine was amazed at the extent of literature and art Ulysses' family had tucked away in the antechamber where no one could see it. The collection process itself had to have taken decades. She could not help thinking, as she continued to work, how most people would love to have just one of the rare objects to display prominently in their homes.

She was in the middle of cataloging a bronze mask with kinky hair and thick features when Catherine came down to inform her it would soon be suppertime.

"The food will be on the table in no more than thirty minutes." The housekeeper looked around the antechamber with dissatisfaction. "You are good to stay down here for such a long time without taking a rest. I myself could not do it. It is too stuffy in here and there are no windows. It is also too quiet. I like lots of noise and activity. I guess that is one reason it does not bother me so much when madame is having one of her moods. I grew up in a big family where something was always happening."

Nadine smiled. "I guess I'm just the opposite. As a child I usually played alone. I really didn't mind. It just gave me more of an opportunity to create my own rules. My own reality." Stretching, she began to rotate her neck. "Anyway, I enjoy my work. It's been anything but boring down here. Plus I can appreciate the solitude.''

"I can understand what you are saying," Catherine replied, "but too much solitude is not good for anyone. Your mind can begin to play tricks on you and you will not even know it. It can become overworked, Miss Nadine." She placed her foot on the bottom stair. "Don't forget about supper." Catherine started to ascend the stairs. "Thirty minutes is not a long time, so I suggest you finish up and get ready."

"I will, Catherine." Nadine glanced up at Catherine's retreating back.

The housekeeper's warning about the mind playing tricks brought back the vision in the hallway. Solitude had nothing to do with that. She was sure Ulysses had spoken the truth when he said he had heard nothing. But Nadine was also sure of what she had experienced. It was possible all of it had been a figment of her imagination. No doubt if she told anyone else about it, they would say just that. But something inside told her there was truth and reason behind everything that had happened since she came to Eros.

That belief placed Nadine in dangerous waters. Anything resembling a belief in what people called premonitions or psychic powers went against the religious teachings she had grown up with, teachings she still embraced in many ways. But there was no way she could cast the vision aside as another person's misguided beliefs. It was not someone else's experience, it was her own.

The very thought made cold tingles run through Nadine, reminding her of the stone tablets that hung around her neck. She knew she could either

let her fears run rampant, and drive her to the point
where even she thought she might be going crazy,
or she could find out why these things were happening. Nadine decided on the latter.

"You do not think it is rather late to start sending out more invitations?" The cold, clipped voice
cut into her explanations.

Nadine felt nervous energy moving inside her as
she looked directly into Ulysses' eyes. His face
looked harder than she remembered. "Not if we
faxed them from the World Treasures Institute. I'm
sure Dr. Steward would have no problem with that.
The more sales we're able to generate, the larger
the proceeds the institute will be receiving. And the
kinds of groups that I have been speaking of are
on the institute's current mailing list. They are
small, but financially capable of sending someone
to the showing even at short notice."

The conversation had been strained from the beginning. Wearing his customary white shirt and
black pants, Ulysses had arrived for supper shortly
after she and Madame Deane. Excitement jarred
Nadine when he entered the room neither slow nor
hurried. Control was the word that came to her
mind, something that she now barely possessed.
First, Ulysses spoke to his aunt and then to her,
scarcely giving her more than a casual look. It
made her feel that much more aware of her feelings
for him because it was clear the feelings were not
reciprocated.

The meal began quietly, so much so that Madame Deane felt it was her duty to make some kind
of conversation. She was at her best and looked it.

As she spoke Nadine could feel the older woman's excitement about the upcoming event.

"It has been such a long time since the hall has been used for anything, has it not, Ulysses?" She looked his way, waiting for an acknowledgment. He nodded his head, and from there Madame Deane began to talk nonstop about the preparations that had to be made to ensure that the evening would be successful. "I hope we will have enough space and food for everyone," she concluded on a note of expectancy.

"Aunt Helen, I hate to remind you, but this is merely a book sale, not some grand social event. And from the people that I have invited and the notices that have been placed on Barbados, I doubt if there will be a need for all the things that you have been talking about."

"Well, maybe I am getting a little carried away," Madame Deane recanted, her slender shoulders slumping as she sat back in the wheelchair.

Nadine could detect some of the sparkle leaving the older woman's eyes.

"I—I guess I just thought we would make the best of the situation," Madame Deane threw in softly as she watched Ulysses' mask-like countenance.

Nadine felt compelled to come to Madame Deane's defense. It was obvious Ulysses found her presence distasteful, but that was no excuse for taking away the joy his aunt was getting out of planning the event. There was already enough unpleasantness in Madame Deane's life. After all, if he had not wanted her at Sovereign, he should not have pressed Dr. Steward to send her.

"If you don't mind my saying so," Nadine cut in, "I believe Madame Deane has the right idea. People love being a part of something they think will be talked about for years, especially when it involves the kind of literature and art that you will be selling. They will be able to purchase a part of history, and the more appealing the food and the surroundings, the bigger success it will be." She looked down at the table momentarily to collect her thoughts. "If you want the advice of a professional," Nadine paused for impact, "I suggest you take Madame Deane's suggestions to heart. It will make the event that much more successful."

Ulysses' eyes bore into her the entire time she spoke. Nadine felt as if she were under the hot glare of interrogation lights, but knowing she was giving sound, professional advice was the only thing that kept her from backing down.

"Sounds like you have got it all figured out, Miss Clayton." The sound of her surname dropped heavily in the informal dinner surroundings. "I suppose with all the grand plans that you have bought into, you are also committed to putting in the work that it will take to pull off such an extravagant event," he pressed.

"Yes, I am," Nadine replied, knowing she was being put on the spot.

"Good. Since I was planning to spend the night on Barbados anyway, I guess I will just stop by your office in the morning and speak to Dr. Steward about your suggestions."

"Good." Nadine's expression gave no indication of what she was really feeling. Stoically, she returned to the pork and vegetables in front of her.

She could feel his dark eyes staring at her as she focused on cutting her food.

He planned to spend the entire night on Barbados! Thoughts of what might be his activities there and with whom, mainly Pamela, nearly brought a flush to her face.

Across the table Ulysses was growing more perturbed as the moments passed. Nadine seemed so cool and detached. Professional was a better word for it. So, Miss Clayton, he thought, all your pretense about having so much to do on Barbados and not wanting to come to Sovereign has just melted away. He watched her slide the fork in and out of her mouth. You're as comfortable as a cat who just happened to show up on my doorstep. I open the door, and not only do you come inside, but you curl up on the divan as if it were yours, taking over the place. Well, that's fine with me, because I have a reason for wanting you here. Your being here will make it that much easier to find out if you are involved with any of the things that have been going awry at Sovereign. No matter how adept at this game you may be, you are still human, and humans make mistakes. I am waiting and counting on yours.

He studied the curve of her face as she avoided his stare. Her hair had been drawn back with a colorful scarf that formed a headband. The blue, black, and gold played up the gold highlights in her yellowish-brown locks. He had never seen her hair so soft and springy, with tendrils around the edges, playing against her skin. She looked so feminine and trustworthy. A profusion of curly lashes hid her downcast, provocative hazel eyes. Suddenly, Ulysses wanted to reach out and touch the curve of her cheek and the cottony twists that lay against it.

He tried to smother the tender feelings that were surfacing, tying his stomach in knots. The feelings forced him to admit to himself that finding out the truth was not the only reason he had arranged for Nadine Clayton's stay at Sovereign.

Abruptly, Ulysses removed the linen napkin from his lap and placed it in the middle of his half-eaten meal. "If I am to catch the next ferry to Barbados I need to be on my way," he said gruffly. He rose and placed a kiss on his aunt's thin cheek, and left the room without another word.

Nadine and Madame Deane looked at one another but said nothing. They both finished their meals in silence. Madame Deane with the slightest hint of a familiar twitch about her lips. Nadine with a similar tremble about her hands.

Chapter 17

 "This is all he could get," John Castle said as he laid the medium-sized package on the desk.

Ulysses looked at the man then down at the package. He did not move.

"Sorry if you were expecting more," John smothered and crushed the remainder of his cigarette in an ashtray, "but I understand he was lucky to get that."

Ulysses leaned forward and took the envelope, then sat back in the leather chair, weighing it in his hand. John thought he was hesitating because of the size of the package. Ulysses wished it was that simple. He was reluctant because he was unsure how he would feel after he had read the contents. "So the job wasn't as easy as he thought it would be?" he asked, looking up at the attorney.

"No, that's not it. My man said it was as easy as pie getting into the place." John ran his hand across his mouth. "He said he nosed around what they called 'uptown,' and he heard that her grandmother, an Auntie Rose, sold antiques. So he posed as someone interested in buying antiques when he went out to the farm." John rested his arms on the chair arms, and began to rock slowly. "He said the place was extremely small, but neat and clean, and the woman was a sweetheart. Claimed she really warmed up to him when he told her he wanted to find just the right piece for his daughter's bedroom, and that he was willing to pay plenty for it." John stopped rocking and leaned on the desk. "Evidently, she took him right inside the house and showed him a dresser. The woman said it used to belong to her granddaughter, Nadine."

"Is that right?" Ulysses continued to finger the envelope.

"Uh-huh," John said, and started to read from a piece of notebook paper. "He says, I didn't have to ask too many questions because the woman talked extensively about hating to part with the furniture, but she intended to surprise her granddaughter and buy her a fancy printer with the money, since she always talked about starting a desktop publishing business." He looked over the rim of his glasses. "The woman seemed to think that would be a way to keep her granddaughter on the farm. She said her granddaughter would be able to work out of the house if she got her the printer." He looked back down at the notes. "He says when the woman went out to get a box for the old papers and odds and ends from the dresser, he made good use of his time. He took all the letters and handwritten papers he could without being conspicuous." John put his elbows on the desk and raised his palms to the ceiling. "And that's it."

Ulysses put the envelope inside his soft leather satchel. "Once again, John, you have done an excellent job. How much do I owe you?"

"Just hold off until we get that tax situation together." John and Ulysses rose from their chairs at the same time. "We'll take care of it then."

"Alright."

The two men shook hands before Ulysses left.

"Hello. I bet you can use some help down here." Melanie's soft voice seemed to reverberate as she came down the stairs.

Nadine smiled, extending her an enthusiastic welcome. "You bet I could. After this I wonder if I'll ever be able to work in close quarters again."

The two women laughed, immediately feeling comfortable with one another.

"Yesterday Catherine brought one of her special mixtures over to our cook who was not feeling very well, and she told me you were back on the island. When I asked her how you were doing, she said you were working very hard to get things ready for the sale. So I thought I would come by and offer you a hand."

"I'm certainly glad you did."

Melanie wandered around the room, her eyes growing large with amazement. "I knew that Ulysses' family had quite an extensive collection, but I never expected this."

"It's overwhelming, isn't it?" Nadine concurred. "I never would have guessed the collection down here could be so extensive after seeing the collection upstairs."

Melanie turned quickly toward Nadine. "Ulysses showed you his private collection?" Her tone was not friendly. Then she realized how she sounded. "I mean . . . it is just so unlike him." She attempted a small chuckle. "He is such a private person. In all the years that I have known him, and as close as we have been, he has never even shown me this." She made a sweeping gesture.

Nadine sought to soothe her newfound friend's feelings. She could tell she was dealing with something, but what, she did not know. "I believe the only reason I saw it is because I'm a consultant. Maybe he wanted to show it to someone who could appreciate it on a professional level."

"Maybe so," Melanie acquiesced. "There have always been rumors about Sovereign's famous collection. The more I would question Ulysses about it through the years, the more closedmouthed he became." Her eyes hardened. "Is it as beautiful as I have heard?"

Nadine's eyes took on a far-off look as she spoke. "I don't believe I've ever seen things quite so beautiful. It was as if I had entered another world. One of love and desire displayed through statues and books." Her voice trailed away as she remembered the intimacy she and Ulysses had shared among his treasures.

"I admire art, as well," Melanie told her, "but from listening to you, I am sure it does not evoke the passion in me that it does in you." She smiled, although her features appeared harsh. "Now where would you have me start?"

Nadine was glad to pull back from the emotional discussion. "As a matter of fact, I've done the labeling on just about all of the smaller pieces. Maybe we can start taking them upstairs into the hall where the tables and stands have been set up."

With the two of them working together, the smaller tables began to fill up quite rapidly and conversation flowed. Nadine and Melanie compared the differences and similarities in their lives as they worked.

"I must say I was surprised to find that English is spoken so well here on Eros," Nadine commented.

"When Ulysses, my brothers and I were school-age we had a tutor."

"That's right. A woman that I met on Barbados named Pamela spoke of a tutor that taught here on Eros. She was with Ulysses," she added with forced calm.

"Through the years my brothers and Ulysses have spent a great deal of time on Barbados. In some ways it has so much more to offer than Eros does," she cast Nadine a meaningful look, "but personally I do not feel it is as beautiful."

"Do you ever go there?" Nadine asked.

"From time to time," Melanie replied. "I shop for things that are not available here on Eros. But the old ways are very much a part of my life. That is the way I like it, and as I believe it should be."

"You know, for the majority of my life I've lived by a strict set of rules that in some ways I've found to be very good for me, but in others I'm not so sure. I've begun to feel as if life may be passing me by." She gave a nervous laugh. "I can look at myself and see why certain things haven't happened for me, but when I look at you, I don't understand why some lucky guy hasn't snatched you up and married you."

Melanie's laugh was melodious. "First of all there are not that many men to choose from here on Eros . . . besides Ulysses. I have had some acquaintances on Barbados, but even so, I do not know how well my marrying someone would be accepted by Basil and Rodney. I am the woman of the house. I believe they would be very lost without me.''

''Why haven't they gotten married? I'm sure there are plenty of women who would say yes. Rodney is quite good-looking, and Basil is charming. I'm looking forward to the dinner he's offered me at Sharpe Hall.'' Nadine repositioned several books.

''You have met my brother Basil?'' Melanie's dark eyes took on a startled, then cautious look.

''Yes, a couple of days ago.'' Nadine flung the words over her shoulder as she continued to work. ''Not long after I arrived back on the island.''

''You must have really impressed him. I cannot remember when Basil has invited anyone to the house.'' This time it was Melanie's turn to sound a nervous laugh. ''He is not as social as Rodney and I.''

''My, that does sound impressive.'' Nadine felt pleased about the special invitation. ''Maybe my charms are working better than I think.''

''Yes, you never know.'' Melanie's steady gaze followed her movements about the room. ''If you would like, I can arrange dinner for this evening.''

''This evening? I'd love to.'' Nadine broke into a wide smile. ''It'll give me something to look forward to other than another late evening down here.''

''It is settled then,'' Melanie said. ''I will make sure I get back in time to tell Cook. It will be exciting having a dinner guest at Sharpe Hall,'' she said before they descended the stairs again.

"I am simply upset because big brother beat me to the punch." Rodney flashed another brilliant smile. "So the least I could do for my brother Basil and myself is to offer to escort you to Sharpe Hall for this all-important event." He chucked a rock at a nearby tree before continuing, "Catherine told me how Ulysses the Terrible had you slaving away in his dungeon, so I thought a walk through the grounds of Sharpe Hall would bring some fresh air and sunshine into your dark life."

Nadine's hazel eyes gleamed with merriment. It felt kind of strange to be having such a good time with Rodney. Caught up in his mood of frivolity, Nadine responded to his antics with due drama, and raised her arms beseechingly toward the sky, then she placed her hands on her hips and said, "Ulysses the Terrible. You got that right."

Rodney's laughter matched her own, but was cut off in its vigor as Ulysses approached them from the fork in the road. Trying to gain his composure as well as warn Nadine of Ulysses' nearness, he began a set of spasmodic coughs.

"Well, hello, Ulysses. Had you been home earlier, I would have invited you to come along and have dinner with us tonight," Rodney said, trying not to laugh again.

"So that is where you are going," Ulysses commented, his visage unreadable.

Looking at Ulysses now, it was hard for Nadine to imagine him being as friendly and carefree as Rodney. For a moment she thought, as she suppressed a rising giggle, he even looked like a Ulysses the Terrible.

An awkward pause followed as Nadine and Rodney struggled to remain serious while confronting the object of their jest. Nadine watched Ulysses' cool gaze slide from Rodney to her. A definite spark entered his eyes as he took in her petite figure clad in an orange top and skirt. Once again she had washed her hair and let it dry naturally, resulting in a profusion of tiny, spongy ringlets which she had attempted to brush away from her face. A pair of rather large ivory and silver earrings, given to her by Gloria, graced her ears.

Feeling obligated to her temporary employer, Nadine began to explain, "A couple of days ago Basil extended an open invitation to me for dinner. It was Melanie who suggested that I come tonight."

A thick eyebrow rose suspiciously at the mention of Basil's name. "I have never known Basil to be so gracious." The words were spoken slowly, ending in a derisive upward tilt of one side of Ulysses' lips. A hint of jealousy descended on his striking features that was quickly masked, but not before Nadine saw it. Her spirits and confidence soared. She was glad she had taken some extra time with her looks: applying mascara, blush, and a light dusting of facial powder in addition to her customary dab of lipstick.

The jealousy she had recognized in Ulysses, and her feelings of high self-esteem urged her on. "I hope things went well on Barbados."

"Yes, they did." A distrusting glint entered his eyes at her obvious pleasure and willingness to strike up a conversation. "I spoke with Dr. Steward. He said he would be glad to send out the information."

"Wonderful."

Another awkward pause followed.

"We will not hold you any longer." Rodney brought the conversation to an end. "I am sure you must be tired after your . . . business on Barbados." He flashed Ulysses a knowing smile, which was not returned.

The meaningful pause before "business" was not lost on Nadine, and despite her feeling of momentary victory, the thought of Ulysses being involved with another woman was very disheartening.

"I hope you do not intend to stay out too long, Nadine. We have a very busy day ahead of us tomorrow."

Before Nadine could respond Rodney came to her aid.

"Why, Ulysses, I never knew you could be such a hard taskmaster."

"Why, Rodney," he mimicked, "what else would you expect from Ulysses the Terrible?" A mock smile crossed his face as he nodded his departure.

Nadine and Rodney walked quite a distance before they let go of another round of laughter, not wanting Ulysses to overhear them again. It had been a long time since Nadine had felt so good, and she was determined to make the most of it.

The two of them progressed together, engrossed in laughter and idle chatter. They cut through a thick cluster of evergreen trees before reaching a road that ended at the steps of Sharpe Hall.

"Well, this is it." Rodney stopped and looked at his home which rose majestically in front of them. "This is Sharpe Hall."

Chapter 18

To Nadine it looked like a miniature palace with columns. A wide, steep limestone stairway led up to arched openings which introduced a similarly shaped double doorway, enhanced by bronze metalwork. She remained quiet as they walked closer to the magnificent structure. Her well-trained eyes took it all in as she assessed the age of the building. Nadine could tell it was old but very well kept. The difference between Sharpe Hall and Sovereign was obvious. Sharpe Hall was much more majestic.

"What do you think?" Rodney asked, seeking some reaction as they climbed the stairs.

"There's only one thing to think," Nadine said. "It's absolutely amazing," she replied, then thought to herself, Not too long ago I probably would have been forced to go through the back door.

"Glad you think so." Rodney placed his palm in the middle of Nadine's back. "Shall we go in?"

A servant opened the door as they approached. Nadine sought to make contact with the young woman's eyes to thank her, but she never raised her face from its lowered position.

Immediately, Nadine felt something was different. There was no sense of camaraderie between the servant and Rodney as he ushered her past the head-wrapped creature without a word.

"I will take you to the salon, and then I will check to make sure everything is ready for dinner. Make yourself comfortable," Rodney advised her before he left her alone.

Like the outside, Sharpe Hall was quite different from Sovereign in the inside as well. The furnishings were more modern, and there were only sprinklings of artwork here and there. As Nadine looked around the room it was plain to see everything was precisely arranged, all the way down to the ashes that had been smoothed out in the fireplace. Nadine thought it was attractive to the eye but it felt sterile instead of inviting.

A wooden stand filled with whips drew Nadine's attention. Their presence seemed to mar the pristine feeling of the room. The whips did not appear to be artifacts that had outgrown their days of usefulness; on the contrary, some were brand-new, while others appeared to have been used quite often. Nadine could not imagine what purpose they served in this day and time. Certainly, even here on Eros where there were many remnants from the past, the whipping of animals would be considered outdated and cruel.

Nadine's thoughts were interrupted when another servant, a much darker, smaller woman, entered the room carrying a tray of tea. Nadine wondered if she was of Ashanti or Egyptian descent. The woman's curious eyes stole a brisk, but assessing look at the guest before she put the tray down and turned quietly away.

Nadine added sugar to the aromatic brew before picking up the delicate china cup with care. Although Rodney had tried to make her feel welcome, she did not feel comfortable in the quiet, pristine surroundings. Just the thought of spilling even a drop of tea rattled her nerves, unlike Sovereign whose organized clutter drew her in, reminding her of the surroundings where she was brought up.

Nadine knew the difference between Sharpe Hall and Sovereign was not only a physical one. The friendliness that existed among Ulysses and Madame Deane, Catherine and Clarence would seem out of place here. Then she recalled how both Melanie and Ulysses had expressed surprise when they heard Basil had invited her to dinner. Now, looking about her, she wondered why he had extended the rare offer. She was draining her cup when Basil Sharpe joined her. He was immaculate in a dark suit and tie.

"Welcome to Sharpe Hall, Miss Clayton. I'm so glad you decided to join us tonight."

"Thank you for inviting me." She reached out to meet his extended hand. His grasp was so strong Nadine nearly winced. Despite the welcome in his words she noticed there was no warmth in his eyes which glowed with a harsh light.

Basil offered her his arm, which she took, and he escorted her into the dining room.

The room was perfectly arranged. Just the right touch of everything. Not too much and not too little. Both Melanie and Rodney were already seated at the silver and china-laden table. Neither one spoke as Nadine and Basil entered the room. On the contrary, Melanie's blank features watched them as they advanced while Rodney never looked

up from the place setting in front of him. Basil
stood at the head of the table and motioned for
Nadine to be seated at his left before taking his
seat. Confused over the quiet reception from Melanie and Rodney, Nadine looked at one of them
and then the other.

Finally, Melanie spoke, her voice strained, con-
trolled. "I'm glad you were able to make it tonight,
Nadine. I hope you like roasted pork. It is one of
Rodney's favorites."

Rodney offered a weak smile, adding, "It definitely is. And after our walk I've worked up quite
an appetite."

Basil released a deep chuckle. "Rodney, you
must be kidding. You tend to be hungry no matter
what. A quarter of Sharpe Hall's fortune goes toward fulfilling your lavish taste in every sense of
the word."

Rodney looked at his brother, but said nothing.
That did not seem to matter to Basil. It was just
the beginning of his gregariousness. As he rattled
on, the same servant who had served Nadine tea
entered with a large pot and ladle. She began to
serve an aromatic soup.

Nadine was relieved someone was in the mood
for talking, although some of Basil's tactless words
were less than appetizing. Still he filled the uncomfortable silence since neither Rodney nor Melanie
seemed to be up to doing so.

"Ah, the callaloo smells wonderful," Basil commented loudly.

The surprised servant jumped as if she had been
spooked, her scared dark eyes darting from Basil
to Melanie. It was obvious she was not accustomed
to any kind of comment, let alone a compliment

from her employer. She managed to mouth a half-audible "Thank you" before escaping with the now-shaking dish.

"Do you serve stew with okra and crab like this in America?" Basil continued his sociable chatter.

"We wouldn't call it stew, at least not in the circles that I'm in. I'm sure it varies according to a person's cultural background. But a dish like that would be considered gumbo."

"Well, callaloo is a very popular stew on Barbados and Eros. I think you will enjoy it." Basil lifted the soup spoon to his lips, making a soft, but audible slurping noise. Afterwards he nodded in Nadine's direction.

"How are you liking your stay on Eros?"

"Everything has been fine. I've been working since I arrived, and there's only so much enjoyment you can get out of that," Nadine replied.

Once again her host laughed, but it rang emptily through the sizable dining room. No one else joined in. Even Nadine's supporting smile faded as she glanced at Rodney's serious profile.

"Well, I must say a woman as attractive as you, Miss Clayton, should always enjoy herself, or should be given enjoyment." His dark eyes looked at her suggestively.

Nadine looked down at her food, but not before seeing Rodney's back stiffen, and Melanie's skin turn rather ashy. The eldest Sharpe glanced around the table at his silent siblings.

"Pretty soon Miss Clayton is going to feel she is not welcome at Sharpe Hall if the mood around this table does not change." Basil's words were said in jest but they held an ominous undercurrent.

A flicker of dismay crossed Melanie's features

and the pulse at Rodney's temple seemed to quicken. Yet that one mild threat was all it took for the two of them to make a concerted effort to change the mood of the dinner. Melanie began to discuss the upcoming book sale, and Rodney asked a question or two just for good measure. It was now Basil's time for silence.

Nadine could feel his hard eyes on her. He made her feel uneasy with his calculating stare. She was glad when the entree dishes were collected and the dessert was served.

"Miss Clayton, I will be accompanying you back to Sovereign tonight. It was very thoughtful of Rodney to escort you here, but since you are *my* guest, I think it is only right that I see you back safely."

These words from Basil seemed to be all that Rodney could take. Suddenly, he excused himself from the table.

"That reminds me, there are several things I need to take care of, uh, immediately. If you will all excuse me." He rose out of his chair and began to exit the room.

"Why, Rodney, I am surprised at you," Basil called out to his brother's retreating back. "I have never seen you take leave of a woman without giving her a proper farewell."

Rodney stopped and turned toward them with a purposeful smile on his face. Nadine could see he was trying to maintain his control.

"You are right, of course." He began to retrace his steps across the floor. "I am sorry, Nadine." He then gave her the customary touching of cheeks and symbolic kiss. As he drew away Nadine noticed an ugly red mark on his face. One that she was sure had not been there during their walk from Sovereign to Sharpe Hall.

"Rodney, what happened? Did you walk into something?"

Automatically, he raised his hand to cover it. "It—it is nothing."

"You will find Rodney is accident-prone," Basil explained in a patronizing, ironic tone. "He always has been, especially when he was a little child." He twisted a large gold ring on his finger.

Nadine could see the anger rise up in Rodney's eyes as he turned toward his brother. Their eyes locked and the tension was tangible.

"Rodney." Melanie called her younger brother's name with urgency. "I know you said you had something to do, but would you mind checking on the cook on your way out? She was sick earlier. Catherine had prepared some medicine for her that I have been trying to get her to take. She does not listen to me very well, but you know how she has always had a soft spot for you."

Rodney's gaze dropped to the floor in a moment of indecision. After a short pause he replied, "Of course I will." Once again he said good night and quickly exited the dining room.

Nadine was glad to see the light coming from the tunnel-like entrance of Sovereign. Even though Basil's chatter had been interesting enough, she felt nervous in his presence. She had not enjoyed her dinner at Sharpe Hall, and there could be little doubt that Basil was the reason.

As she waited alone in the foyer for Basil to escort her back to Sovereign, she could hear harsh whispers in the salon. The voices were deep and she assumed it was Basil and Rodney. She could not make out the words, but she could tell they were not pleasant ones.

This made no sense to her. Why was there so much animosity between the Sharpes? It seemed to have something to do with her, but how could that be? She had just met them, and had not developed or shown any interest in Basil or Rodney.

Nadine looked at the man beside her and felt the urge to hurry to Sovereign's large oak door before he made any further advances toward her. But instead she stood motionless beside him.

"I cannot express how much I enjoyed your company at dinner tonight, Miss Clayton. I hope we can do it again . . . soon."

"What can I say?" Nadine searched for the proper words to express how she felt. "I appreciate your invitation, but I doubt if I'll be able to come back again before I leave the island. The book sale is just a few days away, and I'm sure I'll be very busy. But again, thank you."

"I understand." A mechanical smile spread across Basil's thin lips. "At the same time I am not a man accustomed to being turned away so easily. Maybe something can be arranged. Ulysses is a very reasonable man." A suggestive tone entered his voice. "But it is late and I know you must go inside." Basil leaned over and repeated the customary farewell Rodney had given her earlier. He seemed to prolong the touch of his hot, sweaty cheek upon hers, while holding her arms tightly to her sides, disabling any movement on her part. It sent a cold shiver down her spine. Finally, Nadine was able to pull away.

Something about him bothered her. She thought

about the way Melanie and Rodney were obviously intimidated by him, as well as the servant. With a challenging look in her eyes, Nadine drove her point home. "I don't think that is going to happen."

A semi-smirk crossed Basil's harsh features. He seemed to receive pleasure from Nadine's discomfort. He raised her reluctant hand to his lips. "Good-bye—that is, until we meet again."

As the front door closed behind Nadine, a shadowy figure drew back from an open window. Ulysses' heart skipped erratically, and he felt as if blood was rushing to his head. He wished he could have heard the conversation between Nadine and Basil, but they were speaking too softly for that.

He knew Basil Sharpe well, and what he knew about him he did not like. He was a cruel man with an equally sadistic reputation especially when it came to women. Women of African heritage in particular.

Ulysses knew Basil never invited guests to dinner. As a matter of fact the gossip among the servants and the islanders implied he even refused Melanie or Rodney the luxury of visitors. Ulysses' eyes narrowed as he lit the blackened wick on his wall, a picture of Basil prolonging the touch of his lips against Nadine's cheek coursing through his mind. Could it be they were more than new acquaintances?

The thought of Nadine betraying him with Basil made his blood run cold. Betraying him. What a strange phrase to use. Betraying him how? Financially or physically? Ulysses hated to admit it, but the latter caused the greatest pang. Then he chided himself for even using the word "betray." There was no real relationship between Nadine and him, although betrayal was what he felt. From what he had been able to uncover concerning Nadine's meager beginnings, it would not be far-fetched to think she had latched on to someone like Basil.

At first he was reluctant to hire the private detective through John Castle. But he was determined; if learning more about Nadine Clayton could lead him to the thief who had stolen a part of the Gaia Series, and to Clarence's attacker, he was willing to do it.

The letters he had been given did not indicate she was involved, or ever had been involved, in any criminal activity. But they did reveal another side of her personality.

He sat down and unlocked the desk drawer, pulling out the smooth, tan envelope. Methodically, his fingers thumbed through the pages inside. Ulysses' conscience nagged at him a bit as he looked at the bundle of letters he held in his hands. They told so much about Nadine, and he wondered if John and the detective had read them. He went to the last letter Nadine had received from the woman named Gloria and read the passage he felt was the most insightful.

Well, it seems like you've finally gotten your head together. Going out of the country will be one of the best things you've ever done. And when you find the man who's your ticket to a life of luxury, you had better latch on to him, girl. (Smile) Do whatever it takes to make it work. We both know how long it has taken you to get this far.

Over and over this Gloria had warned Nadine against being so naive. If Nadine had taken her friend's advice about life, love, and men, which from the last letter it appeared she had, she now was well-schooled in the art of female deception. Even her claim of being a virgin could well be a lie, and the way things stood at this point, it probably was, especially if she could take up with a man like Basil. Ulysses put the incriminating letter back inside the pack.

It was obvious, from what he had read, that Nadine had always been on the outer circles of society, and Ulysses wondered if there was a limit to the things she would do in order to break away from the small-town country image she secretly despised. The question was: how far would she go to lose that identity?

Ulysses wished he had known the young woman Nadine had been prior to her becoming a deceitful gold digger. But he knew there was no sense in wishing for the past, yet the new image he had of Nadine did not feel right. If she was a gold digger why hadn't she pursued him or warmed up to Etien Richarde's proposition? Ulysses hung his head and ran both hands through his mass of curly hair. An affair with Etien would not have amounted to much. An affair? You would not have been able to call it that. It would have been more like a one-night stand, and that would not have shown much class. If there was one thing Gloria had drummed into Nadine, it was "Whatever you do, do it with class." How much classier could she get than deciding to become a part of an international literature and art circle, a convenient place for clandestine activities that could be quite profitable.

After all she was not above lying. She had lied about being an historian.

Ulysses' head pounded as he considered the many possibilities. But even after his mental deluge of what-ifs, he still could not convince himself of Nadine's guilt. There was something about her that touched him in places that had never been aroused before. A kind of trusting innocence.

The dull thud of a door closing further down the hall broke into Ulysses' thoughts, and he began to undress. Now that Nadine was back at Sovereign he would be able to keep an eye on her, and whatever he found out, he would not let his feelings for her blind him. He was the owner of Sovereign, and as "the Protector of Eros' Treasures," they must be his first concern, and they must be protected at all costs.

Basil Sharpe approached Sharpe Hall beneath the bright moonlight. A derisive look of satisfaction shone on his jagged features. So the African-American does not like me so much now, after she has been able to compare me to that younger brother of mine and Ulysses. Well, I intend to have some of whatever has gotten Rodney so riled up. As a matter of fact, I am sure after our little discussion today, he will not be giving her a second thought. Basil's features turned even darker. Rodney does not have the right to anything on this island without my permission. I am the oldest Sharpe. The only one who has paid his dues in blood, and I will never allow Melanie or Rodney to forget that. He looked up into the night sky.

As for Ulysses, I have heard the rumors. The servants say he has an eye for Nadine Clayton. That is why having my way with her behind his back will be that much sweeter. What I intend to do with his African-American diversion will not leave any visible evidence. At least not if I am careful.

Basil wiped the back of his hand across his mouth. Just thinking about his intentions caused his manhood to rise. It never failed. All he needed was a new object for his obsessions and it worked like a charm. Instead of going up the limestone staircase Basil took a detour. He had decided to make a quick visit to the row of houses on the outskirts of the Sharpe Hall property line. There, a mixture of workers, some of the less fortunate Bajans and Blacks, made their homes.

Basil licked his thin lips with anticipation while he contemplated his upcoming visit to the neighborhood. A glazed look entered his eyes. This time he would have to be more careful. The last girl was young, and her unexpected expressions and reaction had fanned his passion far too high. He had been overzealous in his actions. But even now the memory of those thin lines of red blood against the dark-brown skin made his breath come in haggard bursts.

Basil stopped at a small shed not far from the rear of the main house. With sweaty fingers he opened the wooden door and felt inside for what he knew hung within his reach. As he walked away the telltale signs of a short, slender whip pressed against the back of his suit as he refastened it. Just the feel of it in his hand brought a passionate shudder within him, and the thought of using it against dark skin hastened his footsteps down the moonlit pathway.

*   *   *

Melanie watched her brother's rapid progression in the direction of the small neighborhood. Her hands grew cold and clammy as she thought about what he would be doing there. Sexual appetites were not as foreign to her as many of the islanders believed, but still she could not fully understand Basil's. His sexual needs disgusted her, and his obvious intentions toward the woman, Nadine, were completely unacceptable. It was one thing to perform his lustful deeds on islanders whose welfare depended on Sharpe Hall, but another to focus his obsession toward Nadine Clayton.

Melanie turned away from the window as Basil advanced out of sight. With deft fingers she removed several large hairpins from the braided ball at the base of her neck. A long black braid tumbled downward, settling against her back. She had not worn the white wrap today. Sometimes she hated it and the ladylike dresses that she customarily wore.

Through the years Melanie had kept her yearnings well under control, away from the prying eyes of the servants and islanders, but that did not mean she was void of feelings. She was a woman just like any other.

In deep thought Melanie removed her outer clothing, peeling down to an exquisite set of black underwear. She ran her hands over the satiny smooth material of the lacy bra and French-cut bikinis she had bought along with several others on Barbados, then slowly, she lowered herself onto the queen-sized bed.

A smile touched her lips as she imagined what Ulysses might think if he saw her in her wicked lingerie. What would they all think? Melanie

Sharpe with her prim and proper ways. The concerned sister. The dutiful woman of the house. Always serene and calm. Always obeying orders and doing the right thing.

An unexpected urge to laugh out loud struck deep within her, and she covered her mouth with both hands in an effort to keep it from bursting forth. Well, Melanie had plans of her own, and it would not do for Basil to botch them by bringing the American authorities here to check on one of their own. No. Miss Nadine needed to be left alone. Things would not go right if she were harmed in any way. And as for Ulysses? She had major plans for him as well. Melanie closed her eyes and crossed her arms as she cupped her full breasts with her hands.

She had hoped Ulysses would have been more receptive toward her proposal for marriage. She had not expected him to say yes right away, but at least say that he would think about it. But Ulysses had been so uncooperative. Melanie's mouth turned into a frown laced with pleasure because of her own stimulation. If they married, many of his financial worries would be over, for she did come with a sizable dowry, and then she, Melanie Sharpe, would be the lady of Sovereign. Sovereign, "the Protector of Eros' Treasures" and the home of the Five Pieces of Gaia.

She looked at the only painting that hung on her bedroom wall. The sight of it reassured her that the papyrus and papers her mother, Evelyn Sharpe, had given her were safely hidden behind it.

But things had not gone as she had planned, and now time was growing short. Melanie had been pretty sure that by now, Ulysses would have agreed to marry her to save Sovereign. She had been wrong. Still, she did not believe Ulysses would make enough money from the book sale to pay the back taxes on the estate. Melanie moaned as one hand remained on her breast and the other traveled downward.

Something had changed his priorities. Something or someone. Maybe she had underestimated the effect the African-American had upon Ulysses. If that were true, Rodney's participation in her plan would become more important than ever. He would have to keep Nadine occupied until the appointed time, and turn her fancy away from Ulysses. Hopefully, Basil would continue to quench his sexual appetite in the workers' neighborhood. Perhaps some extra money to the Brown family would not hurt. Their daughter Nina had come of age; maybe that would persuade them to allow the girl to spend some time with the big boss, Basil.

Several small wrinkles formed on Melanie's brow as she weighed her thoughts and stroked the triangle of wavy hair. Was she really any better than her brother Basil? The question hung in her mind. Yes. Yes, of course she was. Her cause was greater than mere revenge linked with sexual perversion. A cause that her mother would applaud.

Up to this point Melanie's hands had wandered carelessly over her body. But now as she watched the full moon hovering outside her window they became more focused. She had become adept at pleasuring herself, and she sighed as her knowledgeable hands continued their work. But tonight Melanie found it to be somewhat difficult; there was so much on her mind, so much to do. Yet she persisted in her efforts and soon she began to conjure up the images that stimulated her. In a matter of minutes Melanie lost herself in her own desires, letting her future plans slip deliciously away.

Chapter 19

 Nadine looked around for the best spot to place the stack of cartographers' maps. Now the entire hall was almost full, thanks to Melanie's assistance.

Nadine had seen very little of Ulysses during the past two days. As a matter of fact she had barely seen him at all since her return to Eros. He had taken dinner with her and Madame Deane the previous night, but he had remained silent and brooding throughout the entire meal.

No matter how she tried to convince herself differently, Nadine knew that Ulysses' actions disappointed her. She had expected the preparation for the sale to be a joint venture, one that she and Ulysses would work on together. But the only input he had given her so far was his early-morning query, "How is everything going?" to which she would answer, "Everything is going fine." Nadine did not dare show how disappointed she was over his absence.

Even without Ulysses, she was anything but bored. Melanie was a constant source of company, and they were becoming much better acquainted. She liked Melanie, although she felt there was quite a bit about her that she shared with no one.

On a couple of occasions Melanie had suggested going down to the main island wharf to do some browsing, and perhaps even shop a little. She said she knew Rodney would accompany them, and even take them to one of the more upscale taverns. Nadine had been open to the idea, but each time a message arrived saying Rodney had made previous plans and the invitation had fallen through.

Nadine walked to a table stacked with books. She placed the maps on the corner and fanned them out. She stepped back to survey her handiwork.

"From what I can see, you have done quite well with the setup." Ulysses' voice reached her from across the room.

Bright hazel eyes turned in his direction. For just a moment her delight at his presence appeared in their depths, but she quickly concealed it by turning away. "We tried to make good use of the space, yet display the books and art as attractively as we possibly could."

Ulysses nodded his approval as he advanced. "Last night I took the liberty of going through your tablets, and I could see there were some things you had not priced." He picked up a notepad.

"Yes. I had planned to ask you to look at them today. Frankly, some of the pieces are so valuable I wouldn't dare take it upon myself to place a price on them without consulting you first."

"And when did you plan to do that? The sale is scheduled in three days." Ulysses settled a calculating look on her face.

"Well . . . today, as I just said." Instantly, Nadine realized working with Ulysses would not be anything like she envisioned. She could feel herself becoming nervous beneath his unwavering stare. Involuntarily, she straightened her back and tilted her head a bit, arming herself mentally for whatever lay ahead. "Would you like to start now?" she asked, returning his gaze with professional decorum.

"That is why I am here . . . Nadine."

Ulysses knew the exact moment when she called up her defenses. It looked as if her body straightened to its fullest height beneath the aqua-blue, floor-length smock. The puff of natural twists that topped her head tilted backwards as she donned her battle chin, causing several longer twists to lay enticingly against her neck. Ulysses could not help but marvel again at the closeness in color between Nadine's skin and her hair. The only difference was the shiny gold highlights that played amongst her locks. Then, to place such exquisite eyes in the midst of this uncanny picture was nothing less than alluring.

Yet Ulysses knew from Gloria's letters that for a long time Nadine did not think she was attractive. Perhaps a few years ago, before she developed her womanly curves, and with her oval face dominated by thick-lensed glasses, she could have looked quite strange. Even now, Ulysses observed, she was still rather thin for a woman her age.

But nature had filled in the hollows, and the somewhat strange duckling had definitely become a swan, even if she did not know it. Or perhaps she did. Ulysses' eyes squinted in speculation.

He watched as Nadine continued to look at him, antagonism all over her. Why does she feel she has to do battle with me unless she sees me as the enemy?

Nadine was the first to look away from their visual sparring of wills, reminding herself that she was in Ulysses' home as a worker as well as a houseguest. She picked up the second tablet and made her way to the first item on the list without a price. Nadine was determined to make the best of the situation. "If you like, we can start with this novel. I've researched its origins, and it was part of Hannibal's library." She held the leather-bound handwritten document so that she could admire the images that had been carefully pressed onto the cover. "According to my research some of the books from that library were bought during legitimate trade, but more than likely this novel may have been part of a loot or raid. Since it is so rare I thought—"

"You thought my family may have come by it illegally?" Ulysses stood menacingly close as he took the book from her hand. "I guess that is a possibility. Maybe we all have the capability to take what is not ours if the circumstances are right." He looked her up and down crudely as he spoke, and there was no mistaking the accusation that was in his eyes and voice. Ulysses began to examine the book, viewing it from all angles.

Nadine could feel the hair prickle on the back of her neck as she nearly shuddered with indignation. How dare he suggest she might steal something from him after she had been so careful to catalog every single item. She thought of how tenderly she had handled the rare collection, even more so because it belonged to Ulysses, knowing how much he admired and appreciated the objects. Nadine could not contain her anger any longer. "You may be able to accuse me of other things, but a thief I am not. And I would think out of sheer, common courtesy you would refrain from suggesting that I might steal from a place where I am professionally employed." Her eyes flashed furiously. "I am willing to do just about anything that my work calls upon me to do, but I will not be subtly called a thief and insulted by you of all people, Ulysses Deane."

Ulysses grabbed Nadine's chin before she could turn away. His grip, although not painful, disabled her from turning away as he spoke. "So you would do anything, would you?" His voice was silky yet threatening, and his impenetrable eyes displayed a lustful glare. "Don't speak too quickly, Nadine. I can think of some things that could be considered work. According to who you are talking to, and how you approach it."

Moisture began to well up in Nadine's eyes as the faint signs of a cramp ran down the side of her neck. Her pursed lips trembled slightly as she tried to maintain control. Watching her in such a vulnerable position only incited Ulysses more. He longed to shake the truth out of her so the cat-and-mouse game between them could be over. He released his hold on her chin, his fingers soothing the place he had held so tightly. "I did not accuse you of anything."

"Not directly. But you were thinking it," Nadine retorted. The look of desire and something else that she could not read in his eyes made her voice breathy even to her own ears. She held her head stiffly, afraid the slightest movement would break the physical contact between them.

The unshed tears softened her gaze to a soft jade as she looked at him pleadingly, wanting to understand why he did not trust her. For a moment they forgot the battle that raged between them as they attempted to look into each other's hearts and minds. All that they could see was an exquisite burning desire. One that could not be ignored.

Ulysses' face descended toward Nadine's. This time there was no doubt in her mind what she wanted, and her full lips parted in open invitation.

Oh God, he's going to kiss me. How much I want him to kiss me, she acknowledged as he came closer.

Ulysses' mouth was soft and unsure when it reached hers, but when his lips touched the soft buds Nadine offered, an overwhelming wave of desire washed over him. He knew for the first time in his life what it meant to really want, as well as need, a woman. He realized that this vulnerability that Nadine was able to unearth was what had caused him to hold back. Ulysses tried to understand why he had to feel this way with this woman, who might be an ally to his enemies.

Nadine's slightly open eyes gazed into his with longing. She wanted to feel the full force of his firm lips on hers. With anxious hands she dropped the legal pad and placed trembling fingers in the tangle of black curls that crowned his head, bringing her the closeness she craved. Tentatively, Nadine's tongue parted his lips. With tiny strokes she dipped inside, apprehensive, but needing to seek out the moistness that she knew waited there.

Ulysses did not disappoint her. Her inviting strokes awakened him from his indecision. He wrapped her firmly in both arms, tilting her head back to deepen the kiss. His searching exploration of her mouth was passionate, probing, as if through his kiss he could truly know her. Know if she could be trusted.

"What are you?" he whispered as his mouth traveled to her temple and then to her ear. "I want to know the truth about you, Nadine. I need to know." His lips left a tingling trail as he held her against him.

With her head thrown back in sheer abandon Nadine took in his words as a drowning man takes in water, inescapably transfixed by the sound, smell, and feel of him.

Suddenly, their moment of surrender was interrupted by a repeated hissing and grinding sound. Startled, Nadine and Ulysses turned to see Madame Deane laughing hysterically as she thrust her wheelchair back and forth rapidly in the same spot. Her neck was stretched forward and her eyes gleamed as she watched them.

Embarrassed and unnerved by Madame Deane, Nadine quickly stepped away from Ulysses and turned toward several articles behind her. It was Ulysses' calm but stern voice that halted the nerve-racking sound.

"Aunt Helen, you should have said something when you first came in. At least that is how you raised me. You told me to always announce myself when I entered a room." Ulysses attempted to appeal to the rational adult in his aunt. He waited for her to respond but she continued to stare wildly at Ulysses, then Nadine. "Aunt Helen, I am talking to you, and I will not tolerate your refusing to answer me," Ulysses persisted, this time his tone more ominous than before.

Madame Deane's neck curved awkwardly to the side as she lowered her head, her eyes looking up like a wild animal that was about to be struck.

"There you are, madame," Catherine's voice called from somewhere beyond the doorway. "You must not play games like this." When Catherine saw Ulysses she continued to vent her frustration. "I tell you, Master Ulysses, madame is getting where she is almost uncontrollable. I gave her some medicine this morning, but it does not seem to take effect as quickly as it used to. She should have been sleeping by now, instead I found books pulled down from the shelves and on the floor in the library. And the desk in there is a mess." She looked at Madame Deane and stretched out her hands, beseeching an explanation from her longtime employer and companion. "I just do not understand. You have never acted like this before. Never."

By now Madame Deane was agitatedly rubbing her index finger upon her thigh. She looked up at Catherine, her thin pleated lips giving the best interpretation of a pout that she could muster. "I must find it. That is what. I must find it, you hear me." Her voice came in raspy tones. She looked back at Ulysses and Nadine; a secret, unattractive smile crossed her lips.

"Find what, madame?" Catherine implored, thinking of all the work Madame Deane had created for her.

Madame looked at her as if she were a buffoon. "The missing page."

Catherine threw her hands up in frustration and then placed them on her squarish hips. "Well, excuse me for living. I tell you what. I do not care what that doctor says. I am going to give you another dose of that medication." Then, remembering her position, Catherine turned to Ulysses. "That is, if it is alright with you, Master Ulysses?"

Ulysses looked at his aunt and nodded. "Maybe you should also contact the doctor and have him come by to see her."

"I will do that as soon as I am finished with madame." Catherine attempted to push her away.

With clawing hands Madame Deane stopped her. "Ulysses, you will regret that you are having them drug me. Time is running out!" Her eyes were glassy. "Lenora! Lenora! Tell him! Tell him that time is running out!" Her last burst of energy subsided as quickly as it began. The medication was finally beginning to take effect.

Nadine watched as Catherine wheeled Madame Deane away. The urgency in Madame Deane's voice unnerved her. She thought of the animal skin that remained behind her headboard. At first she hadn't given the object much credence because of Madame Deane's eccentricity. But after her stay on Barbados, and deciphering the message on the cliff dwellers' necklace, Nadine was beginning to change her mind. A couple of nights ago she almost opened it, but fear of what she might find stopped her. Somehow she knew inside the skin she would find the answer to the quandary that connected her with the island of Eros.

Nadine had come to the islands ready to work, and with a silent hope that she might discover something about her ancestors, her past. Something that would make her feel she did belong, no matter how much she had always felt like an outcast. But now that Nadine was on the verge of finding out, she did not know if she was ready. She was beginning to feel the answers would be more bizarre than she ever imagined.

A tingling sensation seemed to emanate from the tablets around her neck, another indication of how badly her nerves had been affected by what had just taken place. Poor Madame Deane. Her personality was as mixed up and erratic as Ulysses' reaction to Nadine.

"If that was not enough to bring us back to reality," Ulysses regarded her with veiled eyes, then focused on the legal pad that lay on the floor, "nothing else will." He picked up the tablet. "I think it will take every day up to the sale to get the remaining items priced and ready."

"Yes. Yes, I guess it will," Nadine replied. She thought Ulysses had put emphasis on the word "reality." The reality was, no matter how much she wanted Ulysses and cared for him, his attraction to her was purely physical. He could not care for her because he did not trust her. Maybe that was part of the reason he had decided to supervise the last days before the event.

Nadine recalled the passage in the Bible that said a woman was a man's helpmate, which meant he would trust her with his love, his children, his property. She believed a man who truly cared for a woman would definitely trust her.

As far as Nadine knew, she had done nothing for Ulysses to distrust her, but if that was the way he felt, she would have to accept it. Just as she had accepted the missing onyx slab. Trust. It was hard to know who to trust at Sovereign.

All of a sudden she wanted to be finished with her work at Sovereign. The sooner she was free to leave, the better off she would be, because she knew she had fallen in love with Ulysses Deane, and there was no future in that. It took everything

Nadine had to hold her composure. She drew a deep breath. "Now where were we? Oh, yes, the book from Hannibal's library."

Ulysses' eyebrow rose when Nadine ignored where they really had been before his aunt's tirade. But he did not stop her. There was work to be done, and plenty of time later for other things. Someone was responsible for the troubles that Sovereign had been having, and as enticing as Nadine Clayton was, and as badly as he hated to admit it, she was definitely a prime suspect.

Chapter 20

"Now, if you could hold it still while I refasten this string," Ulysses said without looking up from the kithara.

Nadine quickly lent her assistance as she continued to admire the musical instrument. "You say it is in the lyre family?" she asked, knowing the answer, but enjoying the camaraderie she and Ulysses had developed as the day wore on.

"Yes, it is. The sounding-box of your basic lyre was made of tortoiseshell, whereas the sounding-box of the kithara, as you can see, is shaped from wood. There." His task complete, Ulysses sat back to admire his work. "It's a shame we don't have a plectrum to go with it."

"A what?" This time Nadine's ignorance was genuine.

"A plectrum. It is a small pick that the musicians used to play the kithara."

"You sound like the expert instead of me," she complimented him. "I thought it was supposed to be the other way around."

Ulysses smiled. "Now that I've fixed it, what are we going to do with it?" he said, looking at the instrument's worn strings and bands and washed-out wood.

"It really is in bad shape," Nadine replied. "Maybe we could use it as decoration. I think it will add a special flavor to the setup."

"Sounds good to me." Ulysses turned toward Nadine and stretched. "I don't know about you but I am ready to bring this workday to an end."

"I don't know." She looked out of one of the windows. "It's still daylight and I usually work at least until dusk."

Ulysses watched her concentrated features. "There are other things to do in the daytime, Miss Clayton, such as visit the wharf, take in the beach. Or have you forgotten that our beautiful pink and white beaches are one of our main attractions?"

"I know." Nadine exercised her tired shoulders. "I guess I haven't spent any time on the wharf or at the beach since I arrived. A couple of times Melanie suggested that we might go there together, along with Rodney, but that never panned out. Maybe *we* could go." Her face brightened with the thought of it.

"Let's do it. Since I am the boss here, I give you my permission." Ulysses smiled at her engagingly. "We can get something to eat at one of the restaurants or visit a tavern."

Nadine looked at his expectant features and she did not know how she could refuse. This would be the first time she and Ulysses would do something together that did not involve business. She could feel her anticipation stirring. "Alright. Give me a few minutes to freshen up and I'll meet you in the entranceway."

"I will be waiting," he replied.

* * *

Ulysses dipped and swayed with the rest of the men as Nadine and several other women watched and waited. The music was at a fever-high pitch and the band played tirelessly, while the momentum of the music constantly changed. An elderly man with a black and gray beard yelled, "Goat heaven!" and a responding chorus rang throughout the tiny tavern which was packed to capacity. Several tables and chairs had been pushed aside to make more room on the dance floor.

The men's dance ended in a flurry of squats, leaps, and spins, and then the band began a slow, languorous tune. Ulysses approached Nadine with a swaggering stride, his dark eyes locking with her excited hazel ones. Gallantly, he bowed before her and nodded toward the dance floor.

Nadine did not say a word as she stepped forward. Her heart pounded out the answer. Ulysses' silence thrilled her. There was something sensual about his wordless command. Nadine knew, on the surface, it was an invitation to dance, but the passion that glowed in his eyes spoke of other things, and her quick submission to his demand did as well.

Like dancers entering a stage they crossed the floor one behind the other, and as they walked Ulysses began to remove the black scarf he wore tied about his neck. Adeptly, he matched his steps to the tempo of the music, snapping the black square of material in time with the snapping fingers of other dancers and onlookers.

Ulysses was the first to reach the center of the floor, and he turned slowly to face his willing partner. When they stood face-to-face once again Ulysses snapped the kerchief, and in one smooth motion guided it behind Nadine's waist. He grabbed hold of the loose end as it appeared on the opposite side and pulled her toward him until their bodies were flush. It was the scarf that drew Nadine's body forward, but for all she knew it could have been the sheer male magnetism that Ulysses exuded. Nadine was caught up in the moment and she allowed the sensuous tune to seep into the very depths of her being.

Ulysses' dark, hooded eyes recognized her surrender. It was then he reached down and tied the bandanna around Nadine's waist. Once his task was completed, he wrapped her in his arms and began to dance.

The song lasted for only a few minutes, but oh, how agonizing those minutes were. She could feel every movement of his sinewy body against the thin cotton of her frock, and whenever she looked into his eyes, there was such longing and desire. It seemed to burn straight into her. So much so, that she was forced to pull her gaze away.

Ulysses and Nadine remained standing as one long after the music had stopped. Neither wanted to break the emotionally charged spell of the moment.

Finally, Nadine looked up into Ulysses' eyes, her expression serious. She could tell he was anticipating what she was about to say. "Ulysses," she paused for impact, "do you plan to feed me this evening?" Sensuous overtones glazed the inappropriate question. Nadine knew full well Ulysses was not expecting her to bring up food at such a romantic moment. She could barely keep the corners of her mouth still as she suppressed laughter over his confused expression.

"You little trickster." He grabbed her shoulders and shook her playfully. Then Ulysses smiled. "Okay. Food it shall be. I know a place that makes great macaroni pie."

"You do? Well, lead the way. I'm all yours," Nadine replied, knowing the words held a double meaning.

"Are you now?" Ulysses countered, eyeing her suspiciously. "We shall see."

It did not take long for them to reach the small stand that sold all sorts of foods. Nadine stood by waiting as Ulysses placed the order. Feeling happy in a way she did not know was possible she looked out toward the ocean. Her gaze traveled eastward until it came to a gathering of majestic cliffs. The black, red, and cinnamon rock gleamed as it rose above the sapphire-blue water. It was a powerful sight, a testimony, in Nadine's mind, to the wonder and majesty of the earth and God.

"I never knew that mountains, cliffs rather, could come in such colors," she said as Ulysses came up beside her.

"As you can see they most certainly do," he replied, softly.

"Have you ever explored that side of the island?" she asked, her attention fixed on the cliffs.

"Yes, I have, many times." He paused. "The islanders call it the land of the cliff dwellers. They make their homes there amongst the rocks."

"The cliff dwellers," Nadine repeated the name as she focused on Ulysses' face.

"But it is nothing like most people think it is," he said in measured tones. "They consider the cliffs to be sacred ground. A place to be guarded against strangers." He looked down at Nadine.

She could feel his distrust coming alive again so she looked away, and was glad when the vendor announced their food was ready.

Nadine dove hungrily into the macaroni pie. She realized she really liked it. Or maybe it was just Ulysses' company that made it taste so good. She wanted to get back to the camaraderie she and Ulysses shared before she mentioned the cliffs. Throwing her head back, she locked her teeth together on a long, stringy piece of hot cheese and pulled. She almost choked when she began to laugh at Ulysses who was tossing a piping-hot pie back and forth between his hands like a frantic juggler. "Would you like to put some dance steps to that?" Nadine teased when she was finally able to speak.

"No," Ulysses threw back at her, his eyes brimming with mischief. "But since you found that to be so funny, let us see how funny you think this is." He picked up an abandoned cup of ice, and attempted to toss it down the back of her frock.

Nadine screamed with glee and hysteria as she twisted and turned to avoid the icy bath. Within no time at all the cup was empty, missing her by inches, and she dashed down the darkening beach to avoid any further acts of revenge.

At first Ulysses watched her go, her small but womanly curves silhouetted underneath the airy material of her dress, courtesy of the waning sunlight. Her spongy, tight twists bobbed with the motion of her sprint and the wind. Silvery sprays of white sand sprang forth from her heels, and Ulysses was reminded of the mythical Atalanta, who refused to be with any man who could not outdistance her in a footrace.

Nadine stopped abruptly to catch her breath and look behind her, and Ulysses saw this as his opportunity. He launched a hot pursuit.

Squealing with excitement as she watched Ulysses' rapid approach, Nadine struggled to remove her sandals, knowing her chances of escape would be better without them. Then, as if out of nowhere, her childish game had a dual purpose. She ran for the pure excitement of it, but Nadine also ran because she did not know if she could bear Ulysses' touch without totally giving in to her own desire.

Her mouth parted as she gulped in the sea breeze, her pink tongue tasting the saltiness that came with it. As she ran Nadine could hear Ulysses panting not far behind her, but she dared not look back to see how close he was for she knew it would slow her down.

Ulysses imagined that Nadine's renewed zeal had sprung forth from a deeper source. He could only guess what it was as he drew closer, the scent of her perfume mixing with the salty breeze wafting around him. In a flash Ulysses assessed the distance between them, and he decided the moment was now. He let go a powerful grunt, then leaped. His hands encircled Nadine's waist as he came down, and they tumbled onto the warm, sunbleached sand. Ulysses and Nadine rolled together until they ended up on their backs gasping for air.

"This is the kind of thing I would have been better at ten years ago," he confessed, panting.

"I don't think I was ever good at anything like this." Nadine swallowed, then took another deep breath.

"You could have fooled me," Ulysses replied.

After a moment's respite, Nadine rolled on her side and looked at the now violet-colored Atlantic Ocean. "Oh my goodness, look at that. God, I have never seen anything so beautiful." She marveled at the white sand that had taken on a golden hue because of the setting sun, and the sky which was a masterpiece of orange and red.

"Neither have I," was Ulysses' husky response.

Nadine could feel his eyes upon her, and then the tender touch of his fingers as he outlined her profile. His fingers traipsed over her lips and down the smooth column of her throat, passing the necklaces as they continued their course. His hand opened when it reached her chest and rose with the fullness of her breasts. Softly he squeezed each mound, causing Nadine to moan, and her eyes to close with pleasure.

Ulysses' explorations continued, smoothing the flatness of her belly and running down the length of her thigh, only to come back up the other side. Then he made known to her the center of his thoughts. He could feel the heat as he softly kneaded her beneath the thin material.

"You are the most beautiful woman I have ever seen," Ulysses breathed into her ear. He positioned himself just above her, and gazed deeply into her eyes. "I want you, Nadine. I want you more than I have ever wanted any woman. But there can be no lies between us." His scrutiny of her face continued. "I also want you to be sure that this is what you really want." He turned silent before he spoke again. "I cannot promise you anything. I know that I care for you, but that is all that I can say at this time."

Nadine nodded with understanding. "I'll need some time to think it over," was her quiet response.

"You do that. But please, do not take too long."

A wisp of smoke curled upward toward the fiery sky as Basil squinted, shielding his eyes from its sting. It was also a sign of the aggravation he felt as he watched the couple playing like children on the beach. There was no doubt in his mind what would take place once they reached a secluded spot further along the shore.

He had watched the woman mold her body enticingly against Deane's while the slow tune played in the tavern. From where he stood she appeared ready and willing for anything Ulysses might suggest. Yet on the way back to Sovereign yesterday evening, she had not shown *him* any affection at all. As he recalled, Nadine Clayton had acted standoffish and kept him at arm's length. Perhaps she was playing hard to get. She had shown him none of the hot, ready woman he had seen in the tavern. But he knew that was how women of African ancestry were, hot and ready for any man.

Basil flicked the ashes from his cigarette, then inhaled until the tip glowed red. You cannot trust those women at all, he thought. He knew that from firsthand experience. Basil seethed with lust and jealousy as he imagined what would happen next on the warm sand beneath Ulysses and Nadine.

Ulysses had always been able to attract women. All his life females flocked to him, and although Basil had never heard of him mistreating them, he knew none of them held a special place in his life. But Basil believed Ulysses' feelings for Nadine

were different. It was the way he looked at her
while they danced. The way he held her. And if
that was true—Basil's cynical smile caused the cigarette to hang down—he would use those feelings,
Ulysses' weakness, to his advantage during their
meeting tomorrow. After that Ulysses' mind would
be too occupied with other matters to take care of
that hot African-American of his. Basil chuckled
smugly. *So actually I will be doing him a favor
when I approach her. From what I have seen tonight, it will not matter to her if it is me or Deane
between those slender thighs. It never matters to
women like Nadine Clayton. To them one man is
just as good as another. It is in their blood.*

He took another slug from the flask of rum and
wiped his mouth with the back of his hand. Basil's
mind drifted to his last escapade in the workers'
neighborhood, and his initial reaction was to make
another visit there tonight. But soon he changed his
mind, deciding to save his fervor for Miss Clayton.
*Maybe after I finish with her, I'll offer her to Rod-
ney. Although by then she probably will not be in
the mood for anyone else, and knowing Rodney,
he would not want my leftovers anyway.*

His drunken features registered a frown of disgust as he thought of his sissified brother, who preferred to hide behind Melanie's skirts. Basil
remembered the first and last time he had ever
taken Rodney with him to the neighborhood. He
had thought Rodney was old enough to share a real
man's pleasure. But he had been wrong. Rodney
began to plead for him to stop long before the
Black wench began to whimper with pain. By the
time it was over Rodney's manhood was limp as a

rag, and he was vomiting in the corner of the little shack.

No, I will not waste time with Rodney, Basil thought as he looked out at the dark beach. The African, Nadine, will be all mine.

Nadine closed the heavy oak door behind her and stood with her head resting against its strength. Her body ached for Ulysses, and if it had not been for his last words of wisdom, she would have given herself to him by now.

Immersed in thought she lit the lamp on the wall, and light sauntered forth in the dark room. She decided not to bathe in the large sunken tub tonight. It would be too much, reminding her of when she first actually saw Ulysses, nude, emerging from behind the huge statue of Poseidon. He himself like an ancient god. His muscular body slick with water. His inky curls plastered to his head. No. Nadine knew if she ventured beyond her bedroom door tonight, there would be no way she would not go to Ulysses.

She removed the cotton smock and poured some water from a pitcher into a matching basin. The cool water felt soothing as she splashed it on her face. She stroked her neck as the water trickled down her throat until her hand rested on the smooth stone tablets. This was a night for decisions.

Nadine paced inside the bedroom, thinking of the time she had spent with Ulysses and how the man and the island had touched her. No matter what decisions Nadine made tonight, she knew she would never be the same. She thought of the cliff dwellers, the necklace, and Madame Deane. Somehow the eccentric woman was the only one who

had connected her with the cliff dwellers and the
Legend of Lenora. How had she known?

Nadine walked over to the bed and removed the
animal skin Madame Deane had forced upon her
several weeks ago. At the time she had dismissed
it as part of the woman's fantasies, but now she
wasn't so sure.

With willed calm Nadine unrolled the goatskin
cloth. Inside she found two worn papyri covered
with the hieratic characters of Mu, the petroglyphs
carved on her necklace. But along with that were
several pieces of paper written entirely in English.
She stared at the words written at the top. The Legend of Lenora. It was obviously an interpretation
of the hieroglyphics! Stunned, she sat down with it
in her hands, her eyes quickly sweeping the page.
Nadine wondered who could have interpreted the
writing. But the question was soon forgotten as she
began to read the story.

Thousands of years ago, Lenora lived on the
now-sunken continent of Lemuria, during a time
when one had to do no more than think of what he
or she desired and it would be. Food, clothing, precious stones, water, it did not matter. Honoring the
earth, Gaia, and tapping into one's emotions was
the key to the Lemurian power. The Lemurians felt
closest to the Goddess, although they believed in
the trilogy of God/Goddess/All There Is. It was a
magical time, and happiness abounded amongst the
people.

Lenora was no different from the Lemurians in
that respect, but she was physically different. Her
eyes were a brownish-jade amongst a sea of dark-
brown. Verda, the head seer, had been consulted
when she was born, and she simply advised Len-

ora's mother to love her all the more because of her uniqueness. Verda prophesied that one day, Lenora would play a very important role in the rebirth of the Lemurian culture on Gaia, and the return of the Goddess.

The Lemurians knew they were not the only people in the world. Others lived on the opposite side of the great water. In some ways the Others were more technologically powerful and advanced than they were, and they did not honor the Goddess. The Others believed intellect and logic were the main properties of God, so they confined themselves to those properties. This knowledge did not frighten the Lemurians. Their lives were so fulfilled they gave the Others little thought. The Lemurians simply hoped the lives of the Others were as fulfilled as their own.

By the time Lenora approached womanhood there had been several earthquakes on the continent during which Gaia shook and shifted, each quake greater than the previous occurrence. The Lemurians realized the earthquakes were the result of the Others' technological experiments without concern for Gaia, and that Gaia, an extension of the Goddess herself, would not tolerate it much longer.

The Lemurians began to live in fear because the Goddess had not stopped the Others, and their faith in her lessened. Their decline in faith was manifested in a waning in their capability to materialize their needs and desires, and the times became hard.

Eventually, Verda warned the Lemurians of a great earthquake to come. It would be the last, and it would sink the continent of Lemuria. She told them they would have to leave their island home if they hoped to survive.

Preparations were made. In order for them to muster up the resources it would take for the long journey they knew lay ahead, the group worked together to manifest their needs. Lenora and her mother left Lemuria along with thousands of others. Some took their large watercrafts to the east and some to the west. They traveled for months and over time; many watched their loved ones die under horrid conditions. Lenora was one of them; her mother died before they reached land. Although they believed in reincarnation, the sorrow they felt was overwhelming, and they thought the Goddess had forgotten them.

By the time Lenora's group reached an uninhabited shore that would welcome them, Verda, the seer, was dying. But before she passed away she gave Lenora a glimpse into her past and her future. She told Lenora that unknown to her mother, and through their technology, she had been seeded by the Others. The proof was in her brownish-jade eyes. Then Verda told her that thousands of years in the future, another who looked like her would be born. Deep inside, this woman would house her memories and it would be like she had been reborn. This woman would be important to the reemergence of Mu. She would travel to a distant land. Lemurian descendants who still remembered would be waiting for her. In that distant land, she would be thrust in the middle of turmoil, and ill will would sprout like mushrooms in a field. But, the seer promised, if need be, she, Verda, would be there.

The last thing Verda told her was, "Lenora, you are the bringer of light, the message, and so is the one to come. There must be the consumption of the

dark by the fiery light before the God and Goddess
can reunite to make All That Is. The Dark has been
allowed so that the Light could emerge brighter. It
will be like the balancing of a scale, the payment
of a debt. The one to come will be united with a
man—''

Nadine turned the page with trembling fingers,
but there was nothing else; the last page was missing.

Nadine did not know what to think or how to
feel. She was stunned by the strange tale of Lenora
whose eyes were the same color as her own, and
by the prophecy. She stared at the uneven edges
where a page used to be.

Was this the missing page that drove Madame
Deane to ransack the library? If so, why was the
story in her possession? And what did she mean
when she said time was running out? Nadine
scanned back through the legend, her mind in overdrive. Who was the man mentioned in the prophecy? Could it be Ulysses?

Shaken to the core, she put the book back behind
the bed. But Nadine knew the vision, Madame
Deane, the cliff dwellers, the necklace, and now
this story all warned of something that she inex-
plicably felt was part of her. A part of her had
wanted to deny it, but another part, the one who
dreamed and longed to know about her roots in the
Caribbean, had always known. It was the part that
was determined to accept Nadine's unusual destiny.

Nadine's hand went up and touched the cross
that she always wore, even beneath the cliff dwellers' tablets. *Everything comes from God.* Grandma
Rose's words echoed in her mind as she got into
bed. She embraced those words with all of her

heart, for at that moment she felt if she did not believe them, she would be doomed to hell with all those who worshipped God/Goddess/All There Is.

It was a long time before Nadine was able to fall asleep. Her mind played tricks on her whenever she managed to drift off into a light slumber. Over and over again the last part of the vision seemed to surface, each time coming closer and closer to revealing the man's face. Then the flames would come, bringing illumination. But that was always followed by a wrenching scream.

Chapter 21

It was late afternoon before Ulysses was able to join Nadine in the hall. Catherine had told her more problems with the workers had erupted, and so it was a preoccupied Ulysses who entered the room, a troubled look dominating his features.

"I hope things are going better in here than what I've been dealing with out there," he said, not bothering to say hello.

Nadine overlooked his abruptness. She knew it was not meant for her, and that it was a byproduct of the workers' strike that started earlier that morning. "Yes, I heard all about it from Catherine." Her eyes caressed him from across the room.

She wanted to go up to him and hold him, but from the look on his face a hug was one of the last things on his mind. Instead she began to give him a report of her morning activities. "I've just about completed everything. I used the prices we came up with yesterday. I also did some comparing and calculating. Here are the final results." Nadine passed Ulysses the notepads. She stood beside him as he checked off each item.

"Master Ulysses." Catherine's hesitant voice in-

terrupted them. "Basil Sharpe is here to see you,"
she announced from the doorway.

"Basil?" Ulysses' thick eyebrows went up.
"This is a rare surprise." He quickly concluded
Basil's ill-timed arrival was connected with the
workers' strike. Perhaps he had come to gloat over
his plight.

Ulysses thought of his empty fields. He would
have employed the cliff dwellers but the time of
their spiritual ceremonies had come, and he knew
they would not be able to work. "Alright, tell him
to wait for me in the library," he replied. "I will
be there in a moment."

Ulysses resumed his rapid evaluation of the
prices, but Nadine could feel his thoughts were not
totally there. She could not help but feel a little
disappointed that Ulysses did not mention their
evening together. He made no reference to what
they had spoken of before leaving one another the
night before. He didn't even ask if she had come
to a decision. Nadine did not see a trace of the
impetuous Ulysses with whom she had spent the
evening on the beach. It was like it had never happened.

"Everything looks to be in order." Ulysses returned the pads to her. "If you need me I'll be
available in the library once Basil has left."

"Alright," she said quietly as she thought, He
has forgotten about last night. It was not important
to him.

He turned to walk away, but before Ulysses
passed through the door he turned toward her.
"And Nadine?"

"Yes?"

"I have not forgotten."

Nadine's mouth formed a tremulous smile, and her hazel eyes deepened in hue as she looked at him. "I'm glad," she replied.

Ulysses' attitude took a turn for the worse as he opened the library door and found Basil casually eyeing the paperwork on his desk. Knowing he had been caught in the act, Basil made no pretense. Instead, he slowly made his way to the opposite side of the desk, and plopped down in a large cushioned chair, crossing his legs with great pomposity.

Ulysses' already dark complexion seemed to dim even further as he crossed the room with brisk steps, refusing to greet Basil as a guest since he did not have the decency to act like one.

"What do you want, Basil?"

"Why, Ulysses," he feigned offense, "it has been such a long time since we have seen one another and talked. I thought we could at least catch up on what has been happening in our lives, and with Sharpe Hall and Sovereign." He smiled his most superior smile.

Ebony eyes pinned Basil to his chair as Ulysses gave him an insulting look. "There have been only three occasions that you have set foot in this house that I know of. For my seventh birthday, the day your father died, and today. Three visits in twenty-five years." Ulysses paused to emphasize his point. "So do not tell me this is a social call. You have never liked me, and I have never liked you. So let us keep the record straight." He leaned over the desk. "Now, like I said, what do you want, Basil?"

Basil sat quietly, examining the large ring on his finger. His first impulse was to blurt out everything just to knock the stinking, mixed bastard off his pedestal. Ulysses had always been too high and mighty. Then all of a sudden a feeling of satisfaction coursed through his veins as he thought about the situation at hand. This time we are going to play the game my way, he thought. Basil forced his angry feelings to subside. I am going to see Ulysses squirm before I leave here. I am going to roast him over the pit slowly, until I see him sweat and then scream with pain.

"There is no need to be so hostile, Ulysses. I understand the pressure you have been under with your workers striking, but that does not mean you have to act like a savage. Or is it simply in your blood?" His eyes turned beady with hatred.

"From what I hear, Basil, *you* are the biggest savage on Eros. I understand you cannot get it up without seeing blood, or if it is a man, his drawing yours."

Basil's face turned pasty. He was not proud of what he did with the women in the neighborhood, and he knew some of the workers talked about it among themselves, especially if he had been unusually fervent. But how did Ulysses know about Eric? He had been so careful to keep his rendezvous with him a secret.

Stunned by Ulysses' knowledge of his sadistic bisexual escapades, Basil's anger overflowed. His eyes were much too bright when he looked at Ulysses across the desk. Ulysses greeted him with a cold, disgusted stare.

"You dirty mixed bastard," he spat. "You think you are so much, don't you? You and Sovereign. 'The Protector of Eros' Treasures.'" A derisive laugh rose out of him. "Well, I hope you are selling enough of your treasures day after tomorrow, because if you do not, half of Sovereign's sugar-cane fields will belong to me. To Sharpe Hall. Do you understand that?'' Basil gloated in hearing the words spoken out loud. ''While your withered-up aunt was so busy spreading her legs for my father back in the good old days, he managed to draw up some papers showing that Sovereign had to pay Sharpe Hall back all the money he spent to help bring this place back up to par. Your father and his stinking Egyptian wife let the place go down so bad, it was the only way my father could save it. I guess you people are simply irresponsible. The proof being you also allowed the taxes to get behind.'' Basil wallowed in the vengeful words. ''Yes, I know all about it. That is why you are having this book sale. To pay the taxes on Sovereign. Well, Master Ulysses,'' Basil's eyes burned with disdain, ''now the time has come for Sovereign to pay its debt to Sharpe Hall as well.''

Ulysses' voice, like a snake preparing to strike, was deceptively calm when he spoke. ''You are lying. My father never would have allowed Sovereign's upkeep to fall behind. Henry Sharpe never spent a dime on Sovereign. If anything, he stole from this estate.''

''That is not what the ledger says. It is an account of all the money my father spent on Sovereign, and your aunt signed the paper sealing the debt.'' With that Basil tossed a folded piece of paper on Ulysses' desk.

Ulysses made no move to retrieve it.

Beside himself with pleasure, Basil pressed his position even further. ''You do not have to read it if you do not want to. But it is all there. So if you have any money left after paying your taxes, just

pass it all over to me, because if you do not pay
the debt to Sharpe Hall by next Monday, half of
Sovereign's sugarcane fields will be mine.''

Basil rose from the chair, pretentiously dusting
lint from his black suit. "And by the way, Miss
Clayton has become a pretty interesting player in
this. You can throw her sexual services in for good
measure. I believe she would be eager to oblige."

Basil looked up to assess the damage done by
his last barb. In seconds he saw Ulysses' countenance change from hatred to pure fury as he leapt
across the desk, placing steely fingers around
Basil's throat.

"You stay away from Nadine, you sick low-
life," Ulysses said between gritted teeth. "I am
going to pay back every cent you say Sovereign
owes to Sharpe Hall." He continued his choke hold
on Basil's neck. "But if anything else happens
around here that keeps me from paying that debt,
your life will not be worth one dollar, Basil
Sharpe."

Gasping for air and with his eyes bulging,
Basil's hands flew up to his neck once Ulysses released him, and he fell back into the cushioned
chair. Furious, Ulysses brushed past him, and
strode rapidly through the courtyard. He passed the
hall as he headed for his room.

Nadine had heard loud voices, and she came out
of the hall just as Ulysses was storming by. She
called to him but he did not answer. Automatically,
she started for the library, but she did not get far.
She ran into Basil who was coughing and sweating.

Nadine saw his disheveled appearance and
guessed that things had gotten way out of hand, but

she was so surprised she could not find the words to ask why.

Basil's eyes were still watery as he looked at her. He had threatened Ulysses with the welfare of Sovereign, but it was not until he brought Nadine Clayton up that he became physically violent. Basil stroked his neck. It still burned from Ulysses' strong hands. I will get even with the mixed bastard, he thought. Evidently, Ulysses and this woman had more feelings for each other than he suspected.

"Well, Miss Nadine. Lucky that I have bumped into you." He cleared his throat and massaged it. "It saves me from sending that message. You see, Ulysses' family has gotten itself into quite a bind. They owe a lot of money. Much more than Ulysses thought. He did not include an old debt Sovereign owed to Sharpe Hall."

"And?" She eyed him cautiously. "Sovereign is Ulysses' affair. What does this have to do with me?"

Basil raked her over with an assessing gaze, leaving little doubt of what was on his mind. "You are the only one in a position to help him out." He smirked. "All you need to do is come to Sharpe Hall when I send for you."

Nadine long ago decided she did not like Basil. Now, she knew why. He was nothing less than repulsive. There was a greasiness to his character, and a cruel feel about him. "I don't know what you're up to, Basil, but I'm not having any of it," she retorted.

"Have it your way," he shrugged, "but if you do not come when I send for you, Ulysses is going to lose half of Sovereign."

Nadine shook her head. His words were incredible.

"You do not have to believe me. There is a piece of paper in there," he pointed toward the library, "that explains everything. And Miss Nadine," Basil rubbed his sweaty palms together, "if you say anything to Ulysses about our little talk, I will make sure he loses all of Sovereign."

Basil placed the traditional kisses upon her cheeks and walked away.

Numb, Nadine entered the library. She was stunned to see the majority of the contents of Ulysses' desk on the floor. She sank into a chair, going over the things that Basil had said. When Nadine looked down at the floor she saw a piece of paper sticking out from beneath her foot. She picked it up and scanned the contents. It was a promissory note from Sovereign to Sharpe Hall signed by Madame Deane almost twenty years ago. It was proof that Basil was telling the truth.

All of a sudden Nadine felt as if the whole world was on her shoulders. She thought of Madame Deane and the legend, Ulysses and Sovereign. Ever since she had come to Eros there had been constant signs foretelling she had a tie to the people here and the land. It seemed impossible to believe, that she, a Black woman from Mississippi, would have such a legendary connection, but all the evidence made it real. Now Basil's last words reverberated through her tumultuous mind. "Have it your way, but if you do not come when I send for you, Ulysses is going to lose half of Sovereign."

Nadine's hands trembled along with the paper. Had she been back in Ashland with its down-home ways, the entire story would have seemed preposterous. She would have told Basil where to get off, perhaps reported him to the authorities, and that would have been that. But here on Eros, there was a different sense of reality. Things she would not dare to believe at home seemed highly possible here in this land of legends, myths, and visions.

Suddenly afraid, she asked herself what should she care that Ulysses and Sovereign were in trouble. He was a man from a foreign world, far removed from her own. They were not her problem. But Nadine knew that was not true. She had fallen in love with the foreigner, and she did care. Oh, God, how she cared.

She heard her own sob before she realized she was crying. She looked at the promissory note that Basil was using against Ulysses, and saw that it was wet with her tears. When Nadine read Verda's last words the night before, she had taken the prophesy seriously, but not literally. Today was a rude awakening, for Nadine believed going to Basil was the debt she was destined to pay. Still, she forced herself to close her mind and her heart against the thought, that Basil was the man Verda prophesied with whom she would be united.

Chapter 22

Cassandra pressed her body further inside the gap between the two piles of fruit crates. She had managed to avoid Ulysses while the ferry was returning from Barbados, but as the passengers lined up to disembark down the gangway, she almost ended up beside him.

The smell of rotted fruit filled her nostrils so she held her breath. Only for you, Rodney, would I be doing this, she thought as she watched Ulysses join the passengers at the top of the gangway.

Cassandra had to fight the part of her that desperately wanted Ulysses to know she was there. The part that wanted to taunt him, and tell him why she had gone to Barbados. It would serve him right for talking to her so roughly during the festival at the rum still that day. She was still hurt because Ulysses had not come to see her even once since then, and Cassandra believed it was all because of the American.

As the truth would have it, she was glad when she heard the woman had left the island. She believed things between Ulysses and her would get back to normal, but they never did. Her beautiful, dark eyes burned with scorn as she watched Ulysses progress down the ramp.

When he stepped on land, Cassandra thought, You're not the only rich man on Eros, Ulysses Deane. She bent over and picked up the medium-sized box wrapped in brown paper. For a moment her curiosity almost got the best of her, and she was tempted to tear the package open and see what was inside.

Cassandra had tried to convince the owner of the little shop to tell her what the parcel held. She had used her feminine charms to persuade him. More than once she had leaned forward, allowing him a good look at her bosom. But in the end he had only offered her money for her favors, stating he did not get involved in the affairs of the upper class.

Cassandra tossed her black hair as she made her way into the last group of exiting passengers. She held her head high as she walked amongst the other islanders. Now, she was the woman of a very important man. Yes, Rodney Sharpe had told her as much. Her eyes narrowed as she looked into the future. She had no intentions of remaining his woman for too long without a real commitment, and from the way Cassandra saw it, they were well on their way.

She looked down at the box she carried. Had not Rodney trusted her with this very important transaction? He had said there was no one else that he could rely on, and that she would be playing a big part in his life in the future.

Cassandra smiled and sighed as she pressed through the crowd, rudely hitting more than one passenger with her package. But why should she care? Soon she would be the first wife to be taken by one of the Sharpes.

Rodney watched his sister with mixed emotions. He never thought he would see the day when she would threaten him and call him weak, but that day had come.

"I asked you to take Nadine and me out, or to at least spend some time with her, and you never did that." Melanie made a sweeping gesture with her arm. "You have spent more than your share of Sharpe Hall's fortune on the frivolous things you wanted, even if you did not need them, never thinking of anyone but yourself." She stared into his eyes. "You know there have been many times I have put your happiness before my own, Rodney, and the one time I asked you to do something for me, you could not even do that without thinking of yourself." Her shrill voice reeked with accusation. "I told you to pick up that package from Barbados, but instead you decided to send your newest play toy. Has she turned your head so far that you had to bring her into what I told you should be kept a secret?"

"I never told her what was in the package," Rodney tossed back at her, flustered. "My God, Melanie, the package is wrapped up! How is she going to know what is inside?"

"Still, I cannot believe you did that," Melanie continued to storm. "Have I not always been here for you, Rodney? Spoiling you when no one else would? And that has been from the time when you were small until now." She crossed her arms below her breasts as she paced. "Father had been too busy making money and taking his pleasure wherever he could find it. And Mother,'' her eyes clouded over, ''probably contributed to half of Sovereign's rum fortune with her love of alcohol, and because of that, along with Father's evil ways, she died early and left us.'' Melanie turned toward Rodney. ''So it has always been my arms that have comforted you whenever you were hurt or frightened. Which was often. Now the time has come for you to pay me back for all my loyalty to you, and you do this.''

''I am sorry, Melanie. I know how good you have been to me. My memory is just as good as yours,'' Rodney retorted with hurt residing below his anger. The pain of how Melanie was talking to him overlapped with the hurt of never really having known his mother. ''I cannot recall one week when I was still a boy that Father did not belittle Mother. Calling her a drunk, and asking her what good was she if she could not even perform her wifely duties.'' He sat down on the window ledge and looked out as he continued. ''The three of us, you, Basil, and I, would huddle in a nearby room, and pray that he would stop his tirade before he began to beat her again.'' His voice dropped to nearly a whisper. ''But our prayers always seem to go unanswered. It went on for years and Basil threatened one day he would put a stop to it all.'' Rodney looked down at his hands. ''I do not think I will ever forget the day when he tried.'' His voice recaptured the fear and horror that he felt as a child.

''Neither will I,'' Melanie said, looking at the whips that hung on the wall. ''Basil was only twelve,'' she took up where Rodney left off, ''when he took one of his riding crops and went into the room where they were arguing. You and I were scared to death as we listened in the next room. Father's voice was angry, but there was something else beneath it as he badgered Basil for what he called his chivalry. Now when I think back on it, from the sound of his voice, I know he was receiving a strange kind of excitement from what was happening. Father even laughed when he asked Basil what he planned to do with his little whip.'' Melanie had stopped her pacing; her hands rose and fell as they stroked her forearms. "I was shocked to hear Basil speak up so loud and clear. There was no fear in his voice when he confronted Father, telling him the beatings were going to have to stop. Father laughed.'' She looked up at the ceiling. "To me he sounded like a demon, and then he said, 'So let's see if you will strike me if I strike her.' ''

Rodney went and stood beside his sister.

"That is when Mother screamed," Melanie continued. "And it sounded like there was a scuffle, and then Father's voice was so loud I remember covering my ears, but I was still able to hear him say, 'You will pay for this day for the rest of your life, boy.' ''

"And that is when things got totally out of hand," Rodney said with a loud sigh. "Basil was no match for Father, and he took Basil's whip from him that night and beat him with it severely. After that, the beatings never seemed to stop. They continued almost weekly until Basil was sixteen, and finally he got the best of Father. That time he took the merciless object from him, and reciprocated the punishment that he had received for years. After that Father never touched Mother again, even though she continued to drink.'' Rodney looked at his sister. "So I do remember, Melanie, just like you. And I will do anything for you. But I had to stay here today. Basil said he had to go to Sovereign, and you know it has been many years since he has gone there. He told me I had to stay here to make sure there was no gossiping or dissension between the workers. Although I don't know why there would be.''

Melanie looked into the dark eyes that looked so much like her own, and she wondered what her other brother was up to. She had already decided Basil had paid the workers to strike against Sovereign. She knew it would not take much to accomplish that. Many of them resented Ulysses for using the cliff dwellers to do work they felt they could be doing. Paying the workers to strike would be a major thorn in Ulysses' side and she knew Basil would enjoy that. His jealousy and hatred for Ulysses had grown consistently through the years. "Alright. Alright. Maybe I did jump to conclusions," she admitted, "but you have got to promise me as soon as Cassandra gets here with that package you will send her away immediately. I don't want the servants to get any ideas." She smoothed her hand over her hair. "They know you've got something going with her, but at least, up till now, you have had the decency not to bring your indiscretions to this house. That means if Cassandra stays here too long, they will become suspicious, and they will attempt to find out what brought her to Sharpe Hall in the first place." She placed her hand on her younger brother's arm. "This whole thing is very important to us, Rodney. You and me. I have never guided you wrong before, and I won't this time. So just trust me. After this is all over, we will be the most powerful people on the island of Eros. Not

Ulysses! Not Basil! But you and me, Rodney.'' She gave his arm a reinforcing squeeze.

Rodney could feel Melanie's touch on his arm, long after she had left. The smell of her seemed to linger in the air, the gentle floral scent that she always wore. He gripped the back of the love seat with whitened fingers. He hated when he thought of her like this. When he needed her, wanted her like a brother should never want a sister.

But for years Melanie did not seem to mind his attention. As a matter of fact, she had initiated it on her eighteenth birthday. Rodney was fifteen, and had returned from watching their prize jackass being put to stud with a newly bought donkey.

They had always been very demonstrative toward one another, and this time it was Melanie who needed comforting. He had found her in her favorite place, a tiny room in a far corner of the attic. She had been crying because, she said, no one thought she was attractive, and no one cared for her. Rodney had told her he cared, and that he thought she was beautiful and kind.

Melanie had clung to him for dear life, pulling him down upon her, rubbing her face into his neck and pressing her full body against his. Her long hair had formed a veil across his face and the floral scent of it had been intoxicating.

Rodney did not know if it was the mating that he had just witnessed or his budding hormones that had caused his body to react as it did, revealing to Melanie and to himself that her closeness was causing a very natural involuntary reaction. Eaten up with embarrassment, he tried to cover himself, and attempted to pull away, but Melanie held on to him, preventing his escape. Instead she moaned and claimed now she knew he did find her attractive. They had explored one another in tentative ways that first time, like many others to follow, never taking the game to its culmination.

During a similar, but planned, episode when Rodney was seventeen their secret explorations came to a halt. Rodney's ardor could barely be contained and he wanted more than the petting that his sister had allowed him. But Melanie had stopped him. She scolded him for wanting what she said only her husband should have. She made him feel ashamed and confused. It had been all so confusing. Afterwards she tried to comfort him and make him understand. He had never come to her again.

"Master Rodney." A low voice interrupted his thoughts.

"Yes." His vision adjusted from the past to the present.

"Cassandra Jones is here to see you," the servant announced.

"Alright. Put her in the library. I will be there right away."

Rodney thought about the hot-blooded woman who waited for him so obediently within the walls of Sharpe Hall. His mating with Cassandra was almost like touching a hot-burning coal. She consumed him with her passion. She never needed persuading to do the things he craved. She did them eagerly, leaving him totally satiated and satisfied.

He looked at the gold ring he wore on his finger. He had instructed the jeweler to take small crosses and connect them together in order to create the unique design. He wondered if it lent any protection. In his mind the entire Sharpe family seemed to be doomed to hell. Everyone except Melanie.

Melanie was good and loving. He would never see her as anything other than that.

Rodney started for the door. Cassandra and Cassandra alone had been able to make him forget during those most intimate moments what he had never been able to culminate with his sister.

Cassandra was his soul's salvation, and he did not care what anyone said. The islanders, Basil, or even Melanie. He wanted Cassandra in his life. She was the only escape he had from his illicit feelings for his sister. And he would have her at any cost.

Chapter 23

 "Madame! What are you doing?" Catherine screamed from the door of the courtyard.

At the sound of Catherine's voice Madame Deane's frail body sank down beside the well. She had clung to it as long as she could.

"What are you doing out here?" Catherine demanded as she reached down to help her mistress.

"I thought perhaps I could recreate the time when I nearly died, the time when it all began," Madame Deane said in a breathy but cultured manner, her eyes clear. "But this time, Catherine, allowing myself to die." She looked into her friend's eyes wearily. "I could bring all of this to an end."

"What are you saying, madame?" Catherine asked, frightened. "You were not trying to . . ."

"Kill myself." Madame Deane said it for her. "Yes. That is exactly what I was trying to do," she managed to say between breaths. "Kill myself. Perhaps that would rid Sovereign of everything that has happened since I was pushed in the well at Sharpe Hall. I cannot remember who did it but they should have done a more thorough job. Then I would be dead and not losing my mind."

"No, Madame Helen. Do not say that." Catherine helped her mistress get up. "You are just tired, that is all. And the medication is stronger than you are accustomed to."

Like a lifeless puppet Madame Deane allowed Catherine to place her back into the wheelchair. Afterwards she said, "No, that is not all, Catherine. My life is no longer my own, and it is not worth living."

The muffled thud of Ulysses' bedroom door closing down the hall made Nadine hug her shoulders tightly. Only a few moments had passed when she brought her hands together as if she were in prayer. Her fingers felt chilled and wrinkled when she touched them with her lips.

Ulysses had not shown up for dinner. She had not seen him since his altercation with Basil. Nadine had dined alone. The doctor had come and given Madame Deane a strong sedative to calm her. Catherine was beside herself, trying to deal with her. Nadine had seen her in tears, fearful that madame was on the brink of insanity.

For the first time Nadine believed she knew how easy, or maybe even convenient, losing your mind could be. Her own mind was working overtime. She was acutely aware of everything around her, as if her surroundings were closing in. Yet she had managed to stay back from the emotional waterfall that threatened to engulf her.

Nadine did not know how long she had lain in her bed waiting for Ulysses to return. It was as if she was performing her own private ritual as she lay nude, waiting on the white linen coverlet. The light of a resplendent moon reached through the window and bathed her in a nurturing glow. She examined her arms and breasts, aware of how the natural illumination turned her cinnamon skin to baked gold.

Nadine had gotten up slowly from the bed as she heard his footsteps advance down the hall, and seated herself in the chair before the antique dresser and large mirror.

In silence, with steady hazel eyes she sat and watched her reflection solely by the light of the moon. She had made up her mind. Tonight would be the night she would offer her love and her body to Ulysses. Because it was with love, and love alone, that she wanted to be taken for the first time. Ulysses was the man she loved, and she believed that in his own way, he loved her. He was the only man who had ever made her feel beautiful and worthy as a woman.

Nadine's slightly trembling fingers combed through her spongy, amber twists as she looked at her face that was void of makeup. She had determined she wanted Ulysses to take her as she had come into the world. It was a symbol of her purity in mind, body, and heart. This was very important to Nadine, right down to the minutest detail. It was as if going to Ulysses in her purest form would outweigh and ward off whatever Basil had in store for her.

There was no question in Nadine's mind she would go to Basil. She would go to him because of her love for Ulysses, because she, unlike her parents, would not abandon the one she loved. Nadine would go to him because it was a part of God's plan and she had faith that He would not allow her to be harmed. He had sent her to Eros, hadn't He? This had to be all a part of His plan. When the time came she would do whatever she could to keep Basil from taking any physical advantages of her. But maybe that was not his intention. Maybe he would listen to reason. She had to believe that he would.

Nadine thought about how far she had come in such a short period of time. Only yesterday her thoughts had been filled with the repercussions of making love for the first time, and now the same thoughts were tainted with the possibility of being had by a man whose touch she could not tolerate. Life was indeed strange. Not even Gloria had been caught up in such a whirlwind of strange events.

But Nadine believed a power greater than her own had marked the way. It was her mind that needed logical reasons for the actions she had decided to take. Her heart was sure of its path.

A moonbeam accented the silky gown Nadine had hung on the outside of her closet door. She had been drawn to the small boutique on Barbados where she found it. Nadine knew, even then, that eventually she would wear it for Ulysses.

In the glass she watched the nearly weightless material respond to a feathery breeze. The tail of the beautiful white lingerie began to spread and flutter, bringing the profusion of black butterflies upon it to life. She smiled. It was a knowing smile. A reminiscent smile. Watching the gown was like watching the emergence of the surviving butterfly from the cocoon that had been spared so many years ago. Nadine had felt honored to be there that day to watch it fly away from its humble beginnings.

Tonight she was the butterfly, balancing in that

space between virginity and full-fledged womanhood. A space that had confined and nurtured her
for long enough. Now Nadine was poised on the
brink of sexual freedom, and she was ready.

She slipped the thin white spaghetti straps off
the hanger and held the nightgown against her.
Even through the double layers of the airy material
she could see her brown skin showing through.
Carefully, Nadine allowed the garment to slide to
the floor and with pointed toes she stepped into the
center, easing the lingerie upward; a thick band of
white, elasticized lace caught snugly beneath her
breasts as she slipped the straps up on her shoulders. As she crossed the floor to take a final look,
the delicate material glided in and out of her thighs
and legs.

Nadine could hardly believe the reflection looking back at her was her own. The woman there
exuded such elegance and beauty, and the look
within her eyes was one of knowledge and understanding. Hers was not a face hiding behind Gloria's experiences and understandings, but the face
of a woman who had come into her own.

Some unfathomable feeling urged Nadine to spin
as fast as her feet would carry her, causing the expansive tail of the gown to rise and the wings of
the black butterflies to take flight. At that moment
she felt akin to the almost mythical creatures, for
she knew she was spreading her life's wings in a
direction that would never allow her to be the same
after tonight.

Ulysses sat and gazed blankly into space, unconsciously raising the glass of rum to his lips. The
events during the last twenty-four hours would

have broken a lesser man, and deep in his heart he felt it would be easier to give in and let the forces that fought against him win. But when he thought of who those forces were, and of their motivation, he knew there was no way he would ever quit the fight.

It was true that Sovereign's taxes were overdue, but he had known of other estate owners who had been in similar predicaments and the authorities had allowed them to "work them out" in a time frame that was much less pressuring. Ulysses had made this known to John, his attorney, on Barbados. John had agreed, but he had also confessed that some of the people in power were not too pleased about a man who was part Black owning an estate that for many years belonged to the upper class, two hundred European families that colonized Barbados and Eros.

Ulysses' eyes blazed when he thought of Basil, whose hate for him was born many years ago, and also stemmed from prejudice. He cleared his throat as he finished the glass of rum. He knew far too well how a chain of events during a man's youth could scar him for life.

As a young man Basil had always been a loner. He never had much to say during their tutoring sessions at Sharpe Hall. In retrospect, Ulysses realized Basil's early years had been painful, but as a teenager he thought no one experienced pain deeper than his own.

He remembered once being shocked to see a barrage of new welts and old scars on Basil's back as he caught him changing shirts before one of their lessons. He had gone back to Sovereign later that afternoon and told his Aunt Helen about it. Her only response had been Basil must have done something awful to receive such punishment from Henry Sharpe, for he was a wonderfully kind man. From that day on Ulysses had assumed that Basil was a wicked child, deserving of the abuse he received. He also believed the way Basil treated him proved he was capable of the horrendous deeds that spawned the beatings.

Yet Ulysses recalled a time when Basil seemed to change. It was springtime, and he was seventeen. Ulysses, who was fifteen, noticed Basil had begun to smile more, and would even try to engage him in conversation before the lessons. It was Basil's last year of study.

Basil had begun to show a deep interest in Ulysses' ancestry as well. He would seek him out and ask questions about the Egyptians and their culture. Ulysses would tell him the little he could, but since his mother died when he was seven, his knowledge had been very limited. That did not seem to matter to Basil, who would perk up at the slightest tidbit Ulysses was able to offer. They had even begun to develop a distant kind of friendship.

There was talk that Basil was being seen quite frequently in the workers' neighborhood. Ulysses himself had seen him there when he visited the settlement, or on his way to the cliff dwellers' side of the island. Ulysses found the workers' children and the cliff dwellers refreshing and open with him, despite warnings that the cliff dwellers were a strange lot who could not be trusted.

It did not take long before he found out that Basil was interested in a girl named Salinah who lived in the settlement. She, like Ulysses, was part Egyptian.

Salinah was a very beautiful girl, with large brown eyes and a thick mane of coarse black curls that hung midway down her back. Though she was Ulysses' age, many of the grown men were interested in her. She knew she was beautiful, and she used it to her advantage.

Every other day Basil would bring her a little token of his affection. In return Salinah would caress his face, kiss him gently, and reward him with the most enticing smile that Basil had ever received. He had grown to love her and planned to ask her to marry him. Basil knew the islanders respected his family name and that it would be a great honor for a worker's daughter to marry a Sharpe. But before he went to Salinah's father with his proposal, he decided to tell his father, Henry.

It had been a noble idea, born out of feelings of a young man in love for the first time. From the story the servants told, first Henry had shown great surprise, and then he looked into Basil's young expectant face and laughed harder and deeper than anyone had ever heard him laugh before. When he finally caught his breath he told his son, "I tell you what, when you marry her, you better keep her locked up in one of the rooms at Sharpe Hall. That is the only way you will be able to make sure the whore's children are your own."

The servants say those words sent Basil into a rage and he attacked his father, who continued to say vile things as he fought Basil off. "Get off of me, you crazy fool. Just about the whole island has had Salinah, including Ulysses. You are about the only male who has not."

Almost crazed by the implication of his father's words Basil took one of the donkey carts and rushed to find the girl. It was late, and the majority of his prior visits had taken place during the day. Salinah was not at home when Basil arrived, and he demanded to be told where he could find her. At first her aunt was hesitant to say, then finally she shook her head and crossed herself several times as she pointed to a couple of buildings that sat apart from the main row of houses.

Without thinking Basil rushed over and burst into the first building, and there he found a half-dressed Salinah with one of the island men. He flew at both of them with his riding crop, hurling all of the pent-up hurt and humiliation with each slash of his whip. The workers said the man managed to escape, but Basil cornered Salinah as she huddled on top of the cot, shielding her face and head from his lashes as best she could. In the end it took several of the men to restrain him.

After that day Basil had avoided him like the plague, and as the years passed, they did not speak to one another unless they were forced to. Ulysses gazed down into the swirling liquid in his glass. Yes, he had had sex with Salinah. It had been his first time, and she was the one who had initiated it.

Ulysses stood and removed his white linen shirt, tossing it on the divan. Glancing out his window he noticed the moon was almost at its peak. It brought Nadine to mind, and he thought of her sleeping several doors down. Ulysses began to study the moon. It looked so close, as if he reached out his hand he could touch it. But he knew nothing was further from the truth. Once again Ulysses was reminded of Nadine who appeared to be reachable, but was she really?

When Basil confronted him he had said she was an interesting part of what was going on, and that he believed she would be eager to appease him with sexual favors. Why had he brought Nadine into the discussion? She was an outsider who had nothing to do with Sovereign or Sharpe Hall.

Ulysses closed his eyes against his next thought, but it forced its way through. Unless there was more to her relationship with Basil than he wanted to believe. He continued to look at the moon. What if Basil was using Nadine to bait him? But how would Basil know how he felt about her? He could not unless Nadine had told him. Ulysses' eyes narrowed with distrust for Nadine, and he could not help wondering if her actions were part of a ploy.

He took a swallow of rum. Even if Nadine was involved with Basil, Ulysses doubted she knew the true nature of the man. How sadistically cruel he could be because all women of African descent reminded him of his unfaithful Salinah. Ulysses threw the remainder of the rum down his throat, his body a silhouette against the moonlit window.

Chapter 24

The sound of his bedroom door opening surprised Ulysses. Nadine's entrance into his room astounded him even more. His eyes narrowed as he watched her close the door then turn toward him.

Nadine could feel herself tremble as she looked into Ulysses' face. It was not warm and welcoming as she had imagined it would be; instead it was full of suspicion, distrust. Seeing him look at her that way made Nadine feel disoriented, as if she were in a room with a stranger. More than anything else, Nadine needed Ulysses' support, his understanding, even his friendship, but as she looked at him now, she felt they would never share those things.

She found herself searching for the proper words to say because, at that moment, all of the things she had planned to say seemed obscene and indecent. Nadine had wanted to offer her love to Ulysses, her body, but his cold reception made her intentions seem stupid, ill-conceived.

Suddenly, there was not enough air in the room. Nadine wanted to leave, put as much distance as she could between them, but her feet felt rooted to the floor.

Ulysses' eyes widened as he took in the vision
Nadine made standing riveted against the large oak
door. With her head held proudly, her hands cling-
ing to the door for support, her small breasts rising
and falling rapidly with each breath. He could feel
her fear, and he wondered why she had forced herself to come to him. Had Basil's plan to undo him
changed direction? Ulysses' mind seemed cluttered
with endless possibilities, but his voice was sharp
as a freshly sharpened knife when he spoke. "What
have we here?"

Nadine tried to swallow the lump in her throat
as her eyes grew large from the disarming question.
From it, she could see Ulysses was not going to
make the situation any easier, and Nadine began to
second-guess herself. Maybe she had misjudged his
tenderness during their evening together, and now
that she had come to him, he thought she was
cheap. "I—I thought that . . ." Her voice trailed
off uncertainly.

"I can tell what you were thinking, Nadine. A
woman who comes to a man's bedroom in a sheer
gown, baring all beneath, cannot be thinking but
one thing."

The tips of Nadine's breasts hardened with the
chill of his words, making them more obvious beneath the white material. She grew cold inside from
his insolent phrases, and small chill bumps began
to appear all over her body. "You make it sound
so vile," she said, looking away.

"The act in and of itself is not, but the reasons
behind it can be," Ulysses retorted.

This was not what Nadine had expected at all.
She had envisioned that upon seeing her, Ulysses
would take her in his arms, and begin to whisper

words of love and reassurance in her ears. She had not expected this callous stranger who was saying whatever he could to make her feel unwanted.

A gasp forced its way out of her and Nadine turned to make a hasty retreat, but Ulysses moved swiftly and stopped her from opening the door, trapping her body against it. He leaned his body against hers, then wedged her thighs apart with his knee, rubbing it against the most intimate part of her.

"Is this what you want, Nadine?" he asked, his voice husky, his breath warm against her hair.

"No, no . . . not like this," she replied.

Ulysses turned her face toward him, and said, "How do you want it then?" His dark eyes looked piercingly into hers. "Like this?"

Sensuously, he lowered his lips, placing an intoxicating, languid kiss upon her quivering mouth. Never once invading the inside, but exquisitely punishing her lips with soft nibbles and bites until they were primed and ready for more. When he withdrew, Nadine knew Ulysses could feel her need, so she replied, "I came here wanting to give you my love. To give you all that I am, and you do this."

A slow trail of tears began to make their way down her oval face as she squeezed her eyes together tightly, fighting against the desire Ulysses had aroused in her. Nadine would not allow herself to enjoy it. She felt cheap. Common. Ulysses was like a salesman laying out samples to a potential buyer, a prostitute enticing a john.

Watching her reaction, Ulysses' heart constricted with a pang of tenderness. He hated himself for treating her the way he had. He had not given her a chance to explain why she had come, or what was in her heart. He did not know where she really stood. He had allowed his fear for Sovereign's future and his mistrust of Basil to get in the way. Was it possible she had come to him for the reasons she had just given? Ulysses shook Nadine gently. "What do you want from me?" he implored, his eyes tormented. "Do you have some kind of secret alliance with Basil? Are you working with him to bring me down and steal Sovereign from me?"

"No. No, I'm not. I never met Basil before coming here to Eros. There is nothing between us," she lied, not wanting Ulysses to know about Basil's threat to take all of Sovereign. "I want you, Ulysses. I want your love," she whimpered softly as she willed him to understand how she felt.

"Nadine." His voice caressed and explored her name as he picked her up and placed her on his king-sized bed. Ulysses stood towering above her, a wild hunger in his eyes. "You say you want my love? That is something I have never given to any woman." Ulysses looked at her partially open lips and watched her uncertain hazel eyes transform to a soft jade as she regarded him. "Why should I give it to you? How do I know you will not use it against me?" His tortured voice beseeched her, but he knew, in his heart, she already possessed it.

Hearing his pain, Nadine raised her arms in invitation to reassure him. "I would never hurt you, Ulysses. Never." She shook her head to emphasize her words.

He dropped to his knees and placed his face against the silky material that covered her belly. Hypnotically, Ulysses rubbed his face back and forth, seeking solace from his fear of love which was the cause of his pain.

With quivering fingers, and soothing strokes, Nadine caressed his tangled curls, whispering his name over and over again and finally saying, "I love you, Ulysses."

She heard a raspy noise force its way out of him, as he looked up at her with tormented eyes. "God help you if you lie, Nadine Clayton." Then he was upon her. Kissing her face, her neck, her hair. It was as if Ulysses was drunk with the need of her, and she moaned with relief and apprehension because of his intensity.

"Oh, Ulysses, whatever you do . . . don't hurt me," Nadine implored.

He stopped and looked at her, then rose up on his forearms, extending them to their full length.

Nadine tried to explain. "It's just that I've waited so long . . . I'm afraid it might be more difficult than—"

Ulysses bent down and kissed her softly before she could finish what she was saying. She could feel his body tremble as he restrained himself. "I will try not to hurt you, my precious one," he said as he looked deeply into her eyes. "But if this is to be special, we both must promise to be truthful to ourselves and one another. You know that love is nothing without trust."

"I know," she whispered.

Ulysses rolled over and lay beside her. Side by side they faced one another, drinking in the other's features, rubbing their hands through the other's hair. Ulysses turned his face toward Nadine's palm as it descended down his cheek, kissing it tenderly.

He began to kiss her face once again, but this

time the kisses were tender and adoring as he held her close, and Nadine in turn snuggled closer to him. Upon reaching her mouth, Ulysses returned to the nibbling, succulent motions that he had demonstrated earlier. But this time Nadine reciprocated, imitating the movements of his mouth with her own, until he wrapped his arms tightly about her, and slowly worked his tongue within the moist cavern.

The smooth meandering of his tongue sent shivers down her spine, and she moaned her pleasure, giving in completely to the wonderful feelings.

Slowly, Ulysses released her. Afterwards he searched her eyes. "I have been told there is a big difference in taking a woman for the sake of taking her, and making love to her. Now, at last, I will know the difference. So truly, sweetness, it will be like a first for both of us."

Ulysses buried his face between her breasts, then turning to each mound he tasted the cinnamon-sweet skin they offered. Hungry for more, he traced a small line between them with his tongue, finally climbing to the peak of one of her breasts, where he explored it completely. Just that alone was enough to send Nadine's body into mild spasms and she writhed beneath him, caressing his head and his shoulders, murmuring his name.

She had always imagined how it would be for the first time, but nothing had prepared her for the intensity of the feelings she was experiencing. The movement of his tongue caused a melting sensation inside of her that flowed down to the very essence of her femininity. Like a mounting volcano the liquid began to build inside.

Ulysses could sense her pleasure; her body felt

hot to his touch and her movements were of a woman who was naturally attuned to unimaginable pleasure. The very thought made him burn with desire, and his mouth became dry. Ulysses knew there was only one place where he could quench the thirst that hounded him, and he gently reached down to touch the place that held that special fountain. He had no idea what Nadine would think of him, and what he planned to do. He knew the letters from Gloria had spoken of her religious background. It had been a strict one, and he did not want to offend her. But his urge to please her and himself was very strong. Trailing his tongue down her belly, Ulysses paused as he placed tiny kisses upon her navel.

"Nadine?"

"Yes?"

"You trust me, don't you?"

Her mind tried to follow his line of questioning, but the fire he had started inside her seemed to burn so fiercely it was hard for her to think.

"Yes, I trust you, Ulysses."

Slowly, he nuzzled his way to the top of the tightly curled patch of hair, kissing it softly, then, moaning, "I want you, Nadine," he slipped his tongue gently into the highest folds of her crevice.

Nadine rose up slightly and cried, "Ulysses! No. Wait. I don't know about this."

He spoke with his mouth near the soft triangle. "You said you wanted me to love you; you must let me do it my way, sweetness. I promise not to hurt you."

Still unsure of the course their lovemaking was taking, Nadine began to protest further, but at that moment, he found the seed inside her moist garden and she cried out with pleasure instead. Nadine's head arched back with the electricity of sensations that coursed through her. Ulysses had found what he'd sought, and he assuaged his hunger at the source.

Nadine was in no way prepared for the intensity of passion that Ulysses' assault upon her womanhood provoked. She was snared in overwhelming sensations, and she moved wantonly, unknowingly edging Ulysses on. Her response brought his deepest sexual instincts to the fore. Never before had he received such pleasure in giving it.

Feeling out of control and the most vulnerable he had ever been, Ulysses questioned her between his succulent kisses. "Nadine, what made you come to me tonight?" he demanded, tortured by his own desire. "Why? Why?" He found the essence of her again.

"Ulysses, please, please, don't. Not now. Just love me."

But he stopped and brought his face parallel with hers, his eyes blazing. "You must tell me, Nadine. Tell me now or I will go crazy not knowing why."

"I wanted you to be my first, Ulysses. Only you," Nadine replied.

Ulysses closed his eyes and kissed her deeply before he stood up to undress. He was satisfied with her answer. Ulysses assumed Nadine was thinking of the future. The book sale was today. She would be leaving Eros after that, and it was possible they might never see each other again.

"You need not worry, my sweet, I will be the first," he whispered in her ear as he repositioned himself to take her.

"There is another first, sweetness." He looked

in her eyes while he rubbed himself against her. "I have never taken a virgin before. But now I take you in honor of my ancestors, that you will be mine for now and forever, no matter where our paths may lead."

He entered her smoothly but with force, piercing the veil that held her treasures. Nadine's cry of pain was silenced by Ulysses' kiss, and he lay still within her. Controlling his passion, his movements were slow, almost imperceptible. He was determined to wait until Nadine began to respond to his considerate ministrations. Because this was new to her, Nadine's response was slow, but Ulysses was patient as he murmured words of love and passion in her eager ears. Finally, as her passion grew beneath him, Ulysses' ardor gained momentum as well.

Nadine had willed herself to forget the pain because she dreaded tomorrow, and it was not long before she was deeply immersed in a new world of pleasure.

Ulysses knew when they were nearing the crest. The gratification was familiar, but so much more intense because of his feelings for the woman beneath him. Nadine was engulfed in a series of sensations she had never experienced before. They were wonderfully powerful, but at the same time frightening because of it. She felt as if all of her life's experiences were coming together as she reached for the uncharted peak.

All at once they were there, plunging together into an ocean of bliss. Ulysses gave a loud moan of surrender, and it was joined by ecstatic words unknown to Nadine's conscious mind. In her moment of sheer pleasure her full lips formed the ancient words *"Mu Kam-ma xi!"*

Ulysses nearly drowned out Nadine's strange words. At that moment neither one of them knew or cared what the unusual phrase meant. All they knew was that nothing and no one could take from them what they had just shared.

Before the sun was able to begin its ascent into the eastern sky, Nadine and Ulysses made love again. A strange combination of tenderness and fierce passion. Nadine's uncertainties about lovemaking became minuscule with Ulysses' adept actions. It was as if they both intuitively knew the day's events would throw their already turmoil-filled lives into further chaos.

Hours later their parting kiss was the quintessence of love. Afterwards they stared into each other's eyes, searching for the truths that they felt within their own hearts, and hoped to see the same in the eyes of their lover.

"I love you, Ulysses. I want you to know that."

At first he did not reply. Instead he searched deeper into the hazel eyes emanating sincerity. In the end his words were hesitant, but he said, softly, "I love you too, Nadine."

The spoken words were like a pact between them. They hugged again, and Nadine made her reluctant trip back to her room before Catherine could come and rouse her for the busy day ahead.

The housekeeper was surprised to find her awake and dressed when she tapped on the bedroom door.

"Why, aren't you the early riser," she remarked. "And don't you look lovely today. I am glad someone got a good night's rest. It was after midnight when I finally got to sleep," she continued. "Madame Deane managed to slip back into the library. She had pretended she was asleep, but later when I went to check on her I found her bed was empty. I do not know how in the world she managed to get back in that wheelchair by herself, but she did. When I found her she was cackling like a hen who had laid a golden egg, and repeating the word 'finally.' I must tell you, Miss Nadine, it was the weirdest laugh I have ever heard. Needless to say, right away I went and found those new pills the doctor gave her, made her take two, and that finally put her away. If anything else happens around this place within the next twenty-four hours I think I am going to be the one who will need medication.''

Realizing she was just standing in the doorway babbling, Catherine decided to make herself useful as she talked. She emptied the washbowl out the window and made up Nadine's bed, which had been hurriedly put into disarray when Nadine heard Catherine's footsteps outside her door.

"Ulysses must have returned after I was asleep. I tell you, I sure am worried about things around here. The word is if Master Ulysses does not do well on this book sale he could lose part of the estate. And Miss Nadine,'' her dark eyes were gravely serious, "I think that would kill him. He tries to act tough and all, but I know how much this place means to him.'' She gave the feather pillow a final pat. "In a way he feels his parents died for him, and because of that he believes he must keep Sovereign going. He thinks that is the only way he can pay them back. And of course, keeping that special collection of his here at Sovereign.'' Catherine picked up a dirty towel and placed it over her arm. "So I want you to know, Miss Nadine, how much we appreciate your being here, and helping Ulysses put everything in order. It never would have been set up so beautifully if it had not been for you.''

Nadine tried to lighten the sentimental moment. ''It's all part of my job, Catherine.''

''I know. But I also know you care for Master Ulysses and I think he cares for you.'' An awkward silence followed, which Catherine filled with a curt, ''Well. I guess I better go check on madame. She is probably still sleeping from the dose I gave her, but you never know.'' She left Nadine alone.

Nadine gave her calypso-colored scarf, which she had fashioned into a headband, a final tug. Her cinnamon twists were piled on top of her head inside of it, giving her a regal air. She stepped closer to the mirror and straightened out the matching dress that Catherine had presented to her on her return to Sovereign. Nadine had saved the outfit for today, believing it would add to the ambience of the book sale and social. She had stepped out all the way. Gotten behind her man and his cause, as Gloria would say. The sandals that had been given to her when she first came to the estate adorned her feet.

Nadine's eyes were bright from the love that dominated her night. She was happier than she had ever been, and she felt there was nothing she could not handle.

With that thought she removed the papyri from the animal skin, rolled them into a tight scroll, and tucked them into the pocket of her dress. Nadine felt it was time she showed the papyri to Ulysses. Perhaps with his knowledge of the cliff dwellers he could shed some light on the unusual story, and perhaps ease her fears about Basil.

Nadine made her way to the hall. She looked over the extensive collection of book and sprinkling of art pieces and hoped they would be quickly consumed by the public. Sundry tempting smells wafted past her—smells that had become familiar. She knew Catherine had been hard at work for quite a while in the kitchen. Garlic, nutmeg, seafood, and the sweet aroma of pastries made with guava cheese blanketed the space between the kitchen and the hall, and Nadine was certain the food would be a success with the patrons.

Feeling good, she wanted Catherine to know how much her services were appreciated, so she stuck her head inside the kitchen door. "I hope everyone can pull themselves away from the food long enough to look at what's for sale," Nadine teased as she looked at the trays of roti and tamarind balls. There were baked dishes stuffed with sea urchins, flying fish, pork, and cod dominating several counters.

Catherine turned toward her, giving her the largest smile to date.

"I think you had better keep Clarence away from the kitchen," Ulysses called out. "You know how he is when it comes to good food."

He came up and stood beside Nadine in the doorway. Their arms touched. To Nadine it was a caress. They looked at each other and spoke.

"Morning, Miss Nadine."

"Good morning, Master," she lingered on the title, "Ulysses."

To anyone else there may not have been anything different about it, but to Catherine's watchful eyes and ears, she saw and heard the loving exchange. "Aren't you the cheery one this morning, Master Ulysses."

"I am hoping for good things out of the sale today, Catherine."

"Oh, is that right? We should have a sale around here more often if it is going to put you in that bright of a mood," she retorted.

Ulysses walked over and gave her stocky shoulder a hefty squeeze, then he took a piping-hot roti from one of the trays. "What would we do without you, Catherine, even though you think you know everything." He gave her a playful wink. "Now, if you will excuse me, I have a few things to take care of outside." He tilted his ebony head. "Is there anything you need before I go?" First he looked at Catherine's obstinate back, and then Nadine.

Catherine's no came in the form of a grunt, while Nadine shook her head, smiling infectiously.

Ulysses smiled back. "Then I shall leave you."

He advanced past Nadine and proceeded toward the front entrance. Not being able to help herself Nadine turned to watch his departure. His slim hips rose and fell to the rhythm of his gait, conjuring up flashbacks of their night together. The impact was so strong it caused her to shiver.

Behind her Catherine gave a loud "Humph. Sale indeed."

Chapter 25

 The crowd had swelled to its largest size yet. Nadine could tell most of the late arrivers had come out of curiosity, or just to enjoy the pending social. She was more than pleased with how the day had progressed. Money was no object for the deluge of book lovers from all over the Caribbean, and some from faraway countries. To her delight and surprise the most valuable books were the first to go.

Dr. Steward's beady eyes gleamed each time an extremely expensive set acquired a sold tag, for that translated into dollars for the institute's share of the profits. Nadine could not help but notice that Etien Richarde was amongst those who bought some of the more costly pieces, at his wife Jean's persuasion.

Automatically, her eyes searched the crowd for Ulysses. She found him sharing a chat with a stout, well-to-do female. Nadine could tell the woman was enjoying the attention she was getting from the charming host of the event, if charming was a sufficient enough description for Ulysses' deeds throughout the day.

"Well, I must say, I sure am glad I came to see

for myself,'' a strong female voice declared not too far away. "It just goes to show you cannot always believe everything you hear.''

As discreetly as she could Nadine turned to see who was speaking. She recognized the gray-haired woman immediately. She was part of a group of middle-aged women whose husbands had shown far more interest in each other than in their wives. Some of them, from what Nadine had gleaned, were very influential on Barbados and Eros.

"He is most charming, isn't he? Paul could learn a few lessons from him when it comes to how to treat people,'' her blue-eyed female companion interjected. "And to think we had heard the man was barely civilized.'' She inhaled the fragrance of the purple orchid she held in her hand. "Ulysses gave me this flower,'' the woman announced, smiling like a schoolgirl. "He told me it matched my eyes perfectly.''

Nadine smiled and turned away. There wasn't a woman in the room who had not been made to feel special as Ulysses commented on her taste in literature, clothes, or simply her smile. Yes, Nadine concluded, Ulysses had won the hearts of most of the people attending the sale. She had seen their initial haughtiness and disdain melt into acceptance, then awe. Before today, she had given little thought to the battle Ulysses had to fight being half Egyptian and half British. She felt somewhat embarrassed that she hadn't. Many of her associates back in the States who were deep into the racial struggle would have scoffed at her for her naivete.

As Nadine looked around the room she thought of Melanie. She wished she and Rodney could have stayed long enough to enjoy some of the food, and the dancing that was about to get started, but Melanie had apologized and blamed their early departure on some pending business at Sharpe Hall. Nadine noticed that Rodney appeared to be nervous and high-strung. Still, before they left, Melanie bought a collection of poetry and a decorative dagger.

Everyone appeared to be having a good time, but Nadine would have felt better if Madame Deane could have enjoyed it as well. But Catherine had done what she thought was best, and Madame Deane had been heavily sedated. She had not emerged from her room the entire day.

"Everything has gone wonderfully, thanks to you," Ulysses whispered in her ear. "And after everyone has left I intend to show you how much I love and appreciate you."

At that moment Nadine did not trust herself enough to turn around. If she did she knew she would end up wrapping her arms around his neck, showing the entire room how much she was in love. Instead a tremulous smile shaped her lips, and she looked out into the crowd with as much composure as she could muster, before a shocked expression appeared on her face. That expression melted into disbelief and then utter delight. She could not believe it, but there was Gloria standing several yards away, her hands placed gracefully on her hips.

"Nadine Clayton," she called, her voice vibrant with joy and memories.

"Gloria?" Nadine questioned. "My God, it is you!"

The two old friends rushed to embrace one another, tears streaming down both sets of cheeks as they hugged and cried. Who would have guessed that after all these years they would be reunited on the island of Eros?

A strong male voice boomed nearby, hailing their reunion. "So this is the well-spoken-of Nadine Clayton."

"Yes. Yes, it is." Gloria stood back, holding her friend at arm's length. "Doesn't she look just wonderful?" She looked at the man, then smiled at his nod of approval.

"Never mind all that, what are you doing here?" Nadine still could not believe she was speaking to her old friend.

"Remember in my last letter I told you I was going to be traveling to India? Well, I met Larry there," she linked arms with her attractive companion, "and since then we've been together. We've traveled to Cape Verde together, and now we're here."

Nadine shook her head, exasperated. "But how did you end up *here* on Eros?"

"We had always planned to come to Barbados," Gloria explained, "but about three weeks ago, when we were back in the States, I tried to contact you. So I called your grandmother. And you can imagine how surprised I was to hear you were already in Barbados, working with the World Treasures Institute. I knew during your last letter you had spoken of the possibility of traveling to the Caribbean, but I had no idea it would happen so quickly." She smiled at her college friend. "So anyway, after talking to Auntie Rose, I made up my mind to contact the institute when we got here. Someone there told me you were working on Eros with this sale, and now here we are!"

The two women hugged again and let out a couple more exclamations of "Girlfriend, I can't believe it," while Larry stood by shaking his head.

"Nadine, is everything okay?" Ulysses asked as he approached them through a curious crowd.

"Ulysses, you won't believe this, but I know this woman. This is Gloria." Nadine looked up at him expectantly, then realized she had never told him about Gloria. "Oh my goodness. I'm so excited I forgot I never told you about her." Nadine wrapped her arm around her friend's shoulder as she continued, "This is the best girlfriend I've ever had, Gloria Turner. Gloria, this is Ulysses Deane, the person who is putting on this sale and the owner of Sovereign."

Ulysses acted sufficiently surprised as he reached out to shake Gloria's hand, and then Larry's.

Gloria looked from Nadine to Ulysses. "Queen, I think we've got a lot of catching up to do." She smiled with a special twinkle in her eyes.

Nadine's hesitant chuckle revealed everything, "Yes, we do. We most certainly do." She looked at Ulysses. "But first I need to help Ulysses close down the sale, then once the party begins we will find us a corner and talk," Nadine assured her.

Ulysses could tell Nadine wanted to remain with her friend but was reluctant to leave her work. "It seems to me just about everything has been sold," Ulysses told her. "And if anybody else wants to buy something I can take care of it. You have done more than you should have already. So go ahead. I will take over from here."

"Are you sure?" Nadine looked at Ulysses with adoration.

"Of course I am," Ulysses encouraged her.

"Honey, you don't mind if Nadine and I get together for some girl talk, do you?" With her mild Southern voice, Gloria sidled up to Larry.

"If I did, would it really matter?" His brown eyes glistened as he teased her.

From their exchange Nadine could see that Larry knew Gloria well. She always acted submissive when it suited her, but if there was something she wanted to do, no man or anyone else would be able to change her mind.

Nadine watched as Gloria smoothed Larry's well-trimmed gray beard. "Now darlin', you know it would." She batted a set of curly eyelashes. "But I'm sure you'll be okay. Ulysses will show you around, won't you, Ulysses? Perhaps you can buy me a little something, honey, to remember this trip by." She gave him a peck on the mouth before she and Nadine linked arms and walked away. They had already begun a revealing conversation.

". . . so Larry has just been wonderful for me. Sometimes our friends tease us because of the age difference, but it really doesn't matter. I've never been happier in all my life, and we're thinking about making it permanent." Gloria wriggled the empty ring finger on her left hand. "Now enough about me. I've got to hear all about you. Girl, do you know how much you've changed?" Gloria leaned back and looked Nadine directly in the eye. "You look absolutely wonderful. And for some reason I think Ulysses has a lot to do with it." She paused. "So tell me all about it." She crossed her legs and took a bite of one of the pastries on her plate.

Gloria's plate was empty and so was her glass when Nadine finished updating her on the current events in her life. She had decided to leave out the part about the legend and Lenora. She did not know how to begin explaining it, the vision, and the cliff dwellers. Nadine decided not to broach the risky subject with her old friend.

"So the rosebud has become a full-fledged rose, hmmm?" Gloria kidded her. "Well, honey, from the way he was looking at you I knew if you hadn't, it wouldn't be long before you did," she laughed. "And I believe this was meant to be." She squeezed Nadine's hand. "You know, traveling all around the world I have seen some strange things. In the States we've got this mentality of, if you can't prove it scientifically, it doesn't exist. But after going to Cape Verde and India, I'm no longer sure if that's the approach to take. There are some things that cannot be explained with the mind alone."

Nadine's hand went up and touched the cliff dwellers' necklace. "I believe you're right," she replied earnestly as the band began to play.

"What in the world are they trying to play?" Gloria turned around and looked at the quartet.

"I guess it's an old island tune," Nadine informed her.

"Girl, please," Gloria sighed as they got up. "I'm ready for some Luther or Anita Baker after all this traveling."

Nadine laughed as she led Gloria toward the courtyard. "I'll put in your request, but I don't think you're going to be too lucky tonight."

All the lamps in the courtyard were lit. Soon they would be needed. The sky was already darkening in the east. Profusions of orchids crowded an assortment of flower boxes, adding color and fragrance to the evening. But by far the colorful terra-cotta well was the focal point of everyone's admiration.

Nadine and Gloria saw Larry standing near the well. "There's Larry," Gloria announced. "He looks rather lonely," she pouted. "I should join him."

"You go right ahead," Nadine told her. "I'm going to check with Ulysses and make sure everything went okay."

"Alright. You know, you are working hard for this man, aren't you, queen?" Gloria squeezed Nadine's arm before she walked away.

Nadine found that Ulysses had taken care of everything. The hall had been closed off. The tables in the courtyard had been stocked with fresh appetizers, and the crowd appeared to be enjoying the music and the food as they milled around and talked. The band was beginning to play another tune when an impatient Ulysses appeared at Nadine's side.

"These people do not know how to enjoy themselves." He looked around at the subdued crowd. "They are too tame. They do not know how to let the music enter into their hearts. You understand what I mean?" His dark eyes filled with consternation. "Really take them over." He paused a second before saying, "Come on. We will show them how it should be done." Ulysses grabbed Nadine by the hand and pulled her into the middle of the courtyard. He signaled for the band to strike up a more lively tune.

"Tell them to play something of Bob Marley's," Nadine whispered.

Ulysses agreed and followed her request. As the

musicians struck their first chords Ulysses began to step to the beat. Nadine followed suit, then motioned to Gloria and Larry to join them.

"What are we about to do?" Gloria asked under her breath, looking at the crowd around them.

"We're going to do a kind of island electric slide, that's what," Nadine informed her.

"You mean to tell me we've got all these island people here, and we're going to lead the dance?" she replied.

"You've got that right. And since you can't have Luther, I'm sure Bob Marley is the next best thing. Now just follow Ulysses."

The steps, dips, and slides were easy enough for the foursome. But Ulysses outshined them all, showing that he was born to it, and had mastered the spirit of the dance as well as the technique. Soon Nadine, Gloria, and Larry were dancing with abandon which encouraged others to join them. Before they knew it the entire courtyard was filled with exuberant dancers, including Dr. Steward, Claudia, and Pamela.

When the spirited tune was over Nadine excused herself. "I'm going to check on Catherine and make sure she's doing okay," she told her friends. "Perhaps I'll drop in to see Madame Deane as well."

Nadine was enjoying the feeling of being the lady of the house. She knew it was just for that night, but she intended to enjoy every moment of it. Tomorrow would come soon enough. For once, she was a woman in love who was being loved in return. Nothing could put a damper on that.

She was headed for the kitchen when a woman stopped her.

"Someone is in the foyer asking for you. He said he is looking for the woman involved with the sale."

"Thank you," Nadine replied, wondering who could possibly be looking for her. Or perhaps it was Madame Deane that they sought.

She entered the foyer where a poorly dressed man was waiting near the door. He evaded her eyes as she approached him.

"Hello. I believe you may be looking for me."

The man gave no reply. He simply handed her a crumpled piece of paper he had clutched in his hand.

"What is this?" she asked, looking up. But the man had turned to leave.

Nadine felt a chill. The beauty of the night before, and the busy sale, had made her forget about Basil. But the wrinkled wad of paper created a web of anxiety around her. With shaking fingers Nadine unfolded it. As she read the note her deepest fears began to take shape. It read: This is a reminder of our private conversation yesterday. No further word will be sent to you. I am not a patient man. Basil.

Nadine stared transfixed as she read the simple but clever message over and over again. Basil had made sure if Ulysses got hold of the message he would think it was intended for him—a grim reminder of their confrontation yesterday. But Nadine was certain the note was intended for her.

In a matter of moments, the highest heights of happiness Nadine had ever experienced were plunged into the depths of fear and apprehension. She glanced back in the direction of the music and the happy voices coming from the courtyard. She thought of Ulysses and Gloria, but she could not bring herself to destroy their contentment as well. And Basil had threatened that if she told Ulysses, he would not lose half of Sovereign, he would lose all of it.

There was nothing her friends could do. This was something she had to handle alone.

Stealthily, Nadine appeared in the front of Sovereign. She checked to make sure no one had seen her. When she felt confident she had not been discovered, she quickly headed in the direction of Sharpe Hall. Maybe she could return before they realized she was missing.

Chapter 26

Despite all her caution Nadine's departure had not gone undetected. Painted lips turned into a knowing smirk as the observer watched her hurried exodus on the path to the Sharpe estate. Cassandra had seen Basil's servant, Kevin, trying to read a note by the full moonlight, and then saw his disappointment in not being able to accomplish his clandestine task. Overcome by curiosity, she waited to see what would happen next, and had not been disappointed. Cassandra saw Kevin leave first, followed momentarily by the American.

Her beautiful eyes sparkled as she looked toward the group of workers and servants who had launched their own party outside Sovereign's courtyard wall, and she swayed her hips even more as she advanced. So that is what Ulysses put me down for, Cassandra thought contemptuously. A woman who would prefer a man like Basil to Ulysses.

Cassandra was already upset. Rodney had refused to see her tonight, claiming he had something very important to do. Something that would guarantee his financial independence. He had reminded her that he was not Henry Sharpe's firstborn son, and that meant Sharpe Hall actually belonged to Basil. He and Melanie were only entitled to certain percentages of the profits yielded from the sugarcane crop.

Cassandra looked at the throngs of people inside the courtyard walls. It was not right that Rodney had the money and birthright to mingle with people of stature, and she had to share the music and food with the peasants.

She watched as appetizers were passed through the gate to the workers. She knew it made little difference to Ulysses if they ate inside the courtyard or out, but the poor stiffs were so well-trained to their class that they refused to dine with what they considered to be their betters.

Cassandra picked up a glass of rum and dashed it down her throat, eyeing the crowd within the courtyard resentfully. "I am just as good as they are," she hissed.

Several of the workers looked at her, but none dared to approach her. Cassandra's attitude had become extremely haughty.

She listened as two more songs were played, and the party-goers became more lively at the music's command. By the time a third arrangement was in full swing Cassandra observed Ulysses excusing himself and entering the house. Minutes later he emerged back in the courtyard. This time his expression was serious, and he began to question some of the guests. Cassandra assumed he was looking for the American.

Tossing her hair arrogantly, she knew her moment of revenge had arrived. With a saucy strut she walked through the gate onto the terra-cotta floor. Cassandra cornered Ulysses in the back.

"Looking for someone?" Her voice came across provocatively.

Ulysses was surprised to see her. He had not seen or spoken to her since their dispute near the rum still. His eyes became hooded. "Maybe."

"Oh well, if that is the case, there is no need to tell you what I have seen." She looked him up and down triumphantly, and acted if she was about to leave.

"Look here, Cassandra." Ulysses grabbed her forearm, squeezing it hard.

She looked down at the iron grip he had on her arm, then looked up slowly. Her flashing ebony eyes confronted his. "Are you taking lessons from Basil these days?"

Immediately Ulysses loosened his grip. "No, I am not." Then his voice became smooth and threatening. "And I don't have time to play any games with you either, Cassandra. Do you have something to say, or are you just trying to show me how angry you are for my not getting back into your bed?"

Incensed by his arrogance and the truth, Cassandra could bait him no longer. "Yes, I am angry with you. Angry that you would choose that American slut, who would leave you here tonight and go to Basil. How does it feel now, Ulysses?" She stepped in close enough to feel his heavy breathing. "To be turned down for someone inferior to you." Her laugh was deep and satisfied.

Ulysses grabbed Cassandra's shoulders. "You are lying!"

"You wish I were, don't you? Well, I am not." She shook her hair out of her eyes. "I saw Basil's man bring a note right to your door. Minutes after that, your little American practically fell over herself, she was getting over to Sharpe Hall so fast." Cassandra laughed again.

Ulysses pushed her away. He could tell she was telling the truth, and the pain of it cut into him. With long, quick strides and Cassandra's shouts accosting his ears, Ulysses crossed the crowded courtyard to enter the house. He could not bear her jeering face any longer.

Merry voices rang out as the music's crescendos drowned out Cassandra's cries. Goat heaven reigned with the guests as Ulysses felt his world tumble down around him. Nadine had lied. She did have some kind of secret alliance with Basil or she would not have gone to him.

Basil took another look at the gold watch on his arm. The minutes seemed to drag as he waited for Kevin to return. His palms felt sweaty and he could feel his hands tremble before he rubbed them together with anticipation.

Everything had been set up. When Nadine arrived, a servant would tell her she was expected down in the neighborhood. Basil had made sure the small shack where he had cornered Salinah would be empty. Actually, it was not used that often anymore. Basil thought about how he had permanently disfigured Salinah's face with his whip, making her bitter and her customers few. Now most of the prostitution that took place on the island was on a street near the main wharf, and Basil hardly ever went there. He preferred the young daughters of the workers whose innocence and fear made him feel that much more powerful.

Nervous, Basil wondered if Nadine would have

the nerve to brave the path to the neighborhood alone. He tried to second-guess her and decided that if she was brave enough to meet him at Sharpe Hall, she would also risk going to the neighborhood at night.

He looked down the path that, lit by a full moon, headed toward the small section of houses. The natural light was so bright he could almost see the hovels from where he stood outside of Sharpe Hall's entrance. Basil's lips felt dry, so he licked them with anticipation as he thought about what he was about to do. Yes, Nadine would come, because she cared so much for that near-African bastard, Ulysses. He had seen it in her eyes yesterday, and Catherine had told their cook that Nadine worked so hard because of her feelings for Ulysses. His reddened eyes radiated jealousy and hate.

At first Basil had planned to only rough her up a bit, and take what Ulysses was being given. But through the years he had become an expert with his whip. He knew what kind of lash would leave a permanent scar or just raise the skin a bit. After Ulysses attacked him yesterday, he had decided to leave a more lasting impression.

Basil turned as he heard hurried footsteps behind him. He saw Kevin emerge from a group of evergreen trees. Breathing heavily, his servant explained how he had delivered the note and hurried back because the young woman was not far behind. Kevin had taken a shortcut through the woods in order to arrive at Sharpe Hall in enough time before Nadine arrived.

Basil nodded. "You have done well, Kevin. Now go to the kitchen and tell Mary to fix you an extra plate tonight, along with a bottle of rum. You have earned it.''

A distant breeze carried the faint notes of music being played at Sovereign. Basil had counted on his brother and sister attending the social to keep them from nosing around the servants until his plan was carried out. Melanie had always protected Ulysses and Sovereign, and Rodney—Basil turned up his nose with disgust—was nothing but her pawn.

Basil reached back to make sure his object of perverted pleasure was secure within his pocket. Satisfied, he hastened toward the neighborhood, making sure he stayed clear of the well-lit path.

A whirlwind of anger, hurt, and shock played havoc with Ulysses as he slung open the library door. Pacing furiously, he condemned himself for believing Nadine, and wondered what kind of hold Basil had on her. Ulysses felt the ultimate betrayal because he had allowed himself to fall in love with her, and now realized she held a force far different from love as her motivation. Which one was it? Money or power?

Reluctantly, his mind conjured up images of their lovemaking the night before, and he wondered what kind of woman would give up her virginity to one man, and then run into the arms of his enemy. Maybe if he had told her he wanted her for his wife, she would have abandoned her alliance with Basil. But he was afraid to speak of such a commitment so quickly. Now he was glad he had not. This woman was the worst kind of chameleon, changing to fit whatever situation served her best.

Ulysses cried out in anguish, and in his pain he

struck out, knocking a porcelain statuette to the floor. He was so tormented he did not hear the library door open and Madame Deane wheel herself inside. When she spoke her voice was frail from being heavily sedated.

"My God, Ulysses, what has happened?"

Startled by the sound of her voice, and embarrassed to be seen so distraught, Ulysses turned his tortured face away from his aunt. "There is nothing you can do, Aunt Helen."

"But how do you know? Maybe I can help—" Her weak and distorted voice cut off abruptly, changing to a strong, raspy tone. "There is nothing I can do, but I believe she can."

Despite himself Ulysses turned to look at her. Her spine was ramrod-straight against the back of the wheelchair, her knuckles gone white, revealing how tightly she squeezed the arms of the apparatus. Her eyes held a conviction Ulysses had not seen in years.

"What do you mean there is something she can do?" Fearing his aunt had completely lost all ability to reason in the midst of everything else that was upon him.

"The seer. Who else would I mean?" she threw back at him sarcastically, her eyes extremely lucid. "It is with her help that I speak to you so clearly now."

Dumbfounded by what he was hearing, Ulysses looked up at the ceiling. "Oh my God, Aunt Helen."

"You must believe me. A woman by the name of Verda has been coming to me since my accident. First she was just in my dreams. Then she started appearing in visions and I thought I was crossing over into insanity. But now I know I'm not.''

Overwhelmed by the onslaught of events, Ulysses doubled over with uncontrollable laughter. He did not want to hurt his aunt, but like a spider's thread, laughter was Ulysses' thin line to mental safety.

The metal click of the library door being locked broke his hysteria, and he looked up, exhausted.

"Do you believe me now, Ulysses?"

He was astounded by what he saw. Ulysses' mouth went dry as his aunt appeared to be supported by an invisible force as she stood in front of the wheelchair.

"Could I do this?"

There were no words that would come to allow Ulysses to reply. He watched his aunt descend gracefully into her chair.

"If it had not been for Verda, I would have died from the fall into the well at Sharpe Hall. Verda came to my aid because something I had come across needed protecting. If my life had never been threatened, there would not have been a need for her to come back.'' She eyed him triumphantly. "She would talk to my spirit whenever it felt weak and wanted to leave my body for a more satisfying place. But my body and mind were still needed here. So listen carefully, Ulysses, for this is what I must tell you now.

"Your father and I believed there was a connection between our family and the cliff dwellers. He had been receptive to the idea but secretive about it. Whereas I was driven to know the truth although I feared it. Because, as you know, to most of the islanders the cliff dwellers are almost seen as savages living in the mountains.

"But your father, Peter, had always nurtured a
burning passion to know more about, and to embrace, foreign cultures; hence his love for your
mother, and his interest in the cliff dwellers. This
passion was his destiny, simply another layer in the
events leading up to tonight. He is the one who
transcribed the Legend of Lenora into English that
Nadine has in her possession now. He believed,
like the cliff dwellers, that the woman to come after
Lenora would come from a land rich in western
culture. West is the direction of the sunken Lemuria. So once again the present is a reflection of
the past." She paused and swallowed before continuing. "She would come from a land just beyond
the Atlantic Ocean. The United States of America.

"I found the papyri and the translation of the
legend years after your father and mother died.
Later I discovered the lost page that your father had
hidden for safekeeping. Like your father, I understood the Legend of Lenora and the part you, Ulysses, as well as the Five Pieces of Gaia would play
in it. And like him, I was afraid for anyone else to
know. So I hid it before the accident. And afterwards I could not remember where."

Ulysses could not totally understand what she
was telling him, and he questioned his own ability
to reason when he began to entertain the possibility
that the story she told was true. But he had seen
his Aunt Helen stand, something that was impossible for her to do alone. There was no way for him
to deny that forces he had heard of from the cliff
dwellers and others who believed in the spiritual
realm were at work.

The incomplete passage in the family journal
surfaced in his mind. He acknowledged that his fa-

ther's death was preceded by a period where he was inactive in his journal-writing. But was he on the verge of revealing what he had discovered from the Legend of Lenora? Was that the answer to the unfinished message that had haunted him for so many years?

"Henry Sharpe knew of my search for the truths." Aunt Helen's voice broke into his thoughts. "He gave the things I told him no credence, and reduced it all down to the ravings of unstable females, since his wife, Evelyn, also spoke of the Legend of Lenora when she was drunk.

"Once while throwing his adulterous affairs in his wife's face, Henry told her she and I would probably like one another, since both our minds conjured up the same kind of fantasies. That day I told Henry I had found the lost page of the translations and I thought it referred to you and a manuscript that was hidden between some stone slabs. I told him it was called the Five Pieces of Gaia, a part of the Sovereign collection.

"Unknown to Henry, this was very important to Evelyn. You see, she was not as inept as he thought. Alcoholism had taken over her life and she knew there was no hope for her. But that did not stop her from wishing for a better life for her children, especially her daughter, Melanie. She felt she had relinquished her power and her life to Henry, but she wanted to make sure Melanie did not suffer the same fate. Even if it meant taking power from others.

"It was Evelyn who had delivered the message with Sharpe Hall's seal to me that day. And it was Evelyn who pushed me into the well, leaving me for dead out of jealousy, as well as protecting the future of her child. Only I knew where the lost page of the translation was hidden, but my memory and perceptions had been impaired as a result of the accident. Verda hoped that I would find it in time."

Aunt Helen took a yellowed sheet of paper from the folds of her chiton, and handed it to Ulysses. He looked at his father's handwriting.

"It starts with an incomplete sentence," Aunt Helen told him. "The original papyri was written for Nadine by Lenora thousands and thousands of years ago. A key written for the woman with whom her life purpose was connected, and now, the answer to the exact day and time when the prophecy will be fulfilled." She paused to let her words sink in. "The sentence began like this: 'You will be united with a man—'"

Ulysses took over and began to read. ". . . whose name is exalted on paper and in song, a cunning hero and warrior whose strength has mastered a mighty bow. His blood and his temperament will be dark, split in half, because he was born of two civilizations old." Ulysses looked up, his dark eyes full of recognition tinged with skepticism.

"Yes," Aunt Helen said, "it is referring to you, Ulysses."

He began to read again. "In the year when Lenora's reflection returns, the dark shall plant its seeds when the full moon rises on the second night when the Children of Mu sing. The dark will be enticed by the light, seduced by the Five Pieces of Gaia, and named similar to a melody." He stopped. "What does it mean?"

"It means this is the night, Ulysses, they had all envisioned. Lenora's reflection, Nadine, has returned. There is a full moon, and the second night of the cliff dwellers' spiritual ceremony has begun. The prophecy must be fulfilled before midnight," Aunt Helen declared. "The dark will plant his seed again during a ceremony called the Rite of Commencement. During that ceremony the manuscript inside the Five Pieces of Gaia will be used. You have an important part to play, and so does the young woman, Nadine." Her eyes revealed that she knew what had happened between them during the wee morning hours. With talon-like hands Aunt Helen grabbed his forearms. "Now go. Take the carved bronze chest with you. Find Nadine. She will be in need of you."

Ulysses stared into the bottomless gaze of the tiny, but strangely powerful woman he had known all of his life. The eyes were familiar, but at the same time foreign. She had talked of ancient things of which he had no knowledge, and only now did she reveal her knowledge of the manuscript inside the stones. There was no way for Ulysses to totally understand and embrace all the things she had said, but there was one thing he was certain of. Something or someone supernatural was aiding Aunt Helen now. And no matter how Nadine had betrayed him, he loved her, and he could not let her be harmed. But, Ulysses vowed to himself, once this night was over, and she was safe, he would have nothing more to do with her.

Chapter 27

Nadine's scream rang out piercingly in the moonlit night. It seemed to go on for an eternity before she drifted away into the peaceful oblivion of a dead faint. In her state of unconsciousness she dreamed she was being carried away upon strong, gentle arms, and the voices about her spoke an unfamiliar language, espousing rhythmic, guttural tones. Whenever she attempted to awaken, a pungent but pleasant scent would assail her, tenderly pushing her back down in her cushioned but altered mental state.

They traveled for quite a distance, climbing higher as they went, until they reached an area nestled protectively among several mountain cliffs. There she was taken into an enclosed area and laid upon a soft pile of animal skins.

Now those who had carried her to this strange place were replaced by others, who stripped her naked and bathed her in a lukewarm liquid kept tepid by a smoldering fire. Their ministrations made her think of her childhood. Their gentle, caring hands reminded her of Grandma Rose; she was always there when she needed her, after a fall or brutal words.

The cool trailing of fingers down her arms and legs chilled her, but this soon halted, and shortly afterwards she was covered under a pleasant cloth and allowed to continue her sleep.

Ulysses pushed his way through the crowd of onlookers. After realizing who he was, the workers began to step aside, making a small path for him. His heart pounded as he approached the center of the terrified and curious group. Prayers that he had not said since he was a child formed on his lips as he broke through to the center. Was he too late? Had Basil had his way with her, and then been so brutal and cruel that he left her here at the edge of the woods for dead? A sinking feeling of remembrance surfaced within him.

Ulysses' handsome features twisted into a startled grimace as he looked down, not on the face that he feared, but into Basil's lifeless eyes. The last shock-filled moments of his existence were held for posterity by the beginnings of unkind rigor mortis. A steady stream of blood trickled from his open, but now-pale lips, the only exterior clue to his demise.

Carefully, Ulysses turned Basil's stiffening frame over with a thud. There, planted deep within his back, was a huge, decorative dagger, one that Ulysses recognized instantly.

A large murmur of surprise and speculation began to mount amongst the bystanders while questions poured out of Ulysses like an untapped fountain. "Did anyone see what happened here? Have you seen the American?" His troubled eyes searched the crowd. But it appeared no one really knew what had happened. They had all heard a

terrified scream, and when they thought they had
reached the point of its origin, they saw Master
Sharpe lying as Ulysses had found him when he
arrived. None of them had seen the American.

Another shriek jolted the night, followed by an
uncanny silence. Once again the circle of onlookers
parted, as Salinah, standing proudly with blood-
stained hands, strode forth. Her beautiful eyes
shone brilliantly with the light of triumph. She
stood before Ulysses, her family, and friends.

"It is done." She slowly scanned the crowd.
"No longer will he terrorize you and your daughters because of his hate for me. I have borne the
physical scars of his obsession upon my face, but
you have suffered the heartache of having to submit
to his will. With his family's gift I have killed him.
Now there will be no more pain for you, for me,
or for him."

Spitting on Basil's motionless back, Salinah
turned to walk away. Glancing back over her shoulder, her eyes focused on Ulysses. "The cliff dwellers have taken the American."

Melanie placed the wooden case before the majestic figure sitting several feet away. She tried to
keep her hands from trembling under his watchful
gaze, but it was difficult. She and Rodney had entered the cliff dwellers' settlement under curious
and speculative looks. Initially, they were stopped
by a very foreboding male, who refused to allow
them to pass until she brought forth the wooden
case carved with the cliff dwellers' symbol. Once
he saw it, silently, almost with reverence, the man
had stood aside, eyes remaining downcast as they
were allowed to pass. Yet Melanie could feel the

inhabitants' distrust, and she shivered beneath her black cloak even though the evening breeze was quite warm.

She squared her shoulders as she progressed through the group, determined not to show her fear. Rodney on the other hand was fear personified. His eyes bulged as his mind conjured up all the stories he had heard throughout his life about these strange people.

It was very different from walking along the wharf and seeing them silently offering their goods to the eager tourists who admired their clothing and jewelry. It was as if he had been transported to a different place and time. Even the cliff dwellers themselves looked quite different. Now, most of them wore small painted symbols on their cheeks. The men displayed larger, more intricate patterns on their broad backs. Their headbands and clothing were the most extravagant he had ever seen, and he knew they had all dawned their ceremonial dress in anticipation of the ritual to come.

Rodney stuck close to his sister's side, telling himself it was for her protection, but knowing it was the other way around. If Melanie was afraid, she was not showing it, Rodney thought as he looked at her. Maybe it was because she was the one with the wooden case that commanded respect from everyone.

A small cliff dweller volunteered to escort them, but once again they were halted, this time outside the flap of one of the largest cliff dwellings in sight. Melanie and Rodney stood there in silence, waiting for permission from inside. Several moments later they were allowed to enter.

Both Sharpes were surprised at the color and

splendor inside the unconventional dwelling. The space was filled with shiny, rich earth tones enhanced by burning torches implanted in the walls. The same material that the cliff dwellers used to make their jewelry was the source of the natural beauty that surrounded them. Pieces of various sizes had been used to make all kinds of furniture and tools, ranging from cups to tables.

Melanie marveled at the marble-like tiles that covered the floor. The large blocks had been matched to perfection, rivaling any that she had seen in the finest homes on Barbados or Eros. The unorthodox opulence of the place humbled Melanie. She had never thought of the cliff dwellers as a people with this kind of skill and an eye for such beauty. Great talent was needed to create this kind of environment.

Several male and female cliff dwellers were kneeling silently on fawn skins along the walls of the room. Two others sat in close proximity to the head cliff dweller, a silent younger male and a female whose age was not discernible.

As Melanie and Rodney stopped where they were instructed to, and imitated the postures of those around them, they felt compelled to examine the cliff dwellers who were obviously in power.

Throughout Melanie's life she had seen cliff dwellers on Eros, but never had she laid eyes on either of the three who sat before her. As a matter of fact, she was surprised at the number of cliff dwellers she saw outside. There had been far more than she had ever expected. Again she feared she may have underestimated this strange but intriguing race.

As they knelt in forced silence, Melanie studied

the intricate carvings on the jewelry the head cliff dwellers wore. The headbands of the two males featured the same beautiful stones and a sprinkling of bright gems, while five gold coins carved with the cliff dwellers' symbol dominated the band of the eldest male.

Melanie gasped, and Rodney turned, following her line of vision. To his amazement it stopped on the female's necklace. It was an elaborate decoration with sprays of colorful gems surrounding a much larger crystalline stone. Rodney knew from Melanie's face that her thoughts mirrored his own. The copious stone was a magnificent diamond, and had to be worth a fortune.

With a stunned look still on his face, Rodney's eyes rose to the ebony eyes above the wondrous necklace. But he quickly tore away from her gaze, for it felt as if she were boring into his soul, and that she knew far more about him than he even knew about himself.

Melanie pushed the wooden box toward the head cliff dweller. The scraping sound broke the unnatural silence and drew the attention of the crowd who had gathered away from the two strangers. Low mumbles could be heard throughout the room as the second-ranked male advanced to retrieve the object, then carried it to his superior.

Carefully, the eldest cliff dweller opened the box; his face remained an unreadable mask as he examined the contents. A smooth sidelong look was bestowed on the objects by the regal female, whose face also remained a silent picture.

Finally, the head cliff dweller turned and spoke to his two companions, and without hesitation their straightforward answers were given in hushed tones. Almost instantly Melanie felt at a distinct disadvantage. It infuriated her because she did not speak their language, and could not understand their exchange. She knew the cliff dwellers were well versed in English, and their conversation in their native tongue was purposefully excluding her and Rodney.

As Melanie watched them she began to grow impatient. There were so many things she wanted to know. She had been reluctant to turn the wooden case over to the cliff dwellers without any reassurances. But there was one thing she was sure of, and that was that the cliff dwellers knew the Rite of Commencement could not be performed without the male spoken of in the prophecy, and she had spent much time and energy covering all the bases to ensure Rodney would be accepted as the man referred to in the Legend of Lenora.

For years, preparation for this eventful night had dominated her life, and she had no intention of failing now. Yes, recently there had been complications. Twice her attempt to steal the entire Gaia Series failed, and fate seemed against her. After successfully stealing the onyx and the jade slabs, in her haste she managed to lose the onyx stone. It was then that Melanie devised the plan of forging the missing pieces of the series.

The note to the craftsman on Barbados had advised him to use the basic dimensions of the jade slab when sculpturing the other four. He was known to be one of the best in his field, and the materials he used to make the counterfeit pieces were the best available. Melanie was glad the papyrus her mother had given her displayed detailed drawings of the entire Gaia set: an onyx unicorn, a jade siren, a rose quartz moon goddess, a tiger's-eye scarab, and a citrine sun god. The accompanying paperwork described the manuscript.

Melanie remembered the cliff dweller who used to work for her mother. The first time she ever saw her was down at the wharf selling jewelry with several others, and it had been written all over her homely features how taken she was with the fine clothing Melanie and her mother wore.

Despite Henry's cruelty toward his family behind Sharpe Hall's walls, outside of the house he was the epitome of the loving husband, especially when her mother was younger. He appeared to cater to his wife's every whim, showering her with the finest of jewelry and clothing, only to remind her behind closed doors that the jewels belonged to the estate and not to her.

Melanie had seen the woman for the first time during a period when there was more socializing between the islanders and their strange neighbors. Not to the extent that she had been told took place in the distant past, but more so than the present. Each time, down at the wharf, the young female cliff dweller would seek her mother out under the pretense of selling the stone jewelry she carried, but in actuality she wanted to be near Evelyn's finery and the perfumed scents that she always wore.

Once, Melanie remembered, after shopping, her mother had several boxes to carry back to Sharpe Hall, and she told the young woman if she would assist her she would pay her well. That was the beginning of their relationship.

After that, Kohela would appear at Sharpe Hall's kitchen door from time to time, and she would stand there silently aggravating the other servants.

She would not go away no matter what they threatened, not until her mother appeared and gave her some personal chores to do. After a year or so, Kohela had become a regular at Sharpe Hall, and it was through this woman that her mother gained inside knowledge of the cliff dwellers and their beliefs. It was from Kohela that Evelyn learned of the Legend of Lenora.

Evelyn was already fascinated by many of the strange tales, but it was the Legend of Lenora that captivated her the most. It was the story of how the cliff dwellers believed the coming of one woman would change the bad times that had descended on their people. A people who were one with Gaia, Mother Earth.

It was an ancient belief that the prophesied woman, with eyes of brownish-jade, the light or bright one, would herald the time when the cliff dwellers would no longer be confined to living in the caves and mountain cliffs. It would allow them access to and eventually gain dominion over the entire island, the same as their forebears.

The prophecy claimed this could only come to be true if a virgin participated in the Rite of Commencement. This was to be carried out by the dark one, the proprietor of the Five Pieces of Gaia. Then and only then could "the consumption of the dark by the fiery light" take place.

With time Kohela became very comfortable being a part of Sharpe Hall, and wished she could become more of an intricate part of their society and share their style of living, something all cliff dwellers had been warned against. She knew her people's legends fascinated Evelyn, and she sought to win her favor even more by telling of the jewels that would be unveiled during the ritual. Jewels that were spoken of in hushed tones among Kohela's people who were the last of their kind. The jewels and the papyrus were the only articles the cliff dwellers possessed from the sunken continent of Mu.

Once Evelyn began to drink, she became obsessed with the thought of the jewels. She pressed Kohela to bring the part of the papyrus which described the ceremony and the Five Pieces of Gaia, promising her that she would be allowed to return it. Kohela finally consented, but her naivete brought nothing but tragedy to herself and her people.

Having committed the forbidden, removing a sacred papyrus, Kohela's conscience plagued her tremendously. She asked Evelyn to give the papyrus back to her so she could return it to its sacred place. Evelyn refused and Kohela committed suicide.

Kohela's death caused a bigger rift between the islanders and the cliff dwellers. They knew her demise was connected with the islanders, and from that day forth no communication was allowed between them. Ulysses was the exception, and the islanders believed it was because he had established a rapport with them as a child.

Melanie touched the papers tucked inside her skirt pocket. Her mother's scribbled handwriting had told her everything. Especially about the jewels that would buy her independence. It was these papers that she gave to her on her deathbed, and made Melanie promise to put them to good use. Evelyn told her she had attempted murder to keep Helen Deane from spoiling Melanie's future. Helen was the only person alive who believed Ulysses was the

man referred to in the legend, and with her out of
the way no one would be the wiser when Rodney
was presented in his place. Well, Madame Deane
did not die, but her sanity did, Melanie thought.

She had done everything she could to carry out
what her mother had begun. Actually, it had become her obsession. Her light at the end of the
tunnel when she thought of Basil's cruel nature,
and Rodney's weak one. Melanie knew how her
younger brother felt about her. Their first sexual
encounter was an accident, but soon after that their
mother died, and Melanie's obsessed plan began to
take shape. She wanted Rodney to be like putty in
her hands. She needed that kind of power over him.
She had borne his intimate fumblings willingly, but
she had determined no man would ever truly possess her. They were all animals, just like her father,
including Ulysses. Had she convinced him to marry
her, theirs would have been a loveless marriage.
Her real purpose was to gain access to the manuscript, the Five Pieces of Gaia, and eventually the
jewels. Just one of them would give her enough
wealth to live as she pleased. A life independent of
men.

Melanie's becoming features took on a strange
twist as she thought of Salinah and the talk she had
with her earlier that day. She had warned Salinah
that Basil would come to their settlement tonight
for her fourteen-year-old daughter. Melanie had
been quite convincing in her display of concern,
declaring that she wished there was some way he
could be stopped. It was then that she offered the
woman the dagger she had bought at the sale, telling her it had belonged to Basil. Melanie offered it
to Salinah as a token of her goodwill. She said it

was valuable and could be sold for a comely price.

Melanie knew the dagger had been used as she had planned. She could not bring herself to kill her own brother, but she could not allow him to destroy her plans by harming Nadine Clayton, with her brownish-jade eyes, and the necklace presented to her by the cliff dwellers at the rum still. She had known that Basil would take action against the American today. It was the only day he could. She was scheduled to leave the island early tomorrow morning.

Melanie cut dark, disdainful eyes toward Rodney as he sat beside her. He had vomited behind the group of trees as he watched Salinah plunge the dagger into his brother's back, several feet away. Everything happened so quickly that Rodney had frozen with fear. But Melanie had watched with expressionless features, and chastised him for his weakness, saying he should be glad. Now he would be the owner of Sharpe Hall.

A strangely accented voice rang out in the cavern, calling Melanie back.

"So you would have us to believe that this is the dark one that is spoken of in the legend?" the second-ranked cliff dweller asked in English.

"Yes, he is," Melanie responded with conviction. "As you can see he is the proprietor of the Five Pieces of Gaia as is required by the prophecy."

"Yes, it is required, but from what my eyes can see you are the proprietress of the ancient stones, and he is simply here to do your bidding."

Three sets of perceptive eyes assessed Rodney who was now visibly trembling from the cliff dweller's candid words.

"It is not true," Melanie answered.

"Then if it is not," the female interjected, "let him speak for himself."

Glancing into his sister's piercing eyes, and thinking of Basil's untimely death, Rodney found his voice, albeit a shaky one. "I—I am the dark one spoken of in the legend."

"This man is lying." A loud, clear voice interrupted the gathering. Ulysses walked toward them.

Chapter 28

 Rising out of the well of unconsciousness, Nadine's eyes fluttered open. They focused on a spherical object with shiny points suspended from a ceiling.

As her sight adjusted to the soft light around her, the sphere transformed into an intricately carved lotus flower with eight scalloped petals. The pistil was created by an entourage of yellow citrine stones that twinkled incessantly because of the torches.

Slowly, the evening's events unfurled in Nadine's clouded mind: the unkempt man with the note from Basil, her arrival at Sharpe Hall, being told she was expected at the workers' settlement, Basil's lifeless eyes staring up at her from a small clearing beside the path. She shuddered at the image, then realized she must have fainted from the shock of it.

Still feeling woozy and aware of her nakedness, Nadine rose up from a bed of skins enclosed in a translucent net. She held a soft cover against her as she focused on her surroundings. Nadine's movements drew the attention of a female cliff dweller who had been waiting patiently not far from her bed. Swiftly, she went to a container submerged in a tiny pool of water near the center of the room, and opened it. She poured the golden contents into a goblet, then brought the object to Nadine.

Nadine took hold of the cup as she stared at the woman. Was she dreaming? The cup was real enough. It felt cool to the touch. No, Nadine determined, she was not dreaming. The contents had been kept cool by the convenient reserve of water. Her parched throat constricted at the thought of the smooth liquid, and she gazed at it longingly. But the memory of a strange smell assaulted her, and she knew the scent had kept her unconscious. Nadine was afraid the drink would render the same effect.

The female waited momentarily, then understanding surfaced in her eyes. Nadine watched her pour another glass of the amber liquid and drink it. After she emptied the contents of her glass she nodded in Nadine's direction.

Nadine was satisfied the drink was safe. She drank the liquid and passed the empty container back through the gossamer net.

Finally, everything was beginning to come together. Nadine realized the strange dreams she had experienced were no dreams at all. She had been literally carried in several pairs of strong arms, and then given over to a group of women who had tenderly bathed her. All of the people were cliff dwellers.

Nadine reached for the necklace the cliff dwellers had given her, and found the tablets had been replaced with a more elaborate strand. She looked down and saw a large tablet suspended below the rest. It carried the cliff dwellers' symbol with a pink rose quartz adorning the center.

Nadine raised one of her painted arms and studied the delicate designs of lotus blossoms, spheres, and half crowns. The succession of white symbols also appeared on her other arm, her legs and thighs. Despite the signs of reality about her, Nadine still found it difficult to believe what was taking place. The translation, the vision, and the necklace had all linked Lenora to a strange fantasy world of legends and prophecies. But in her mind she had never completely accepted that she was linked to this mystical being.

If this is real—she gazed about her—then I, Nadine Clayton of Ashland, Mississippi, am very connected with this Lenora. Somehow her purpose and my purpose for being born are a continuation toward a collective goal. The thought alone was mind-boggling, but it was evident the cliff dwellers believed every word of it.

Nadine knew the young female watched her with eager, covert glances, quickly averting her gaze if Nadine looked directly at her. Her clothing was like that of the first female cliff dweller Nadine had direct contact with at the rum still, except this one was dressed totally in white. The symbols that embellished Nadine's arms also adorned the woman's top and skirt, stitched in a precise pattern. Her thick black hair hung about her shoulders, held neatly by a decorative headband.

The ceiling of the room in which they sat was slanted, rounding off at the edges as if they were in a cave; the walls were a rich chocolate-brown. Nadine noticed stalactites and stalagmites of various sizes present throughout. The elongated forms of the latter had been carved into functional pieces such as stools and tables, or hollowed out to serve as storage spaces for a vast array of things.

Nadine was amazed at the imagination and craftsmanship displayed by these carvings, like the decorative flower which hung above her, carved from a huge stalactite. The objects teemed with color from years of mineral deposits coming together in streaked multicolored forms.

As she looked about her, Nadine realized the cliff dwellers' jewelry was crafted from remnants of larger carvings, like the ones she observed now. The earth-tone tablets of orange, brown, slate-gray, and beige had been taken from the natural formations on the floors and ceilings of the cliff dwellers' homes.

Nadine was startled by two females speaking rapidly, and casting furtive glances in her direction. On light, silent feet, the woman who had attended her uncovered one of several storage receptacles and retrieved a garment very similar to her own. As she brought it closer, Nadine could see how the now-familiar symbols were designed on the white material by arranging and attaching tiny gemstones of various colors. Fringes surrounded the bottom of the robe-like garment which had a high collar covered with gems.

Nadine watched the women holding the robe in readiness as the third assisted her in rising from the pallet. They all helped her place the splendid garment about her slender frame. White sandals were produced for her and Nadine was silently beckoned to follow their lead.

She knew her evaluation of her surroundings had been correct; she was in a cave, and was being led through a maze of well-lit tunnels branching out from the cavern.

The walls were covered by the hieroglyphics Nadine had seen on the papyri and on the onionskin document that uncannily presented itself in the office on Barbados. These were the same symbols that she had seen in the vision.

The women approached an opening to what Nadine assumed was another cavern. It was covered by the same fabric the cliff dwellers seemed to favor, a heavy linen. One of the women slipped inside.

Nadine thought she could hear her heart pounding as she stood outside the opening. The walk through the tunnels had allowed her time to gather her thoughts, and fear grew deep within her. She had no idea what would happen next. She tried to remember some of the passages from the translation. They had mentioned a man involved with the debt she had to pay. She had assumed it meant going to Basil and saving Ulysses and Sovereign from his greedy intentions. But that was not possible now. Basil was dead.

No matter how she tried she could not imagine what lay ahead. So far the cliff dwellers had treated her with extreme kindness, but what would they expect from her now?

Nadine could hear loud voices coming from inside the cave. They sounded vaguely familiar although she could not understand what was being said. Then the woman who had left returned, and ushered Nadine and her attendants inside. To her astonishment, Melanie's angry voice was the first thing she heard.

"This man is the one who lies," she spat back

at Ulysses, pointing an aggravated finger in his direction, her voice rising in pitch with each word.

Seeing Ulysses, Melanie, and Rodney gave Nadine a jolt back to reality. Melanie's anger stunned her. This woman was nothing like the Melanie she had come to know.

Ulysses, his eyes narrowing with speculation, was even more stunned by Melanie's malicious outbreak. He watched her as she pointed a threatening finger while Rodney knelt obediently beside her. Ulysses had not known what to expect when he decided to follow Nadine to the cliff dwellers' settlement.

In light of all that he had seen, and what his aunt had told him, Ulysses still remained somewhat skeptical that his aunt was speaking the truth. He had to admit his main concern had been for Nadine's safety, although he knew the cliff dwellers better than anyone else on the island, and knew they were a peace-loving people. There was one thing about them that Ulysses knew very little. The cliff dwellers' spiritual rituals. That was one aspect of their lives they had not shared with him. It was taboo to speak of the rituals with outsiders.

Ulysses tore his eyes away from Melanie to focus on Nadine. She was frightened. He could see that. But Ulysses wondered if her fear came from being brought to the cliff dwellers' caves, or had it been magnified as a result of seeing Basil dead? Ulysses' jealousy gripped him. Was Nadine heartbroken over the murder of her would-be lover? He considered the possibility that the killing had occurred before her very eyes. Yet Nadine still appeared devastatingly beautiful to him, even now when he knew she had betrayed him.

The soft material of the cliff dwellers' ritual robe clung to her. The slender fringes at the bottom of the robe began high on her toned thighs and fell softly about her sandaled feet. Evenly spaced slashes had been made at the top of the garment above each breast, allowing tempting strips of her cinnamon-brown skin to show through. The remaining strands were decorated with sparkling, colorful gemstones. Ulysses could feel his blood coursing hotly through his veins and he knew he wanted her, regardless of her intended infidelity.

Frightened brownish-jade eyes focused on Ulysses' stony features, and her full lips formed to call his name. No sound came forth as she took in the loathing in their depths. In a matter of seconds Nadine's sudden rush of hope, that Ulysses had come after her out of love, plunged in the dark recesses of his eyes.

They were pitch-black and hard as obsidian stones. With the weight of her circumstances pressing on her, Nadine was numbed by this last blow, and her body reflected her resignation.

Now all eyes like Ulysses' were upon Nadine, and her own gaze traveled to the three figures seated near a large, blazing fire. She watched as the female rose to her feet, walked over to her, and offered her hand. Taking it like a child in need of guidance, Nadine allowed herself to be led to a place near the elders.

She recognized Ulysses' bronze case sitting beside a wooden container. The head cliff dweller opened both lids and examined what appeared to be identical pieces inside each one, except Ulysses' case did not contain a jade slab.

Nadine watched as the oldest cliff dweller

looked at Melanie, Rodney, and then Ulysses. There was no anger or even surprise on his lined features; to the contrary, he embraced them all with an understanding gaze.

Slowly, he rose from his seat and approached the three of them. He extended his knurled fingers and placed his leathery palm upon each one of their unsuspecting heads. As if on cue several cliff dwellers who were seated silently along the walls began to play a slow melodious tune on reed instruments, while others lit braided sticks of unusual twine, creating a light, sweet cloud of smoke within the cavern walls.

The melodious, soothing, high-pitched notes vibrated in the night air like a ghostly reminder of things of which only the cliff dwellers knew the true meaning. One by one sparks of light ushered forth from several lines of participants holding objects like lighted candles, their flames appearing to sway to the melody of the soul-searching tune.

It was apparent to Nadine that even though she, Ulysses, Melanie, and Rodney had not known the evening would end with all four of them gathered together like this, somehow the cliff dwellers had known.

Without saying a word the elderly man held out his hand to her, calling her forth. What else was there to do but to consent to his request, and Nadine found herself seated by Ulysses' side. Strange words began to pour from the cliff dweller's withered lips. They had a rhythmic sound, a calming sound. Soon he was joined in his chanting by the woman and the man seated upon the stand, and then their voices were joined by many others.

The cavern was filled with cliff dwellers, and

those who could not fit inside chanted outside under the stars, their voices joining together, low and raspy, but beautiful all the same. In a strange way the cliff dwellers' unity made mockery of the outsiders' anger and distrust.

Melanie was stunned into silence by the transforming vibrations of the music, the trance-inducing smoke, and the cliff dwellers' chant, but the guilt upon Rodney's face told the entire story.

As if by secret command, five young girls carrying tiny mounts fashioned from the cliff dwellers' stone came forward and stood in a semicircle beside the high elder. The four outsiders watched as the head female took the jade slab from the wooden case and placed it within Ulysses' bronze one. Afterwards she brought the bronze case which now held the original Five Pieces of Gaia forward, and stood among the other females.

The high elder's lips turned up in an almost imperceptible smile as he looked over the contents of the ancient bronze case, and his wise gaze rose and held the supportive gaze of the eldest female.

Slowly, she extended the case forward, and with reverence he removed his headband, laying it inside the open lid. One of the female cliff dwellers who attended Nadine stepped forward and gave the papyri Nadine had placed inside her pocket to the elder. He held the papyri in one hand as he slid apart the carved bronze sheets inside the lid, revealing the secret compartments. Then, with reverence, he unrolled the pages and placed them inside the lid, before concealing them behind the shield. Next, one by one the elder removed the gold coins, with their images of the cliff dwellers' symbol, from the headband, and placed them inside the carved medallions on each of the slabs. When the elder turned the coins they acted like ancient keys, opening the stones. This allowed the female cliff dweller to remove the manuscript. Afterwards the slabs were closed and put on the mounts held by the five young attendants. Once the last stone was mounted, the onlooking cliff dwellers brought their soul-satisfying melody to an end.

Chapter 29

The high elder looked out into the throngs of his fellow cliff dwellers and began to speak. First he motioned toward Ulysses and Nadine, then Melanie and Rodney as he talked in his native tongue. Ulysses was the only one of the four who understood his message, and despite his obvious indignation toward her, in a voice that sounded far off even to her own ears, Nadine could not resist asking what the cliff dweller was saying. Ulysses responded as if he were in a semi-trance, translating the ceremonial words.

"The Rite of Commencement could not take place without bringing together the symbols of good and evil." His rich voice reached out to her through a pleasant mental haze. "Both were part of the original cause. Evil, the dark, had to be born to prove the power of the light, for all comes from God/Goddess/All That Is. Everything from the tiniest stone, to every human being, to Gaia herself, is an expression of the trilogy. The uniting has begun and in the end darkness will be no more."

Melanie could only hear the low hum of Ulysses' voice, and although the trance-inducing smoke was taking hold, she visibly blanched as she stared at

the five original pieces in their sacred holders. Her
mind resisted understanding that all along the cliff
dwellers had known who the true owner of the
manuscript and the Five Pieces of Gaia was. She
had underestimated these people who appeared to
be uneducated and uncivilized. How could she accept that all the years she and her mother had spent
dreaming of owning the cliff dwellers' jewels had
come to naught?

Melanie had come to the cliffs believing she
could outwit these primitive people, but in reality
they had not only outsmarted her, but had prophesied her coming to their settlement as well.

She thought of how her life might have been
different had she not become obsessed with pos-
sessing the jewels, and she thought of all the hid-
eous things she had done to obtain them. The
jewels had been her sole motivation in life since
her mother first shared the secret with her. A secret
Evelyn felt would free her daughter, but had actually chained her to a life of evil intent, and had
contributed to creating the twisted person she had
become.

Melanie thought of the years she had seduced
her youngest brother, inviting him to know her in
ways that were indecent, obscene. How she had felt
triumphant and powerful at the confusion in his
dark eyes. Eyes that longed for motherly love.
Their mother's love. Eyes that had witnessed the
death of their brother. A death that she had wanted.
Planned.

On the verge of hysteria Melanie rose up, crying
and laughing melodiously. The sound rang within
the quiet cavern as her glazed eyes scoured her
brother then Ulysses and Nadine. With Melanie's

rise the cliff dwellers' music began again, this time a combination of rich, even tones, flowing from instruments created from seashells.

The music seemed to coerce Melanie further into her madness, and she began to spin and turn in a maniacal primitive manner, working her way toward the platform and the ritual fire. To Nadine it was like watching a strange ballet, Melanie's display of animated madness accompanied by the cliff dwellers' song.

Melanie danced about the ring of fire, her wild, flailing arms graceful in their insanity as she swayed perilously close to the edge. In the beginning the wailing was almost indiscernible it mounted so slowly. First, like a distant calling, the high feminine voices of the cliff dwellers were hypnotic as they accompanied the concluding notes of the ritualistic music. Their peaking notes foretold the end was near.

By now the trance-inducing smoke was in full command, and as if in a waking dream, Nadine, Ulysses, Rodney, and the cliff dwellers watched Melanie take a final leap into the ring of fire. There were no cries of anguish or terror from her or the hypnotized onlookers, only the vibration of a shrill final note struck on the quivering strings of an instrument resembling a lyre.

Unmoved by the scene before her, Nadine continued to stare at the ceremonial fire that had become Melanie's funeral pyre. Words which seemed like her own filled her mind. The dark will be enticed by the light, seduced by the Five Pieces of Gaia and named similar to a melody. Melanie.

Somewhere behind her she heard the sound of grating stone. The bizarre incident was over, and was accepted by all as the rightful end to Melanie's horrid, tragic life.

By command Nadine and Ulysses rose and followed the head cliff dwellers through a newly revealed opening to an adjoining cavern. Several males and females followed before the stone door was closed behind them. Rodney remained in the outer cavern in blissful silence.

A rainbow of colors met Nadine and Ulysses as they entered the space on the other side of the stone. It was breathtakingly beautiful. Small fires had been lit and placed strategically throughout a grotto. The flames were enclosed in mounted rings of quartz crystals, amethyst, rose quartz, jade, and tiger's-eye; therefore each fire was encapsulated by a tiny wall of white, purple, pink, green, and brownish-gold. The marvels created colorful, natural spotlights.

A profusion of long streamers made of blossoms and green leaves hung throughout the grotto, decorating uneven walls of cliffs and crannies. It was a natural fantasyland with several small waterfalls tumbling into a sapphire-blue lake. A boat fashioned like a scallop shell floated silently upon it. The masthead on the tiny bow was an exquisite young girl, delicately holding a butterfly in her hands.

Two males led Ulysses to a cliff where he was undressed and bathed under a trickling waterfall that fell into the crystal lake. His dark-brown skin gleamed from the water's touch as he stood beneath its gently massaging fingers. The shower plastered his black curls to his head. Ulysses' face turned up toward the source of the water, and his thick lashes imprisoned the luminescent beads like a silken spiderweb.

The sound of the gently rushing waterfalls pressed upon Nadine's consciousness as the ceremonial white robe she wore was removed from her slender shoulders. Coaxed, she was led to the tiny boat trimmed in peonies and orchids. Nadine sat obediently as the tiny craft was steered through the clear water toward the platform where Ulysses waited.

Despite the silent cliff dwellers who watched at a distance, and those who assisted them, when Ulysses and Nadine looked at one another they could have been the only two human beings on earth, existing in a phenomenal haven so far removed from the reality they had always known. Their actions reflected their feelings as he guided her behind the translucent shield of the waterfall, where a soft covering of pummeled reeds awaited them. Like Melanie, they too had a predestined role to play. Their union would mark the beginning of a new way of living for the cliff dwellers on Eros that would reverberate throughout the indigenous peoples of Gaia, Mother Earth.

It was all part of the prophecy. Melanie, the dark, whose hidden passions had distorted her view of life, allowing greed to be her master, had been consumed by the fiery blazing light. Ulysses, the dark, who had never let the light of love shine fully upon him, would soon be physically consumed by the fiery passion and pure love of Nadine, the present reflection of the light one.

Closing his eyes, Ulysses sat cross-legged upon the reeds and waited for the warm feel of Nadine's nude body to descend upon him. She wrapped her supple lower limbs around the base of his back, then they held each other tight, their bodies flush.

Initially, they sat very still, inhaling the mellow aroma of the smoking braided twine that burned in nearby crevices, their only conscious thought being the smoothness of the other's body, and the sound of the other's breath.

But soon their breathing turned deep and synchronized, and their bodies resembled one flowing instrument as nature took its course. Small moans escaped Nadine's lips as Ulysses' hands began to explore the velvety softness of her back. His fingers strummed up and down her spine as if they were playing an instrument.

Nadine's hands also began to explore, and she combed through the ebony curls that nestled at the base of Ulysses' strong neck. They felt slick and cool to her touch, and the need to get even closer to him overwhelmed her as she nestled her face in the space between his neck and shoulder.

Tiny whimpering noises like those of a young animal in need of love and affection formed deep in Nadine's throat. The sounds were answered by Ulysses' mating call, a throaty guttural noise, and the couple nuzzled each other in an affectionate primitive display.

At first their kisses were meager samples of the other's lips. Tiny, testing strokes of their tongues. Soon they evolved to slower, more languid explorations, their lips welding together as the passion mounted between them, until the kisses were deep and draining. The potency of the kisses plunged Ulysses and Nadine into a drunken state of unparalleled eroticism.

The cliff dwellers who had been watching from a distance, all except the head female, left through the stone entrance. With decorum she turned her back, and began to read from the manuscript hidden within the original Five Pieces of Gaia.

Ulysses and Nadine were oblivious to the goings-on around them. Somehow they had been transported to a place and time where love and sex were the epitome of communication and giving between a woman and a man. The movements and murmurings were sacred.

Free of the societal guilts that are present to lovers, Nadine gave of herself to Ulysses, pressing her small rounded breasts against his eager lips, urging him on with strange utterances that he reciprocated as he traced each bud with a feverish tongue.

With escalating intensity she gave back the loving attention, each one wanting to give the other the ultimate pleasure. Their bodies positioned themselves to ensure their desires were carried out, and they focused on the most sensuous spots of their being, until neither could take any more. The ache for their physical union had become a burning force.

Nadine opened to Ulysses with complete abandon, and his entrance itself sent intense pleasure throughout their bodies. Bright sparks of color passed rapidly behind her closed eyelids as the fluid motions of their bodies propelled them forward. Now their union became more than a physical experience as Ulysses and Nadine shared the same mental pictures. They saw themselves hurtling together toward a center of light. The closer they came, the more intense the pleasure grew. When they entered the light's core their bodies and minds exploded in ecstasy.

Again Nadine called out the strange phrase, *"Mu Kam-ma xi!"* Mu shall rise again! Then she and Ulysses both passed into a sleep of oblivion.

Chapter 30

 Nadine awoke to bright sunlight pressing against her defensive eyelids. She wriggled down further into the soft, comforting covers. She wanted to remain in the world of dreams where her body coveted a soulful satisfaction it had never known before. But she could not avoid the pull of reality as her hazel eyes opened under the white coverlet. Was it a gossamer net? Or . . . then Nadine realized she was lying in her bed.

She pulled the covers down from her head, and looked at the familiar surroundings of her bedroom at Sovereign. Bits and pieces of memory floated in her mind, but there was no continuity as she tried to separate reality from her dreams.

The last place she remembered being was in the cliff dwellers' cave, kneeling beside Ulysses. She was hurt by what she had seen in his eyes. They told her he loathed her. But that was all she could remember, and she wondered how she had gotten back to Sovereign.

Nadine threw back the linen coverlet to look for the markings the female cliff dwellers had made on her legs and arms. There was no trace of them.

Quickly, she put on her robe and dashed down the hall to Ulysses' bedroom door. Before she could knock the door opened. There he stood, fully dressed. She could smell the fresh soap from his morning bath.

"Ulysses . . . for a moment . . . I tell you I am totally confused," she said, then rushed on. "I woke up and realized I was back here, at Sovereign." She stretched out her arms for her own benefit as well as his. "The painted markings, and everything associated with the cliff dwellers' cave is gone. I don't even remember how I got back to the house." She raised her hands, befuddled. "Did you, I mean, do you remember what happened last night?"

"You know better than I do."

"What do you mean?" Nadine took a step back when she became aware of the distant look in Ulysses' eyes.

"Just what I said. You know what happened last night better than I do." His voice was cold.

"But you were there in the cave beside me," Nadine persisted, all the more confused by Ulysses' attitude. "You were translating the cl—"

Ulysses narrowed his eyes as if he could not believe what she was saying. "Alright. If that is where you want to begin, that is fine with me." Suddenly, he seemed detached. "I think I passed out from all the smoke. Beyond that, I do not remember a thing. But all that matters to me is, it is over, and Sovereign is safe and sound." He paused. "Your work is done, Nadine. The game is over. It may not have ended the way you thought it would, but it is still over."

Nadine looked down at the floor. Ulysses' concern about Sovereign and not her welfare hurt. She tried to follow her first train of thought. The smoke. That's right. So I must have passed out as well. Of course that's what happened. We weren't accustomed to the smoke like the cliff dwellers, and we must have passed out in the middle of the ceremony and the cliff dwellers brought us back to Sovereign. Nadine put her hand up to the side of her face. So I could not have done whatever the cliff dwellers had expected me to do. Her breath trembled as she sighed. I guess it was all for the best, and it proves I am not the fulfiller of their legend. I am not connected with Lenora, the bringer of light. Nadine felt as if something had been taken away from her. Some of the magic that had transformed her on the island of Eros into the woman she believed herself to be.

She looked back up into Ulysses' face. What did he mean, the game was over? For a moment Nadine thought she saw the same look on his face that she had seen the night before in the cliff dwellers' cave. Did she disgust him? The thought struck cold fear in her heart. Is that how he really felt? Had the night they shared together, her first and only night of making love, been part of a bizarre game?

All of a sudden Nadine noticed how Ulysses stood so close to her, but he felt so far away. Not wanting to believe it, she looked deep into his eyes. She searched for the love she hoped would be there. But there was none. None at all.

Nadine covered her mouth with her hands. Had Ulysses made love to her on a whim? Had he taken the virginity she had offered so willingly, knowing it was no more than a one-night stand? The doubts that Nadine had lived with all her life descended

on her with fervor. Had she fooled herself into believing that he loved her, an over-the-hill, inexperienced, twenty-six-year-old ex-virgin from America,
looking for substantiation of her womanhood and
self-worth in a foreign land?

Nadine tucked the robe in around her body. She
felt hurt and angry, but most of all, she was tired.
Perhaps, if she felt so inclined, she could have
fought against his hatred. At least she would have
known he had some kind of feeling for her. But
from the way he looked at her it was obvious she
meant nothing to him. It had all been a game. One
that her fanciful imagination had bought into. One
that was almost as far-fetched as the Legend of
Lenora.

"This is your last day," Ulysses began, "you
will be leaving sometime this morning." It was
more of a statement than a question.

A heavy feeling pressed against Nadine's chest
as she answered, "Yes, I will." It was such an
indifferent way for the first man she ever made love
to, to say good-bye. With those words, what they
had shared had been reduced to nothing, and to
think she had put herself in jeopardy to save Sovereign because she loved Ulysses the only way she
knew how, with all of her.

There were so many things she could have said;
instead Nadine stood silently in front of him, feeling a medley of things. Finally, acceptance etched
itself on her face that was suddenly older.

"From what I understand, your friends, Gloria
and Larry, left a message for you last night before
they left. They said if you plan to leave Barbados
for the States tonight, the three of you can fly back
together."

"Is that right?"

"Yes." The word hung in the air between them. Nadine cleared her throat as the pain inside nearly took her breath away. But she would not give Ulysses the pleasure of seeing her pain. He had stolen her love but he would not steal her pride too.

Of its own volition, love intertwined with hurt surfaced in Ulysses' eyes. He looked down quickly to conceal them. When he was in control again he raised his head and focused on Nadine's face. "Good-bye." The words were a breathy final sound.

It took a concerted effort to control the tremor in her voice. "Good-bye, Ulysses Deane," Nadine replied as he passed her.

Ulysses could feel her eyes on his back as he walked away. Then he heard her bedroom door close softly. He wondered what Nadine had remembered from the night before; his own memory was limited. But there was one thing that was clear. There was no way for him to forget. Nadine had gone to Basil of her own free will before she ended up in the cliff dwellers' cave. Finding out had nearly torn him apart, but it was best that he knew. It did nothing but substantiate his nagging suspicion that they had been involved all along. Ulysses did not care to focus on how. The bottom line was it meant all the things that had happened between Nadine and him had meant nothing, and whatever Basil had offered her had meant more than the love he had to give.

Ulysses' lips settled in a firm unyielding line. The one time in his adult life he had trusted enough to love, that trust had been blatantly betrayed. He took his hand and pressed hard against his abdomen, detesting the flutter in his stomach that had started the moment he opened the door and found her standing outside, her beautiful eyes filled with confusion and obvious need. But for what? Why had she sought him out? Did she think he might seek revenge against her for siding with the man who sought to take Sovereign away from him? Was the need he saw in her gaze a need to be assured that he loved her so much he would never take any action against her? In his mind there was no reason for Nadine to have come to him at all. It was over. She was safe, and would soon be on her way back to the United States.

Ulysses painfully recalled the moment when he felt himself weakening, and how he had to fight the impulse to take Nadine in his arms and demand to know why she had betrayed him. It was no consolation when he realized, despite all he knew, the love he had for her could not be ignored. But for Ulysses, it was easier to close off the love and the pain. The only place he felt strong was behind an armor of silent pride.

He exited the house through the kitchen, and decided to ignore how Catherine and the cook from Sharpe Hall stopped whispering as he passed by. Ulysses understood that it would be a long time before what happened yesterday was forgotten on Eros, if ever.

Back inside Nadine sighed as she stood looking in the small closet of her room. It was a sound of resignation and resolution. She had no idea when she came to the Caribbean what destiny would send her way. It had sent an awful lot. But Nadine had determined when she boarded the plane to come here, that no matter what she experienced, she would grow as a result of it. At the time she had been thinking about her career. She did not have the courage to acknowledge the small spark of hope that love would find her, but in the end it had.

Eros had been quite a teacher. She had become deeply immersed inside a world of literature and beauty far grander than she had ever imagined. With her own hands she handled priceless novels and art never known to the masses, but would be treasured from now until posterity as the result of her efforts. Nadine had finally experienced the loving touch of a man, one whose emotions ran so deep, even he was afraid of their depths. Ulysses was so much like the works of art that surrounded him; able to be touched physically, but his essence remained a mystery.

It had always been a mystery to Nadine, the feelings that flowed inside artists that enabled them to create works of beauty. Equally mysterious was a man who could tenderly bring her into the knowledge of what it meant to be a woman, yet, a day later, with no remorse allow her to fly away to her country.

Nadine gathered her few belongings together. As she did so, she tried to make peace with herself as well as mentally prepare for the life that lay ahead of her in the States. A life that would seem so different now, because *she* was different. A life that would be . . . different without Ulysses.

Yes, she was tired, drained, and Nadine knew that accepting that Ulysses would no longer be a part of her life was the most important thing in her preparations to leave Eros. Without doing so, with all that had passed on the small mysterious island,

she feared she would not have the strength to leave
at all.

With her suitcase in hand, Nadine went to Madame Deane's room and knocked on the door.
When there was no answer she opened it slightly,
and saw that she was sleeping. Even from across
the room Nadine was surprised at the rich color of
her cheeks and the smoothness of her brow. She
was glad to see Ulysses' aunt looking so well, and
she bade her a silent good-bye before closing the
door.

Nadine's eyes missed nothing as she walked
through Sovereign in search of Catherine. She did
not want to forget all that she had seen here and
experienced. Nadine knew she would not.

"Miss Nadine," Catherine called from the foyer.

She saw her standing by the statue of doves in
flight, a feather duster in her hand. Nadine remembered the first time she entered the room. It was
her first night at Sovereign.

"Clarence told me you wanted him to bring the
cart out front. Are you leaving already?"

"Yes, Catherine." She looked at the woman she
had come to know as a friend. "It's time for me
to go. Tell madame good-bye for me, would you?"

Catherine nodded, causing her head wrap to slip
forward. "We are going to miss you around here."
Her eyes were shinier than usual. "Things will not
seem the same. They already are not with Salinah
killing Basil."

"Salinah?" Nadine questioned. Catherine's
words nudged hazy memories surrounding the
events of the night before. An image of Basil lying
near the road to the settlement surfaced.

"She is a woman who lives in the settlement on

the edge of Sharpe Hall. It seems she paid him back for some things he has been doing for years," she sniffed. "Not that anyone deserves to die like that."

"My God." Nadine covered her eyes with her hand.

"I do not mean to upset you before you leave, Miss Nadine," Catherine apologized. "There is some good news. Madame Deane appears to have gotten better overnight."

"Is that right?" Nadine replied, mentally switching tracks. "Yes. As a matter of fact she looked much better. I went to say good-bye to her before I came looking for you," Nadine explained, "but she was asleep."

"She is much better," Catherine chimed in. "It is like a miracle."

They became silent.

"Madame says your coming to Eros had a lot to do with it," Catherine said softly, moving her hands as if she did not know what to do with them.

"I don't know about that, Catherine," Nadine protested before the housekeeper hurried on.

"She says things will never be the same on Eros. I, along with many others, believe that."

A lump materialized in Nadine's throat. She knew her stay on Eros had vastly changed her life.

"We are all glad that you came," Catherine said as Clarence opened the door. He stood looking at them, tugging on the bill of his cap.

"You take care of yourself." Catherine gave Nadine a hug. "I wish things had worked out between you and Master Ulysses. They should have, you know," she added before hurrying into the courtyard.

Nadine rode beside Clarence in silence. Although she was deep in thought she could feel him looking at her from time to time. The cart jolted as they hit a particularly rough part of the path.

"Miss Nadine," Clarence said, his voice raspy. Hesitant, he cleared his throat as if he feared he might be interrupting her thoughts.

"Yes." Nadine looked at Clarence's deeply creased face, and realized of all the people who lived at Sovereign, Clarence was the one she knew the least about.

"We all will miss you when you are gone."

"I'll miss you all as well, Clarence."

"But you leave at a good time," he continued to Nadine's surprise. "There will be much sadness on Eros; both Basil Sharpe and Melanie are gone."

"Basil and Melanie?" Nadine turned toward him, shocked by his including Melanie. "Catherine told me about the woman in the settlement being responsible for Basil's death, but what do you mean that Melanie is gone?"

"One of the workers at Sharpe Hall just told me about it when I was bringing the cart around." He tightened the reins on the donkey. "It seems Cassandra found Rodney on the other side of the island late last night, near the edge of a cliff. He had injured his head, but he did not know how. He told her he could not remember a thing." Clarence adjusted his cap. "He said Melanie was with him when he went out last night, but Cassandra said she never saw her. They are searching for her now." He turned the cart onto the paved road of the business district. "They fear she may have fallen over the cliff and her body has been washed out into the ocean."

"Poor Melanie!" Nadine declared. She shivered as she thought of it.

"It is sad, but the Sharpes' lives have always been full of problems." Clarence looked at her from beneath shaggy eyebrows. "So maybe their deaths are not so bad for the rest of the island."

It was a strange thing to say, and Nadine felt as if Clarence knew more than he had been given credit for. From that moment on they traveled toward the wharf in contemplative silence. Clarence remained with Nadine until the ferry disembarked for Barbados.

Chapter 31

Two restless children, a young sister and brother, had made Nadine, Gloria, and Larry's plane ride a little more animated than they had anticipated.

The little girl, Patrice, had taken a liking to Nadine, and talked to her incessantly, even if she was already engaged in a conversation with someone else. By now Nadine felt she knew far more about the little girl's family than they would have liked her to know.

Nadine looked at the children's mother. She was a young woman, but she appeared to be exhausted from traveling with the two- and four-year-olds. It appeared she simply did not have the energy to keep them under control.

"Patrice," she called. "Turn around. Read your book. I'm sure that lady has had enough of you by now," she said in a patronizing, but warning voice.

Patrice obeyed her mother, but a few minutes later Nadine saw her pinch her sleeping brother. "Bobby, wake up. Nell wants to talk to you." She placed her worn Cabbage Patch doll near his ear.

Actually, Nadine did not mind the commotion. She and Gloria had literally talked for hours while the children slept, doing more catching up on the past as Gloria became her sounding board for the more recent events in her life. Nadine began to realize just how much she had actually changed during her three months in the Caribbean. She saw herself differently, and despite all the things that had happened there, she had developed a greater sense of self-worth.

Nadine unbuckled her seat belt, stepped out into the aisle, and headed for the lavatory. She wanted to brush her teeth. She closed the door behind her and stepped into the tiny room. Nadine looked at herself in the mirror that was a foot and a half away, sighed, and began to dig in her large purse, searching for her toothbrush holder. She stopped when her hand brushed across several smooth, cool objects. Nadine looked down into the bag and was surprised to discover the cliff dwellers' necklace. She had searched for it earlier in her room at Sovereign. But when she didn't find it she concluded she had lost it the night before. Tears came to Nadine's eyes as she began pulling it out of her purse, but surprise turned to shock when she saw a brilliant diamond nestled in the middle of the center tablet.

"Lord! Oh, my Lord! I don't believe this!" She stared at the necklace. Somewhere, almost as if it had been in a dream, Nadine vaguely remembered seeing the same necklace hanging around the neck of a magnificent female cliff dweller.

Slowly, she drew the entire ornament out of the bag. There was a small piece of papyrus wrapped around one of the tablets. Her heart fluttered as she removed it, and studied the images. One showed the onyx unicorn slab in the middle of a table filled with books. The other depicted a smiling female giving a large, glowing stone to another, as a group of proud onlookers observed the transaction. Nadine was shocked. Did the cliff dwellers place the onyx slab in the library/museum knowing she would find it? And was it possible the cliff dwellers had actually given her the necklace during the ceremony? Nadine tried to separate what she thought were distant dreams from reality. If any of it was true, it meant she had fulfilled the legend, and that she was connected with Lenora, the bringer of light.

Her trembling fingers caressed the images on the papyrus and the carvings on the tablets. Nadine could not begin to guess the value of a diamond like the one she held in her hand. Just the thought of being treasured so highly by the cliff dwellers, a mystical group of people living in the Caribbean, was payment enough. It made her understand how connected all of mankind was, no matter how separated they perceived themselves to be. If she, a young woman who had grown up in a small town like Ashland, Mississippi, could be such an intricate part of the cliff dwellers' life on Eros, Nadine realized, the connection between the entire human race was just as powerful.

She fastened the necklace around her neck and covered it up with the scarf she was already wearing. Nadine brushed her teeth quickly and returned to her seat.

"Is everything okay?" Gloria asked as she sat down. "You look kind of funny and you were gone for a long time."

"No. Everything's fine," Nadine answered, then looked out the window. She could not tell her friend about the magnificent necklace. How could she? Nadine could not explain to Gloria what she herself did not understand.

Hours later the plane taxied in. Shuffling along within the crowd, a growing feeling of sadness descended upon Nadine. She was finally back in the States. Memphis, Tennessee, was a long way from Eros, and the possibility that she might never go back again was tough to bear.

Once she was inside the terminal Nadine hugged Larry and Gloria for the last time. Their connecting flight to Tampa would be leaving in about forty-five minutes.

Gloria held Nadine at arm's length while tears welled up in her eyes. "We can't let so much time pass before we see each other again."

"No, we can't," was Nadine's shaky reply. "It's been so good seeing you, Gloria."

The two women hugged and held on to one another. Finally, Gloria pulled away and made an effort to smile. "Who knows? Maybe in a few months we can plan a trip to Mexico or something."

Nadine began to shake her head. "I—"

"No. I don't want an answer right now," Gloria stopped her. "Let a little time pass." She knew they were both thinking about Ulysses. "Get yourself settled, and we'll talk about it then," she encouraged her.

"Sure," a weary Nadine acquiesced. "We can shoot for that."

They hugged again, then Nadine watched as Gloria and Larry were swallowed up in the airport terminal traffic.

Chapter 32

The sun was beginning to scorch Nadine's ankles as she sat in the grassy meadow observing the colorful picture being painted. Sadie's tiny hand held the brush tightly as she stroked her interpretation of the landscape.

"My cow's head looks too big." She puckered her lips in disappointment.

"Not really," Nadine encouraged her. "This painting is supposed to represent how you see the landscape and the cow. It doesn't have to be perfect in the general sense of the word. As a matter of fact," Nadine donned a serious expression as she studied the brown heifer, "I think Bessie's head just might be a little larger than the other cows. What do you think?"

The little girl turned her head from side to side, finally nodding in agreement. "Yeah, I think you're right," she said, suddenly satisfied with her painting.

Nadine gave her small shoulder a squeeze before moving on to the next child's painting. She was pleased with the way things had turned out over the last two months. The first week after returning to Ashland had been the most difficult. Drained from traveling and the events that had unfolded, she barely left the farm. She had done the best she could in telling Grandma Rose about her international adventure, but there were so many things she could not tell her. Nadine felt there was no need to disturb her grandmother's way of looking at life, just because *her* life had been rocked.

Despite Nadine's decision not to tell her grandmother everything that had happened on Eros, Grandma Rose told her how much she seemed to have changed. She said she liked the way Nadine looked with her contacts and her natural hair worn loose and free. She also liked her clothes, which continued to be modest, although they were now arranged in a manner that enhanced her figure. But Grandma Rose said there was something within the depths of her eyes that had changed the most. "They look confident, baby. And you no longer hide behind your education, trying to cover up other personal things that you feel insecure about," she had just told her this morning. "I see deep understanding in your eyes now. Yes, I believe my Nay-Nay has come into her own."

Even so, in the midst of all of this, Nadine felt a vast ocean of sadness and a longing that only a woman in love could know. Grandma Rose had pressed her to share the pain, but Nadine had refused. The hurt was still far too new, far too real.

But things had worked out okay. Nadine was gathering information on how to start a desktop publishing company. In the meantime Grandma Rose felt good when she used the computer she had bought for her to organize a summer art camp for children. Nadine had put together a proposal for the board at Rust College to interest them in funding the venture. The members were highly impressed with her credentials and experience, and agreed to back the project for five weeks.

There was no problem finding youngsters who wanted to participate; as interest began to increase, Nadine had to limit the age of eligible participants in order for the program to be effective. When the classes began she had fifteen students, mostly girls between the ages of eight and thirteen.

Nadine shooed the bee that was determined to follow her as she examined each student's work. They could not have asked for a more beautiful day, and the children were glad this assignment had been scheduled outside on Auntie Rose's farm.

Gingerly, Nadine stepped around the splattered palette of one of the young artists, only to arrive at Lavern's blank canvas. The young, gangly girl sat cross-legged at the base of the wooden easel, using the end of one of her brushes to poke at a soft mound of grass. Nadine had tried over and over to reach Lavern, but it was proving to be a difficult job. It bothered her all the more because she knew the girl had potential.

As she looked at Lavern's bowed head she remembered how, on her own, Lavern created a beautiful flower from a collage of dried petals. Nadine had praised her highly, but before the session was over Lavern had destroyed the picture.

Nadine had purposefully set up the lesson today on the farm where she had grown up. Lavern lived with her mother in a rural area far away from the college. Her father had left them several years ago. The only time Nadine ever saw Lavern was during the art sessions. She had set up the session today with the young girl in mind.

"Lavern, why don't you take a walk with me back to the house. I've got some drinks and snacks for everyone, and I'll need some help."

The eleven-year-old's eyes perked up immediately at the thought of being chosen to help "Miss Clayton."

Nadine knew all of the girls looked up to her, and over and over again she would hear them whispering about how smart, nice, and pretty she was, and how they wanted to be just like her when they grew up. Although Nadine also saw admiration in Lavern's eyes, she never heard the girl voice her feelings about anything to anyone. She was the loner of the group, never reaching out, and in return, no one ever reached out to her.

Nadine watched Lavern get up rather clumsily. She was taller than the rest of the children, all legs as Grandma Rose put it. Her thick, natural hair was constantly worn in two cornrows with bangs. Even though her clothes were comparable to the other children's clothes, sometimes her sleeves or pants legs rode a little high on her long limbs. From personal experience Nadine understood why. Lavern was extremely thin, and had to wear the smaller sizes in order for her clothes to fit.

Upon entering the house the girl silently followed Nadine to the kitchen.

"Have a seat, Lavern." Nadine pointed to a chair tucked under the kitchen table. "I'll be right back." She went inside her bedroom and reappeared with a photo album.

"Why don't you take a look at this while I prepare the snacks. It's my old family album."

Nadine couldn't help but smile at the glow of pleasure on Lavern's thin face as she took the oversized book and began to turn the crackling pages.

"I know where this is." She pointed. "That's down off of Pegues Street. And I know her too," she said as she perused the photographs. Lavern's curious gaze came to a halt at a photo of another young girl about her age. She frowned at the gangly child standing awkwardly by an old well with several small chickens about her feet. So engrossed was Lavern in examining the picture, she never realized Nadine was standing behind her.

"That's me." Nadine's soft voice broke into the child's concentration.

Lavern looked up at her with disbelieving eyes, then returned to stare at the creased black and white shot.

"That's you, Miss Clayton?" Surprise filled her high voice.

"It most certainly is. Surprised, aren't you?"

She nodded her braided head fervently.

"Time brings about all kinds of changes, Lavern, inside of you and also on the outside. If things always remained the same there would be no progress. Sometimes, even when you're an adult, it's a little hard to realize who you are and your purpose in life. But always remember you are a very special part of Creation, and if you believe in yourself, anything is possible." She gave Lavern's thin shoulder a squeeze. "Remember that and look forward to it."

Their trek back to the field with refreshments was a short one. Before the afternoon was over, Nadine noticed some tentative smiles passing between Lavern and a couple of the other girls. Smiling to herself, she released a deep sigh. At least she knew the art session today had been a whopping success.

Later that night Nadine climbed into bed. She thought about the letter she had sent off to Gloria, telling her all about her strange experiences on Eros. Nadine did not know how many times she had searched for Gloria's old letters. Not being able to find them totally baffled her. She closed her eyes. She had found all of her other personal papers stored inside a boot box put away by Grandma Rose. Nadine had finally given in to the fact that Gloria's letters were gone. Perhaps Grandma Rose had accidentally thrown them away after she sold her bedroom set while she was in the Caribbean.

Nadine felt saddened by the loss. The letters had held such rich memories of the years of her young adult life, the closest thing to a diary she had possessed.

She lay there in the new full-size bed, thinking of what she would do once the summer was over. She had heard about a couple of projects. There was even a letter from Dr. Steward praising her work with the World Treasures Institute. He said the donation from Sovereign's book sale had far exceeded their expectations, and the word was, it never would have been so successful without her efforts. He had regretted an onyx unicorn shown to him by an islander was not one of the legendary Five Pieces of Gaia, although it was an excellent replica. He was beginning to believe the set was just that, a legend. Dr. Steward expressed hopes of having her aboard when the project went into phase two later on in the fall.

Through the open window Nadine listened to the symphony of cicadas and other insects that always began to play as darkness approached out in the country. She opened her eyes and stared at the ceiling. She wondered if she would have another dream involving the cliff dwellers, Ulysses, and Melanie. The images always presented Melanie as the dark one. She did not understand why in her dreams, Melanie, as kind and generous as she had been toward her, would be represented in such a way. But night after night the message was always the same. The darkness of hatred, ignorance, and greed would eventually be obliterated by the light of love, truth, and understanding. Nadine thought it was a beautiful message. She hoped for the world's sake, someday it would come true.

Then the dream would take an erotic turn, and Nadine was ashamed to admit she found physical solace in the passion, although the effects often spilled over into her waking hours. It was in the daytime when the dream became a burden.

There was such stark vividness surrounding the lovemaking she and Ulysses shared while she slept, that afterwards, during the first moments of her waking hours, she felt either totally satiated, or aroused to the point of frenzy. It was a burden because even on the nights she did not have the dream, it was most difficult fighting Ulysses' presence in her daytime thoughts.

Nadine believed during the day she was winning the battle by filling her time with the art camp, the farm, and Grandma Rose's antiques. But at night she was totally helpless, completely swept away by the inner workings of her mind and heart, revealing to her what she knew to be true. She loved and missed him terribly.

Chapter 33

"Ulysses. Look at your hair, and your face," Madame Deane said, her voice weak. She patted the bed beside her child-thin body. "Sit here and tell me, where did that handsome nephew of mine go?"

Ulysses smiled slightly as he followed his aunt's instructions. "He is here, Aunt Helen. I have been waiting for you to come back to us. You have been . . . sleeping for nearly two months now," he said, holding her bony, cold hand. "Do you think you have had enough rest?" he teased, relief over her miraculous awakening apparent. The strain of her coma had left its mark on his face. Ulysses looked over at Catherine and Clarence who were standing quietly by the hospital door.

"Two months. Has it been that long?" she asked, her eyes seeming to go out of focus. "I guess I am in need of my rest," Madame Deane said, her words barely audible. "But let's not change the subject. I want to talk about you." Her weak eyes focused on his face. "Look at you. Your hair is too long. You have not shaved in days and your clothes look as if Catherine has not had her hands on them in God knows when. Why are you mistreating yourself so, Ulysses?''

"I have been worried about you, Aunt Helen,'' he replied, touching her cheek.

"Now that is a half truth. It is not a lie,'' she raised her index finger a bit, "but it is not the whole truth either.''

Ulysses sat quietly watching her.

"I wonder if your father and mother have been made aware of why the Five Pieces of Gaia were so important to our family and the cliff dwellers.''

Ulysses listened, thinking his aunt's mind was more unstable than ever. Still the mention of the Gaia set brought a sparkle to his dull eyes.

"Oh, I do not know why I asked that.'' Madame Deane closed her eyes. "I know they know. *She* told me they were aware of it.''

Ulysses' eyes searched her face.

"Verda told me.'' She opened her eyes again. "And I know for sure that I am not losing my mind.'' Her lips turned up in a thin smile, her eyes lucid. "Your father knew the cliff dwellers would be important to you and to the island of Eros. Even though he did not know about the manuscript, he knew the Five Pieces of Gaia were connected with them and that's why they were the most precious of his treasures. I did not know about the manuscript inside the stones until Verda told me, right before I confronted you in the library.''

"Well, somehow the Gaia set ended up back at Sovereign, but the manuscript had been removed. The bronze case was sitting by my bed when I woke up the morning Nadine . . . left.'' It took effort to say her name out loud although he had

thought about her more times than he cared to remember.

"Nadine." Helen Deane repeated the name. "I
was right. She was the woman who was prophesied
to come after Lenora. I was right." Her voice
trailed off.

Ulysses leaned closer.

"Yes." The word sounded like an exhalation.
"My brother knew the Five Pieces of Gaia would
be important to you," Madame Deane continued,
her speech slow. "Somehow he knew through them
you would find love, Ulysses."

"Love." Ulysses mouthed the word, the look in
his eyes distant.

"Yes, love," his aunt proclaimed, softly. "You
love Nadine Clayton, Ulysses, and she is worthy of
it."

The room grew silent and Ulysses noticed his
aunt's paper-thin chest was barely moving. "Aunt
Helen. Aunt Helen," he called gently and picked
up her hand. Catherine began to sob softly in the
background.

Madame Deane's eyes opened again. "Let me
go, Ulysses." Her voice was barely audible. "I will
be happy with your father and mother, just as you
will be happy if you go to Nadine," Aunt Helen
declared before her eyes shut for the last time.

Chapter 34

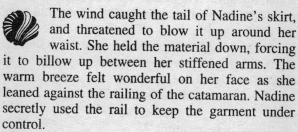 The wind caught the tail of Nadine's skirt, and threatened to blow it up around her waist. She held the material down, forcing it to billow up between her stiffened arms. The warm breeze felt wonderful on her face as she leaned against the railing of the catamaran. Nadine secretly used the rail to keep the garment under control.

The line of patrons was diminishing as they climbed aboard the boat for a late-night ride along the downtown shoreline of Miami. Most of them, couples like Gloria and Larry, had already settled down on the long cushioned seats outlining the twin hulls of the boat.

At first Nadine had been reluctant to go on the five-day trip to Mexico. She felt as if she would be the odd man out traveling with Gloria and Larry, without a partner. But Gloria had been her old persistent self. She told Nadine the cruise was free. She had earned it through a frequent traveler program. All Nadine had to do was come to Florida.

So here she was on the beautiful ocean-trimmed, palm-sprinkled peninsula. Her room in the International Omni was tasteful but not extravagant. It faced the bay, and further out the Atlantic Ocean.

Nadine had felt like a true woman of the world as the porter brought up her richly colored tapestry luggage. Not Gloria's taste in travel gear, of course, which her girlfriend voiced to her in no uncertain terms, but solely her own.

Gloria was in particularly high spirits as she waved the pear-shaped diamond engagement ring about whenever she talked. She and Larry planned to tie the knot in her hometown of Atlanta four months in the future.

"Isn't this just marvelous, queen?" Gloria's softly accented voice crept into her thoughts.

Nadine looked out over the bay, at the diverse Miami skyline, and finally at the sky littered with stars.

"It really is beautiful."

"Almost as beautiful as the Caribbean . . . but not quite." Her friend's voice trailed away as soon as she realized what feelings and memories her words evoked for Nadine.

"What do you mean, not quite? Nothing compares to the Caribbean, especially the island of Eros." A deep sultry voice pressed its way into their conversation.

Nadine turned. Her brownish-jade eyes enlarged with disbelief to find Ulysses, black curls longer than ever, blowing wildly in the nighttime breeze.

"Well, it's about time, Ulysses, I was wondering if you were ever going to make it," Gloria exclaimed. "They nearly scared me to death when they said you hadn't checked into your room. The last time I asked was before we came down here to the catamaran." She was so relieved to see him that all her clandestine actions were forgotten as she spoke openly.

Nadine looked from Gloria to Ulysses, her heart pounding. Gloria's words were a blur as she wrestled with Ulysses' presence beside her in the United States.

"Hello, Nadine." His dark gaze focused on her flushed face.

Breathless, Nadine managed a barely audible "Hello."

"I'm going to leave you two alone. I know you've got all kinds of things to talk about, and I'm not one to stand in the way of progress. I've done all I can do to get you two back together; the rest is up to you." Gloria sauntered back to Larry, a satisfied look on her face.

Ulysses' unexpected appearance unnerved Nadine to the point where she had to take a seat on the cushions; her wobbly knees would not hold her. She turned her face toward the shoreline and the water beyond. Nadine was so full of emotion she felt as if she might explode, and she dared not assume too much. She knew if she looked into Ulysses' face for any extended period of time, her eyes would tell everything she was not prepared for him to know.

While they sailed within the bay, Nadine and Ulysses carried on a conversation like two tourists just getting acquainted. They kept the conversation to the sights and sounds around them. Nadine did not realize it, but they both felt comfortable with this approach.

Ulysses dared not press his position too far after the uncertain reception Nadine had given him. But it was obvious to both of them—a man did not travel from the Caribbean to Florida just to talk about skylines and sea breezes.

The slow gliding catamaran ended its round within an hour, and the two couples disembarked and made their way back to the hotel. As they approached the towering building, Larry announced he could use a Bloody Mary, and automatically the foursome began to drift toward the bar.

Something inside Nadine would not allow her to walk contentedly at Ulysses' side as they strolled toward the outside entrance of the hotel lounge. Gloria and Larry's lackadaisical acceptance of Ulysses' presence had become an irritant. Everyone had known he would be in Florida! Everyone but her, and within one hour her life had turned topsy-turvy because of it! Not being able to bear the incredibleness of the situation any longer, before they sat down at a table, Nadine excused herself from the cozy group. She needed space to explore how she really felt about Ulysses resurfacing.

She was not in her hotel room for long before a bold knock shook the door. When she opened it a somber Ulysses was standing outside.

"Well. May I come in?"

Silently, Nadine moved to the side.

"Mmmm . . . you do not have anything to say to me? Any kind of welcome?" Ulysses asked, his voice low.

"What do you expect from me, Ulysses? Three and a half months have passed and I didn't hear a word from you. Not a phone call . . . letter . . . not even a card." The pain and bitterness of her loneliness crept more openly into her voice.

"Now you pop up here in Miami on a catamaran and everyone tells me we're booked on the same cruise ship for Mexico. You've always been presumptuous but how do you know I want you back in my life? How do you know I haven't arranged to meet some man tomorrow at the dock?" She threw up her arms in desperation.

The few minutes alone in her hotel room had helped to clear away the cobwebs of surprise and confusion. Nadine had finally adjusted to the idea that Ulysses was actually here and sailing to Mexico with them on the *Princess*, but somehow it still felt threatening.

"I knew there was no man, and there would be no man, Nadine, Gloria has told me everything." His seductively accented voice reproached her.

"Good old Gloria. The mouth of the South." She marveled at her girlfriend's audacity.

Ulysses understood her frustration. He could see resistance in every part of her body. He needed to make her understand why he had come, and why it had taken him so long.

"Let me tell you why I have stayed away. At first, after you left, I had made up my mind to forget you. I thought you had betrayed me with Basil," he looked down at his large hands, "then I found out the truth. You had gone to him because of your love for me."

His words were a knife, opening an old wound. A deep, naked hurt appeared in her shimmering eyes as Nadine remembered and felt the pain of his rejection. "You should have trusted me, Ulysses. I had given you all of me. Bared my soul and body to you . . . and you still did not trust me. How can I believe you can trust me now, or ever?"

The question hung between them.

Ulysses had prayed during his entire trip to the

United States that he had not waited until it was too late. Now as he looked at Nadine he still was not sure. "First I had to truly trust myself," he confessed. "Nadine, when my parents died, a part of me died with them, even though I was very young. Then I met you. And feelings I had never felt made themselves known to me. Life began to change drastically as we shared some extraordinary experiences. I realized it was my ability to trust and love that died that day on the path to Sovereign." He watched her fold her arms protectively across her chest. Ulysses saw her arms as a barrier between them, just like the one he had erected, but at least she was listening, and at the moment he felt he could not ask for more.

Ulysses walked over and leaned against the television stand. "As I grew up, whenever I felt even the slightest hint of love or caring coming alive in me, I would will it away. To say it plainly, I was afraid." He paused. "Loving and trusting made me remember, and I could not stand the pain of it, or the memory." Ulysses sighed. "Then as a grown man, I learned to seek my pleasure with many women. It provided a sense of satisfaction, but I made sure I never gave them my heart. I never gave it until I met you." His dark, thickly fringed gaze burned with intense feeling as he continued. "It was not my intention, Nadine, to love you. It was my fate."

Numbed by Ulysses' fervent pronouncement, Nadine did not know what to say. All she had dared to hope for had been fulfilled by his words. She trembled with relief as she stared at his open features.

Ulysses crossed the room and touched her for

the first time. He caressed her cheek where a single tear traveled down the velvety softness. "I am sorry that I have hurt you in my process of finding myself. But now that I have found myself, I have come to find the woman I love, and claim her for my own."

He wrapped her quivering body in his strong, muscular arms. Then he kissed her. The taste was unbelievably sweet with an underlying passion, and an unfulfilled need lit a liquid fire within them.

Reeling from the effect of the kiss, Nadine's body became limp, so ready was she to give in and ease the torture that had plagued her nightly since her return to the States. Yet her mind and her pride were more difficult to persuade. Her newfound self-acceptance and love demanded more than a few words and a kiss.

Nadine pulled away. She forced herself to walk over to the sliding-glass doors and out onto the terrace where the wind whipped her spongy cinnamon twists away from her face, and repeatedly popped the material of her wide circular skirt. "But how could someone else's words convince you of my sincerity, when my own could not?" Her voice was carried on the wind.

Ulysses came up behind her and placed his hands on her upper arms and his face in her soft bed of locks. "No one else's words did, my sweet. It was responses to your own words that convinced me I was wrong. Each night I would read the pages of Gloria's letters that addressed your thoughts and feelings about life—"

Shocked, Nadine moved away from him, pushing back the hair the wind kept blowing in her face. "How did you get my letters?"

"I wanted to find out more about you . . . so I hired a private detective." He spoke hesitantly. Ulysses knew how incriminating his words sounded and how wrong he had been. "He was the one who bought your old bedroom set."

"What! How deceitful can you be?" Nadine asked in full-blown indignation. "I hope you got your money's worth," she said, disgusted.

"I did and more," was his throaty, remorseful reply. "But there were so many things that caused me not to trust you, Nadine. You knew of the cliff dwellers' symbol, but you claimed you had never been to Eros. You never spoke of the onyx carving that was hidden in your drawer. The same carving that had been stolen from Sovereign only weeks before. I did what I thought I had to do to protect Eros' treasures and learn more about you," he confessed. "But in reading those letters over and over again, I discovered the woman they had been written to. They were responses to an unbreakable belief in the goodness of humankind, and how you planned to make a difference, not just in your hometown, but in the world. Your dreams were so grand for one so naive with no experience." Ulysses smiled and his eyes softened as he spoke. "And I knew that kind of resolve could never be broken in a human being. Not for money or glory. Not for anything." He looked at Nadine, and he could tell she was listening once again. "Then Gloria contacted me about some of the things she had purchased at the sale. She told me they had become such a hit amongst her friends and family, and then of course, you became the focus of our communication. It was Gloria who told me what actually happened the night of the book sale. About how you found the carving with the manuscript inside among the artifacts at the library/museum, and how Basil had threatened you with my losing Sovereign if you refused to meet him or told me. A person who could love so unselfishly, Nadine, could surely find it in her heart to forgive.'' His dark, searing gaze bore into her leery hazel one.

"I can't believe you." She held on to the anger she felt against him. For some reason it felt more comfortable than giving in to the love she knew she harbored inside. "You deceived my grand-mother with some phony antique lover, read my private letters, and now present yourself as Honest John, is that it?'' She laughed, almost out of control. "Well, you can take—"

Ulysses grabbed her and picked her up in his arms before she could finish her rebuke. "No. I don't need you to tell me what I can take.'' The passion behind his words was a living thing. "But I don't want to take it, Nadine.'' The feeling of her soft body against his was edging him on. "You gave yourself to me once before, my sweet, and will do so again before this night is over if I have anything to do with it."

Ulysses was incensed by her refusal to accept his apology. He crossed the threshold of the sliding-glass doors with a flailing Nadine in his arms, then plopped her unceremoniously down on the king-sized bed.

"What do you think you're doing?'' she asked, breathing hard.

"Whatever I have to do.'' Ulysses pinned her to the bed. His hungry lips sought hers, but Nadine evaded him, twisting her head from side to side, the only part of her body she was able to move freely, her small frame being no match for his larger one.

Instantly, she was terrorized by the thought that he was trying to best her physically, and she resisted him until he pinned her arms above her head.

"I love you, Nadine Clayton. I have told you everything in my heart, but that does not seem to be what you want. I have wanted no other woman since having you."

He managed to capture her lips as her head lay turned to the side. Like a man dying of thirst he drank of their moistness. Ulysses forgot about tenderness as he probed the inner recesses of Nadine's full lips, while continuing to restrain her.

The kiss felt like an eternity, as he demanded her submission through his expertise and fervor. "Stop fighting me, Nadine, and love me as I want to love you."

Nadine's heart answered his plea, and she wanted to return his loving ministrations, but a residue of hurt was still there. "Let me go, Ulysses," she commanded through clenched teeth.

He looked down into her squinting eyes filled with resolve and drew back.

"You hurt me, Ulysses. You hurt me like I have never been hurt before. I gave you everything I had and you rejected me. Thought I was some kind of fraud, when I was totally innocent. I never lied to you, Ulysses. Never." She poured out her feelings as she remembered it.

"But you did lie," he quickly retorted. "You said you did not have any kind of secret alliance with Basil, and even though it was to protect me and Sovereign there was no way for me to know that." He probed deep into her gaze, his forehead crinkled. "All I knew was you had left my home, full of guests, and even your dearest friend to go to him. I did not know anything else until I spoke to Gloria several months later. Nadine," he paused, "you must understand, of all men, Basil was my enemy. He hated me for who and what I am and he wanted to steal the only thing I had left of my parents from me, Sovereign. And in my eyes and in my heart, the only woman I had ever loved had betrayed me with *him*. I could not bear it, Nadine. And if it were true now, I would not be here." Their gazes remained locked as they searched for the truth in the other's eyes.

Slowly, the flame of anger in Nadine's eyes was replaced by the fire of love. Although her mind had fought against it, Nadine knew she loved Ulysses, and as she probed his gaze she knew he loved her.

Ulysses recognized Nadine's surrender. He began to lower himself toward her, murmuring tender words as he kissed her hair, her eyes, her face. "You forgive me for staying away so long? Please say you forgive me."

"I forgive you, Ulysses," Nadine said, as her body involuntarily arched against his. She wrapped her arms around him. They hugged for a prolonged period of time until their closeness sparked the passion that their long separation had nurtured. Now, no matter how close they were, it was not close enough. They needed more.

As Ulysses made love to her body, he spoke of their separation. "I would see you when I closed my eyes, when I walked the land at Sovereign and in the statues and busts in the treasure room."

"You haunted me as well, Ulysses," Nadine confessed, softly.

A strange look entered Ulysses' gaze. "Nadine," his voice was husky, "you must let me see you as I have envisioned all of these lonely months. Your memory has nearly driven me insane over the miles that separated us."

Nadine nodded, unsure of what he meant, but she wanted to please him in any way she could, and she knew Ulysses would not hurt or abuse her.

Nadine watched Ulysses cross the floor and close the curtains in front of the glass doors. He looked about, then chose an ornate crystal boudoir lamp. Ulysses placed the lamp on the floor near an empty wall. When it was turned on the little light shone surrealistically inside the dark room. Ulysses stepped back from the illumination, and turned and reached out his hand to Nadine.

"I just want you to stand in front of the light. Stand as still as a statue with your arms outstretched before you, and your feet spread apart. So many times have I envisioned you this way. So many times have I stroked the cold stone of the statues of my private collection only wishing it was your warm skin beneath my hand. In my mind's eye you became one of the objects of art," Ulysses told her with passion in his eyes. "Your arms perpetually reaching out for my love and affection. Would you do this one thing for me, Nadine?"

"Yes." The word was hesitant, breathy.

Nadine crossed the room to stand in front of Ulysses. With reticence she raised her arms, and stood deathly still, her eyes focused on his face, several feet in front of her.

His heated gaze trailed from the top of her head, pausing momentarily on her face, her breasts, then the covered triangle between her tender thighs.

"There is nothing in this world as beautiful as you are." The soft phrase poured from his lips as the gentle lamplight outlined Nadine's reddish-brown skin in a golden glow. In Ulysses' mind she was the epitome of womanhood, as her shadow loomed behind her.

Silently, he came toward her and descended down on his knees, placing pliant kisses on her feet, then traveling upward.

Nadine shook from the pure pleasure of it, and it was impossible to stand still as he continued his assault on her senses, calling her name over and over again. It was not long before Ulysses reached the core of her femininity. Tenderly he invaded the soft folds, exploring all of the components. It was far too much for Nadine to bear, and her knees nearly buckled. She cried out, and reached down to engulf his face within her hands. "I can't stand any more of this, Ulysses, you must take me. Take me now."

Moments later he entered her, his movements reflecting his long period of abstinence. As new as Nadine was to lovemaking, even she was able to surmise it would not be long before Ulysses reached his peak, so she wrapped her arms about his body and began to speak of love.

"I am yours for eternity, Ulysses," she professed. In the last throes of their passion, she once again shouted, but this time it was the impassioned call of her lover's name. "Ulysses!"

Chapter 35

Ulysses and Nadine climbed the stone-sprinkled path together, passing under the centuries-old stone doorway that led to the Mayan ruin Tulum. Spread before them were the remnants of a civilization that was still a mystery to tourists like them who came to walk within its walls. The pyramids and sacred buildings seemed to silently declare the spiritual beliefs of the people who built them.

For a moment Nadine felt swept away to another place and time, and she grabbed for Ulysses' hand to bring back a feeling of reality. She could tell he could feel it too. The presence of a culture that thrived long ago was strong.

"Ulysses?" she hesitantly called. "What happened to us back in the cliff dwellers' cave?"

He paused for a few moments before he spoke.

"I am not sure. But it is amazing how many things have changed on Eros since it all happened. Evidently, there were several large gems along with your diamond, and the cliff dwellers asked me to help them sell the stones through a jeweler I know on Barbados. With the money they were able to buy up a lot of the land on the island. Much of it came from Rodney. He did not want the burden of managing all of the sugarcane fields. He said he and Cassandra, who he recently married, had no need for them.''

Nadine tried to imagine the cliff dwellers as the owners of sugarcane fields previously owned by the Sharpes. It was perplexing.

''But although things are changing for them, the cliff dwellers remain the same in many ways,'' Ulysses continued. ''They still refuse to talk about their sacred rituals and beliefs, and more than once I have felt uncomfortable under their admiring looks, as if I have done something extraordinary.'' Ulysses looked out over the blue water that edged the ancient ruin; his eyes took on a distant look. ''I cannot tell you what happened in the cliff dwellers' cave, but to me, whatever happened, it is just one more thing that proves you and I were destined to be together.''

Ulysses gave Nadine a peck on the lips.

''Destiny, what an interesting concept,'' Nadine mused. She thought about the dreams and the Caribbean stories that had been sprinkled throughout her childhood. She thought about how destiny and a strong will to go to the islands had landed her there. But most of all she thought about the manuscript and the Legend of Lenora, her legend. ''Can you believe the cliff dwellers gave me that diamond?'' she asked, still in awe of it all. ''It's got to be worth a fortune. I have kept it locked away all this time because I couldn't bear looking at it. It reminded me of Eros and you.'' She shoved him playfully as a Mayan boy came by passing out pamphlets. ''Thank you,'' Nadine said, taking the paper.

"Evidently, they believed you deserved it." Ulysses put his arm around her. "And like them, I cannot think of anyone else who deserves love and riches more."

But Nadine wasn't listening as she read the black print on off-white paper given to her by the boy. "Ulysses, look at this," she said, feeling as if she had been struck by lightning.

"Lemuria rises again," Ulysses read the headline out loud, then continued. "Three months ago, in accordance with the Mayan calendar, the prophecy was fulfilled. The seed was planted for Lemuria, Mu, the mother continent, to rise again. According to Mayan belief, this heralds the beginning of a new time on Mother Earth, Gaia. A time of peace, love, and harmony."

Ulysses and Nadine looked at each other.

"Could we really have—" Nadine began the unbelievable question. Ulysses simply looked at her, raised an eyebrow, and smiled.

Together they turned and looked out from the top of the pyramid into the vast blue waters of the Gulf of Mexico. Although Nadine wasn't sure if she and Ulysses had actually played a part in it, deep down inside, her soul joined with his and smiled at a job well done.

Dear Reader,

Julia Quinn is quick becoming a rising star here at Avon Books, and next month's Avon Romantic Treasure TO CATCH AN HEIRESS shows why. A case of mistaken identity provides Caroline Trent with the escape she needs from her stuffy guardian. But Caroline escapes right into the very strong arms of sexy Blake Ravenscroft. Julia is pure fun to read, and if you haven't yet joined in the fun you should!

Lovers of Regency period romance shouldn't miss Suzanne Enoch's BY LOVE UNDONE. Four years ago, Madeline Willits was found in a compromising position. Now she's rusticating in the country, but when handsome Quinlan Bancroft arrives at the estate she's once again caught up in passion and discovered in *another* compromising position! Poor Maddie...all she ever seems to do is fall for the wrong man—but then Quinlan proposes marriage...

If you're hooked on THE MEN OF PRIDE COUNTY series by Rosalyn West, then you know you're in for a treat with next month's THE OUTSIDER. Starla Fairfax has returned to Pride County with a secret. She accepts northerner Hamilton Dodge's proposal of marriage for one reason only: he can protect her from her past. But Dodge has more in mind than a marriage of convenience...

Contemporary readers: be on the lookout next month for Hailey North, an exciting, new writer. Hailey's got a winning writing style, and in BEDROOM EYES, her debut book, she's created a magical, sensuous love story. A prim-on-the-outside attorney, Penelope Sue Fields has dreams of finally meeting Mr. Right. But lately all the attention she's getting is from Mr. Wrong—ex-cop Tony Olano. Will Penelope ever find true love?

Enjoy!

Lucia Macro

Lucia Macro
Senior Editor

AEL 0698

Discover Contemporary Romances
at Their Sizzling Hot Best
from Avon Books

SIMPLY IRRESISTIBLE   *by Rachel Gibson*
79007-6/$5.99 US/$7.99 Can

LETTING LOOSE   *by Sue Civil-Brown*
72775-7/$5.99 US/$7.99 Can

IF WISHES WERE HORSES   *by Curtiss Ann Matlock*
79344-X/$5.99 US/$7.99 Can

IF I CAN'T HAVE YOU   *by Patti Berg*
79554-X/$5.99 US/$7.99 Can

BABY, I'M YOURS   *by Susan Andersen*
79511-6/$5.99 US/$7.99 Can

TELL ME I'M DREAMIN'   *by Eboni Snoe*
79562-0/$5.99 US/$7.99 Can

BEDROOM EYES   *by Hailey North*
79895-6/$5.99 US/$7.99 Can

Avon Romantic Treasures

*Unforgettable, enthralling love stories,
sparkling with passion and adventure
from Romance's bestselling authors*

❋❋❋❋❋❋❋❋❋❋❋❋❋❋❋❋❋❋❋❋❋❋❋❋❋❋

WALTZ IN TIME *by Eugenia Riley*
78910-8/$5.99 US/$7.99 Can

BRIGHTER THAN THE SUN *by Julia Quinn*
78934-5/$5.99 US/$7.99 Can

AFTER THE THUNDER *by Genell Dellin*
78603-6/$5.99 US/$7.99 Can

MY WICKED FANTASY *by Karen Ranney*
79581-7/$5.99 US/$7.99 Can

DEVIL'S BRIDE *by Stephanie Laurens*
79456-x/$5.99 US/$7.99 /Can

THE LAST HELLION *by Loretta Chase*
77617-0/$5.99 US/$7.99 Can

PERFECT IN MY SIGHT *by Tanya Anne Crosby*
78572-2/$5.99 US/$7.99 Can

SLEEPING BEAUTY *by Judith Ivory*
78645-1/$5.99 US/$7.99 Can

Avon Romances—
the best in exceptional authors and unforgettable novels!